Demon Seed

Demon Seed

Guy Jones

Strategic Book Publishing and Rights Co.

Strategic Book Publishing & Rights Co., LLC
USA | Singapore
www.sbpra.com

For information about special discounts for bulk purchases, please contact Strategic Book Publishing and Rights Co. Special Sales, at bookorder@sbpra.net.

ISBN: 978-1-68181-500-8

This is the sequel to *The Journeys of Rowena Sunita Singh*. It is a more in-depth look at the trials and tribulations of a fragmented family that believes that their mother had squandered their rightful inheritance, treating her with disdain and cynicism throughout their lives.

It's about how life can be wasted when relationships could have grown and flourished. Yet for those of demon seed, poison soars in the veins and vengeance shades their hearts. They see as if under a shrouded cloud, for they live in the darkness.

And in that darkness are seeds set to grow . . .

So, Beelzebub's legions of dark lords scattered their demon seed,
Like dandelion seed heads, perfect and round.
They germinated in fertile hearts all over the globe,
Ensuring that destructive values like trouble and strife abound.
No trust, no loyalty and no love that can flow,
Instead, disharmony, resentment and jealousy in each and every heart
does show,
So that life under this blanket of darkness is neither safe nor sound.
Yet as there are lords of darkness, there are warriors of light,
Who enable that light to seep in through every crack in every brick,
rock, and slate,
In order to tip the scales towards love and light and taking us out of
all hate,
Warriors who are often burdened and stumble but never fall,
In their eternal campaign to bring light where there is destructive
darkness,
And relieve the burden withal.

Chapter 1

It was a dank, drizzly day in October. Guy held on tightly to his mother's hand as she, most decidedly a woman with a vision, walked rapidly trying to get out of the *drich* atmosphere. They were going to the post office where she was to collect the allowance that her eldest son, Pedro, had organised to leave for her.

Pedro was in the army, a move that Rowena felt glad that she had had instigated. Pedro had become what she often termed a *gunda*, a Hindustani term for a delinquent or wastrel. Some months down the line, he arranged to mail ten shillings of his weekly pay to the post office nearest to her.

Before Pedro went into the army he was involved with a local gang, whose chief aim was burglary – at least to begin with – and after she had witnessed his several severe brushes with the law, it prompted her to take immediate action, especially once they were under police surveillance.

With Guy by her side, she duly went to the counter and exchanged some pleasantries with the post office assistant, whom she had got to know, and with a rather grave face the woman told Rowena that the money had been stopped.

"Are you sure there isn't some mistake?" Rowena pleaded. "I've not been informed of any changes."

It was apparent that Pedro had stopped the money, but she relied on those ten shillings to buy groceries and necessaries for

Rowena's small family at home. When the post office woman told her, and Rowena connected with what Pedro had done, she felt a cold iciness in her heart that she had known many times before in her life. It was an old and haunting accomplice to her mood swings. So, with what money she had in her purse, she endeavoured to buy what victuals were needed, but on a lesser scale. She tried her utmost not to take it out on Guy, yet she withdrew from the world, as she so often did.

Guy experienced his mother emotionally disappearing, even though she remained with him in the flesh. He experienced it all through his tender years, which gave him much confusion, yet he learned to understand later on in his life just what ambivalence meant.

Later that evening Rowena told Joseph what had occurred, and he tried his utmost to commiserate with her. However, she could not be consoled from the fact that Pedro reminded her so vividly of his father, Raghubir Singh, and the feelings of betrayal and violation that she had known so well in her past encircled her now as she looked blankly at her beloved, saw his mouth moving, but did not hear his words.

Yet she also realized that the money from Pedro was never intended to be a permanent arrangement, and it was bound to end one day, especially when Pedro had plans for his future. It was just a shock that he had not had the courtesy to let her know. He knew that she would go to the post office to collect the money and then be denied it; perhaps that is what he wanted to do.

Rowena and Joseph had met on the boat coming over from Bombay to Tilbury Docks, and there were memories that they both shared and often talked and laughed about, especially the time when Joseph first approached Rowena, a woman with five young children of varying ages. Her eldest daughter of Raghubir

Singh was just fifteen and extremely beautiful, with green sparkling eyes, olive skin, and long flowing dark hair; she was a princess. In fact, all of her children were comely – that was the one thing they were blessed with. Yet Beelzebub had claims on other aspects of them.

However, rather like a ferocious lioness protecting her cubs, she snarled at Joseph Gordon, naturally thinking that he was hovering around Venema, her eldest daughter who had grown into a stunning young woman. She was astounded to discover that he was interested in her, a woman, a mother of five children whose prime concern was for their safety and welfare, yet he told her so in his polite and inoffensive way.

She warmed to him, though her suspicions of men clouded her judgement and clear thinking, and she continued to be hostile to him. Gordon was not perturbed by this. Somehow he knew intuitively that this beautiful woman, clearly with a complicated history, was no wild and common shrew. She was a sophisticated woman, though also a naïve and wounded young girl at heart.

He was not wrong, and as time went on they grew to love one another like no other two people in love in all of history – at least that is what they both felt.

With her complex ways, Joseph learnt to travel down those dark and haunting corridors of her mind that were so often dappled with excruciating memories. Yet he too was human, with his own concerns, and there were times when Rowena turned into a she-devil and he had to retreat and leave her in her own quagmire, for she excluded even him in here.

A letter came in the post some days later from Pedro, stating that he had other commitments now that he was getting married, so he needed every penny that he earned for his new life. As an afterthought he wrote, "Maybe I'll bring Janet around sometime when I have leave."

Rowena was pleased that she took this philosophically and focussed her thoughts on his marriage, which she thought may be good for him, but she feared history would repeat itself.

It was some weeks later when Pedro finally brought Janet to meet them, but sadly Rowena did not take to her. She sensed that Janet was doing most of the chasing, and Rowena felt that this always looked banal in anyone, especially a woman. It transpired that Janet was pregnant, and the wedding was planned to be within weeks.

Rowena also sensed that Pedro did not love her, for he was akin to his father in all ways, and here before her very eyes history was repeating itself. Pedro, like his father, had chosen a white novelty. Pedro, like Raghubir, was fit in body and extremely handsome. In the army he had excelled in athletics, and there were various photographs of him performing the high jump, in which he appeared to be a master.

Janet did not intend to let him slip through her fingers, especially now that there was an engagement ring on one of them and his child within her womb.

They married in a registry office in Aldershot, and Pedro sent Rowena some pictures of the ceremony. Rowena had never been asked to any of her children's weddings; this one was the first.

They were to live in accommodations that the army offered them, and over the course of time they had four children, all of whom would come to visit. The atmosphere was always fraught with hostility and tension. Neither Rowena nor Joseph took to any of them, and they were generous, spirited people. They found Janet to be a woman lacking in basic hygiene and of limited intelligence; but she was shrewd, and she knew what she wanted and bee-lined for it. Despite that, she tried to raise the children as best she could. Anyone who recalls those early days only remembers Pedro shouting at his children and never really spending any quality time with them. Sadly, this continued for all of their lives, and they knew first-hand what it was to be brought up in a dysfunctional family.

Pedro and Janet's eldest and first born, Jeanette, was seven when they decided that they would emigrate to Canada, and this they duly did in the summer of 1964. Rowena remembered the preparations that were made for this, and recalled how her eldest daughter, Venema, now in a successful modelling career, accompanied them all on a final shopping spree before they eventually left England for Canada.

Guy had accompanied them all, and it was probably one of the loneliest days of his young life, as he was discounted and brought along like a trailing stray dog that wasn't wanted. When they returned to her home and celebrating how many bargains they had found, Rowena noticed that no one had even bought the stray dog a lollipop to chew on.

Venema was another story.

After her alleged affair with her uncle in Wales, Venema had been out with boys. Naturally, they did not compare with a mature and experienced man like her uncle, so she grew bored very easily with most of them, and dumped them – that is, until she came to London and met a Greek man, Theodosius, who seemed to satiate her hungry appetite.

Now an extremely beautiful woman, tall, with an hourglass figure, sparkling green eyes, and a winning smile, she exuded her sexuality. She was a successful model to a degree, but her animated eyes were probably too individual, and she shone much more than the gowns she modelled.

Venema was a prime example of the saying "That which glitters is not always gold." This young woman most definitely glittered, and she had such a persuasive and manipulative way about her that she often won over the opposition.

Yet she clashed dramatically with Joseph Gordon, for he saw through her like a sheet of glass. He tried, chiefly for Rowena's sake, to get along with her, but as someone who could see beyond the false persona, he saw the poison that lurked within her. She reminded him of a rather impressive cobra who attracted his victims, and then gave a sudden dart and killed with its poisonous extended fangs. Her hostility towards him was so apparent that even her honeyed and manufactured way of speech could not hide it.

Joseph understood that he could never be a replacement father, especially for the elders of the Singh tribe, because they were now too cynical and rejecting of anyone who might offer this to them, and they also resented their mother for having "another man in tow" (their words). The fact that they knew that Rowena and Joseph loved one another impounded their animosity and drove a stronger wedge between them, firing them onto the other side of love. And how well they knew hate, as it became the easier option. Fired by Venema's dedicated zeal to poison the others' minds – or at least endeavour to, for it worked with Pedro and Freddie; it became a crusade they never seemed to tire of. What wasted energy!

Whenever Venema came to visit, flouncing in in her usual flamboyant way, like some main character in a West End play, she was disdainful of any attempts Rowena and Joseph had made to furnish their humble home. She had no time at all for Guy, who was someone she ignored, and he always remembered that there was strife whenever she visited and discomfort after she had gone.

Rowena often reflected that was she cursed in some way, especially when she tried to find common ground on which they could at least try to get along. She understood that Gordon tried, but in his defence of his beloved and their hearth and home, he could not help but verbally strike out at Venema at times, especially when he witnessed her cruel and condescending remarks that she always aimed quite pointedly at her mother.

There was a time when Guy had a friend around after school, and Venema was waiting for their mother to return from work. There was a particular Corgi car carrier that was recently out, and Guy chanced his arm in asking her for the money. He distinctly remembered her speaking to him in a hotly disdainful way; it is surprising to adults *just* how perceptive children are, and he pondered then if all beautiful people had this abrasive and cutting way about them.

"You know what your mother would say if she knew you were asking for money." Yet she still handed him the money for the car carrier, though with contempt in her eyes.

Guy never knew if she told Rowena, for nothing else was ever said about it, but she must have wondered where he got the money to buy it, as his pocket money was not due at the time.

On the way to school the next day Robert, Guy's friend, said, "Your sister is gorgeous! What a figure."

Guy did feel pride at this, because he agreed. No one could ever deny Venema her beauty, at least what showed on the outside. It took many years of seeing her fleetingly before he realised that there was no chance of building any type of relationship with her, because she was, in fact, quite a dangerous person. Evidence of that would appear later when he was a teenager.

There was always trouble whenever Venema and Barbara came in contact with one another, and Barbara said after one of Venema's flouncing, in-and-out- visits that she always felt overshadowed by her.

It is so easy to see events occurring and then make a judgement on only those that meet one's eyes at the time. There was an intense and turbulent history between all of the Singh family, especially when they lived in India.

Venema was very much the head of the family – something that she had assumed because she was the eldest. Not only that, she was a bully by nature. She adored Pedro from the time he was born to this very day, even though he still drinks profusely and is an embittered and prejudiced cynic. Frederick, Freddie, she always considered thick, yet he was part of their true blood bond, as the three of them were Raghubir Singh's children. So she just about included Freddie in her "gang," yet he fired her superiority because she saw him as no threat to her.

She treated Gerald and Barbara, Chunny's children, with disdain and a cold, dismissive superiority like they were her private ayahs. Sadly, when they all grew up and travelled from the East to the West, Venema's attitude did not change. She exhibited a persona of steel-like queenship, even though it could well have reflected a lost and lonely girl within.

For any young child growing up in an atmosphere of constant strife and arguments, especially whenever any of the Singh family was together, it was to say the least, confusing. Yet Guy often reflected on these times when he was older, and saw it all as a sound education in human dynamics; he never, ever believed that "blood is thicker than water," because he witnessed more betrayal amongst family than he ever did between people who were not related by blood. Or it possibly made him more resilient, as he had experienced it vividly first-hand from blood relatives, and thereby strengthened his mettle.

One day Joseph and Rowena were talking, and he was always baffled as to why there was hostility from Raghubir's children towards Rowena.

Rowena began, "You know, Joseph, when I left India I left everything behind me. Riches really meant nothing to me. I went to India with nothing, and I left with my children. My prime concern was bringing the children with me to England and starting a new life –or at least try to. I knew it would not be easy, especially having to go back to that hovel in Wales, but it was the only address I could give the government at that time, and as you know they had to have an address in the country of destination, otherwise they could not help me.

"They believe – well, Venema seemed to set the seed in the other's minds – that I kept all of their rightful inheritance and squandered it. On what? Perhaps they thought it was on you and our son. You know that I didn't; and when I told them that I left it all behind, they then called me a fool.

"But what would have been their destiny if I had left them behind? They were half-caste children in a country of absolute turmoil and revolt. Do you think that their father's would have stood by them? We saw Chunny at Tilbury Docks, and you sent him packing. He wanted to take care of me he said! I wouldn't trust that man to give me a glass of water if I was thirsty!"

Joseph interjected, "I know that you put their welfare first. When I first saw you on the SS *Ranchi*, I could see that you were a good person with a heart full of giving and love, but you gave off a tough exterior. Having to bring five children with you to a land that they had never seen before was a huge thing to do. I admired you."

"You are very sweet, Joseph. If only they could see how it really was! But this belief that I swindled them seems to have poisoned their hearts. Yet in India, Venema was a sweet girl, and everyone seemed to take to her–"

Joseph cut in, "Sorry to dash your good memories there, darling, but she always knew how to manipulate, and perhaps this was seen as niceness. She is a cobra, my dear, and will never

fail to attack with her poison when she has no use for someone
or if they see through her."

"It is so hard. When I see them I see their fathers, and to
be honest, I don't like what I see. They are *them* in every way –
conniving, maudlin, manipulative, and selfish. Joseph, forgive me
if this sounds extreme, but the thought . . . do you know what
haunts me? The fact that they are all from demon seed."

The atmosphere grew thick and heavy, and they both looked
at one another knowingly.

Chapter 2

Rowena and Joseph received an official letter one day, one that they had been expecting. Joseph was a devoted Catholic and wanted to marry his beloved, but it was hindered until the whereabouts and status of Raghubir Singh could be established.

The official letter that arrived stated that Singh had passed away from heart failure sometime around September of 1965. Rowena was full with vivid and varying memories, superimposed with mixed and fierce emotions. There was sadness knowing that Raghubir was dead, and she wondered if he was now facing how he had treated people and come to realise just how much sorrow he had caused many people. *Judgement of our actions comes to us all*, she thought, *whoever does the judging*. But she mused that the best judge of those actions is us, we who do the deeds.

Now, Joseph and Rowena could be officially married, yet one more obstacle remained. Gordon was advised by his local priest that permission had to be granted by the pope before the marriage could go ahead, and now that Singh's demise was confirmed it was put into action. Two weeks later Joseph spoke to the same priest, who had received the letter from the pope sanctioning the marriage.

Joseph and Rowena were married in a local registry office in Croydon in the summer of 1967. Guy remembered the photograph well as he looked over snapshots of family and friends. He thought they both looked regal and most definitely suited to one another.

Rowena had found work in a factory in a local industrial estate within walking distance of her home. She, being an industrious worker, got along fine with her work, and her foreman, a Welshman naturally nicknamed Taffy, saw her potential and asked her if she would consider working in the accounts office. Rowena declined, for she had had no experience or training in accounts; moreover, she had no affinity for numbers. There was a woman who also worked at the same place, Dot Richards, who spread it about that Rowena and Taffy were having an affair. Quite soon after that, when gossip had grown rife and was assuredly believed, Rowena left.

Freddie was a seriously troubled soul, and he'd dated a few girls before he met Dot Richards' daughter. There was a girl, Doreen, who was a school teacher, and Guy remembered her well because she was extremely nurturing towards him and his schoolwork. Sadly, Doreen was seen no more, and Freddie talked of her dismissively, even though others had good memories of her.

He then met Ava Richards, and within a short span of time they were engaged. Freddie then announced his plans to go to Yorkshire, as Ava's mother was moving there. Evidently, Freddie moved to the woman's decree, for she came along with Ava one evening to speak with Rowena about him.

It was a cold and frosty evening in November when Mrs Richards accompanied Freddie and Ava to evidently state their cause. Rowena could not help but feel a surge of contempt for her son, who stood before her with downcast eyes, looking the image of his father. She had the penchant to condemn men, and she felt that Freddie was spineless and constantly looking for someone to lead him. He did not rely on his own strength to make decisions, and his eldest sister's poison towards Joseph coursed through his veins.

Freddie had one week left to qualify in welding at a local factory, and Joseph pointed out that doing so would give him a trade. Freddie was adamant that he had discussed this at length with Ava and her mother, and he had made his decision. Surely, if it was care and concern that prompted the decision, then Freddie would have been encouraged to qualify in his trade, yet it appeared that what Mother Richards decreed others obeyed and followed without question.

Rowena looked at him with disdain, and asked, "Are you sure that this is your decision, Freddie?"

Mother Richards interjected quickly and sharply, "Yes, Freddie has made up his mind, and we'll be leaving this coming weekend. I've sold the house, and everything is wrapped up. Freddie also wants his rent back that he paid you."

Rowena retorted, now with sharpness in her voice, "I was actually asking Freddie. Do you now speak for him?"

Then Rowena looked at Freddie, who could not meet her eyes, and continued, "This all seems very quick. Freddie has only just met your daughter, and now you're sweeping him off to Yorkshire – and what has the rent money to do with you?"

Mother Richards returned, "Well, he won't be here if he's coming to Yorkshire, so he'll need it back to help with his new life. I hope that you won't try and put obstacles in his way."

"Now why would I want to do that? It all seems to be arranged and decided on, without a word said to us," Rowena replied, and then went to look for her purse for the ten shillings Freddie had given her.

She tried to hand it to him, but Mrs Richards took the money. "I hope you see the whole situation now," she said.

Rowena replied, looking again at Freddie, "I think we all see it *very* clearly."

Rowena remembered the fierce and scheming way in which the woman had spread ugly and salacious rumours about her and Taffy at the factory, yet just looked at her with contempt. The further startling fact that hit Rowena was that Mother Richards actually believed her own machinations. They all scurried out of the front door, and Rowena and Joseph again just stared at one another.

Joseph said in wonderment, "Life is indeed strange. This is the same woman who spread those ugly rumours about you at work, and she is Freddie's new religious leader. Good luck to them I say; Freddie will need it."

Rowena remained silent and ruminated, Joseph said no more.

It was sad for Guy, because he and Freddie had bonded and often played together. Their games often involved serious rough and tumble, and Freddie would say affectionately to his youngest brother, "I love you, Butch." This was his nickname for Guy, who always had a crewcut hairstyle.

When Freddie moved up to Yorkshire Guy and Freddie wrote to each other every week, and Guy so looked forward to getting Freddie's letters.

Guy even spent time with Freddie and Ava. They first lived in a flat in Sheffield, and Freddie often took him up on his Lambretta. Guy would always remember the sore backside he got during the journey, but he gladly suffered it to be with his brother.

Guy often debated with Ava about evolution, for the Richards family were staunch Jehovah's Witnesses, as Freddie now was. Yet even as a young boy Guy sensed that Ava was jealous of the bond between the two brothers, and now it was as if he had entered a new coven and the Richards family wanted Freddie to belong exclusively to it and them.

Mother Richards had two other children, Radleigh and Yvonne. As they were about the same age, Guy and Radleigh spent some time together. Guy also took to Yvonne, as she had a mind of her own, and they shared some humour together. They were all now a part of the coven.

As time went on and Guy grew up from that plump little mischievous child to a tall and slender young man, Freddie seemed to change towards him, and Guy sensed an animosity and a sense of judgement from him. However, Guy was angry with Freddie for abandoning him for a religion that seemed to have tight strictures about whom they associated with. Their closeness drifted away as if it was built on sand that washed away with the tide. Guy was heartbroken for a long time afterwards; he was often the farceur, the court jester, in this complex web of family strife and warfare. Yet for some time after he was quiet and withdrawn, which concerned both Rowena and Joseph.

The last time that Guy and Freddie spoke was after Freddie had been to see his mother after Joseph had died, and he flew at her about blaming Joseph for his shortcomings. When Guy heard of this he telephoned Freddie and asked him how his father was to blame for the decisions that Freddie had made. Freddie did not answer, and said something nonchalant like, "I'll see you around some time."

That same day, the news told of the tragedy of Hillsborough.

Sometime after that, Guy telephoned Freddie's home because he had heard that Freddie had suffered a nervous breakdown. Ava answered the call and told Guy that Freddie could not come to the phone. Guy persisted, and asked her to tell Freddie that he was on the telephone and wanted to speak to him. Guy heard Freddie say "no" limply in the background.

Guy recognised the same feeling that their mother might have felt when Freddie had stood there in her lounge with Mother Richards. He couldn't help but say the same word – spineless.

Freddie and Guy never spoke again. Yet many years later his son Thomas, now a grown man with children of his own, reunited with Guy. Thomas had always respected his uncle and admired his individuality. He told him, and also added, "I've missed you, Uncle Guy."

All Guy could think was *so the father and so not the son.*

Although Freddie had decided to leave and make a new life for himself, both Rowena and Joseph wished to give their blessing to his venture, and when they secured a position as matron and warden of a nursing home in Croydon, they gave Freddie most of their house furnishings for their new home in Barnsley.

There was a time when they were established in this business when Freddie came to visit one dark and mysterious night. He seemed anxious and said that he had brought a friend with him, who was in the car outside. Freddie had a motorcycle license at the time, which allowed him to drive a three-wheeler, so outside sat his paramour in his Robin Reliant. It was clear that Freddie intended to remain taciturn – something that came very naturally to him – but both Rowena and Joseph asked instantly where his wife was.

As it happened, there was a vacant apartment upstairs, which Rowena and Joseph allowed them to stay in overnight. Quite early the next morning Freddie and his paramour disappeared as quickly as they had arrived.

Freddie and Ava clearly reconciled after this peccadillo, and the result was that Ava gave birth to another child, now giving them four.

After Joseph died they all visited Rowena, and there was an occasion when Guy also came. Their youngest son and Guy seemed to bond, and as he was arriving at the front door, young Andrew ran to greet his uncle, but Ava decidedly pulled him back.

Rowena saw it and openly said to Guy, "Consider yourself an outcast."

Guy took up the thread and replied, "I do."

So this was how it ran for Rowena and Joseph; everything that they tried to build with any of her children crumbled. It resembled building castles in the sand. However elaborate and attractive they might be, they undoubtedly fell and disintegrated as soon as the tide came in, and washed away all of the good intentions and toil that went into trying to build a family unit.

If this was classified as a drama, it would represent a farce/tragedy that left every good-intentioned person totally confused.

Chapter 3

The only ones who really lived with Rowena and Gordon were Guy and Barbara. Out of all of those evidently cantankerous and pugnacious adults, Guy only ever lived with Barbara. Gerald, after pursuing his interests with boxing, exceled in it and won the championship of Croydon, but Rowena would not agree to let him take it up professionally. She felt totally protective, and became dictatorial in her decision, and much to his chagrin, she would not sign papers for him to go ahead.

Gerald would always work at something, however, and worked on a fruit and vegetable stall in Surrey Street in Croydon, often bringing home produce for the family. Gerald had his demons to deal with, and his boxing seemed to give him an outlet where he could at least activate the rage he felt within. He was an immaculate dresser, and Guy looked up to him as a role model, often watching him and admiring him.

Guy also remembered Gerald often becoming extremely emotional. Yet although others were with him, he always seemed to cry alone and act out his private inner play on his own stage. No one could console him, for he seemed oblivious to anyone's presence. This was later greatly enhanced when he drank profusely and became foully abusive to anyone near him, or the world in general.

His tantrums were phenomenal – as they still are to this very day. His rage seemed to have graduated into fury over the years, and the root of his malaise had evidently not been eradicated. Yet it comes over very clearly to anyone with any insight that he definitely wants to hold on to the canker that eats away at him within.

We often hold on to what is the most familiar, even if it is the most destructive, both for us and our relationship with others and life. That which eats us away we cling to as if it is our best friend; yet, sadly, it is also our greatest saboteur. This is when we see betrayal and fractured connections – when the trust has been brutally battered by our bloodline links – as the only sea on which to sail our ship.

From the time when they were all children in India, Gerald and Barbara had been the outcasts from the Raghubir blood gang. Venema, their leader and dictator, influenced both her brothers, Pedro and Freddie, to look at them as such, and that rift exists to this very day. What a waste of energy and time!

When we look at how certain things have progressed in the society that we live in, for example, how fast a book manuscript can be sent to a publisher in a matter of seconds, and some of the major breakthroughs in technology, it is so pusillanimous and pathetic how people hold on to useless and time-wasting personal vendettas that do nothing but add excess and unnecessary baggage to our load that we carry in our lives.

In the course of time, all members of the fractured Singh tree came together for some reason or another; yet there was never a time when there was not some trouble, argument, or discord between them. Verbal, and even physical, abuse often ensued; it was as if they were all walking time bombs, and each one had the potential to light the other's fuse and engender an explosion.

So Joseph understood when his beloved said those words to him, and they rang in his head very often afterwards, like the bells of a nearby church tower, "Demon Seed."

He also recalled when they shared many tales of their travels in India. Like the time when Rowena, who was going around with Chunny, a giggly girl in a strange eastern land, went to see a fakir for a reading of her hand. The fakir looked at her with penetrating, deep eyes, and said, "I will not read your hand, my child. Please go in peace."

What he must have seen and understood was this woman's future and the load that she would carry. How it often drained the life from her, and she could feel the blood go cold in her veins, when she witnessed the troubles that were promulgated – chiefly from the cobra queen's poison – by her children. Yet she also felt contempt and was totally dismissive of how easily led they were, especially the elder sons, how weak they appeared in her mind's eye.

It did not take long before her hatred for men wafted back into her consciousness and give a snarl to her features. She had realised just how strong she had to be when she recalled how both the men in her life in India, Raghubir and Chunny, went off the rails, and how she had to work with the British Government to journey back to England with her five half-caste children, watchful all of the time, overprotective, austere. It is unfortunate that negative things can be so easily remembered and focussed on, whereas actions that emanate from a pure heart are often forgotten or go unnoticed.

Unfortunately, her youngest son, who was naturally the love child of her beloved – the twin who lived – often bore the brunt of her total withdrawal. Naturally, he thought that it was something that he had done. Rowena's withdrawals were phenomenal, especially so on a Sunday. The reader will understand why after reading the previous account in *The Journeys of Rowena Sunita Singh*.

The pain that she suffered in the past, and now seeing her children fight and hate one another gave her an emptiness and dullness within that forced her to emotionally retreat, burnt out with it all. It also pained her that she made both Joseph and Guy suffer, so this added guilt and shame to her load. How the complexities of our memories haunt our consciousness.

"I need to go to my island in my mind where there are no people to hurt and confuse me anymore."

Much to everyone's chagrin, she also took up chain smoking, probably as a psychological prop to lean on, something strongly habit forming, but which fed her orally. Whenever you saw her she had a lighted cigarette in her mouth, and another was lit as soon as the former reached its stub.

After their travels in halfway houseville, Joseph and Rowena, along with Gerald, Barbara, and Guy, had uplifting news one day. Joseph had been cleaning windows for the director of social services at the time, George Fantanini, who seemed to be a generous-spirited man. Because Rowena had been out of the country for as long as she had, she had to live in England again for a minimum of five years in order to qualify for council accommodation. The period was now up, and they received a letter from the council offering them a house in New Addington, Surrey. It was a three-bedroom house in a semi-rural setting on corner plot, so there was a double-fronted garden, and an extensive one at the rear.

Rowena and Joseph were delighted and felt that a huge burden had been lifted from their shoulders. They could not help but think that Mr Fantanini had a hand in helping the process move along faster. Joseph, when he did the latter's windows for the last time, thanked him and shook his hand. They both exchanged a knowing look, and Fantanini said that he understood now that, as he had a new home which was some distance from here, he would understand if he finished cleaning his windows. It was an elegant show of diplomacy, and Joseph understood, thanking him again on behalf of all his family.

The small family ate their fish and chips on newspaper on the floor of their empty house, as they had no furniture in their new home, and none to bring in. This was actually a cleansing experience for Rowena and Joseph; they started from the bottom with nothing and wished to build on this premise, and at least now they had the means to build a family unit – or at least try to. After their many travels and travails, at least they now had a permanent base that they could call their own home. Yet life was to unfold with further experiences.

It was not long before Joseph was cultivating the gardens in the back and front, creating a large vegetable patch at the very rear of the back garden. The two flanks of the front garden on either side of the front door were laid to lawn, with rose bushes and other border plants and perennials carefully positioned for their volume and colour. Joseph was exceedingly talented in garden design and layout, and he later entered competitions, and always came within the first three. His roses were his pride and joy.

When he was preparing the deep beds for his roses, the local milkman passed by and made an inane remark about Joseph digging his grave. Rowena told the man not to deliver milk to them anymore. When Joseph remonstrated that the man was joking, Rowena responded curtly that they did not need jokes made at their expense, but at least it was done to their faces and could be dealt with immediately.

Venema had always accused her mother of being hard, but although still a wounded little girl inside, Rowena showed the world her toughened persona, which was often mistaken for callousness, yet she was a tender-hearted girl who was hurt easily.

So, both Rowena and Joseph were thankful for this new enterprise, and excited at the same time. They now had somewhere they could create some security, both for their love and their small family.

As was stated in *The Journeys*, the Raghubir blood gang kept strong connections with Wales, until they decided, or rather the cobra-dictator did, that they would quit Wales and most definitely *not* live with their mother. They considered Gerald and Barbara traitors, and would not have accepted them to be with them. So, Venema took up lodgings in London and pursued her modelling career. Pedro and Freddie were nomads for a while, and Freddie stayed with Rowena and company sporadically. Pedro got into all kinds of trouble and was totally offensive to her and Joseph. This was when Rowena had acted swiftly and signed him up for the army.

Freddie, as has been mentioned, eventually went off to Yorkshire under the cloaks of his new mother-in-law, Ava, and the new religious coven that he had joined. Gerald joined the Merchant Navy, and from a very early age saw a great deal of the world. He would come home for visits when on leave, and those times were always fraught with tetchiness.

Gerald was often either angry or emotional, yet he performed on his own stage. He never seemed to want to bring anyone else into his own drama, though he wanted to perform for any audience. Gerald respected Joseph, and the latter often steadied the young fiery, emotional youth with his placid and active listening.

Chapter 4

Bob and Bertha Farleigh lived next door to Rowena and Joseph's home. They had four sons, one of whom, the eldest, Bobby, was married and lived away from home. Bob and the other boys often tormented Bertha. Bob was rather more sinister towards poor Bertha, reiterating that she had lost things, or that she was getting more and more careless – an experience the parallel of the 1944 film by George Cukor, *Gaslight*. Rowena, incidentally, had a striking likeness to Ingrid Bergman, who played the lead female character.

One evening during the first week they moved into their new home, Rowena and Gordon decided to burn some rubbish at the end of the garden at the rear of the property. A couple of days later when Rowena went to the local shops to buy some groceries, an assistant, who happened to live further up the same road from Rowena, called her aside and gently told her that Bertha – for she was well known to the locals –had spread a rumour that "those red Indians next door were sending smoke signals late in the evening."

Rowena taken aback at first, but then smiled with the woman and they shared a sympathetic and knowing look that the poor wretch needed to be forgiven. Joseph also felt compassion more than anything else when he learned of it from Rowena later on that evening.

What was often heart-rending was the way in which Bob mentally tormented his wife, to the point of her believing that he was right in everything, and this was reflected in the way in which she began everything, "Bob says . . ." It wasn't long before Bob had Bertha committed to the local mental hospital, and Guy distinctly remembered visiting her there once or twice with Rowena and Joseph. Bob was then comparatively free to continue his affair with a woman up the road, Doris, whose hair was often a different hue each week.

Barbara did quite well at school, and her school was adjacent to Guy's. Barbara and Guy were the only two of the flock who really shared the same home on a day-to-day basis; they had their usual sibling strife, but they got along to some degree. There was a lingering resentment in her heart for Guy, whom they considered an unnecessary addition to their already fractured family. This often showed in outbursts towards him as being spoilt; perhaps in their eyes he was. He had a biological father who loved him, and actually stayed with him, while they did not.

Many a time when Guy was a babe in arms and being pushed about in his pram, he was let go of often at the top of fairly steep hills – all apparently done as a joke. Rowena did not agree with the sentiment, and that two word phrase often rang in her ears; the reader must have gathered this by now.

Apart from Freddie for a time, Guy did not genuinely bond with any of them. He never gave up trying – they were insecure attachments overall – until the day when he decided that he needed to divorce himself from them, as knowing them always seemed like walking on sand, and building on this medium, he knew through experience, was fruitless.

Before this mental divorce, which happened when he was way into his middle years, he tried in many ways to build bridges and mend things, yet they were always rejected or scorned. When Barbara married and returned to stay with Rowena and Joseph with her young daughter, Natalia, when she decided to file for a divorce, Venema came to visit and swanned in in her usual dramatic way. It was not a good time for Barbara, especially seeing her eldest half-sister, who she sensed would gloat over the events. This was when Rowena and Joseph ran the nursing home for Croydon Social Services. Guy was around and witnessed them sneering at one another.

Guy and Venema shared an interest in antiques, and he had a pair of figures that Venema had her eye on. In an attempt to make peace between them, he offered Venema the two figures, on the proviso that she make up with Barbara. He learnt from that day that no truce could work between them. Venema rather half-heartedly made the attempt, but they ended up in yet another fiery argument, and Venema duly left with her prize. Guy formed the opinion that day that there are some people who seem to have an unending supply of energy for squabbling and bickering.

Barbara had dated boys, and occasionally she brought them home; one or two lasted a while, but most did not. Even one of the Farleigh's sons next door asked her out. Barbara was stunning in her own unique way. With jet black hair, often in a beehive, and extremely well-groomed clothes, she cut a dashing figure. Yet Barbara created a subtle impression rather than the ostentatious one that her sister conjured.

After she left school, Barbara worked as a stenographer for a company in Croydon, and then went on holiday to Deal with some of her girlfriends from work.

Prior to this she had been seeing Bernard, a French boy whom everyone liked. He was energetic and likeable, and was devoted to Barbara. Bernard had a few months to complete his studies in architecture, and wanted to marry Barbara when he was finished. During the time he went back to Paris, Barbara met Johannes in Deal, who was also on holiday from Berlin. She was besotted by Johannes, and came back with such a passion burning in her heart that she was adamant that she wanted to marry him. She was also pregnant.

Rowena and Joseph told Barbara that she need not feel obligated to marry him just because she was pregnant; they would give the child their surname to prevent any stigma. Yet Barbara insisted that she wanted to marry Johannes and live with him in Berlin. So that happened, and again photographs of the wedding were sent to Rowena and Joseph.

Natalia was born in due course.

Barbara visited Rowena and Gordon, with young Natalia in tow, some five years later with a strong desire to divorce Johannes because she had found evidence of his adultery. Johannes visited them, and after reconciliation and a further consummation, the divorce proceedings were halted. They all returned to Berlin and a second daughter was born, Karin. However, there was the solicitor's bill to be paid.

Rowena got a job in a nursing home within walking distance of their home, and they actually saw it being built. She was accepted as a caregiver, and thoroughly enjoyed her work. Always a conscientious worker in whatever she did, sometimes her worries and anxieties prompted her to be a workaholic, and she always accepted whatever overtime was available, and seldom refused whenever she was asked in to cover other's shifts when they had not turned in or were off ill.

She got along fine with the matron, a Mrs Tanner, the successor of Miss Michelle and Miss Douglas – the reader will have read about them in *The Journeys* – and a devoted husband who was excessively possessive of her. Mrs Tanner told Rowena in confidence one day that they never married, and this shed more light on his possessiveness.

At weekends Guy helped at the home for the elderly. It accommodated 40 residents, with substantial flats for both the matron and deputy at the top of the building, along with large guest rooms as well. It was a red-brick, flat-roofed building that had its problems with wet seeping in after ten years.

Over time Rowena became a very trusted employee, and was often asked to act as deputy matron when the Tanners were away, living in the accommodation upstairs. The hierarchy system that governed the whole setup was comprised of a superintendent matron and three deputy superintendents, each of who had three or so of their own homes to supervise.

The superintendent, a Mrs Wainscot, drove about in a silver Ford Capri, a car that was considered *de rigueur* by some at the time, and there was a Mrs O'Hanlon, Miss Bruin, and Miss Schell, all quite different women with different backgrounds and experiences.

In her time with Croydon Council, Rowena was to have dealings with all four of these characters, and this will unfold as time goes on.

Chapter 5

Joseph had worked as a night porter in a Croydon hospital before they came to live in New Addington. He would cycle to Croydon and back, and did this for some years. The job gave them some security whilst there were so many things to deal with, and before Rowena began earning, Gordon's was the household's only income.

The household seemed much less busy now that everyone had left and married; the only one left was Guy. Venema had now married an Englishman who had chased her for some time, and he was a thick-set rather bull-headed type of person who saw that brawn spoke louder than brains. Venema often released small doses of poison into her new husband, Bruce, specifically about Joseph, and most definitely about her mother, whom she blamed for most of her shortcomings. Nevertheless, the seeds had been planted, and this tactic was one of the cobra dictator's finest.

When there was some strife between Rowena and Joseph when they ran Mooreland Rise – for even here they were not free of the troubles that Rowena's children brought them. Venema had visited her mother, and naturally being overwrought about work and the relevant pressures, Venema stepped in and took her home with her, leaving a message for Joseph about what she had done.

Joseph had strong forebodings about this. Guy was out with friends, and when he returned that evening he thought that his father had an abscess in his mouth, because it was severely swollen. Joseph related that when he went to collect Rowena from Venema's house, Bruce had answered the door and instantly started laying into Joseph, and in the background the cobra was spitting her poison and fuelling the episode. Rowena did not return that evening, and the cobra twirled and slithered about in glee at her achievement, whilst Joseph writhed about on the floor, but eventually got himself up in his own dignified way.

The situation was eventually resolved, and it became much clearer to Rowena that her daughter was growing in her hatred and vengeance. Rowena was contrite towards Joseph, and they got on with life, putting this down to yet further experience. Yet something inside of her died towards her daughter; she saw her for what Joseph had always said that she was. She could not deny it any longer, and perhaps she had always known it. But does not a mother live in hope that their child may change for the better?

When Rowena thought of her past experiences, or when memories of her two paramours came flooding back into her mind, she often felt an empty vacuum. Memories can indeed be our saboteurs. Yet somehow they can haunt us, especially in our darkest and loneliest of times, as if they are our hunters and we the prize game for their sport. Even though her beloved often tried to comfort her whenever he knew that she was reminiscent of that distant, yet memorable, past, Rowena could not get it out of her mind that she was to blame for the poisonous vengeance that her children carried with them.

Nagged by this inner anguish, Rowena paid a visit to a clairvoyant one day to have a reading. She had always had an interest in the occult, which was intensified by the many strange and fascinating things she had seen in India. The reader told Rowena that her Karmic path had a great deal of tribulations that she had to endure in order to rectify events from a past existence; there had to be a balance, which would occur when she had undergone these trials.

This made sense to Rowena, yet it still did not ease the discomfort that her many burdens brought, but having the understanding why they were there helped her understand the *raison d'être* behind them.

It seemed as though she had gone through the love and then hate of her two erstwhile paramours until there was an empty vacuum, which was an underlying force for her children, and this brought immense conflict for her. On the one hand, she had maternal feelings for them, yet the more they reminded her of their respective fathers, the less she liked them as people. It was a powerful dichotomy that haunted her most of her days.

Joseph was now working for Croydon Social Services, while also floating at other homes in the borough. After they had stood in as acting deputies for the home whilst the Tanners were on holiday, Mrs Wainscot approached them with a proposition. There was a home in Addiscombe that needed a deputy matron. The position came with accommodations, and she offered it to Rowena.

It was something that they would both have to discuss. The home in Addington was now far too large for their needs, and Guy was fifteen and could travel to school from Addiscombe with little difficulty. They had grown used to standing in as relief deputies, and were accustomed to both the residents and the staff, yet this was another challenge in a new place.

Joseph now also worked for the service, and reflected that he was now working in the same organisation whose director he once cleaned windows for. Gordon was in favour of Rowena taking a promotion, and also with further challenges, so they both agreed that they would take the position, and preparations were made right away. This was the time when they gave most of their possessions and furnishings to Freddie in Yorkshire, who had now secured a house in Barnsley.

Mrs O'Hanlon was from Leeds originally, yet had lived in the south for some years. She still had a pronounced Lancashire accent, which was often extremely entertaining, especially when Joseph and Guy mimicked her voice. Her mother was alive, yet quite elderly and cantankerous, and Mrs O'Hanlon had a husband whom she had married later in her life. A nephew lived with them, whom, after she got to know Rowena much more, she spoke a great deal about.

She seemed to get along very well with the matron of Mooreland Rise, a Mrs Skane, who lived in the top floor flat with her husband and rather growly dog, Candy, who was not at all sweet. The Skanes were from the same part of the country, so they all naturally had an affinity with one another.

Nora Skane was a small-framed woman who with a perceptive eye, yet her rather over-confident, even arrogant, persona housed a more vulnerable and nervous disposition. Ted Skane was a rather unsociable, gauche type of man, who appeared to have few social graces; he would grunt whenever he saw someone, rather than utter a word of greeting. Their dog seemed to take on his personality, as it was unapproachable and could not be petted without it baring its teeth, which they both would cover, saying that it was all harmless.

Nora showed all the pleasantries of accepting her new deputy, yet it was not too long before she began to intimate that Rowena was not as experienced as she was and had a long way to go. The latter took these comments and let them ride over her head, because she was so absorbed in the new position and new life to worry too much about other's remarks. Rowena always believed that events will always change and wrongs will be righted during the course of time, even though it could happen at a frustratingly slower pace than we anticipate.

In the lodge there was a large proportion of West Indian staff, with whom Rowena, Joseph, and Guy got along amicably. Gordon and Rowena were well-travelled people, and their horizons were far reaching, so they had a natural affinity with people not native to England. Over the course of time, however, Rowena noticed that Nora Skane's relationship with her staff was comparatively fractured, and her authoritarian attitude towards them did not help to build bridges between them.

On one occasion, both the matrons were on duty together because of a particular meeting and stock take, when Nora put resident's plates and teacups in the staff cupboard for their use. Ida Hill, the cook, who was a fiery, rather militant West Indian, found this to be an insult, and placing them on the floor, slid them to both matrons, saying that they were staff and not residents and they would not be using that crockery. Furthermore, she was aware that there was staff crockery and that they should use it.

"But wait, nah, you tink dat we are residents as well, Matron. We are your staff, and you give us de same plates as de residents? No, we don't want dem, Matron," shouted Ida.

It was a difficult situation, and both matrons had to withdraw to talk about what to do. Rowena pointed out to Nora that it was not advisable to put resident's crockery in the staff cupboard. Nora did not like hearing this, even though she intuitively knew that everyone would have something to say about it, but eventually got the staff crockery out from storage and had it duly washed and put into their cupboard. To Rowena, this reflected just how relations were between Nora and her staff.

From that time on, Rowena noticed that things seemed to decline. Nora was beginning to look more and more tired in the mornings, and was irritable during the day. Rowena concluded that Nora was taking heavy medication to sleep at night, as the latter had let that slip on one occasion. It was not long before there was talk about it, and one day Mrs O'Hanlon wanted to speak with Rowena about the situation. She felt like she was trapped between a tight corner and the deep blue sea; she did not want to appear disloyal, yet was also concerned for the well-being of her matron.

It was easier because Mrs O'Hanlon said that she had noticed the change in Nora, and that even when she had telephoned the lodge and Nora had answered, she did not seem as coherent and lucid as she normally was. Rowena gave her observations, which confirmed the deputy superintendent's theory that Nora needed time off, so Mrs O'Hanlon spoke with Nora and advised her to take a month off.

Unfortunately, Nora believed that Rowena had plotted this against her, and when she returned to work she was never the same towards her again. Nothing can be done when someone believes their own theories or deductions about someone else. As groundless as they may be, they then gather momentum within their own belief system.

When Nora returned to work, she found that the lodge was running smoothly and what problems there had been had been dealt with. The residents and staff were as happy as could be expected. They also liked their deputy matron, as she had a way of approaching people, calmly yet decisively. Nora did not revel in this harmony, but felt resentment towards it, and before too long she was at loggerheads with Ida Hill again.

It can be so apparent to anyone who observes that when certain people come into a gathering or room of people they can bring harmony, and some bring negative feelings that usually result in some kind of animosity or upheaval. Nora Skane promoted this action, whether purposefully or not, it happened and it grew in intensity until Ida Hill – clearly the self-appointed spokesperson for all the staff – asked to see Mrs O'Hanlon.

The meeting took over two hours, and Ida's loud, emotional, and penetrating voice could be heard from afar. She was a forceful woman, originally from Clarendon in the West Indies, and was an extremely buxom woman with a strong, even controlling, personality. Although militant in her attitude, she endeavoured not be insubordinate. Yet the chemistry between her and Nora was intensely negatively charged, and Ida Hill sensed acutely that Nora was racially prejudiced, and that she could not help but react to most of what her matron said in her own defence. I became clear that nothing was actually resolved that day, because Ida believed that Nora's attitude should change, and the latter's ego prevented her from seeing that she had done anything untoward.

Ida Hill put in for a transfer.

The next day when Rowena was on duty she spoke with Ida, whose bite she understood was much less than her bark, and persuaded her to reconsider her transfer. It seemed as though Ida needed this reassurance, and she was persuaded to stay, but vociferously stated that she had tried but could not get along with Nora. When Rowena planned the next staff rotas, she organised it so that Ida and Nora met as little as possible.

Over time this eased the situation. But Rowena watched Nora's decline – at first gradually, and then quite rapidly, as she became totally dependent on heavy night medication, which did not help her in the long run of things. When Nora was seen by two night staff taking medication from the locked medicine chest in the doctor's room of the lodge, it was reported first to Rowena, who then had to act. She duly spoke to Nora, telling her that she would have to report it to Mrs O'Hanlon. This turned Nora entirely against Rowena; she now believed that Rowena's intention from the outset was to oust her out of the job.

Rowena was in a dilemma. If she kept quiet about the incident, especially with her staff knowing, somewhere down the line there could be repercussions for her. If she reported it, it would definitely create ill feelings; Rowena took the risk of saying nothing.

Within the week, Nora was given the opportunity to resign, and Rowena remembered well the hostile way in which both the Skanes treated everyone who they came into contact with. She did learn from Nora that she was returning to the north, where they were thinking of taking early retirement.

On the day the Skanes left, Nora found Rowena in the lodge and asked to speak with her privately. She duly handed all her keys to Rowena, and with an acrid smile, said, "So now that you have what you planned for, my dear, I hope you'll be very happy with yourself. You're welcome to all of this, because in my estimation it's not worth the effort anyone puts in. Here are the keys, and it's *all* yours."

Rowena saw nothing more of the Skanes until one day after Joseph had died and they had moved on from Mooreland Rise. She and Guy saw them in a supermarket buying some groceries, but the Skanes remained quite insular.

"Lord Jesus, de woman gone! Me never believe dat she want to leave. What a relief, me dear sir."

Rowena was approaching the staff room and overheard some banter from Ida, and she smiled to herself. She did not believe for an instant that there would not be further issues with Ida, as she was a shop steward at heart, and was always swift on the uptake whenever her ego was even slightly brushed against. Yet aside to this, Ida had a great personality and was a very capable cook.

It was at Ida's home where Joseph first suffered his angina and later died in the hospital. For all of Ida's brashness and reactionary turns and twists, Rowena liked her, for she was honest, and in her mind, Rowena lay strong foundations so that they could both at least endeavour to build a strong working relationship. Ida was reliable and steadfast, even though her militant proclivities flooded into her objectivity many a time. Rowena found her to be a challenge which she welcomed, for she understood that they were to learn a great deal from one another.

Chapter 6

As time went on, Rowena found herself settling into the role, and overall she got along fine with her staff, which she would interview and select. Rowena had worked, socialised and interacted with people of other races, beliefs and customs, which gave her a wider horizon from which to view people overall. Other than her intuitive perceptiveness, her first impressions, which never let her down, were accurate, and she had learned to take notice of them after many years of being the fool and not noticing the signals. Now, she trusted her gut feeling and went with it, rather than against it or not take heed at all.

She had always sensed that Nora was jealous of her, and she often wondered why. Nora was experienced within this field of work, yet did not have that guile that Rowena possessed, and she still had an air of naivety, even though coldness and cynicism shadowed her heart from her many experiences to date. It often plagued her heart that Nora thought that she had designs on getting her dismissed from the job – it was the furthest thing from Rowena's mind – yet she understood that people will believe what they want to, irrespective of the truth.

Rowena and Joseph often talked at length about their journeys together, and now that all of her children were married and lived away in different parts of the land, it gave them room to ruminate and share laughter along with the heartaches and negativity. It was as if the Gordon and the Singh families were like detracting magnets, for the force that pushed them away from one another seemed a natural phenomenon rather than a contrived one.

Guy had grown up in a confused and eventful household, with one person quarrelling, verbally fencing or physically fighting another. Unfortunately, he never forged strong bonds with any of his stepfamily, because he always felt there was too much useless and excess garbage in the way which prevented clear-cut developments. To this end, he could be straightforward, and at times brusque, in his dealings with the Singh clan. Yet their responses always (predictably) came back to the same bone of contention – that he had it easier than all of them – but the difference was that Guy had a mother and father, and a father who stayed the course and was not errant. He was a man who loved with a huge heart, and felt the same level of anguish and pain when he saw Rowena's children hurting her time after time with their cruel words and actions.

Guy could not change this, so the resentment was hurled at him until he finally understood the reasons why. With his long journey in the study of psychology, he also eventually understood his own actions and reactions when certain words and behaviours smarted him. What is so desperately lamentable is when people spend their whole lifetime holding onto resentment and vengeance, which clouds their way of seeing life and their whole *raison d'être*.

In Venema's case, she blamed her mother for leaving what she considered her rightful inheritance in India when she took her children, with the assistance of the British Government, back to England. Neither Rowena nor Joseph was able to communicate to Venema the reason. What was a mother to do in a time of rampant and violent political uprisings, leave her children to fend for themselves with their errant fathers? Perhaps the Singh tribe would have had what was rightfully theirs materialistically, but where would the care and nurturing be that a naïve woman intrinsically gives freely to her children?

Here again, Venema was set in her the belief that she now had to struggle along in life, as opposed to living in ease and luxury with the means which her father had given to her! So, with this demonic seed in her mind, she set the same belief in her other siblings, the Raghubir blood gang.

"But, Venema, what else did your father do for you and your brothers?"

"What does that matter? If one can live a life of ease, because although daddy was an errant artist, he had money which I could live off now, so that is indeed better than what *love* has taught or brought me! *She* brought me up and then dragged me across to the other side of the world where I had to ward off the harsh remarks and bitchiness from other women because *my* beauty outshone theirs.

"But I learned how to survive, and I developed my personality so that no one could resist me and my gold-plated charms, even though underneath the real gold my mettle had been poisoned and was now black as pitch. I became the master of the double entendre, because I enjoyed cutting people down in their complacency, especially when they grew puffed up with pride with my exaggerated compliments, and then I'd watch them crumble, my honeyed-sword tongue cutting them down!

"But she and that other one that she married – although he was a match for me and I could not handle his clear-sighted directness peering through me – were to blame. Yet another man taking her away from us. Yes, *she* always had a man. Damn her!

"I was glad that Bruce beat that Joseph up. I enjoyed watching him squirm on the ground, and I did it. But now, on reflection that they are now both dead, I am not glad. I also remember when she told me that he had died, and I remarked in a cavalier way, 'Well maybe I might see more of you now.'"

It is about there being a man in the way. Is it not, dear cobra queen? But now they are together in eternity, and there is nothing that you can say, think, or feel that will harm their eternal bliss. They do not worry about anyone, because they know that we all have to face our own Karmas; no one can do it for us.

Another phenomenal element about the Cobra Queen of Poison was that she had a decidedly poor memory. But then one asks if that is not a natural progression for someone who chooses not to remember their past and thereby waylay all reckoning. Although one can live a lifetime choosing not to remember thoughts and actions, they still have to be faced and addressed, and the part that we played in their epicentre has to be acknowledged.

What became the focal point of Venema's life were the children she produced, for they could do no wrong, as they were her creation and were naturally perfect in all respects – especially in those ways where others had let her down most drastically.

She and Bruce had a boy child they called Piers, who happened to be a beautiful child, yet who also died whilst asleep in his cot one night. It was a tragedy and such a wrench for both parents who mourned his loss for some time after. Later in her years, Venema had another boy and then a girl, both of whom she idolised.

Rowena's connections with her grandchildren were as fractured an affair as her relationship with her own children. Yet what grandchildren she saw at times took to her, and welcomed her playful spirit and winning ways.

It was not until Gordon pointed out to his beloved that her eldest daughter was jealous of her –something which she had always dismissed, for it challenged the concept of humility that she held of herself, and this could often be noticed with the jibes and course comments Venema made towards her mother – did Rowena begin to understand the motives behind Venema's behaviour towards her. Jealousy and resentment can be such powerful and destructive saboteurs that they prevent any real and heartfelt feelings to develop. Instead, they influence the mind with dark and destructive thoughts that prevent any true bonding between people.

"What a waste of time and energy!" Joseph would often exclaim when he and his beloved would talk and reflect together. Rowena would look at her foot cross-legged over the other and reflect in silence.

Rowena often thought about what went through her children's minds and agreed with Gordon that if only there could be more to share and grow together with, rather than experience this fractured affair that could not be called a family. Although she knew that she needed to be strong and rise above all the criticism and judgements hurled at her from them, at times she grew weak and fell prone to crying, and even dark and bleak moods where she'd withdraw and hurt those who she knew loved her dearly.

Yet it can also be just as easy to get into the same game and play as the others, with spears ready to attack when blame is cast out like a net. Rowena had to understand that her eldest daughter sewed poison; this was her forte. However, to continue to blame her for this likened her to the Cobra Queen of Poison, so that she became a persecutor in the game just like Venema.

As time went on, over the years of experiencing different things, Rowena learned through her own research just what forgiveness actually meant. She always had an interest in the occult, which had been intensified by her travels in India. She met a woman one day who did a Tarot reading for her, and they saw one another from time to time. They often had long talks about the meaning of life and the *raison d'être* of being.

Whenever Rowena thought of the word and the act of forgiveness, she recalled a stern-faced Baptist minister evangelising on the sins of the people and announcing, "The wages of sin is death." She never understood, beyond the threats and the instilling of fear in people, just what such men ever meant. It never inspired any real belief or feeling in her, more like self-loathing, and the word *forgiveness* also had religious and judgemental connotations to it.

Yet one day she discovered just what forgiveness really meant. She first understood, after searching at great length for a synonym for it, but none could be found that adequately paralleled it; it is a unique word, as is its action. To truly forgive, she learned, was to completely let go of all memory of something painful, thereby freeing ourselves from its burden. In this way, the whole action can be considered selfish, but in a self-protecting way, rather than to see it in a judgemental way of excluding the feelings of everyone else. She understood, too, that one would naturally be aware of such a person who has caused hurt, but all memory of what they had inflicted would need to be forgotten – not an easy task, especially when holding onto such memories has been a habit. It does, however, have the power to release us from the bondage of vengeance and resentment, because there are no more emotional or mental ties to them.

As time went on she practised this, and it gave her some respite, at least from what her children believed that she had not done for them. However, the void that was left when her beloved died could never be filled, until she believed she would see him again in spirit.

Both Joseph and Rowena had become so reliable and industrious within their roles, and as they now both worked for the corporation, the joint running of Mooreland Rise was offered to them. After some deliberation, it seemed the most advisable step to take – yet no one knows just how much pressure is involved in living and working together until they do it.

The secret that she had kept all her life about her father raping her still lingered deep within her, yet it was not yet the time for it to rear its buried head. Actually, Rowena was not strong enough to verbalise it until later on in her sojourn at Mooreland Rise. There was another recent thought that kept occurring in her mind whenever she thought of Nora Skane. Rowena could not help but feel a strong sense that Nora's demise was prophetic of her own circumstances. And again, this would unfold in time.

Rowena and Gordon took up their respective posts in running Mooreland Rise, and as they were both travelled people and had known other cultures, they got along well with their staff, which was predominantly West Indian. They were able to share humour from time to time, which assisted the demanding work.

Chapter 7

Ida Hill was as strong and domineering a leader in her home as she was at work. She was married to Terry Blackthorne, a man who came over as rather eloquent and knowledgeable, yet his ego used the tool of arrogance, which rendered him defensive and at times argumentative, as he was always attempting to gain the upper hand.

With Ida, Terry endeavoured to use logic, which helped some of the time, depending totally on the mood that Ida was in. However, during the times when her emotions ran to the highest level, he could not appease her and retreated. When Ida was in "cyclone mode" it was best for everyone to just leave her alone, lest anyone get caught up and trapped in her merciless whirlwind.

Ida and Terry both had children from previous marriages, and they had married one another in their forties. Terry was from another part of the West Indies. Ida had a sense of fashion, as well as a streak of subversiveness, where she might wear pink with red, or another item of clothing which would be of her choosing, rather than what fashion dictated to her. Terry was more conservative in his appearance, and overall was a handsome man.

Ida had a sister, Pearl, some two or so years younger than herself, yet they were often at loggerheads. Ida disagreed with how her sister brought up her children, especially the girls, who Ida described as being slack in morale fibre.

Ida's remonstrates to her sister ran something like: "You know, Pearly, dose gals will have pickneys before dem old enuff, becas you na give dem enuff discipline, girl." *(Those two girls will have children of their own before they are old enough, because you don't give them enough discipline.)* And sure enough, two of Pearl's daughters had had children before they were fourteen.

Ida and Pearl had another sister called Jo, who had a daughter, Antonia, when she was very young. Jo could not handle Antonia once she reached her fourteenth year, so she sent her to live with Ida until she was twenty-one and decided to emigrate to America. Antonia got along with Ida most of the time, and learned like everyone else to avoid her aunt when she sensed that there was a storm brewing. There was always a strained relationship between Jo and Antonia. Yet somehow Antonia had a soft spot in her heart for her volatile aunt, and would not hear an adverse word said about her.

Ida was from Clarendon in Jamaica, and came to Great Britain in the 1950s when there was a large immigrant population explosion there, chiefly from the West Indies. Ida was but a young girl when her mother and father brought her and her two sisters over on the boat from Jamaica. Like many from their homeland, they all found it a challenging experience with a different culture, different ways of living, and most of all different values. Sadly, that which is not understood can often be seen as threatening, and Ida had her fair share of animosity, adverse remarks and rejection from "dem white folks."

One evening Ida and Terry asked Rowena, Joseph, and Guy over for a meal. Rowena and Ida had become sound work colleagues, and Ida, although often headstrong, always gave to both her managers their due deference as her superiors.

Work at Mooreland Rise was becoming increasingly burdensome for Joseph, as he was doing all of the work; Rowena was now drinking heavily and the pressure on his shoulders was intense. Rowena's outbursts at him and Guy were vitriolic, but in the light of the new day Rowena was always contrite and ashamed of herself, often not even remembering what she had said in her drunken stupors. Ida, being a perceptive woman, thought that an evening out would do them the world of good, and so invited them over for a Jamaican meal.

There had been some friction between Guy and his father, and the pressure from the explosive situation in their small family environment was reaching its crescendo. The evening out at Ida's seemed to be a release valve, and it did ease the tension somewhat, yet ironically no one knew that this ease was to portend tragedy.

Ida did herself proud with her Jamaican feast. She had prepared fried snapper served with rice and peas and callalou. She gave strict instructions to "Mind de bones of de fish, Matron, cos me na wan you to suffer. Just eat your fill in comfort now." The spread was indeed splendid, and Ida washed down her repast with a hearty glass full of rum.

During the meal, Joseph was sipping a whiskey and suddenly looked drawn and his face went ghostly white. Everyone was immediately concerned, and then his head drooped and he fell into a slump over the table.

Ida dramatically shouted, "Lord Jesus, de man sick! Antonia, call an ambulance, gal, and tell dem a man here is dying."

Ida, in her spontaneous, dramatic and prophetic outburst, rang that bell of imminent death in everyone's ears, and then there was a loud knocking at the front door. The paramedics took Joseph and Guy to the local hospital, along with Ida, who took the lead and suggested that it would better for her to go, as Rowena was inebriated.

It was a frightening and worrying time for everyone, and whilst Guy waited with Ida outside the ward where Joseph was rushed to, they both heard him screaming for life – a sound that haunted Guy for many a dream afterwards. Ida held Guy's hand affectionately, but he was distracted and looked ahead into space. Then they all watched lights flashing and medical people in white coats rushing to the where Joseph was – and then there was silence, like the aftermath of a raging storm.

Ida and Guy gave each other knowing looks, and then a doctor approached Guy, telling him that the medical staff did what they could to save his father, but to no avail. His father had passed away in the early hours of that morning. When Guy thought about it, he knew when he had seen his father go pale at the table that his sojourn on this plane was approaching its end, and the screams for life he'd heard from his father in the hospital were for care for those he was leaving behind. Guy knew that life would not be easy without him, but he knew that he would have to take control.

When they returned to Mooreland Rise, Rowena looked up at Guy and said, "He's not coming back is he? He's . . . gone!"

Chapter 8

The funeral was a daunting affair, yet Guy knew instinctively that he had to take control. Sadly, he did not have the space to vent his own grief or sense of loss of his father. He became the rock to which his mother held fast, which naturally could not replace her profound loss of her beloved, yet he was a scaffold whereon she could safely lean.

Joseph was a highly respected man, and many people attended his funeral, and a stunning array of wreaths and flowers bedecked the antechamber to the church. Barbara had come from Germany, and she gave what comfort she could to her mother. Guy felt that it was good that their mother had another woman to be with.

Venema's words often rang in Rowena's mind like a huge tolling bell, "Oh, he's gone, so can I come and see you more often." This was when Rowena was struggling to resume her work, and when she telephoned her eldest daughter one day to tell her of Joseph's demise. And she remembered the time when Venema stood over Joseph, gloating when her husband, Bruce, had attacked Joseph. She could never seem to forget that gleeful smirk on her daughter's face. Memories . . . often thoughts can appear like poisoned arrows or hovering assassins to our equilibrium; they can often taunt and undermine an already troubled mind.

Rowena knew that there had never been any great fondness between Joseph and Venema. Still, the coldness and lack of feeling in those words cut her deeper than the cruelty that she and her beloved had encountered since beginning a new life in England.

How would she be able to overcome this, this mightiest wrench in her life to date? It seemed as though a huge part of her had been torn out of her body, and she wondered if that cavern within her would always reverberate its hollowness. Of the people Rowena had known intimately in her life, Joseph was the one person who tried his utmost to understand her often bizarre and exasperating ways, and he was the one person who she had given the most heartache to.

In her quietest of moments, Rowena often reflected just how strong the irony in life is, that the one man whom she was devoted to had been the one she very often dealt with the worst. In the aftermath of her greatest loss, she lamented him with her whole being, and she felt tortured by the memory of how badly she had treated him, recalling the vitriolic tirades that she threw at him. This was probably the most heart-wrenching experience of her life, because her guilt was as rife and prevalent as her grief. And this time it was not shame for what was done to her, but sheer and absolute guilt for her own miserable self-indulgence.

Yet clichés have their uses; it's only when they're used about death do they become tiresome and trite. Rowena's clairvoyant friend told her that "wounds do heal, and great loss gets easier over time," yet who can believe that at the time?

The interesting twist in the tale was that no sooner had Rowena outed the horrific secret that had plagued her all her life, and in this way released it by verbalising it, she then had this major loss to deal with.

Her drinking did not abate, and it came to the stage when both Guy and Barbara went to see their family doctor to tell him of the situation. After hearing about it, Dr Fleishman told them in an absolute way that their mother would never give up drinking. Guy found this to be defeatist and voiced his opinion to the doctor, saying that there had been times in the past when he had made these absolute remarks about other ailments that Rowena had had, and he, the doctor, had been as negative.

"What you are saying is surely beyond your knowledge, and is not helpful to us or our mother." Barbara tried to quiet Guy, but he continued, "So what do you advise that we should do?"

"I will arrange for her to be admitted to an alcohol recovery unit immediately."

When they both left the surgery the doctor said, "I hope everything works out all right." Guy turned and looked at him and said nothing. Yet his look travelled deep.

The cold day came in mid-winter when Barbara and Guy took their mother to the alcohol rehabilitation unit; Rowena was like a feral cat, snarling at them both. When they all went to the room that was allotted her, Rowena was wringing her hands through her hair, and snarled, "You're putting me away, and I'll never forgive you for it. Get out of here!"

The memory of that day haunted Guy for a long time afterwards, and at the time he wondered if her words were true or just a reaction to her children's' plan of action.

Dr Fleishman had known Rowena since she moved to her home in Addington, and Guy had known him all his life. Fleishman had told Rowena some extremely thought-provoking things in the time that he was her family general practitioner. Then, some years after Rowena had moved away from that practice, it came to light that he was not a medically trained doctor at all – he had done a brief correspondence course and bought his medical degree.

When Rowena had had some pain in the joints of her left hand, Fleishman had told her that it was arthritis and that in time she would lose the use of the hand, as this was how the condition deteriorated. Another time Rowena had some troublesome pain in her stomach, and Guy came in after work one day to find her in a severely withdrawn state of mind, looking ghostly pale. It happened to be voting day, which always falls on a Thursday, and Gerald was visiting, yet was well under the influence of alcohol at the time and much more intent on showing his mother pictures of his hot tub in Canada, and naturally did not notice that his mother was ill. When Guy asked her what was wrong, she told him that Fleishman had told her that she had cancer – something that she had feared, as her mother, Bessie, had died of this. Guy insisted that she get another opinion, and went along to the same practice to see another partner in it. She was sent for relevant tests and was admitted to hospital for gallstones.

So when Guy heard Fleishman say that their mother would not recover, it sent off red alert signals in his mind, and because Barbara did not know of the history, she could not share this with him, so naturally thought that Guy was being impatient and rude to the doctor. How easy it is to misjudge without knowing the facts.

There is a quote from the New Testament that Christ said to one of his disciples, "Hope doesn't disappoint us." Guy certainly had hope that each time he saw a member of his stepfamily there would be an opportunity to build a relationship, yet every time his hopes were dashed. Collectively, it would be safe to say that there was too much excess baggage in the way of any clear development along those lines.

Each time he saw Gerald, who had decided to call himself Gerard and had made a base for himself in Canada, there was trouble. For some time Guy wondered what he had done wrong. In calling himself Gerard he had developed an accentuated American brogue, which seemed to intensify the more he wanted to impress people, and when he had drink he was nothing less than unbearable to be with. When he later gave up alcohol, he described himself as the performer on his own stage, and saw everyone else as his audience who was there to listen and pander to him.

Gerald also believed that people were after his money. He did help people out – even lent Guy money over the years – but there was a cynical aspect to his nature which had to mention the loans sooner or later, in the pretext of "I've given you my money, so now you serve me." When he was challenged in discussion, or someone exercised their own individuality, he got angry with the attitude that they had no right to an opinion. He was like his true blood sister Barbara in this – they command and others obey.

Gerald wanted to hold onto his own demons, because as they were familiar – however destructive – he let them sabotage his way of thinking clearly and constructively. It just took him further and further into the bowels of the labyrinth wherein he snarled and barked at the world, and especially at his mother and father. Even though he evinced closeness to his mother, he harboured a deep resentment that she had not done enough for him. And regarding his biological father, he wanted to kill him over and over again.

When Guy was a young teenager, Joseph and Rowena searched out Chunny and telephoned him, arranging to go and see him with Barbara and Gerald. He lived in a remote part of Devon bordering the moors, and the meeting was brief and fraught with tension. Joseph had suggested the idea to Rowena, and then to Chunny's two children, that they visit their father. There was indifference at first, and then rejection of the idea, but they changed their minds and went to visit him.

When Rowena saw her ex-paramour, she winced; he had gained weight, was balding quite dramatically, and she sensed that he was a troubled man. Chunny had married an English woman, Annabelle, who did not seem too welcoming of the visiting family. Gerald and Barbara had little to say to their father, as they never really knew him, and sensing the tension, Joseph and Rowena decided that they should all leave. There was no more contact between the two parties; Chunny remained the absent father.

Soon after that visit Gerald returned to sea with the Merchant Navy, and Barbara was withdrawn for some time after. Gordon tried many times to tie up loose ends or bring together what seemed permanently fractured between members of Rowena's nuclear and extended family, yet it was not possible. In the end, he accepted that parallel lines just don't come together, so get used to it.

Chapter 9

When Rowena was in India, another one of her brothers, Ernest, came to visit her, and she had a photograph taken along with Chunny and a very young Gerald and Barbara. Ernest was on military service and was posted for a short time in Bombay, so decided to look up his younger sister.

Ernest was not as burly in build as their father and looked somewhat more refined in features than their brother Frederick. Ernest seemed to take their mother's swarthy Mediterranean complexion and had distinctive black hair, which gave him the look of an Italian or Spaniard.

At the time, Rowena and Chunny were moving quite well together, which was well before he started using heavy drugs. At the outset everyone seemed to get along – and who does not look like they get along in a photograph – but there was an undercurrent that disturbed Rowena. She did not fully trust her brother's intentions.

He was not intending to stay long, as he only had a short leave, and he seemed to gel to some extent with the two children.

Rowena had persuaded Chunny to invite Dr and Mrs Mystery next door to dinner one night, along with her brother and another friend of the family, Mahatma Gandhi. Everyone dressed formally for dinner – Rowena had hired a dinner suit for her brother.

Gandhi was as gracious as ever, yet he no longer wore western clothes and was now wearing his own white home-spun robes that reflected his own purity of heart. Rowena always enjoyed his company and felt totally safe, and was always warmed by his conversation, even though she understood that he had a mission to fulfil, so his arguments could get directional.

Ernest, without realizing the extent of the work that Gandhi was doing for India, still respected him, yet was somewhat baffled by the conversation when it took on a political tone, and then of course all general discourse is diminished as soon as either religion or politics comes into play in any gathering.

Whilst the ayahs cleared away the used utensils after the meal, Rowena took her brother out onto the veranda to ask him about Wales. There was a full moon that night, and the veranda was lit up like there were many floodlights on it; the moonlight was that strong. There was a warm breeze engulfing them, and Rowena was dressed in a rather stunning sari with varying shades of blue. Her dark eyes were enhanced with some kohl, and her lips were stained with a ruby hue.

Rowena pointed to some seats and gestured for her brother to sit down. After they both sat she asked him how it was in Wales. "It's been so long since I was there, Ernest. How is mother?"

"Well . . . I . . . need to tell you that mother passed away last week, and within a few days father died too."

Rowena looked at him fixedly. "Was she in pain, Ernest?"

"Apparently not, she went in her sleep, and it looked as though father couldn't manage without her; he just declined and went soon after. Other than that, everything and everyone is the same. Nothing seems to change," he said in his heavy Welsh brogue.

Rowena actually saw her father in a totally different light for once in her life. The only picture she had in her mind of him was that he was a drunken brute who violated his daughter and bullied his wife. Into this one-sided picture came a different nuance of light and shade. It was as if the black-and-white negative had been infused with some colour.

She actually felt that he did have feelings after all, and was as vulnerable as anyone else. Bessie, although frail by stature and submissive by nature, was Frederick's backbone after all, and he, a brutish bully was really a weak and dependable man. For once in her life she actually felt some warmth for her father, though it was just a waft that passed through and over her.

Ernest approached his sister and knelt down in front of her. Rowena felt self-conscious and uncomfortable; there had never been any affection felt or shown between them, so this was a surprise. He took her hand and squeezed it, then soon after his hand wandered and ran down her thigh.

She instantly gathered the intention behind his actions, and stood up, saying, "I think you'd better go, Ernest."

"I'm sorry, but you are a beautiful woman."

"And I'm your *sister*! Just get your things together and leave," she hissed.

Rowena felt sick to her stomach and wondered if she might vomit up her revulsion, but she had to do this with dignity, at least for the sake of her guests.

She followed Ernest into the lounge. There were rather heated discussions being shared by all, but she spoke up. "Excuse me for interrupting, but Ernest has decided that he needs to be on his way. There was some confusion about his deadlines."

Ernest left trying to say a goodbye to Rowena, but she ignored him; she was still in a state of shock. Even though she realized that he was fighting in the war and she may never see him again, that did not prompt her to say anything to him. How that steel claw gripped her heart once again.

Rowena was looking over some photographs, and that family shot with them always prompted that memory. She also noticed that many pictures had been ripped out of her album, and she wondered what memories they would conjure up for her children, who she knew had taken them.

On further reflection, that phrase still rang like a huge bell in her mind – demon seed. She thought about both her and Joseph's extended family, and still that bell in her head rang even louder. Many years after Rowena and Joseph settled in England, Rowena heard nothing of her extended family. Now that she knew that her mother had passed away, she had little inclination to contact any of her other siblings; growing up was a very fractured affair.

When Rowena returned to Wales after leaving India, her eldest sister, Sylvia, was also in nursing. Sylvia was like their father, domineering and wilful, and was always full of criticism of her sister's actions. When Rowena and Joseph came to London she lost contact with Sylvia, and honestly saw little point in getting to know her, because she seemed to be a female version of her father, fundamentally a bully.

However, Joseph prompted Rowena to take the step to bridge any rifts that lay between her and her family, and when they were established at Mooreland Rise, they decided to get in contact with Sylvia again. Rowena had heard from the grapevine that she was the sister in charge of a hospital in Kent. When Rowena telephoned the said hospital asking for Sister Cousins, she was told that there was no sister by that name, but there was a Nurse Cousins. Rowena never let on to Sylvia that she knew that she wasn't a sister, for she thought that because Rowena was now a matron of a nursing home, Sylvia did not want to be her subordinate.

Sylvia was married to Bert, a rather gauche and course man who could come over as being common. He had no art of conversation, but was always trying to get people into a jovial mood, for that way he felt that he had won people over. His opening gambit was always a joke of some kind, and usually at someone else's expense. He enjoyed schadenfreude, but guised it with humour.

Rowena and Joseph remembered, and often talked about, the very first time they met Bert. His opening gambit was a joke that ran thus: "Anyone know where the word bungalow comes from?"

Joseph offered that it could have derived from a place called Bangalore in India where there was always low-level housing, to which Bert interjected in his raw cockney accent, "Na, two builders ran out o' materials one day, and one said to the uvver, '*bung a low* roof on that one.'"

Bert found this so funny that he laughed for some time afterwards, as if to himself; others could see the connection, and were mildly amused.

Bert had been married before, and had two daughters by that marriage who were now in their teens. When Sylvia married Bert and went to live in his house, she ordered him to burn all existing furniture in the home out in the back garden, and she forbade his two daughters from ever coming to *her* home. Bert complied and followed all orders to the tee. Sylvia allowed Bert to see his daughters, but she did not want to know when or where.

This dictatorial and controlling streak ran through the paternal side of the Rees family line it seemed, and at times when Rowena looked at herself, she realized that she had to be controlling over her children when she came over from Bombay to England in that cold winter of 1951. She hoped that she was not like what she saw in her eldest sister. Rowena had always found that people who want to control so totally are often the most insecure, and the outward show of bravado really reflects their fear of being lost.

Sylvia had two children together, two sons, who also had the dark swarthy Mediterranean look of their grandmother. It was an interesting twist of fate that after Sylvia so often vilified Rowena for getting involved with "darkies," her youngest son married a West Indian girl, whom Sylvia claimed she adored.

It later came to pass when Rowena and Joseph met up with her other sister, Rhoda, she relayed to both of them that Sylvia had told Rhoda that Rowena wanted nothing to do with her. Rhoda also went on to say that her husband, Derek, had asked Sylvia to leave their home one day because she was interfering too much and causing unrest and friction in their home.

Rhoda had suffered with rickets when a small girl, which left her legs slightly bowed. She was like Rowena in many ways, and it looked as though their father had raped Rhoda as well after Rowena left for London to work in the Simmonds' dairy.

Rowena often reflected, whenever she thought about any of her family, that the enjoyable moments with them were minimal, and the course, strained experiences with most of them often left her feeling empty.

Is it an illusion when one sees others with family or friends in a state of unison and feels that the grass is greener on the other side? This was something she often asked herself, and at times she became envious of the harmony between others, because she wanted it so badly, yet had never seemed to hold it within her grasp. But Rowena was not intrinsically a jealous person, and such surges of jealousy of others' harmony were transient.

Even her relationship with Rhoda, however enjoyable, did not last. Those castles were again built on sand.

***

When Rowena lived with Chunny in Dehra Dun, she gained the reputation of being a healer. This came about when she tended one of her ayahs who had a severe gash on her hand, which had happened whilst she was preparing lunch. The cut was deep, as the knife had slipped and reached the bone. Rowena tied up the woman's arm and got her to hold it up so that the blood stopped rushing to the hand; it was a simple process really, yet clearly done with such attentiveness that her reputation as a healer spread, and soon other locals came to her for remedies for various things. The ayah with the cut hand, Manjeet, was so indebted to her that she always greeted Rowena afterwards with her hands together in a prayer position and head bowed, like the traditional Eastern greeting, yet it carried more devotion in it, and Rowena was touched.

Although the relationship with Chunny was changeable in comparison to her married life with Raghubir – which really existed when he returned from his peregrinations and wanted his conjugal rights – it was exciting. Rowena realized after meeting Chunny that the buzz that one could feel through such exhilaration reached deep within and was a great energising force.

Unfortunately, there was a cruel streak in Chunny which Rowena witnessed to her great sorrow one day. Rowena had a black cocker spaniel named Chuchy, which everyone loved and the children often played with. Dr Mystery had a piebald male spaniel, and they both agreed that it would good to have them mate.

Chunny was beginning to drink quite heavily, much more than just having a little more than usual after a meal. Whenever Rowena mentioned this to him he naturally became defensive. Chuchy was now pregnant, and she happened to be in Chunny's way when he was stumbling about one day. He kicked her out of his path and she tumbled down the stairs to the bottom, howling in a state of confusion and pain. Sadly, she lost all five of the puppies that she carried, and Chunny later feigned concern, but Rowena did not feel that he meant it – she always wondered if he was jealous of her love for her dog.

Rowena's doubts about Chunny's stability and trustworthiness began to deepen, and naturally, Dr Mystery was questioning his trust of his neighbour, leading him to become suspicious of his motives. Chunny was also prone to severe mood swings, and could have a nihilistic attitude when under the influence of drugs. His son, Gerald, inherited this trait, as his moods swings were also phenomenal.

His mood swings suddenly culminated one day when he aimed a loaded rifle at Rowena after she had made a cutting remark to him about his substance misuse.

"Just look at what you're becoming, Chunny. The children are afraid of you, and I never know how you're going to be from one minute to the next," Rowena pleaded.

"Don't you speak to me like that," he replied. "What do people think about you then, the great and respected Sunita, the accomplished whore of Dehra Dun, favoured of the great and wise Ricchypal Singh? I'm tired of you and all this baggage that comes with you. Now leave me alone before I blow your brains out!"

Rowena screamed loudly then, and soon after somebody was thudding on the front door. Dr Mystery then ran in and asked what was going on; he said that he'd heard the shouting for some time.

This was when Chunny's mood swung once again to one of sheer remorse. He dropped the rifle and broke down, sobbing like a lost child. The rifle went off and the bullet hit the wall. Rowena screamed again and then went to comfort the children.

Dr Mystery gingerly picked up the rifle, looked at both Chunny and Rowena, and told Rowena that they had to leave the madhouse before someone got killed. He then offered that she and the children could stay with them.

Dr Mystery spoke to Chunny peremptorily, "I will keep hold of this firearm, Singh, before you do actually kill someone with it. Whether you like it or not, Rowena and the children are coming to stay with us."

Chunny said nothing; he just stared fixedly at the floor and then slumped into a chair saying, "I'm so sorry."

***

Still withdrawn, Rowena sat alone in the alcoholic rehabilitation unit after a group meeting. Used to burying the sordid details of her life, she naturally found it difficult to verbalise them. However, she knew that she had to speak of being raped by her father and how her disgust for herself and her hatred for men had grown within her like some uncontrollable phantasm that took form when she wanted to attack so she would not be hurt again.

She understood deep down that what Barbara and Guy had done was for her own good, because the quantity of alcohol she was consuming every day would easily have felled a Tyrannosaurus Rex. So her anger towards them both had abated, and so had her rage at Guy for shopping her to the psychiatrist for drinking at home at weekends. She felt truly cornered, without any props to hold her up. She had to face everything now, and life was not as hectic as it used to be to curtain all those dark, haunting secrets.

Some would call this a Shamanic rebirth. Rowena was to begin again, her foundation built this time on solid, truthful ground instead of deceptive sand as it had been before. Anything that frightened her was *not* to be buried and hidden from view. From now on it was to be faced. Slowly, the more she did this the easier it became. Of course, the first step was the most excruciating, but she began to gain strength within herself. It felt strangely powerful, but in a pure and strong way.

She no longer felt fractured, even though her children and events outside were. She realized that it was just the way it was. She was growing inside, and for once in her life she felt that she was maturing solidly, no longer that haunted and frightened child, but a free child of the universe. Somehow, her resentment and bitterness of past experiences lost their hold over her, and she was able to look at the tapestry of her life with clearer objectivity and much less pain. This was when she understood the meaning of forgiveness, to be able to let go.

When Rowena had first come into the unit she was not responding to anyone coherently, and she was so full of retaliation, revenge and hatred that little could be done for her. In a semi-comatose state one day, she heard an attending doctor ask the question, "Who is her next of kin?"

In the distance Rowena heard Venema's voice, "I am, Doctor."

Rowena was eternally grateful to her eldest daughter, the Cobra Queen of Poison. For in hearing that egotistical yet cold statement, it fired the blood in her veins once again and she felt reborn. Rowena had made the decision to pull through this period in her life, and she prepared herself for the mental and physical assault that she knew instinctively would make her whole.

Chapter 10

Joseph Gordon's plans for his sizeable gardens were already buzzing about in his head the first day he set eyes on them. Although they were somewhat overgrown and gone to weed, he nevertheless could see their potential. It was a double-fronted garden, as the home was on a corner plot, a red brick three-bedroom house built around 1930.

What he planned was to have the two flanks on either side of the central path leading to the front door laid to lawn, with round beds in the centre and borders encircling the perimeter to grow colourful annuals in the summer, and have masses of daffodils and narcissi underplanted for a rich spring carpet. In the two well-prepared round beds he would grow his roses – his greatest passion. He was eager to grow Ena Harkness, which were named after Violet Carson (Ena Sharples) of *Coronation Street* fame, and newly out.

In borders around the path and the rose beds he had low-growing perennials, with room to put in annuals for a mass of colour every spring. He also had underplanted many narcissi, which later came up as a thick carpet of yellow. His favourite here were jonquils, which he let Guy initially plant and feel pride over when they came up every year. On the right flank, looking from the road to the house, adjacent to the door leading into the back garden, was a rectangular area where he cultivated an Alpine plot with various shaped rocks and granite. As it became established it looked rich and verdant.

In his travels in search of garden materials he had found some Victorian edging stones with a classic twisted shape at their tops. Some were terracotta and other were shades of graphite and black, and he used them in one colour when lining a bed, rather than integrating them all in, and this gave more of a uniform and ordered appearance. Guy wanted to integrate them but he did not get his way there.

The rose beds he prepared with much diligence, digging down a good six feet before he put in organic matter and horse manure. Riders often passed by on their horses, as there were stables not too far away, and he shovelled up the fresh droppings and fed his valued roses regularly; it became a standing joke too.

"Nothing like fresh manure for the roses," he would say with a smile. This practice, along with his diligent pruning, evidently paid off, because his roses bloomed to perfection every year.

He cultivated a vegetable patch in part of the bottom end of the back garden and grew green beans, broad beans, sweet corn, tomatoes, radishes, lettuces, and of course potatoes. Guy often helped him weed the patch, and he was allowed a space where he grew items of his choice. The larger part he laid to lawn again, with borders with masses of daffodils standing like soldiers in the springtime sunshine, and annual scarlet impatiens or deep red begonias or pelargoniums. To the right of the house as you approached from the back door, further down from the shed, he planted a shrubbery and put in buddleia bushes of different shades of lilac and purple, and always took Guy to watch the Red Admiral, Peacock, and yellow Brimstone butterflies as they sunned themselves on its bracts.

These were interspersed with cordylines, Laurel and Hebe veronicas – some green and some variegated – which all added thick and voluptuous vista after a few years of getting established. At the rear of the back garden on the flank opposite the vegetable patch, he had cultivated a compost heap, which became very productive in the summer, and he would feed this organic compost to his prided gardens; tea leaves were naturally kept for the roses.

The house was well situated because faced east. Joseph explained to his son that this was the best aspect, just as churches were built on the same axis, to get the sun in the morning and enjoy the sun setting in the west in the back of the house in the evening – Christ rising in the morning and resting at dusk.

Joseph Gordon was a captivating story teller. Guy was often spellbound by the tales his father told; he was like Odysseus mesmerizing the troops in between battles whilst waiting to invade Troy. So often in the cold and dark winter evenings, very much like Scheherazade, he would engage his audience.

In Calcutta there was a man named John Fleury who was the chief engineer of the railways. He had started working as a labourer, digging trenches for telegraph poles, clearing rubble and laying down railway tracks.

John Fleury was a man with a vision, and he was taught by his father, who was known for his wisdom, to put his heart and soul into everything he did, however menial it seemed and no matter how much ridicule was thrown at him.

John worked diligently day in and day out, often with aching limbs and an excruciatingly sore back. Yet still he continued, for his vision to be someone of importance fired him on, and that gave him some respite from the toil and sweat he spent on the railroads.

One day his foreman was taken ill. John had noticed that the foreman had not looked well for some time, and had a strong premonition that he would not live much longer. John was asked to step into the position, much to the chagrin of the elder members of the workforce, who resented the move immediately.

John saw beyond the jibes and vitriolic retorts that he got from the older men, and soldiered on with his plans. He had noticed that the existing foreman would often favour the older veterans and speak harshly to the new recruits. He was determined to level out this modus operandi and treat everyone the same. John referred to his mental notes that he had made whilst he watched the foreman at work. He had noticed that his work and level of command over the men had deteriorated – probably due to his illness, but perhaps more to do with his inability to lead the men. That was when the production line often dwindled and the deadlines were never met.

However, John led the workforce as a solid team. Anyone who did not want to work this way was told that they had the option to find work elsewhere if this did not suit them. Few of them left, for they knew in their heart of hearts that John would get the job done despite any obstacles, which was what happened. They were very often ahead of schedule and were rewarded with bonuses that John Fleury instigated.

News reached them that their foreman had died of his illness, and John was elected to be the new foreman. The work progressed and all deadlines were met.

As time went on, John Fleury's dedicated workforce and his own charisma took him through the channels of promotion, and after studying engineering at night school he became the chief engineer of the railways in Calcutta.

Because he had an eye for the unusual, even exotic, John was given a black panther cub from a friend who was a zoologist – it happened to be an unusual case where the cub had been found abandoned and brought to be reared in the local zoo. John trained the cub, and over the years his panther, Midnight, accompanied him everywhere, and he became the toast of the province.

One day the high commissioner was visiting the station to see just how John's plans to modernise it had fared. The commissioner stepped off the train with his Alsatian dog and saw a small group of men talking and looking over some blueprints. The commissioner liked to arrive unannounced, as he felt that this gave him a more authentic view of how the station was run.

When they realized it was the commissioner, they greeted him cordially, but as soon as his dog saw Midnight he launched into an attack, barking vociferously and baring his teeth at him. Midnight hunched in defence, hurling a blow at the dog with his mighty paw, killing it instantly. There was a shrieking yelp and the dog lay motionless on the platform station. Of course, Midnight had to be quarantined. He was imprisoned in an iron-barred cage, and John was advised not to see him.

Other engagements took John away from Calcutta for a while, and he was gone for at least a month. When he returned he went to see Midnight, and was appalled to see how emaciated he had become. He was told that the panther had not eaten anything since the day the Alsatian died.

Confidently, John said to one of the keepers, "Open the cage; Midnight knows me. Open the cage!"

As soon as the cage door flung open, Midnight charged at his master and tore out his throat, killing John Fleury. Midnight was shot dead."

Joseph often ended the story with, "So, what was the moral of the story?" which would promote deep thinking to all listeners of the tale.

Like Odysseus, who held soldiers spellbound with his fantastic tales often told at camp fires whilst they ate their meal, or like Scheherazade, who told the tales of the *Arabian Nights* to save herself, here was young Guy listening to tales being told as well as those two proficient storytellers who claimed that their tales were all true. This is how he understood that truth can be stranger than fiction.

***

When Joseph went to search for accommodation, his first thought was his family, and so he contacted his brother Theodore, who he knew lived near Cambridge. Joseph thought that he'd write first, rather than just turn up at Theodore's home. The letter ran thus:

> *Dear Theo,*
>
> *I hope this letter finds you in good health and that you are well settled after leaving Calcutta. I wrote and told you that I was going to Dundee, Scotland, to take up that position Mr Chalk had found me, but I met the woman of my dreams on the boat coming over from Bombay, and my plans have since changed. Rowena is a Welsh girl who married a Singh from the Punjab. Since the troubles in India, the British Government helped her come back to England, and her destination address is with her brother in South Wales.*
>
> *We don't plan to stay here, but things are getting tight, as there are five of us! Is it possible that you can help us out for a while until we get established? We will gladly pay our way*

and not impose on you; as I say, it would only be for a while.
We're not quite sure yet where we will establish ourselves, but
as you know these things can take time and a lot of planning.
So, I'll carry on my search and hope to hear from you soon.
Your brother,
Joseph

The reply came very shortly afterwards.

Dear Joseph,
Thanks for your letter, but we cannot help you at all. Our
doors are closed to you.
Sharla Gordon

Joseph had never met Sharla, Theodore's wife, and as he and
his brother had not talked at length, he did not know whether
Theo had met her here or in Calcutta. Nevertheless, Joseph was
stunned by the reply and its brevity. He gathered that they did
not want anything to do with him, but why couldn't Theo have
written? Was he that weak and under his wife's control to that
extent?

He did not tell his beloved, as he felt that it was just another
setback that they could do without.

Although Joseph had never been particularly close to any of
his brothers and sisters – there was always a harboured resentment
that he was favoured by their parents – he hung on the thread of
belief that because they had all come to England from Calcutta,
it would give them a common denominator and there would be
no hesitation in one helping the other out in a crisis. Perhaps this
was the hope of the child, and in many ways Joseph was naïve,
which actually added to his charm. This heavy blow of rejection
toughened him over time, and as he had a philosophical way of

seeing things, he carried no burden of resentment or hatred for Theodore's lack of courage.

Rowena and Guy eventually met Joseph's relatives, and when they finally met Theodore many years later, Sharla had died.

Both Joseph and Rowena knew the adage *Blood is thicker than water*. Their addendum to that would be, "Yet blood clots but water runs free."

They had now both been rebutted by their own blood relatives, yet had found kindness from total strangers, like the Bells, who the reader will know from *The Journeys*. So they had no more illusions about trusting and relying on kith and kin. It certainly did not mean that a blood relative would not let you down or betray you. They had matured from trusting children to toughened adults, and they were getting tougher in order to face life. Yet they did not grow to be cynical, because they fortunately could always raise a laugh, which was always a tonic, especially in the harshest of landscapes where there seemed to be little if any assistance.

Melville, Joseph's eldest brother lived with his wife in Bedfordshire, and when Guy was in his teens they all went to visit them. Melville, still very much the colonel in civilian life, called his brother "Johnnie boy," which seemed rather out of place, though Joseph did not object and let it rise above his head. It came across that the Colonel needed to enforce his rank both in a military and filial way, which culminated in a kind of farce with no real meaning behind it all.

Zandra, Melville's wife, reminded Joseph, Rowena and Guy of the Cobra Queen of Poison, as she was another doyen in the art of the double entendre – I'll flatter then I'll flatten! She too took on the regimental hierarchical system, for as she was the Colonel's wife, she treated both Joseph and Gordon as new recruits, and Guy was an unwanted brat who was expected to shut up until spoken to.

They had two daughters who popped in and out and were busy preparing to do some world travel, but what short glimpses they got of the girls, Joseph and company thought kindly of them, as they had warm smiles and greeted their newly found relatives cordially.

At the time when Joseph visited Melville, he had a professional position and was fairly affluent, compared to earlier when he had nothing but his beloved and her five children; none of his family was interested in him at all then. And over the years when he became established, he paid them fleeting visits, and some of them did the same, yet there were no strong bonds formed. *Is this the way of the world?* Joseph asked himself repeatedly, because if he had been asked to help his brother or sister he would have, and later did, having no vengeance in his heart for their earlier rejections of him. Then the saying *Do to others as you would want them to do to you* came into his mind, and it confused him.

Other than his parents, who were genteel people with dignity and breeding and whose values he treasured, he loved his beloved, because she had in her the same core values and characteristics that his kindly mother had – strength, compassion, steadfastness and love, to name but a few of the many others that he loved her for.

How he often thought of them and missed them until his heart ached. Yet he knew that he had always respected them, and had no compunction leaving Calcutta when he did. They had both passed away, Mother first and then Father, within a few days of one another, and he believed in his heart that they were together and happy. He remembered his father's gentle disposition and wisdom, which Joseph passed onto his own son, who he would have been proud of. In the last days, Father was heavily burdened with many troubles, and then when his eldest son was murdered his world seemed to begin to crumble.

Edwin was the firstborn of Roberta and Gareth Gordon. The Gordons were of Anglo-Indian stock, and Edwin had a head of red, thick hair, with a lighter complexion. It is often said in mixed race lineages that when there is a light-skinned or dark-skinned child, that they are a throwback. Edwin was considered so because he had no Eastern colouring at all, yet this fired him up to be quite a gangster. He was notorious around Calcutta for being the leader of a smuggling gang, and no one crossed his formidable character. It was as if his unusual colouring gave him a kind of Herculean status in his mind, and so he went on as if he was invincible and beyond the law. Yet Edwin was also shrewd, and always used careful strategy whenever he planned any illegal enterprise.

He caused his parents a great deal of grief because they knew that he had no intention of changing his ways, but eventually they told him that he must leave their home and make one of his own.

Edwin did so, and definitely prospered from all his illegal activities, until ironically he was killed one night in a disagreement with his second-in-command, who wanted more money for a job they had just done. It started with a brawl, and then the second-in-command drew a knife unexpectedly and stabbed Edwin straight through the heart when he was unaware; he died instantly. It was the opening the police needed to break up the smuggling ring, and the second-in-command hanged for Edwin's murder.

This event tipped the balance for Joseph to leave Calcutta, and all the Gordons did so after Edwin's demise, their parents having passed away in the interim.

Joseph and Rowena often talked and reflected on the phrase that had become an accepted term to them now, demon seed. But what if they were it and everyone else was not? Yet deep down within they knew that they meant no harm to anyone and wanted peaceful relations with whomever they met or knew. Unfortunately, the reverse is what they experienced time after time.

Yet deep within their hearts, Joseph and Rowena nourished their own creation, and even though they were a small boat out to sea a lot of the time, their hearts were warmed by this love connection – so warmed that there was another story on a winter's night when the fire roared in the hearth.

Sam Da Costa was a wildlife photographer for National Geographic and other wildlife magazines. He had earned himself a reputation for capturing authentic images of wild animals in their natural habitat, and he definitely seemed to tune into the animal before he took snapshots of it.

Sam was a bold sort of man, and the kind of situations he had found himself in over the years would vouchsafe that he certainly wasn't squeamish. There was an occasion when he was charged by an angry rhinoceros on the plains of the Serengeti, and it was only due to the quick thinking of his companion, Mwangi, that they both got out of her charge in good time and then away from her completely; she then went back to her young calf which she was suckling. Later when things had calmed down, Mwangi gave Sam strict instructions to never go near a wild animal when they had young because the females were ferociously protective.

Sam listened to the advice, but added, "Okay, I'll remember that, but at least I got some great shots of that mother!"

Sam Da Costa was a likeable man, and Mwangi, a Kikuyu local, told him many stories about Africa and the rivalry between the Kikuyu and the Massai, although it was no longer as ferocious and tribal as it once was.

Then Sam came to India on an assignment he was given for a wildlife magazine. He had written to his friend Alistair, an old army buddy who was working in Delhi on a research project that was funded by Oxford University, and who was delighted that Sam was coming and happy to accommodate him. They both shared a keen interest in animals, and Alistair was a zoologist.

Alistair was working on the behaviour of the Indian elephant, and he wanted to compare their whole modus vivendi with their African cousins to see if there were any changes in their hierarchal system – this was a part of the entire project which was to do with the study of animal behaviour in the wild – and to compare how it differed from animals in captivity.

The two friends shared many memories of the war, where they had been posted, and how they looked out for one another, and this nostalgia took them well into the early hours after drinking a sizeable bottle of Jack Daniels.

Alistair invited his friend to accompany him one night to take pictures of a particular herd that he'd been tracking, Sam was delighted and agreed that he would accompany his friend. A sturdy platform had been built, suspended between two cedar trees quite high up from the ground, enabling a clear view of the surrounding area, and the two friends took up their positions. There was a full moon that night, and the full moon in India is so bright that you could read a book.

When Alistair and Sam were settled and could hear the indigenous sounds of the night, around 3am they heard rustling in some brush just 50 yards to their right. It was a huge bull elephant with one of his tusks broken off severely, and there was blood at its stump.

Alistair whispered, "It's a rogue, been ousted from the herd by a younger stronger male. He's now on his own and is a very angry beast because he has no herd. He's considered an outcast by his own kind."

Sam looked on with amazement and could see plainly that the beast was agitated and irritable, not keeping still for too long.

As an elephant's eyesight is not very strong over long distances, so this rogue did not spot the observation platform immediately. However, when he did he trumpeted fiercely and then began to charge, to his left there was some rustling in the bushes and a tiger emerged from what looked like a sleep, but when he came into the light it was obvious he had wounded his left paw quite badly.

Both animals looked at one another, each in battle mode and threatened by the other. Again the rogue trumpeted loudly, and the tiger roared in response whilst positioning itself to pounce straight at the elephant's face. Seconds later he did just that and landed on the top part of the elephant's head, grabbing on with its incisor–like talons.

The rogue began swaying his head from right to left, and the two men on the platform watched in amazement at the strength of this creature. The tiger eventually was slung off, and before it could turn and slam the elephant with its mighty paw, the rogue encircled the tiger, put its trunk around its middle, and raised it above his head; the tiger was roaring ferociously. Seeing a fallen tree ahead of him, the rogue ran to it and smashed the tiger down on it, breaking its back immediately. After a few moments of twitching limbs, the tiger lay dead. The rogue raised its trunk, trumpeted again loudly and ran off from the combat arena.

Sam and Alistair were dumbstruck for some minutes after the incident. The sheer immediacy of the event held them in stasis, until Alistair spoke, "I've never seen anything that dramatic in all my life. Did you get any pictures?"

Sam replied, "I was too scared that if I clicked or flashed my camera they would both turn on us. But what a battle! We should at least take the tiger back with us as a memento of this night."

But neither of the two men had recorded any of the events, but what they had was a story to tell others in their travels and the appreciation of the strength of those two mighty beasts.

Guy learned that day that the moral of the story was that not everything has a saleable value and some experiences are sacrosanct. What those two friends shared was for them to hold, remember and value.

Joseph had a habit of making up nicknames for people, which in some way was a secret code of language whenever he was talking to someone else who knew the code. There was a woman who lived further up the road who had a thick head of ginger hair, so she naturally became Ginger Nut. And of course a neighbour, whose surname was McVitie, became The Biscuit. There was a pigeon-breasted man who he named Buster, and another corpulent man who would always nod a greeting that he was called Fats. The woman about four doors up the road, who was having an affair with Farleigh next door, was called Dye, as she changed her hair colour so often no one ever knew what her natural shade was. The name also had smatterings of Wales when Rowena's brother tried to get her married to Dye, the old man with bed bugs in his bed.

Yet whenever Bertha talked of "My Bob," it was always with absolute deference, and whatever he said was right.

It was Bob who put Bertha up to saying that Rowena and Gordon were sending smoke signals when they first burnt some rubbish in the back garden soon after they had first moved there, seeing them as "Red Indians." Rowena and Joseph had enough compassion to overlook what they were told at the local shops, as they knew that Bertha had her burdens to bear, and as she repeated everything that Bob told her, she saw no wrong in it.

Whenever the ice cream van came about on a Sunday lunchtime, Bertha would queue up to get ice creams for "Bob and the boys" in her worn leather sandals that curled up at the toes.

It was not too long after the Gordons had moved into their home when Bertha was sectioned at the mental hospital, and Farleigh was then free to see his paramour, Dye – still clandestinely, as he would jump the fence at the rear and enter through her open back door.

Bertha returned for a while, but Bob never let up on his treatment of her, and she eventually completely collapsed and was sectioned. Joseph and Rowena always wondered if this *fait accompli* by Farleigh would ever play on his mind, but were finally convinced one day that it would not. Rowena and Joseph had looked after a young dog for a colleague whilst they went on holiday, and there were some complications and they could not take the dog back. Having a dog was not viable at that time, as it would have spent a lot of time alone in the house, so Rowena mentioned it to Farleigh and he said that he would take the dog.

Purely by chance, Joseph was in the local woods gathering leaves to make leaf mould for the garden. He heard continual barking from a dog nearby, and he found the same dog that they had given Farleigh tied to a tree. It looked as though the man had a cruel streak running straight through him.

When they confronted Farleigh, he denied all knowledge of it and said that he had given the dog to someone else. Joseph found another home for the dog; he gave it to Mrs Fillip, who was married to Dominic and his family of Anglo-Indian heritage.

Mrs Fillip would always raise a smile on Rowena and Joseph's faces because she had a permanent drone of a voice, and when she spoke she never took any breaks; she would relate the entire day's episodes in one continuous sentence. Joseph often mimicked her and put Guy into fits of laughter. Rowena would outwardly scold their schadenfreude, but would smile to herself, appreciating the funny side of it. It later became clear to Guy, when he reflected on those times, just how vital humour is in the journey of life; it tempers the tragedies and lightens the load.

Chapter 11

From a tender age, Guy had lived in an environment that was hectic and ever changing, and it would be fair to say that it was dysfunctional. What he experienced was a never-ending flow of conflict, temper tantrums, sulking and fragmented relationships, built on sand that washed away with the tides.

Yet the nucleus that was his parents and himself gave him some sense of security on the one hand, but on the other it was continually addled by Rowena's ambivalence towards him whenever she fell victim to her dark moods and withdrew from all humankind, especially men. And because Guy was male, it went sorely against him in maintaining any equilibrium. He was a forceful child, probably because he had to work at being acknowledged at times, which also gave him the reputation of being precocious – but then he was bright and had an analytical mind at an early age.

That lineage of men in Rowena's history, memories that haunted her, at times all culminated into an inner rage that led her to punish those who were nearest and dearest to her heart. Then the blight she caused on their innocence added guilt to her shame, and she slipped further down into the maelstrom that soared within her, hating herself as well. There was often an oppressive atmosphere that lingered afterwards, and she, an indigenous nurse, just did not know how to give it first aid.

So Guy lived in a place called Pandemonium, even though his parents were trying desperately to build a home. Unfortunately, others wanted to tear it down. Guy saw his mother as a nurturing beautiful angel on the one hand, and on the other she was a ravaging Harpy that tore through flesh and bone, leaving the soul bare and undefended. When he surfaced from and over this tide of ambivalence many years later, he came to understand his mother's behaviour, but how can anyone convey to a child such anguish that lives within their soul.

For many years Guy lived under a cloud of unknowing, until psychology taught him the reasons behind adverse and ambivalent behaviour. Nevertheless, a parent with haunting demons can be deeply disturbing to an infant mind. Shadows disappear when light seeps in, and in the light everything has the chance to grow.

Guy had always tried to build a relationship with his stepfamily, and whenever something seemed to grow, from sharing an interest in common or just getting to know one another, it dissolved again like elaborate clouds formations in the sky that vanish in minutes. He wondered for a long time if this continual lack of tenacity was his fault, but after he looked at their dynamics, and listening to what they had to say in their own way about how they saw life, he grew to understand that because they carried so much excess baggage – in regrets, recriminations and resentment – this blocked the channel for any true and long-lasting development. They also wanted things to be on their terms.

One of Guy's characteristics was that he liked to build and enjoy things as they developed, but he found himself always confused and frustrated with the Singhs, especially because there was that major division between them, the three and the two, which intensified all the feelings that ran very deeply and became buried. So where was the room for him in their lives?

He was sad to learn that one day, and he tried not to be bitter, but was angry with some, especially Freddie whom he had loved as a young boy. What they became focussed on was their own lives and the children that they were to produce. This was their achievement and reward in their lives; a younger half-brother was no reward at all. So perhaps that was why they were never very interested in building a relationship with the product of a man whom they despised – Joseph Gordon. Guy could not help but speak of them collectively, because he experienced the same pattern of rejection from all of them, though each handed it to him in their own way. It may have been because of their inability to build or contribute to any relationship because they had known abandonment early on in their lives, at least from their fathers. But their mother stood by them and tried as best she could, with the knowledge that she had to be both parents to them. In their eyes she had failed. She left their rightful inheritance in India, and it would be a mammoth achievement to have our own inheritance, would it not?

One day Guy made the decision that he would no longer be the whipping boy for their rejections, so he divorced them in his mind and trained himself to be less and less emotional about them until he could speak about them, and whenever necessary, to them with objectivity – not an easy task considering how much emotional turmoil had been thrown at his mother, father and himself. And for what reason?

Guy had never known Pedro, and only remembered him shouting at his young children or telling crude jokes. Then he went to Canada when Guy was a small boy, and had no further contact until his youngest daughter was 21 and they both came over on a visit to see their mother. Guy was also there.

Guy did not like him then. Pedro was an inveterate drinker, never going anywhere without his rather large hipflask of rye whiskey. He was severely overweight, and he was also bigoted and acutely prejudiced of all "foreigners." Apparently, he had no time for anyone who he considered foreign – this was naturally a subjective criterion and to do with the people he disliked the most, so they became foreigners. He later lived with a Filipino woman, but that kind of foreigner was fine because she was subservient to him.

He drove buses in Manitoba, Canada, yet had not pursued his skills or felt any sense of fulfilment about himself or life it seemed. He had produced four children and had no real or loving relationship with any of them – and he was estranged with their mother, Janet. *If this is achievement, give me none of it*, thought Guy to himself as he listened to Pedro at their mother's on that brief and scarce visit he paid to England. He wanted to see Rowena's eldest sister, Sylvia, for what reason no one ever knew, as they were never close. But he did spend time with his sister, the Cobra Queen of Poison, but after a few days they were squabbling; alcohol was Pedro's closest companion.

Guy watched his mother as she looked at her eldest son, and there seemed to be a vacuous and distant gaze that both went deep yet reverberated back, as there was nothing to really value or hold on to as a warm or positive memory. It was difficult not to see his father, impounded by the living example before her that he was his father in most things, except for the ambition that Raghubir had had that was totally lacking in his son. However, other things like arrogance, bull-headedness and chauvinism were definitely there.

Guy's heart sank when he tried to make conversation with his niece and steer her away from talk of her father's drinking. He mentioned the native American Indians, and she dismissed them as "dirt." Was her father's prejudice running through her veins as well? Yet on the other hand she had grown up seeing them as a disillusioned race of people, languishing on reservations and drinking excessively. If Pedro had informed her of their history, perhaps she would have had further insight into their plight. Guy did not feel that it was his place to enlighten her, as he knew it would have landed on a closed mind and deaf ears.

There seemed little point in talking more to her, so he wished them all well and left them to it. Pedro did not stay long anyway. Notwithstanding the long trip from Canada to England, he wanted to get back post haste.

The last time Guy saw Pedro was at their mother's funeral, and Pedro made no real attempt to speak with him. He later went off with the Cobra Queen of Poison, and stayed with her until his return flight to Canada. Guy had chosen the music, a piece by Mozart called "Laudate Dominum," and he had hoped that the eldest son would have prepared an eulogy –with a due deference to tradition – but then perhaps the Singh blood gang had no praise for their mother. But did any of them really know or understand her? Guy remembered feeling that one should have been prepared by the elders. He also reflected on the term "elders," and when he thought of them he held no respect for them, although he wanted to.

Guy's relationship with the Cobra Queen of Poison had seen times of enjoyment. In the beginning he was fooled by her winning charm and what came over as charisma, but over time he realized that where there's poison it must ooze out in some shape or form. There were times when she tried to engage him in talk of others, and he tried to remain loyal to the others, but it was difficult. And at times he spoke of them to her, only to discover that she had conveyed it all back to them in some way or other. She and Guy shared an interest in antiques, Victoriana and furniture of the period, and often went to auctions together.

Venema was also quite free in what she told him about her private life, which he found too much information at the time, but later realized that that was Venema. She was renowned for having a big mouth, something that has been called logorrhoea. Also, any memories about Wales were blocked out, and she never wanted to talk about her Uncle Frederick, whom she would not leave when Rowena and Joseph sent for them after having found accommodation in South London.

Venema adored Pedro and only spoke honeyed words about him. In her eyes, her youngest brother, Freddie, was "thick," and Chunny's two children were not of her tribe. Neither was Guy really, but at that time he thought that he and Venema were building a sound relationship – something else that was to dissolve after the tide came in.

Venema always maintained that Guy had it much easier than they ever did, so this was how he realized that resentment of him ran through all of their veins, chiefly because his father did not run off and was a loving man to his wife and child. This is something that he was despised for instead of being prided for. How bizarre is human nature!

Guy remembered the Cobra Queen's words at Rowena's funeral. Guy joined her as she was looking in a small aviary after the funeral service, and as she looked at one of the birds she said, "Do you think that mother is there, Guy?"

"No way. She is now a free spirit and has flown," he replied, but he wanted to add that she was now with her beloved, but held his tongue.

Another thing she said had stayed with him was, "Remember now, Guy, we have each other, so let's keep in touch."

This raised hope in Guy's heart, and he tried many a time afterwards to keep in touch with her. However, Venema was either far too busy or nonchalant, and told him several times that she had lost his telephone number. So again, what little was there dissolved away.

It always seemed that if the Cobra Queen did telephone it was because she wanted some information, but never to genuinely know how Guy was doing. Her two children were her creation and life, and this gave her a kind of superior air above all of her siblings, and a means by which she could cut off all connections with them – except Pedro of course. Yet when he visited her from Canada, because of his excess drinking, there was little in the way of communication between them.

After many years without communication, Venema seemed to find Guy's telephone number to ask for Freddie's address, as Pedro was making another of his fleeting, random visits from Canada. Pedro did not telephone Guy; there was a reason for this, which the reader will learn of later.

Speaking to Venema again was a strange feeling for Guy; it was someone he knew, yet didn't at the same time.

"Hello, darling, how are you?" she asked.

"Venema, what a surprise. To what do I owe this pleasure?" he sarcastically replied.

"Darling, do you have Freddie's address? Pedro will be staying with me for a week, and we both want to visit him."

"I'm sorry but I don't. I don't have any communication with Freddie. The last time I contacted him he was living in Holmfirth, but that's all I know"

Guy emailed Gerald, now Gerard, and he had the address and sent it to him. Guy called Venema back and gave her the information. He did not want to get into any further conversation with her, because he knew that his childlike heart would hope again. So he kept it short, despite her bombardment of questions – just idle curiosity really – so that she could pass it on and assess just where Guy was in his life and what he had gained materialistically, which he recognised and thwarted. It was the last time they spoke.

One good thing came from it, because Guy believed the theory that something constructive always comes out of chaos. Freddie's eldest son, Thomas, telephoned his uncle, and they reconnected after many years and a lot of water rushing under their bridge.

There was a rapport between Bruce, Venema's husband, and Rowena, from when they first met —this more than likely caused jealousy in Venema — and there were times when he visited his mother-in-law that they would chat at length, often helping one another out in their darker moments. This could have been why Bruce was so angry at Joseph when he had attacked him in defence of Rowena, as Venema had added as much fuel to his fire before and after the event. Many people were drawn to Rowena's inner wisdom and calm acceptance of things, and they often felt better after talking with her. Unfortunately, this same reasoning force does not always have the same effect on our personal travails. Perhaps it's hard to see the wood for the trees.

When Joseph died, Rowena chose to take early retirement, and because of her devoted years of service to the organisation, they found her accommodations, a maisonette very near the famous St Saviour's Road. Rowena was comfortable financially, as she had both her own and Joseph's superannuation and respective pensions. Because Bruce was going through some financial difficulties, Rowena agreed to lend him some money —the amount was strictly between them.

It remained a mystery why Bruce did not make an appearance at Rowena's funeral. Guy knew that they often talked, and he sensed that there was a bond between them, because she always spoke respectfully of Bruce. Guy was again confused by another person's behaviour.

He saw Bruce one day in a local restaurant, coincidentally when Gerard was visiting. Bruce looked haggard, but Guy did not feel the drive to speak with him, though he felt that Bruce had seen him. This was the last time anyone heard of Bruce, as soon afterwards he and Venema divorced.

When Barbara left school she got a job in Croydon as a stenographer. She was a diligent and industrious worker, and had been steady with her academic work at school. Barbara was quite stunning in her own way. She had naturally jet-black hair, which she often wore in a beehive style, and her dress sense was impeccable; she turned many a head in her direction. Whereas Venema was much more of an extrovert and brash, Barbara was the reverse, introverted and at times taciturn. She was renowned for her sulking which could last days, an element of strong control that she exercised.

She once told Guy that she always felt belittled by Venema. He tried to console her by telling her that she was beautiful, but the dynamics that ran between the two she-cats lay far below the iceberg, and he knew intuitively that he was only dealing with the tip, which was immense as well.

Because Barbara was shy and withdrawn at times, no one really saw just how wild the other side of her nature could be. She had a huge amount of pent-up rage and resentment. Guy had experienced her outbursts, which could be disturbing to say the least. Guy was no angel either; he was prone to teasing people, probably for some kind of recognition or return, and he recalled how once when she had come in late from being out with her friends or boyfriend at the time, Rowena was confrontational with her, and Barbara was insolent in return. Rowena, at the end of her tether at that time, slapped Barbara hard across the face, telling her fiercely that she was never to speak to her in that way again.

Guy tried to console Barbara, but she did the same and slapped him across the face. She could be a fierce wildcat that could charge and attack at random; this also showed that there was a lot beyond the tip of the iceberg.

The reader will recognise that each and every one of us has our own demons to deal with, and facing them rather than burying them is by far a securer path if we want to have equilibrium. How easy it is also to criticise others for their actions and thoughts. Yet no matter how perverse those actions are there is always a reason behind them. However, knowing that still does not make them less oppressive to others.

Rowena's children had had a traumatic life, brought up knowing only an Eastern culture, however affluent. Then, in a time when there was insecurity in their homeland, they were brought to the opposite side of the world to begin again, without the support of their respective fathers. On the other hand, as we have the ability to remember and blame, we also have the ability to accept our lot. There were many people who suffered in other ways – for instance, those who had to stay in India because they did not have the means to leave. We can spend our lifetimes lamenting the past and being anxious of the future, the one bringing us regret and the other anxiety, but what we know we have is the very powerful now.

When Guy came home from school one day he came in through the back door via the kitchen. There was a visitor sitting there, and Joseph introduced his Uncle Freddie from Wales. At the time, Guy knew nothing of the experiences that his parents had had with Freddie in Wales, and he just shook his hand, Freddie making the comment that he was going to be a big lad. "Look at his hands," he said in a thick Welsh brogue.

Rowena was present too, and she looked apprehensive, but was strengthened by the fact that Joseph was there. She would have found it much harder to cope with without him. Joseph was in his heart a peacemaker, and always attempted to building bridges where conflict and acrimony had worn them down; his philosophy was to build them again with a fresh start, forgetting past experiences.

After talking with Rowena about this, she contacted her brother and they invited him over for a visit. They did not feel that they could visit Wales again with an open heart. This was some fourteen or so years after the events in Wales when they all first arrived after travelling from Bombay.

Later on in her life, when she had ample time to reflect, Rowena learned and practiced the art of forgiveness – the reader will have read this in *The Journeys* – but at this moment in time she had not quite graduated to that point, and there were still raw feelings in her heart for her brother. She had mixed feelings, because on the one hand she knew that Joseph's intentions were true, yet she also felt a sense of being patronized by a wave of Christianity that came from the edicts of Joseph's church.

However, she tried with all her might and endeavoured to be as detached as she could. After all, she had been the successful hostess to many a dignitary and had often been revered by them, but still she administered her duties appropriately. There was no way that she could like Freddie, but she showed a detached yet polite persona that would have fooled only those who did not know her.

Guy recalled how alike Freddie and her sister Sylvia were, both in looks and demeanour. Domineering and controlling, he met her later when he had left school. Then she had tried to take control of a situation that involved him and some of his friends.

They were all going out for the night and were dressed up in a new wave style. Sylvia had said to some of his friends while looking at him, "I hope you're not going out dressed like that."

Guy remained silent for a while because Rowena had silenced him with a look to say *hold your peace; she is your aunty after all.* He respected that for as long as he could, yet he felt that she was bullying her younger sister in her own home, and he naturally felt territorial for his mother's sake.

Sylvia had cooked something which Guy knew that Rowena had not made, and he told her so. That was when Sylvia, coming from the bathroom, said, "I wouldn't allow my son to speak to me like that."

Guy interjected, and by now had had enough of this bully, despite the fact that she was his aunt, "I wasn't talking to you, and how I speak to my mother is my business. And what right do you think you have to criticise me and my friends. This cauliflower cheese dish you've made is vile; it's like wallpaper paste with a few grains of cheese thrown in, but I'm sure you think it's marvellous."

There were further remonstrations from Sylvia, calling Guy insolent and that his father would turn in his grave. He then reminded her of whose home she was in, taking the lead as if it were her own. She was actually staying over for a weekend, and Guy ensured that he did not return that night. However, he met her in the morning, and said, "Oh, you're still here, are you?"

But she had sewn mischief from her packet of demon seeds she kept with her. She telephoned Venema and they exchanged notes on the unruliness of Rowena's youngest son, Guy. He also reminded her of the cost of the calls, for she rang many people to complain about his behaviour towards her.

Guy remembered the elder-sister chat she had with him in a state of righteous indignation on behalf of Sylvia, telling him that he had always had it easy by comparison to how they were brought up. That sank into his subconscious then, but he did not realize the impact of it until later. She did this without even hearing his side of the tale that dear auntie had spun, that she had been insulted for no reason at all. Gracious, what injustice! Queen Sylvia had been affronted!

Probably because he had seen so much conflict, strife, betrayal, rivalry and even condemnation – it was definitely as strong as the Tudor Royal Court – Guy had had enough of having to put up with such things and became the very person who would be blamed for his outspokenness and intolerance of all the emotional chess games. He also rejected all attempts at being controlled, and that caused him to be an anathema for Sylvia, who wanted to be obeyed by all. Guy realized then how easily his stepfamily could be swayed against him by a domineering, meddling, mischief-making aunt whom they had no strong affinity with.

Freddie did spend time with her at one point when he was in his teens, and they seemed to form a bond. He did odd jobs for her, for which she paid him.

Rowena always wondered what Sylvia would do if she told her that her husband had made sexual advances to both herself and Barbara on separate occasions in the not-so-distant past. Rowena imagined the response tainted with prim indignity, "What are you saying? My Bert would never do any such thing! Your imagination is running away with you again, my girl."

Rowena saw her father saying the words through Sylvia, for there was no way that she could ever believe that Bert found another woman attractive, let alone make advances towards her. If she found out it was true, she would have them all burnt at the stake.

There seemed to be this Tudor mercilessness than ran through a part of the Rees family tree. Yet Rowena had an affinity with her other siblings, Gwendolyn, who had died young of cancer (in her forties, and soon after Rowena returned to England again), and of course Rhoda, whom she, Joseph, and Guy met up with later. It looked like there was a dichotomy between the father's line and Bessie's, two different sets of genes entirely. What would Darwin have propounded about that? Are the domineering, bullying genes stronger than the gentler and more nurturing ones?

When Rowena looked analytically at her lineage, she could put all her siblings into two distinctly different camps, with King Frederick the head of one and Queen Bessie, at the head of the other. That was the court that she had descended from, and given the opportunity, King Frederick would most certainly have been at war and tried to conquer, rape, pillage and burn things that he felt would come with ease, as it would be with his heir, King Frederick II.

Yet having said this, there were many times throughout her life when Rowena was that fighting warrior, ready to avenge the many injustices and heartaches that had been put her way by men. In her heart of hearts, her war was with males, even the ones whom she dearly loved and had borne. But at the end of the equation, they were males too and had to suffer at times.

The truth of the matter was that Rowena had only known a hectic and fractured life, always filled with extreme and diverse experiences that catching up with extended family took years to put into action. Sadly, when this did happen, she lost some of the very people she would have loved to know and share friendship with. There were times when she seriously and wholeheartedly lamented her lot. Even though you might understand the *raison d'être* behind life's journeys, it still doesn't stop them from being tough to deal with.

Chapter 12

Rowena always sensed strongly that Barbara had never really settled in Berlin. After eighteen or so years she had eventually divorced Johannes on the grounds of infidelity. He had been brash enough to have had his sexual liaison in their marital bed, which naturally wounded Barbara that much deeper and set her wholeheartedly on the path for divorce.

Interesting how her two offspring were girls and the eldest, Natalia, also had a daughter; this was mentioned because that gene from her mother could well have been in play – give birth to no more men; they are nothing but trouble!

When Barbara took up work on a fulltime basis, she got a position with the British Army, which was stationed in Berlin. She worked for a Colonel Williams, and thoroughly enjoyed her role as his PA. They enjoyed a wholesome working relationship. Barbara, efficient and industrious, carried her work out conscientiously, and Williams valued her input.

Johannes's mother, Stephanie, was an intelligent and caring woman whom Barbara had struck up a close friendship with, and was extremely helpful to her daughter-in-law over the years, especially when Johannes had two-timed her. Apparently, he had had other liaisons. However, it looked as though Barbara wanted to sever all links with his family, and over time when she had divorced Johannes, she chose not to see anymore of Stephanie. It seemed sad that their friendship could not carry on, but everyone deals with these things in their own way.

Johannes looked acutely Aryan, and would have fit in perfectly with Hitler's idea of a master race of blue-eyed, blond-haired super beings. This had a lot to do with her total infatuation with him when she first set eyes on him all those years ago in Deal, Kent.

Barbara organised a short trip away to Deal with a group of work colleagues at the time she was engaged to Bernard, a French architect student from Paris. Bernard was returning to Paris to do his architectural finals before returning to marry his beloved. Unfortunately for Bernard Builder, Barbara met Johannes and her whole world was turned upside down. She was bowled over by his Germanic features. Bernard was informed of this and was heartbroken. Barbara was determined to marry Johannes, and duly did in Berlin some months later when everything had been wrapped up in England.

Stephanie's mother, whom everyone knew as Oma (grandmother), was a hale and active woman in her early eighties who was extremely likeable. A Russian refugee who had settled in Berlin after the Second World War, Guy met her once when he made an unexpected visit to see Barbara when he was sixteen. It was the day when the old currency in England changed to the new decimal type in 1970.

Then the time came when the British pulled their troops out from Berlin. Now that the wall had come down under Gorbachev's regime in 1989, many estranged families could at last be reunited with their loved ones. Yet for many, the actuality of it was devastating. Even though they had been imprisoned in the east all of their lives in some cases, it gave them some form of *modus vivendi*, and the freedom was just too much for many. Unemployment also soared, as many sought work in the west, which also caused resentment and strife with established workers already settled there.

Barbara met a man who had actually escaped from the east before the segregating wall came down, and he had managed to get through, well hidden, in the boot of a car. Barbara struck up a friendship with Gerhard, and before long they were romantically involved. Gerhard often said publicly that he adored his princess, and Barbara revelled in the adoration – it suited her inner wish to be worshipped.

They both paid Guy and his partner, Jaime Diaz, a visit one weekend in the summer. Barbara was the one of Guy's stepfamily who had been to all the places he lived. Guy had always considered himself ultra clean, yet when he visited Barbara and Gerard, respectively, in their own environments, he was able to make the comparison between cleanliness and neurotic cleanness. Barbara would only have white accoutrements in the bathroom. It had to be white tiled all over, and a wet room that had to be washed down daily. If anyone used a towel after rinsing their hands, she would ensure that the towel was in the washing machine and a fresh one put out. Gerard also had a strong obsession about towels; they were washed after every use.

However, Barbara had gone out shopping with Gerhard. Guy could never do that, as she could literally shop until she dropped – and that could be without buying anything. She was ceremoniously unravelling something on the kitchen table, and from a distance it looked like onyx, but it was plastic. Then he realized that it was a toilet brush, so his first thought was that she had bought it for herself. He then asked if she had changed the colour scheme of her bathroom, as he knew that she only liked white.

"No, it's for you!" she replied with excitement, and even urgency, in her voice.

Guy was dumbstruck, and wanted to handle it as diplomatically as possible, but he was irritated at the fact that Barbara again was buying people things that she thought they should have. "We don't use those things here, Barbara, because they harbour bacteria and germs."

Naturally she was upset, and in her arrogance she got tetchy, justifying the purchase by saying that she needed to clean the toilet after use.

Gerhard in his broken English said, "*Ja*, you use like so," demonstrating with his hands.

"I know how to use one, Gerhard, but I don't want one!" Guy replied assertively.

"Well, throw it away then!" retorted Barbara.

Guy realized how complicated this had all become, all over an object which he thought was a poor choice to buy anyone. Perhaps it could have been discussed beforehand, but Barbara took it upon herself to buy one, concluding that because she didn't see one in Guy's bathroom that he had not got around to buying one, or had not even given thought to cleaning his toilet. Also, because she had decreed that he needed one, he needed to accept it without any argument – I decree, you accept.

She had often sent Rowena clothes that Stephanie wanted to pass on, and a lot of the time Rowena found good use for a great deal of them, yet some she did not take to and passed them on herself. When Barbara visited her she became quite angry when she saw that they were not all there. She seemed to find it hard to believe that Rowena would give them away.

Anyway, Guy made them all some refreshments, and he persuaded Barbara to sit down, as she suffered with thrombosis in one of her legs, trying to forget the incident. It is difficult when you cannot get through to someone that the gift they have bought is not suitable or acceptable. Barbara would not recant, and believed that Guy was ungrateful.

Later that evening the three of them were having a drink together. Guy was drinking a Diamond White cider, and Barbara was fascinated by the transparency of the liquid and thought it was wine. Guy offered her one and she drank it.

Barbara was starting to throw recriminations at Guy, but he tried to take it in an adult way, so he asked her why she had slapped him so hard the time she came in late and Rowena was harsh with her and he tried to console her all those years ago. She did not answer and began to snarl, as she did when angry.

Guy said, "Do you know, Barbara, I've had enough of all of you."

With that, she said to Gerhard in German that he'd just told them to get out. She went upstairs and rapidly packed her bags. Jaime came out from the lounge and asked what was happening, and Barbara repeated as she went up the stairs, "He just told us to get out!"

They were both gone within fifteen minutes. Guy remained seated and thought, *She is an adult and if she chooses to leave, that is her prerogative*. If it had been a child throwing the same tantrum he would have intervened. Guy and Barbara never spoke again.

A few years later, after she had told everyone that Guy had thrown them out of his home, Gerard had had some contretemps with her - the reader will hear of later - and decided to believe Guy. However, Guy tried to make contact – possibly a trait he'd inherited from Joseph – by getting Barbara's email address from Gerard and writing to her.

Her reply came, a royal decree. *I've discussed it with my husband, and I am not ready at this time to have contact with you.*

Guy's reply ran, *I didn't actually write to your husband, but to you. Forget it, Barbara, and have a good life.*

It appeared that she had told Pedro about being thrown out of Guy's house, because on his last fleeting visit he did not telephone Guy. Barbara and Pedro had become friends, despite the fact that she'd considered him a chauvinistic bore in the past. What a reputation Guy had, but he really didn't care. He knew what the truth was, even if no one else wanted to believe it; somehow he had known this before.

So Venema had only telephoned Guy that last time to find out information – her usual tactic – and Pedro was with her; they were planning a trek to see Freddie.

***

Gerald, after working in the Merchant Navy for some years, decided that he too would make his home in Canada. He had met up with Pedro on occasion, yet the only thing they had in common was that they had the same mother. Pedro was a highly prejudiced individual who always hated different races of people, and his close relationship with booze made it impossible for him to have a relationship with anyone else. They had never grown together over the years and remained in that feudal chasm where the fact of having different fathers was the segregating factor, coupled with the fact that they just did not like one another. If they were work colleagues they would have walked different paths.

Gerard had a global awareness, as he had travelled the world since he was a teenager, and had a thorough knowledge of different countries' customs. Unfortunately, he also had a prejudicial streak that ran through him. When he lived with Joseph and Rowena – stayed with them, rather, when on leave from sea – he was wont to get highly emotional and cry, but would never let anyone console him. He also had a pet hate for Jews, whom he would call *Yids* in an inflammatory and derogatory way. Joseph and Rowena corrected him severely, and told him if those were his views he was to keep them to himself. Was this a case of the oppressed being oppressive? Most of Rowena's children had suffered from racial insults in some way, and Gerald had taken up boxing, which enabled him to vent his feelings. Unfortunately, the act never had a therapeutic effect, for his fury remained with him, and he has it to this very day.

In fact, Gerald was asked to curtail a lot of his own strong opinions, and he was advised that if anyone was interested in them they would ask him. But of course, his regal bearing disagreed with this, and he felt intuitively that everyone must hear his views.

Although Gerald respected Joseph and looked up to him as a mentor, possibly a surrogate father, there still lingered within him that all-consuming rage which would throw him into temper tantrums. When he had paid a visit one day when Rowena and Joseph ran Mooreland Rise, Ida Hill had heard him in one, and she respectfully said to Rowena, "Matron, de man so mad him will tear off roof top!"

She had put that succinctly, for no one actually knew what he would do when in such a rage. The crux of it was always because he couldn't get his own way. Barbara had the same trait, but it was veneered over and did not come across so obviously. Instead, she would sulk and then explode later, but in action she was most definitely a wildcat who had been caged up and then let out. Then things buried within her, like acute resentment, came flooding through.

Once, when Gerald was visiting Barbara in Berlin, his journey took him via Jordan. He was detained by airport security and questioned about his intentions and reasons for travelling to Berlin. Gerald had a killer look in his eyes that seemed to come straight from Beelzebub, for everyone moved away from him. Acting on his suspicious behaviour, and also because he fit the description of a renowned terrorist, they blew up his briefcase in a secured unit. When he was cleared they bought him a new one, and he was given abject apologies, for although he was not that terrorist, he was fighting his own terror in his heart and soul, and perhaps this emanated out.

Under his blanket of fury there was a little, hurt and wounded boy whose daddy had deserted him, but the only way he wanted to deal with the memory was through severe outbursts, which were triggered by everyday mishaps. The outburst was disproportionate to the cause. Gerald would not allow anyone to come close. He moved deeper onto his own emotional island where he could view the world in a detached and isolated, yet desperately lonely, way, covering that existence in saying that he wanted to be anonymous.

As we have seen with Rowena, experiences happen that often leave wounds and hurt, and then heal, which later turn into scars. The memory of those scars can cause us the most discomfort. But they are only memories; it's our choice how we see them. We can hold on to them with venom and resentment that can eat away at us, or let go of them as experiences that we had to go through to better understand of life, which can help us to be fuller and more contented beings.

In Gerald's case, his hatred and resentment of what had happened to him as child and teenager became his best friend and saboteur. Without it he feared he would not exist, as it fired him from his root chakra.

All of Raghubir's and Chunny's children never really had a bond that grew over time – except of course Venema and Pedro – but even in the end she knew, but would never admit, that his drinking blocked all real intimacy. Barbara had always said that she was the one person who understood Gerald, yet she eventually betrayed him over some property, which the reader will hear of later.

When Gerald came home on leave from the sea, he often aimed for goals that seemed unrealistic. And although Joseph had instructed him to have his dreams, as these fire our imagination and can be a driving force in our lives, having delusions of grandeur is another matter that really takes us into ferocious and dangerous territory. Joseph and Rowena often wondered who he was trying to impress, for the delusions were vivid and aggressive. Was it himself, an empty phantom that was his absent father, or everyone who had laughed at him for having a dark skin? Perhaps it was melting pot of all those things and more. The conglomeration of these issues, however, fired Gerald on negatively, as he was much more prone to be arrogant than confident.

He married a beautiful young woman, Cecile, who was the daughter of his boss. Gerald had now left the Merchant Navy and worked on the oil rigs for various companies. He always got a huge buzz from being offshore, whether it was a ship or now an oil rig positioned way out to sea, it gave him that feeling of anonymity and elusiveness he could never feel on land.

His boss, Kurt Waylend, was of Doukhobor stock, a southern Russian sect who fled their home country in 1899 after being persecuted for their religious beliefs and political views. Their exodus was assisted by the Quakers, and even Leo Tolstoy, who shared the same beliefs.

Gerald could know people at a distance very well; it was only when anyone got too close did he turn into Beelzebub's apprentice. One could conclude that there were deep, running attachment issues here. With strangers he was instantly liked, and was well-mannered and amiable.

He respected Kurt, and it was mutual, because Gerald was like his sister, an industrious and efficient worker. Kurt often asked Gerald over for dinner when he was on leave, and that is when he met Cecile. Gerald liked the image of being with a beautiful woman; it fed his persona of being that terrifically successful business tycoon with a heavy American brogue, eccentric and individual.

He now lived in Vancouver and had a substantial house with swimming pool and hot tub, pictures of which he always carried around with him, and always felt the need to show them off. He would work three month stints on the rigs and then have one or two months off, and during that time he drank profusely. He always had this notion that he had no unmanageable problem, because in the time he was at work he drank not a drop of alcohol, which convinced him that he was in total control. But the underlying reality was that he was an alcoholic, and his moods and temper tantrums became terrifyingly disturbing to others.

On one of his leaves, Rowena visited him and only ever remembered him being drunk, loud and bombastic, or sober and tetchy. She had an interesting experience, however, in the local bar that Gerald frequented and often bought people drinks. She was stared at quite intently one day by a man across the bar.

When he became aware that she saw him, he came over to her. He first apologised for staring at her, and then mentioned how expressive her eyes were. It turned out that he was a Hyder Indian chief and lived on a local reservation. He said, "You have many depths in your eyes, lady, and you have been through many journeys. Will you be here tomorrow? I would like to give you a gift."

Rowena somehow trusted this peaceful man; he reminded her of Gandhi, and she felt the same sense of tranquillity. She said that she would be there the next day; she was curious what this man had for her.

On the next day, he had carved her a foot-long totem pole, and told her that it would bring peaceful spirits to her home; she was to hang it on her front door. Rowena was delighted by this pure-hearted gift and thanked the man with all her heart and her biggest beaming smile. They chatted for a while, but he told her that he was a fleeting spirit in her life and they would never meet again.

Gerald, on the advice of Cecile's mother, now estranged from Kurt, advised him to change his name from Gerald to Gerard, and of course this added to his grand persona. And was there some attempt at shedding an old skin for a new?

There was no one who had conquered so much - he cherished the biography of Genghis Khan – and no one who had suffered with such intensity as he had. No one was as rich as he, and certainly no one had achieved as much as this newly reborn Gerard. Everyone else's experiences and hardships were merely drops in the wide Atlantic Ocean compared to his, which were gargantuan tsunamis. These beliefs that he held would be reflected in the nonchalant way in which he would hear someone else's problem, with a disdainful look that said, "It doesn't matter what you say; you just haven't suffered like I have."

But it was all to crumble and disappear . . .

When Rowena and Joseph ran Mooreland Rise, Gerard and Cecile came to visit. This was the last of her children's marriages that she would know about, and she had been asked to none of them. Again she looked over photographs, which were naturally of an impressive celebration. However, it was clear as crystal that the newly married couple of some months were not getting along at all. They were squabbling, and Gerard would not tolerate being contradicted or argued with – it offended his dictatorship. Cecile was inclined to do this a lot. The tension that was accruing was a time bomb waiting to explode, and the friction between the two was obvious to anyone, regardless of their level of perception – it was that apparent.

On one occasion, Joseph was taking them in the car somewhere and they were in the back. Cecile argued with Gerard about something trivial, and he slapped her so hard across the face that the whole car shook; it left an eerie, chilled silence.

Cecile was very much a daddy's girl, who had been given whatever she had asked for. She wanted to be a society girl and shop on Bond Street and Chelsea whilst in London. The image had suited Gerard's narcissism, but he had grown tired of her because she challenged him too much. Naturally, their marriage did not last and ended in divorce. Cecile had suffered a great deal of Gerard's temper tantrums and excess emotional baggage, which broke down her spirit for some time afterwards.

Cecile saw Barbara from time to time, and they would shop together and naturally share girl talk. Cecile had confided all of her experiences with Gerard to Barbara, and none of them were pretty.

There was such a long path of violent outbursts from Gerard towards Guy that the latter often wondered what he had done to warrant such tirades, but then that was Gerard. There was a time after Joseph died and Rowena lived in the maisonette very near St Saviour's Road, where they had begun their nomadship in South London with the memorable Mrs Andrews, when he had called his mother a prostitute, and then turned on Guy because he was defending her and told him to go in a corner and commit suicide. Rowena thought of only one other person then, Gerard's father, Chunny, who had pulled a loaded rifle on her that day in Dehra Dun.

Gerard had helped Guy out at times and always mentioned it to someone. When Guy attempted to pay him back, Gerard would always magnanimously say "forget it." After his continuous vitriolic outbursts, Guy felt no compunction about the money, but still had the intention to send it back with interest one day.

On another occasion, Gerard visited Guy in his flat in Brighton, and Rowena was there too. Guy had to go out to the local shop for something. When he returned he saw Rowena's face looking grave, and she said to him confidentially, "Don't leave me alone with him again. I was frightened; he's been snarling at me like that wild beast again, ready to kill."

Soon after this, Rowena had a minor heart attack. Gerard never knew about it or what she had said to Guy about him.

When Gerard had worked for a particular drilling company, he was based in Pakistan. The sanitary conditions were less than primitive, and he made several written complaints to the executive chiefs. Very little was done over a period of some eight months, and Gerard was taken seriously ill one day.

Naturally, because he had the reputation of being a heavy drinker, it was concluded that he had psoriasis of the liver, and even the doctors were flummoxed as to what the illness was. He remembered that he was put into an AIDS ward, and in a semi-comatose state he remembered a cold-hearted nurse saying as she was leaving the room, "That's what you get from being promiscuous."

He was in excruciating pain during the night, which eased off in the daylight hours. After further tests, it was finally discovered that he had contracted a disease called Q fever. The bugs which had attached themselves to his liver slept in his bone marrow during the day, and at night they fed on his liver, hence his anguish. He had picked these bugs up from the poor sanitary conditions where he had been working in Pakistan.

He sued the company. It took many years for the case to come to fruition, but twelve years later he was awarded a moderate sum for his incapacitation. Gerard had asked Guy to introduce him to his bank, with the view to opening a bank account. He instructed Guy to tell them that he was an international businessman. Guy did no such thing, as the imagination can run to odd lengths when told this. However, he had been awarded a substantial amount of money, which really could not compensate for the years of discomfort and hardships he had suffered because of negligent sanitary conditions.

It was interesting how Gerard wanted Guy to be with him in the interview, because he wanted to open both a US dollar account and a Canadian dollar one too. After all the preliminaries were over, the accounts were opened in his name and he made a definite point of having the woman bring up on the screen exactly how much money was there – a kind of trophy to himself, and an example to Guy of just how much he was worth.

At that time, Guy needed some help with the studies he was finishing and had asked for help. Gerard said to the bank clerk, in his finest American brogue, "Drop my brother a thousand."

For the course that he was doing Guy had to have so many hours of personal therapy, and he related this to his therapist, as he felt guilty that he was not grateful enough. She turned it into a parable:

He was a wine merchant with huge vineyards. It was a scorching hot day, and the wine merchant took his younger brother through them to see how plentiful they were. His younger brother said that he was very thirsty. The wine merchant plucked him a single grape from a large bunch and gave it to his thirsty brother to quench his thirst.

Gerard would always give you something so that he could say, "Well I gave you money, didn't I?" This was irrespective if the amount met the other person's requirements.

There were numerous times when he had given Rowena money, but he never seemed to be able to keep this information to himself. There had been times when Gerard had fallen on hard times, and Guy got together some clothes that he thought would be helpful to Gerard – which were focussed on warmth rather than fashion – and later when they met for the last time, Gerard said to Guy that he should have sent him money.

Yet the interesting thing about Gerard's makeup was that there seemed to be a conflict within him, which on the one hand led him to be materialistic and egotistical – being the big I AM, as Joseph would put it – and on the other the spiritual disciple in search of inner peace and harmony with himself and the world. When Gerard was down and out and lived in trailers or his car, he was the most natural person to talk with, no Americanised accent, and his ego slept. Guy telephoned him regularly at those times, hoping that they would be able to build a relationship. It looked as though Gerard had touched his inner humility. But this was to change again as soon as he started working. Guy also told Barbara, as she was not in contact with her brother, yet in knowing this she helped him out and they became friends again –to end yet again, and this last time, finally.

After his settlement, via some contacts that he had kept, he was offered work again, which was a healthy sign for anyone. Again, being based all over the globe, he took on work as a health and safety officer on oil rigs.

He had bought some land from a friend of his, which could be considered by some to be an idyllic location, far away from any development, no neighbours, and breath-taking views with clear air. He had built the trailer that he had lived in on the site, and developed out the rest of the living accommodation to high standards. It suited him, because Gerard could not successfully live with anyone – not man, woman or beast.

His work became his life, and his home on the mountain was his retreat from work and life. It could be an idyllic way of reaching one's goals if there was contentment and acceptance in one's heart. Instead, Gerard had fury and anguish.

He had paid for Barbara to come over with Gerhard for some years, again when he was on leave. Then he concluded that instead of bequeathing the whole site to Barbara after he died, he would change his will so that she could be the beneficiary of it now. When they were about to sign the new codicil, Barbara seemed to get greedy and told him that if she became the owner then he would not be able to live there; he would have to find alternative accommodations. Of course, Gerhard was backing anything his princess said.

Naturally, Gerard was gutted like a fish, for of all people, he never thought his true blood sister would betray him; so that is how their relationship ended. She was vindictive to him afterwards, telling him that he had never had a proper job in his life. And so the feud continued and the demon seeds were sewn again, though it looked like this time they were sewn on barren ground.

Gerard started to telephone Guy once again, and it looked like he wanted a relationship – because it suited him. They arranged for Guy to visit, and the Gerard used up his air miles that he accrued from his world trips for the ticket. Once again Guy saw Vancouver, Calgary, Kelowna, and the outskirts of Silverton where the great Gerard lived on his mountain top.

The trip was planned for a month, and to also celebrate Rowena's birthday on 2 September, but it did not last a week. Gerard was still ailing after the Barbara episode and was projecting his rage and betrayal onto Guy, but the latter would not take it anymore. It ended by the flight being brought forward, and Guy saying to him, "We have *nothing* more to say to one another"

Guy had had enough. All his life he had experienced Gerard's (and Gerald's) tirades, like he was the many-headed Typhon, and he was now at the end of his tether. He was not prepared to witness any more childish outbursts, which only wasted time and precious energy.

Gerard knew that this was the last time he could push and push and push without there being an ending, so he got it. He had driven everyone away from him because he wanted to feel that no one could cope with him – in that he had succeeded, but what an achievement and ambition! It would not be too difficult to imagine how he would justify it all. *Look what I did for everyone, and they kicked me when I was down. Look at the money I gave people, and see what they've done to me!* But one would need to ask him what hand he played in the prolonged drama.

It is impossible to get close to some people, and in knowing this history, any further attempts to do so with these entangled individuals surely leaves he who tries as the fool, or the masochist, knowing the anguish that they will cause sooner or later. It is better to sever all links and wish them a good life; that is what Guy did that day in Canada. He apologised to Rowena for not celebrating her birthday, but he gave her his greetings in his heart, and she knew it. What also surged through Guy's thoughts was if Gerard really cared for anyone. Guy remembered that had never come to Joseph's and Rowena's funerals.

During the counselling-psychology course that Guy took, one of his tasks was to interpret a dream for the Carl Jung term. He was concerned and anxious, for he had not been aware of having dreams for some time – though apparently we dream all the time but are not always aware of them – and feared that he might not be able to come up with the goods.

Then one night he had a vivid dream, which turned out to be part of a sequel.

He entered a room which was bare except for five chairs placed in a semi-circle around a single one that faced them. He intuitively went to sit down on the single chair and faced the others. Seated on the other chairs were five faceless human effigies that sat motionless. As soon as he sat down it was as if he powered their movement, for they looked as though there was life injected into them.

That was when the first dream ended. The next night he dreamed the sequel.

He entered the room again and the effigies were his step relatives, each looking ahead without any particular expression. He looked at each one individually for a few heartbeats, noticing fully their features and absorbing their ethos.

Then he spoke to them:

"I tried to be friends with each and every one of you, but you've all rejected my efforts and either vilified my name or told lies about my actions, and you've most definitely hurt me. We were given the opportunity to have a strong family union, but none of you wanted that. There has always been an underlying resentment of me from the day I was born; now I see it, and now I reject it. I see no point in trying to have any form of relationship with you any longer. I free myself of all thoughts of you, yet I carry no hurt, blame or recriminations. I am free – how you are is up to you."

As he finished speaking there were a few heartbeats of silence, and then they all disappeared from sight until the empty chairs remained.

Guy thought to himself, It's ended.

He had to represent a lot of his academic work, but with this dream analysis he sailed through. His tutor's comments ran, "It looks as though you were being controlled by a family bond that you wanted but did not exist; now you have taken control and feel empowered."

He felt that he was no longer the foolish child who wore his heart on his sleeve, but a mature person who could see things much clearer and objectively. Yet he still rejected that little eager child within him who was eager to love and be loved.

Guy had been brought up in chaos, yet intuitively knew that he was conceived in love, which gave him anchorage or ballast in perpetually stormy seas. Even though he knew that Rowena loved him dearly, as a young boy he was so utterly confused by her ambivalence and severe mood swings that he did things to be noticed. He also had the reputation of being into everything – yet even to a forceful and precocious child full of energy, constant pushbacks from someone who claimed to love him had its effect, and at one stage in his teenage years he became withdrawn and morose. It passed, and his later delving into the study of human behaviour helped him understand things better.

He held onto no recriminations towards his step relatives, even though he had tried to build bridges. Then he later realized that the pain he was causing himself was his own fault. They just were not interested in him, and it took a great deal of time for him to accept that. When he did he had the dream sequence. We can shut off from a past that is ours and block all its memories, yet the actions during that past have to be faced one day. We do not escape the residue that they have accrued.

Chapter 13

Rowena and Joseph's hearts were heavy the day they left their house. This home in Milne Park West had seen laughter, tears, betrayals, tantrums, fights, sulks, misery, doom and gloom, and many other things that would be a story to tell one day. It all contributed and became interwoven into the rich tapestry that was their life together. Yet there was a bright horizon unfolding before them, for they were both to begin a new career and work for the same organisation.

They had come to realize, from their many journeys together so far, that it was futile to hope that everything would be smooth sailing, because the sea is never the same for too long; it's changeable and fluid, just like life, and their lives provided many twists and turns and ducks and dives from the myriad of experiences that were to come.

The night before, Rowena, Joseph and Guy had packed up all the belongings and were prepared for the new journey ahead in the morning. The home was as empty as it was when they moved in. They had given all of their furniture to Freddie for his home in Barnsley; they just kept their beds and kitchen paraphernalia.

Joseph had another tale to tell:

There was a man named Pak Chow. A man of mixed origins, his father was a Chinese rice merchant, and his mother was

Burmese. Pak was always an industrious and innovative individual, and when he was a boy he helped out at an itinerant circus which stayed for a while in India, as it was travelling through the many provinces.

Against his father's wishes, Pak worked for the circus as an elephant trainer – his father had designs for him to take over his rice export business, which was quite lucrative, but Pak had other ambitions.

Pak Chow had an affinity with animals, and he got along well with the elephants, developing a strong rapport with one young bull called Raja. Raja always was happy when he saw his friend, not only because Pak fed him, but because they would play and enjoy each other's company. Raja also responded well to Pak's training techniques, which were gentle yet assertive.

The elephants were allotted a ration of rice, which Pak Chow weighed out and fed them the same time each day – the elephants liked consistency. Pak, having an insidious side to his nature, thought of a plan: if he took a portion of Raja's rice everyday he would have more for himself.

He began his clandestine plan, and Raja assessed its weight as usual in his trunk and then put to its mouth. This happened for some months, and Pak Chow tried to take a little more, but he knew that if it was done too often Raja would know. So he was careful, and on some days he took none, and on others, more.

The interaction between them changed, and Raja was not as forthcoming as he used to be with his erstwhile friend. But Pak Chow did not register this and continued in the same way. Raja became more inclined to look at Pak from a distance and with distrust, rather than the loving friendship as before. Still, Pak did not read the signals.

Time passed and the circus moved on; Pak Chow found work elsewhere.

Many years later, Pak had his own itinerant circus and was a very successful showman who had gained a reputation for putting on remarkable entertainment. He had used all his observations and knowledge he had gained from all the circuses he had worked as a young man, and put them into a creative and entertaining performance.

He eventually needed to buy some more elephants, and he always chose them himself, because he was the master of ceremonies when it came to elephant training and performances.

He duly went to a dealer he knew and surveyed what beasts he had. He was dumbstruck to find that Raja was in this man's collection. He greeted his old friend, but Raja was distant and pulled away from him. Raja then turned quickly, picked Pak up around his waist with his trunk and hurled him to the ground. Pak lay motionless and Raja trumpeted loudly. It was thought that Pak Chow was dead, but there was movement. However, his back was broken and he never walked again.

While he was recovering, he realized why Raja had done what he had. Pak had betrayed his friend and stole his food, and this was his repayment. Pak Chow reiterated to himself the adage that an elephant never forgets. Raja could have easily have killed him outright, but he wanted to teach him a big lesson – there is a price to pay for betrayal.

Guy and Rowena said playfully, "And the moral of the story is … ?"

In this case it was self-explanatory, and Rowena added that she had heard stories of how elephants never forget things.

Guy had his conflicts with Rowena because, like her, he also had a strong spirit and wouldn't be controlled – and for this he was called all kinds of derogatory things, which at times got to him. In fact, he even started to believe them. How easy it is to take on others' negative criticisms of us, especially when we in our formative years. But when the time comes that we no longer accept the script we've been given – as in transactional analysis – we have the right to change it and add our own desires and goals to it. Too often we can achieve for others – our parents, peers, brothers and sisters – and can forget who we are. If we take the road to self-discovery, we are often labelled as selfish.

It was understandable why Rowena had become much more controlling of her children. When there was no father in situ, she became their dual guardian and protector, especially in coming across a great sea from India to England without any knowledge of what lay ahead. But old habits die hard, and her way of parenting had stayed with her. But to the strong-willed Guy, she seemed to be even stronger in her will over him. He rebelled from a very young age, and when he was recalcitrant and obstinate, the one thing that acted as some form of deterrent was threatening him with boarding school. To Guy, this seemed like imprisonment, but it was a useful tool that wielded great power for Rowena.

We all grow up with derogatory words and phrases thrown at us, and often they wound us because they hit us deeply, like poisonous arrows that leave their venom long after the attack, rearing up to remind us of the event when the wounds have healed. It can often take a great deal of mental training to emerge from under that heavy critical blanket, but it can be done, and when the whole scenario is looked at with objective eyes, the entire picture can be seen with greater clarity.

Mooreland Rise was of contemporary architectural design that reflected the flavour of the distinctive 1960s. To some, this era and use of building materials had seen the construction of many a structure that led to the phrase "the concrete jungle." It had built around the same time as Addington View, where Rowena first worked as a caregiver, and she had watched its construction when she lived in Addington.

Mooreland Rise was mainly constructed of red brick and wood slats with a flat roof. The main nursing home area was to the right as one approached from the road, whilst the three apartments for the staff were positioned to the left. There was a private entrance door to the flats, though one had to walk through the lodge's main thoroughfare to get to it. This meant that there was no privacy when one chose to go out.

Adjacent to Mooreland Rise was another sixties wonder of architecture called Rees Heights, and Rowena wondered about the coincidence. It was a five- or six-story block, again with a flat roof. It was actually the hub of the council, containing the head offices of the district nurses, social services, human resources, housing, financial services, mental health outreach and other facilities.

The living accommodations for the staff were two-bedroom flats, all atop one another, as opposed to Addington View where they were laid out in a long line across the top of the building. The matron lived at the top, the deputy at the bottom, and the middle flat was let out to a Mr and Mrs Cummings at the time; he worked for the corporation, and she had psychological issues.

After the demise of Nora Skane, Joseph was appointed the deputy, and Rowena the matron. Mrs O'Hanlon continued to be their deputy superintendent matron, and Mrs Wainscott was the superintendent.

There was a lot to organise for Rowena and Joseph, as these were not only new positions for them – and a huge challenge – but a new home as well.

Rowena had made many observations whilst she had worked with Nora Skane, and whereas she knew that two of the easiest things to do in life are to judge and find fault, she tried to learn from her erstwhile matron. She did learn a great deal, even if it was how *not* to do certain things. Rowena had an intuitive knowledge of how to handle people in most situations – her travels had given her a great deal of experience – and although she naturally gave a due deference to Nora, she was sure that she would have done many things differently. Now she had the opportunity.

The one thing that she knew she had to tackle was the staff's morale, as she felt that it was off-balance, which then emanated towards the residents. She felt that a lot of the staff had not been understood for who they were, and in regular staff meetings she endeavoured to bring out their talents, giving them different tasks to carry out. She also promoted training as often as the budget allowed.

The occupants of the first floor apartment, Mr and Mrs Cummings, were an interesting couple. Dennis Cummings, a pigeon-chested man in his mid-forties, most definitely had the gift of the gab. According to his wife, who seemed to feel no compunction in telling people quite freely – much to his chagrin when he found out – that Dennis Cummings had been born with three ears; the surplus one had been removed surgically removed when he was an infant, which left a furrowed scar in his later years, but could only really be detected if closely scrutinised. So it appeared that Dennis had adopted this often overpowering garrulousness, probably to deflect anyone from noticing his facial scar. Dennis worked as a caregiver in another one of the corporation's homes for the elderly.

When Rowena and Joseph first moved to Mooreland Rise and took up their respective positions, over time they were aware that Peggy Cummings was housebound due to neurotic and personality issues. She would play her selection of vinyl 45s every day at a certain time, singing along with them to her heart's content. Peggy had no real experience with people, and whenever she came across anyone she always looked nervous and apprehensive.

Rowena very discreetly broached the subject one day to them both, as she was short of a caregiver, if Peggy would be interested in taking up the position. It seemed to be a win-win situation, where Peggy would have something to occupy her mind, and Rowena would have another member of the staff whom she knew something about already, and who actually lived on the premises.

Rowena often wondered what exactly the Cummings had in common, yet she knew that it was not a *Gaslight* situation, as it had been with Bertha Farleigh. Peggy could be quite fiery, and often had outbursts in reaction to Dennis's dogma. Although Rowena knew, by living beneath her, that Peggy was neurotic, erratic and tetchy, she was prepared to give her the chance to see how she would handle a job, as she had never really held down a job.

Another thing that Rowena had learnt through her experiences is that some people cannot be helped, because they believe that everything that comes their way is their due, so have no gratitude for it. Peggy Cummings was like this, yet she was also quite shrewd and did not begin to really show herself until her three-month probation period was up.

After that, Peggy became childish, reactionary, and petulant, very easily led by other members of staff who had a militant way about them. Peggy could also be the scapegoat for others who were the agent provocateurs; they would load her gun and she would fire it, but she did not recognise how she was being used.

Peggy also clashed quite strongly with Ida Hill. Ida, who did not tolerate fools easily, was blunt and straightforward with her, something which Peggy had not experienced before and was always ready to react and complain about. It was really like trying to nurture a recalcitrant and lost child who was now a grown woman.

As Rowena understood Ida – and was trying to understand Peggy – she brought the two of them together in a meeting in order to attempt to draw some compromise out of the friction that lay between them. It threw a great deal of light on Peggy's dynamics, as she was never prepared to make any form of compromise, and held onto the belief that Ida did not like her and that she wanted to insult her every time she saw her.

The conflict between them was rife that day. "Every time you set eyes on me, Ida, you want to say something to hurt me or make fun of me," Peggy said.

"Me no know what you're talking about, Peggy," Ida retorted. "I am who I am, and everyone understand dat. I am a straightforward person. So wait, you wan me to give you special treatment? Every time *me* see **you** me wan to insult you? What a liberty, Mrs!"

Peggy burst into tears, and Rowena noticed that they could be turned on and off very quickly. Even though she tried to mediate, Rowena knew that she would get nowhere, because Peggy's mind was set that Ida Hill was there to hurt her. She endeavoured to keep them away from one another as best she could, while still monitoring the situation.

So that very something that Rowena and Joseph tried to bridge, prejudice, seemed to come back and bite them viciously. They had both seen prejudice take many forms – race, religion, gender, status, birth, class, a person's sexuality – and it looked as though that enemy would always be with the world. The demonic seed within peoples' hearts – especially when it's popularized by a group of people – can become solidified and justified by anything that is done in its dark and destructive name.

Rowena and Joseph knew that to try and combat it would leave them helpless and disempowered, so they endeavoured to go with its ebb and flow – just like the tides cycles, always in motion – trying to use logic wherever possible to appeal to the better side of people's natures. They tried not to see it as an insurmountable cliff face to scale, but a force like the adverse side of nature that we have to accept. Joseph always reminded his beloved of the ancient adage, "Keep your friends close, but your enemies even closer."

One day there was a serious confrontation between Ida and Peggy over what Ida considered a racist remark that she claimed Peggy made. Naturally, Peggy denied it flatly, but then she had not gained the reputation of telling the truth, so Rowena looked into it.

Peggy Cummings had asked Ida if they wore shoes in her country of origin, and even though it could have been an innocuous question, it greatly offended Ida, who immediately flew into a tirade. "What you asking me, woman? You tink that we live like savages or cannibals in Jamaica? Look 'pon your foot, woman. You na wear na shoes either. Damn cheek, sometimes you white people tink dem so knowledgeable and cute, but you all just damn fool!"

"All I did was ask a simple question, Ida, and I can't wear shoes because of medical reasons," Peggy replied with a rather superior tone, but she intuitively knew that she had overstepped the mark. However, she clung onto the fact that Ida had used the term "you white people," and mentioned this as a racial comment in her favour.

Rowena was at her wits end with the pair, and she knew that once Ida had dug her heels in there could be no persuading her to see another view. She acknowledged that Peggy had also been indiscreet, but the connotation was implicitly there that shoes were for more advanced peoples. The unfortunate thing about it was that Peggy actually found it quite amusing, and Rowena overheard her laughing with Mona Blade, a senior carer whom Rowena had inherited from Nora Skane's matronship, whilst they were having a tea break one day.

Rowena had a word or two with Peggy privately, but the latter became petulant and stormed out of the office up to her apartment.

The next day she was handed Peggy's resignation by her husband, who said nothing other than, "Peggy asked me to give you this; she is still very upset."

Rowena was not prepared to discuss it with Dennis, and he knew that, because he just gave Rowena a knowing look, smiled and left. Rowena said nothing, but thanked him in a cool, business-like way.

Peggy Cummings worked out her one week's notice, and Rowena made it crystal clear that she would put up with no more heated interactions between her and other staff – because it was not just Ida Hill that she had issues with– and Peggy was surprisingly humble, contrary to how Rowena imagined she would be. She'd assumed that, as she was leaving, she would have been purposefully difficult.

Within the month the Cummings left Mooreland Rise for good; Rowena and Joseph breathed a very long sigh of relief. Clearly these plans had been underway for some time, and Mrs O'Hanlon told Rowena later that they were leaving the area to make a fresh start – evidently something they did often, probably due to Peggy's unmanageable behaviour.

Nora had given Rowena a verbal assessment of the staff that she had employed, and Rowena had naturally later looked in their files to check the details, as more often than not assessments can be subjective. Yet Rowena discovered that Nora's analysis of Mona Blade was accurate; she was a militant person who had a strong shop-steward-like approach to things. She was a devoted union member, and seemed ever ready to make a point when she thought that others had not noticed something.

Rowena had also assessed that Mona had been the main *agent provocateur* behind Peggy, preying on her gullibility and lack of maturity. Naturally, Mona would disappear into the backcloth, whilst Peggy would fire the metaphorical gun that Mona had loaded, getting the blame for the outburst or confrontation.

Yet in knowing this, Rowena could not have given Peggy another chance, though she had considered that, but her intuition led her to accept her resignation. Then it all fell into line when she learned of them leaving their flat; it had taken its natural course. Peggy had an opportunity to have some independence in earning her own wage, but it was clear that she was not able to handle it. Rowena was never in too much of a hurry to help someone out in such a way again. She still tried not to let it influence all her decisions to help others, because she knew that everyone is an individual that can be influenced by mass opinion or belief.

Chapter 14

Guy was with the grownups as much as was possible from the time he was young – often before he was shooed off by them, or they would curtail their union until Guy had gone. He enjoyed listening and absorbing what was going on. And in all honesty, there was so much happening on a daily basis when he was an infant that he was well on his way to a degree in psychology, or at least the dynamics between siblings.

This all, of course, began with total confusion, because he could never understand – until he was old enough to analyse it all – the constant miasma of strife that existed between everyone. He survived it by becoming the jester of a very fragmented court. Even though the king and queen would laugh at him in jest, did they really understand what was behind the farceur? Moreover, did the others in his stepfamily?

From this bustling atmosphere that he knew when he was growing up in Addington, life at Mooreland Rise was comparatively quiet. Yet the work that both his parents did brought with it a fair share of conflict and strife. It made him ruminate if this was the way of the entire world.

As Rowena had always lived a hectic lifestyle, from the time when she left Wales at 17 to her travels in India and then back to England to begin again, there had been very little time for the ugly, repressed memory of her father raping her to emerge and see the light. But somehow it reared its ugliness, and she felt its darkness rise within her, to the point of having vivid and frightening dreams.

Rowena was never really a drinker, but she was starting to drink on a daily basis. It seemed more fitting to call her malaise compulsive drinking rather than alcoholism, but this was by no means a euphemism for it, because, either way, the condition caused disruption and anguish. Compulsive habits, because of their regularity, are never hidden for too long, and Rowena's dependency on alcohol became acute; she also lost the appetite for food.

When dusk fell Rowena became the snarling banshee she-devil who only hurt those nearest and dearest to her. When dawn broke through into a new day, it was as if the spell had lifted, and she was Rowena again, the contrite little girl who felt ashamed of what she had done yet had no memory of it.

So, as Rowena's drinking increased, Joseph dealt with all the administration and management of the nursing home; he was more than heavily burdened. Then the fateful day arrived when Ida and Guy heard the man screaming for life from the emergency room in the hospital whilst they waited impatiently outside. Then they saw red lights flashing, heard buzzers sounding, and saw medical people rushing to his side; then there was silence.

"We did all we could for your father. I am sorry for your loss," came the doctor's voice, breaking Guy's reverie as he stared ahead. Ida took his hand in hers and pressed it hard. It was some comfort to him, but he knew that he had to remain steadfast for his mother's sake.

When they arrived home, Rowena was perched upright in a chair and bellowed, "He's not coming back, is he?" The silence and grave looks from Ida and Guy answered her.

Over the next week or so, Rowena and Guy saw Joseph's relatives as they came to pay their respects – Theodore with his twin daughters, Carmel and Michelle, big brother Melville and Zandra, Thelma and Dulcie – but as quickly as they appeared, they disappeared like the mist over a mountaintop.

Rowena was under a drinking spell, until Guy's friend, Reynald Waters, exorcised the demon sent to her by two of the people she had employed. The greatest surprise was realizing the fact that the two women had done what they did. Rowena did not do them any harm – yet neither had she done any harm to Sita when she sent black magic to kill Freddie.

No, it was not about that. It was about jealousy. The two women, who were from the same province in Jamaica, and had apparently known each other since they were young girls, clearly delved seriously in the black arts, and hoped that they would destroy Rowena.

When Rey described the two women, Rowena and Guy both knew immediately who they were. The other disturbing thing was that Rey vociferously said that the demon of alcohol that they had sent to her would be returned to them and do the same to them with interest. Evidently, conjured spirits are like mercenary soldiers; they are not loyal to any master, but do the work of the highest bidder.

Rowena had always complained about a huge weight that lay on her shoulders at night, to the point of her dreading lying down – and of course because of her drinking, no one really took any notice, thinking that it was a result of that – yet when Rey exorcised what he did, she slept soundly after a long period of torment.

Guy had met Reynald at a neighbouring nursing home where Guy worked for a spell while he was studying. It was an impressive Victorian gothic building about ten minutes' walk in Addiscombe. The site was at the end of a short road which ran adjacent to the railway line. The building was an impressive example of Victorian gothic architecture, with the original mullioned casement windows with distinctive gothic arches above them and the doorways. The facia was a notable red brick, with the architraves in contrasting plain, but weathered, concrete. The council owned it, and had designated it to be a nursing home for fifty or so elderly men.

Reynald was originally from Barbados, a muscular man of about six feet in height, who took care with his appearance and presented himself in a smart, casual way.

In charge of Davies Lodge was Bert Kinley, a Northumberland man with a distinctive north-east brogue. He was an insular type of man, and reflected the sergeant-major, as he was still regimented in the way he carried out his work. He lived on site with his wife.

His deputy, Ron Bissel was quite the opposite in character to Kinley; he was coarse, and drank a great deal with other members of the staff. Bissel was a cockney and revelled in sharing crude jokes, especially when they were flavoured with someone else's misfortune.

The monthly matrons' meetings were held at Davies Lodge, because its vastness accommodated a large gathering.

Reynald Waters worked there as an orderly, and was working to save money to help his beautician business in Barbados, where he was intending to return. After living in rented rooms about the Brixton and Herne Hill areas, his patience paid off. He had put his name down on a housing association register for accommodations some years prior, and he was eventually offered a comfortable conversion flat in Brockley.

By nature, Reynald was quite a direct man, and before Guy really got to understand his manner, he used to get offended and sometimes wounded by his brusque and matter-of-fact way. He appeared as though he had a very low tolerance level, and Guy often bore the brunt of this. Guy had learned a lot from being with people from the West Indies, and he knew that they could be direct and absolute; any form of wavering in decision was often considered weak. Spending time with Ida Hill had taught him a great deal, but there was something much more here when Reynald Waters dealt with Guy.

At this particular juncture in his life, Guy was feeling very vulnerable, confused and disoriented, and what would have helped was a nurturing tone of voice, rather than Reynald Waters' harsh and often irascible one.

Guy later understood why Reynald had been that much more abrasive with him. Waters had had romantic inclinations towards Guy, which he did not reciprocate, so Reynald had thought that he was playing coy, but this was not the case at all. Guy was so preoccupied with his mother's heavy drinking and his father being overburdened that he felt that his world was crumbling around him; any romantic pursuit was out of all thought at the time, and any form of a relationship with any member of his stepfamily was non-existent. He could not talk to any of them –they were all involved with their own lives and were not interested. He sometimes considered himself a fool for hoping that they would ever be.

However, it was at Guy's twenty-first birthday when Waters met Rowena and Joseph. It was a small gathering of some of Guy's friends and some staff from Mooreland Rise. Of course, Ida Hill was present, as she had a big place in her heart for Guy, as he did her.

Guy remembered how Ida had chastised him sorely one day when Guy had ignored Rowena for about a week because he had had enough of her outbursts and excessive drinking. He was watching her destroy herself and he felt helpless. He felt that any action at all might help, however negative.

"What is dis nonsense about you na talking to yer mother, bwoy?" she bellowed at him in private one day. Then her voice softened, "Me know Matron is going through some hard times at the moment darlin', but not speaking to her is killing her. Please talk to her, okay darlin'?"

Ida's caring talk opened his heart to feel the compassion for Rowena, for he knew she was hurting. He was willingly doing it to make her understand what she was doing to the ones she loved.

There were times when Rowena was such a lost little girl that it made him grieve that he did not have all the answers for her. He also felt anger at the others, for he knew they were not interested in him or his struggles, and definitely not their mother. Sometime after he realized that he probably expected too much from them, but just some interest in how his life was going would have been something.

He ruminated on a motto he got from a Christmas cracker one year which ran, "We are born crying, we live complaining and we die disappointed."

How much longer, he thought, was he to be in the cesspit of troubles and strife and all things not very nice?

Chapter 15

When Guy visited Reynald in his new home in Brockley, it turned out to be quite an event. What was intended to be a simple "let me show you around my new place" was transformed into a spiritual revelation for Guy. He was not closed to the occult, or rather spiritual matters, as his mother had talked a lot about such things – especially her occult experiences in India – so it was not so much the experience that flummoxed him, but the sheer suddenness of it.

After Reynald had shown Guy around his flat, they sat down to have a coffee. Reynald was folding his bandanna into a triangle to tie about his head when he went very still and stared straight ahead of him. He finished tying the bandanna and then got up and rushed to the bathroom, almost chanting, "Wash the boy, wash the boy."

When he returned he brought with him a bottle of eau de cologne and started fiercely dousing Guy with it. He then sat down again, and after what seemed a long time – probably not to him, but to an onlooker – he seemed to return to the room and focussed again on Guy.

"She has been here protecting you and your mother, and now as her duty is done, she wants to go back to her homeland," said Reynald.

Somehow Guy intuitively knew who he was talking about, yet his conscious mind asked, "Who?"

"Your mum's friend from India. She always dressed in cotton dresses and had her hair tied up so." He gesticulated a twirling motion about his head with his hands.

Guy remained still because he was silenced into the realization that he had never said one word about Rowena or her life to Reynald. There was no other way he could have discovered the same information, as he only knew Guy and had never come in contact with anyone else who knew Rowena or her family. Benny had contacted him through spirit; there was no doubt in his mind that is what happened.

When Guy returned home he never knew how he would find Rowena, as she was still drinking heavily, but it looked as though she had slept off most of what she had drunk that day. Guy related to her the events at Reynald's, and quite calmly Rowena said, "Yesterday, when I was walking out, I'd had a lot to drink, and when I tried to cross the road I stumbled and nearly fell as a bus was nearly on me. I felt this arm go around my waist and pull me upright, and there was no one there, but I know now that it was Benny. Bless her."

There was a noticeable calm look on Rowena's face, and she had the most serene smile that Guy had seen in a long while. That furrowed brow had gone, and she looked like she felt cared for, not just physically, but totally. It appeared that even though Rowena had to leave her friend when she left for England all those years ago, Benny had never left her in her heart, and even though she had passed away, she was with Rowena in her darkest days.

Prejudice can very easily block clear sightedness and curtain a clear horizon with negative energy, which can be like the regal horse of the shire with blinkers on – tunnel vision. When it's coupled with being judgemental and backed up with religious fervour, it is a mighty destructive concoction.

Karma teaches us that living a life is about addressing the issues that were not dealt with in a past existence or incarnation, acknowledging and owning all of our actions – cause and effect – no matter how banal or heinous they were. If we have not done this, those same actions will have to be faced in another lifetime so that we recompense for any injustice caused to someone else. That is why we have discomfort or pain, because we are readdressing these actions. The whole process is about living, dying, and living again in another body – as these are our vessels that carry us through an incarnation – and being constantly connected via the spiritual umbilical cord that is our soul.

Recorded in the soul or spirit are the Akashic records, the log of everything we have done since we came into existence, very much like a database or hard drive on a computer. So, all injustices, wrongs, discomfort, and pain that we have ever caused anyone else has to be acknowledged and addressed, with our realization that we caused them and now have to face the effects. Once we take responsibility for our actions we evolve and grow spiritually. Perhaps it is synonymous to the repenting of sins for Christians; then there can be forgiveness.

Bearing this concept in mind, the very people who are in our present environment have usually played other parts in other existences in this overall drama that we call life. For instance, our brother or sister in this incarnation could well have been our daughter or lover in a past one. We have also, apparently, been different sexes. This is often why we can have different feelings for someone at different times, because the energy from that past life surges through the present one, which can leave us confused or make them think that we may be unbalanced.

To illustrate this point, Joseph had another tale on this subject:

There was a man who had recurring dreams of the Circus Maximus in ancient Rome. Then one day when he was crossing a road, he was knocked down by a speeding car and was badly injured; he had to have his leg amputated below the right knee.

After his injuries healed some months later, he started to have the same dream again; this time he saw people in the Circus Maximus and wild beasts running about. He was advised to go for a regression session to establish what had happened in a past life, and as he was open to such things, he did.

What was revealed to him was that in a past life he was a Roman centurion who had been posted in the arena when there was a bout of Christians being slaughtered by ravenously hungry leopards; it was when Caligula ruled Rome and he saw this as a novel slant on having lions do the same. There was a Christian man who was being attacked by a leopard, and it bit off the man's right leg just below the knee; the centurion stood and laughed. When the man recalled the car accident, he remembered that it was a Jaguar, and he distinctly remembered the chrome symbol of the pouncing jaguar on the bonnet of the car standing out in his memory.

Who knows what the connection was between Rowena and Benny in a past life, but there was definitely an unbreakable link that connected them. One would look out for the other, no matter what, and Benny showed this to Reynald as the agent between planes. Because Rowena had experienced so much fragmentation in her life, she somehow lost the feeling of being whole, but the spiritual connections she felt with Benny, Ricchypal, her father-in-law, Mahatma Gandhi and her beloved Joseph kept her connected to this wholeness, however battered it was with everyday wear and tear. They were still the lights that never went out in her heart.

Benny and Reynald clearly communicated, because he had first-hand information that no one else could have given him. Guy did not have a closed mind to such things, as he and Rowena often talked about the occult and spiritual matters – Rowena's interest in such things was often ridiculed by her children – and so he felt a connection with Benny after this unforgettable experience.

What also rang like a bell in his head was the quote "One day is as a thousand to God," that there is no concept of time in spirit, only the physical world. Rowena knew Benny all those decades ago in the flesh, but she was only a heartbeat away in spirit.

Benny must have also been in a great deal of anguish, because on the physical plane she was attracted to the same sex and loved Rowena romantically, yet knew that this was not reciprocated in the way that would have made her happy. However, her love for her friend proved to be pure and steadfast, as she never told her and remained a loyal friend and confidant, and clearly did to the day that Rowena passed away.

Reynald also had his fair share of extreme experiences, which he relayed to Guy, as he felt he trusted him. Guy learned from his friend that there was a great deal of prejudice amongst what Reynald termed "my own colour" that was not necessarily apparent. Reynald spoke of adverse comments and jibes thrown at him from people who were from neighbouring islands in the Caribbean. He told Guy that the level of darkness can be discriminated against in dark-skinned races, and in his knowledge of collective opinion, Reynald said that very dark-skinned people can be considered to be under the influence of evil – probably the same theory could be attributed to left-handed people being considered servants of the devil, sinister (in Italian, left is *a sinsitra*).

The interesting thing here is that the two women who sent Rowena the demon of alcohol were from Jamaica and extremely dark skinned, quite black in fact – and one was left-handed. A coincidence or an example that could swing the decision that way?

Guy had learnt that just because there are several people who might be of the same race, country of origin, religious belief or sexuality, it never guarantees that they will get along. This was confirmed by what Reynald told him, and gave him insight into Reynald's world and field of perception.

Reynald was a spiritual person who had strong Christian beliefs, even though he did not follow a particular denomination. He told Guy that in his estimation there were too many Christian sects, each one promoting their own version of the message that Christ gave out, and somehow the original message had got corrupted and distorted.

Rowena saw this in action in India. With many different people with varying religious beliefs, it opened up a wider horizon for her to look out on. From the mainstream Hindus and Moslems, each had many tributary cults/sects that were considered heretical by the more traditional followers. Rowena remembered Joseph telling her of the cult of Kalika, which became the godhead for the band of men who called themselves *Thugee* (the English derivation became thugs), who robbed people and murdered them in the name of their goddess, Kali– her temple was in Calcutta, where human sacrifices were made at one time, but now goats suffice.

Kali is said to stand for the ferocious and frightening elements in life that have to be faced before we can move on spiritually. Because she was depicted with a terrifying appearance

– fang-like teeth and unkempt hair garlanded around her neck, with human skulls, and sprouting several arms – she was seen as the patroness of destruction, which must have justified the Thugees' actions. Many people were killed, by a particular form of strangulation, and robbed by the *Thugees*, yet they appeared to have no compunction about this, for their collective belief was that Kali sanctioned it and this was their calling in life.

Reynald had encountered Obia women before – those who dealt in black magic – and had suffered at their hands too. He related an experience to Guy that a particular West Indian woman, with whom he'd met through a work connection, had had designs on him. When he rejected her advances, she sent him what he described as "spiritual bees" that infested his home on two occasions. At other times, when there had been visitors, they had left certain elements to break down his strength of mind. He was shrewd, however, and detected the signs quite quickly. He was an acutely aware man, both of his own behaviour and his environment, and sought help to eradicate those impediments to his well-being.

So Reynald and Guy had a spiritual connection, in that they could talk about such things at great length. Unfortunately, the element of the unrequited love was an impediment. Some time later Reynald returned to Barbados, and Guy telephoned him on occasions, and of course they spent a while in conversation, but it was costly. Reynald wrote to Guy a few times, but then it dwindled away – the fire was not kept alight. But Guy would always remember his experiences with Reynald and how he was introduced to Benny in that most unorthodox, and even surreal, way.

Chapter 16

When Rowena and Joseph ran Mooreland Rise, Mrs O'Hanlon, their deputy superintendent matron, became quite friendly over time, and they met socially at times.

Mrs O'Hanlon had married in her later forties to an architect, who she described as a brilliant man in his line of work, but an airhead with everything else he had to deal with. When she got to know Rowena more, she confided about her experiences with Tom and all his eccentricities. Although she was from Lancashire and had a distinctive brogue – which was a point of mirth for Joseph and Guy, who shared mimicry of her distinctive accent – her mother was Irish, and being in her eighties was inclined to be cantankerous, and the latter lived in sheltered accommodation, but pestered the life out of the warden who was employed to oversee the apartments. He often had a word with Mrs O'Hanlon about her mother. All to no avail, however, as Margaret Battle was this by name *and* by nature.

Elizabeth O'Hanlon did not like the superintendent matron, Mrs Wainscott, and when she was on an intimate level with Rowena, she would often call her "a stupid bitch." In her eyes, Mrs Wainscott was a coquettish bimbo with a position who thought she was flash because she drove about in silver Ford Capri. It did come to light that Mrs Wainscott had marital difficulties on and off, and her husband had had other affairs. She also had the reputation of flirting with men whenever there were social gatherings. Apparently, she and her husband had violent quarrels, which could be seen in the behaviour of their dog, Gypsy, who accompanied Mrs Wainscott everywhere. Rowena and Joseph looked after Gypsy on occasion when the Wainscotts went on holiday, and whenever there was any shouting between Rowena and Joseph, Gypsy would immediately take cover under a bed.

As time went on, Mrs O'Hanlon began to spend more and more time with Rowena and Joseph, to the point of overkill. She was a heavy drinker of whisky, and was often too inebriated to drive a car, so Joseph would chauffeur her about. There was an occasion when Mrs Wainscott made a sudden appearance to the home, and for some reason – which Rowena suspected as a ruse – wanted to check on the curtains that she had had made for their lounge.

Mrs O'Hanlon was there and had to hide in the cupboard in the lounge until her superior left after chatting for some time – people liked talking to Rowena, as she was a receptive and active listener.

When Mrs Wainscott finally left, O'Hanlon came out of the cupboard, rather the worse for drink, and immediately asked, "Well, what did that silly bitch want?"

Rowena started to feel that this whole situation was getting out of hand, and now O'Hanlon was expecting to be driven about by Joseph wherever she needed to go. They were both in a quandary because, after all, she was their superior, but she had overplayed the part and taken advantage of their hospitality.

Guy took the lead one day and gently spoke to Mrs O'Hanlon, pointing out how he saw the situation and that his parents were being put upon by her. She became quite reactionary.

"Why, you young whippersnapper, how dare you tell me how to carry myself and hinting that I have designs on your father! What cheek!"

Guy made it clear that he did not want to upset her feelings, but reiterated that he felt that she was making too many demands on his parents and they were suffering as a result. She would not listen to reason, however, and stormed out of the apartment, still saying that she thought that Guy was rude and insolent.

Guy was scolded by Rowena for interfering, but in her heart she was happy that it was done and the burden was spared her and Joseph, as they did fear that there would be repercussions if they said anything.

It was at this time when Gerard announced that he was paying a royal visit to London – this was before the fracas with Cecile, as he had not married her yet – and asked Rowena and Joseph to dinner one evening. They both went in good faith and met up with Gerard for aperitifs in the hotel lounge where he was staying, before going into dinner.

Gerard was still bombastic and as egotistical as ever, speaking with his adopted American twang, which seemed as though he thought added grandeur to his whole bearing, when it actually made him look course and unfeeling. Gerard related his experiences to his mother and stepfather, with the underlying theme of the racial prejudice he had suffered at the hands of workmates and people in general. Joseph could relate to this up to a point, as he had experienced derogatory racial remarks and jibes over the years, but there came a point when he recognized that Gerard was being maudlin – and of course, the more he drank the worse he became.

Joseph glanced at Rowena, and they understood each other's thoughts. Even trying to change the subject did not work, as Gerard wanted to talk about himself and his universe. It became clear to them that day that Gerard was not proud of who he was, but he bemoaned it, and this ethos probably emanated out, and others took the cue to taunt him with it.

How they hoped, as they watched him and listened to his empty words, that he had grown and matured into a man who accepted who he was with pride and wanted to show respect to his mother and the stepfather, whom he always claimed he revered. But unfortunately he had become more churlish, defensive and reactionary, which saddened them both deeply. They also had a strong premonition that there was to be some high drama during the course of the evening.

Joseph mentioned to Gerard that the boiler suit he was wearing – marked heavily with the logo of the oil rig he worked on at the time – would probably not be accepted because of the dress code of the hotel. Gerard made some egotistical remark that he would wear what he chose to and would not be dictated to by any hotel that he stayed in.

They approached the entrance to the dining room, and the floor manager asked, "Good evening sirs, madam, have you booked this evening?"

Gerard told him who he was and the room number, and the manager checked it off his guest list for the evening. Rowena and Joseph sensed that Gerard was peeved because he wasn't instantly recognized.

"But could I point out, sir, that we do have a dress code, and what you are wearing does not meet with it," the manager said.

"I'll come to dinner in what I choose to wear, and I'm changing for no one," Gerard responded petulantly with an even more exaggerated American twang.

"I'm sorry, sir, but I cannot allow you in dressed like you are," replied the manager.

Joseph stepped in and discreetly said that they could easily eat somewhere else that evening, but Gerard was adamant that he had booked a table and that he was going to eat there, however he was dressed.

The situation had reached a stalemate. Rowena and Joseph knew that they had to adhere to their codes of behaviour and dress, and it was clear that Gerard's ego had been denied; Rowena knew above everyone else what he could be like when that happened.

She had to be forceful, and said, "Gerard, we are going to eat somewhere else. Join us if you like."

With that, she took Joseph's arm, walked out of the dining room and headed for the door to the street. Gerard followed soon after, still remonstrating about the hotel's modus operandi and how it infringed on guests' liberties.

The meal that they had in another restaurant was not enjoyable because Gerard could not leave the subject alone; he did not get his own way and now he wanted to cause a civil war. Joseph and Rowena came home with heavy hearts, despondent about Gerard's whole mien and attitude.

They also wondered if there would be repercussions after Guy had spoken to Mrs O'Hanlon, but what they noticed was that she kept her distance, appeared only on a professional basis, and made no plans to see them socially. She could be a matter-of-fact woman, and dropped all confidential and personal links. Rowena was not displeased, and it gave them some time for themselves, which never really lasted too long, as there was always some drama happening, if not externally, then internally with Rowena's demons.

Joseph was getting to be more and more overburdened. He had taken his driving test a few times and failed, but he eventually passed. Their first car was a Morris Minor traveller, which gave them some means of getting them away from the home and all its worries. Yet Guy remembered vitriolic rows in the car when they stopped off somewhere, when Rowena was in one of her demonic tirades, blaming everything on Joseph. It was very much like the exchange between Richard Burton and Elizabeth Taylor in the film *Who's afraid of Virginia Woolf?*, the same line snarled by Rowena, "You're no man . . ."

However, with frazzled nerves and the weight getting heavier on his shoulders, Joseph ploughed on, as if he was the only ox that was driving the plough in icy, hard terrain.

Chapter 17

After Joseph died Rowena was in a strange and lonely place. Fortunately, she could hold on to the only living reminder she had of her beloved, their son, who by now was nearly at the end of his road of tolerance.

Rowena was in the alcoholic rehabilitation unit from Monday to Friday, returning to Mooreland Rise at weekends, but she was till drinking secretly, which Guy discovered quite soon. Under the influence of alcohol, Rowena was a merciless banshee who would put any Harpy to shame, but this time with professional help as a support blanket, Guy knew that he had to take action immediately, as indulging Rowena in this destructive path would only lead one way, and that was further down into the abyss.

When Guy smelt the drink one day, he asked her outright if she was drinking, and of course she denied it. He then told her that if she continued to drink whilst she was at home on weekends from a unit which was helping her to get off the booze, he would not hesitate to tell them about it.

Either Rowena thought that he would not do it, or she was testing providence, because she continued to drink the poison water and Guy kept his word and told them. He ignored her remonstrances, and on the advice of her consulting psychiatrist, he paid her no attention for a while and did not visit her in the unit. She had a rough road to go down, as the unit's policy was a course of tough love, which gave the patient a metaphorical rubbing down with course sandpaper.

To relieve Rowena's position was a man Guy had known from Davies Lodge – one of the "drinking club" that drank incessantly with Ron Bissel, the deputy warden. Paul Koble was a corpulent ruddy-faced man, who habitually smoked a pipe and gave off the persona that he was an educated and world-wise man. However, beneath this mask lingered a frightened, insecure and insidious little boy who would use his position to get anything that he wanted. This he proved whilst he stood in the matron's position at Mooreland Rise.

When Guy spoke to the psychiatrist in the unit he felt much better, because the latter told him to think about his own future, and that it did not have to be totally revolve around his mother. They were there to help her professionally, which would relieve the burdens from him. It helped Guy to see that he had a right to live and be happy, instead of being caught up in this entangled cesspit that Rowena was in. There were times when he desperately needed a sister or brother to help, even to just talk to, but there was no point in wasting thoughts hoping for that.

One evening at the weekend, Rowena, feeling somewhat better because she was leaving the drink alone, wanted to have a chat to her staff, so went along to see some of them. Whilst she was chatting with some of them and also saying hello to some of the residents, Paul Koble appeared and announced that she was not permitted to come anywhere near the home, and that she was strictly restricted to her apartment.

Rowena replied with a quick retort, "You make it sound like I'm under house arrest, Mr Koble, but I will return to my flat and will talk to you about this another time."

She handled it with her usual sense of decorum and dignity, and Koble felt belittled in front of the others. The very thing he wished to do backfired on him mercilessly.

However, as time went on, it looked as though he sought his revenge. He reported to the superintendent matron that Rowena was stealing the residents' money to buy alcohol, some of which was kept in the medicine chest in the doctor's room for those who were mentally confused to buy them odd sundries. It looked as though he wanted to ruin her reputation.

Rowena was called into a meeting at the unit to face this accusation, and was more astounded by its sheer fabrication than anything else. Yet she had sensed that Koble would seek revenge for the spot she had put him in the other day, but she did not think that he would go this far. But then, it was easy for him; he was in a position of authority and wanted to ingratiate himself in order to curry favour for his own promotion. On the other hand, Rowena was in a vulnerable position, and who would believe her over the very capable Mr Koble, who drank profusely himself daily whilst on and off duty at Davies Lodge.

It transpired that Mrs Wainscott met up with Rowena. They discussed an early retirement, because looking ahead to face Mooreland Rise without Joseph was a grim prospect indeed. Rowena did not really want to do that, so retirement seemed the better option. Mrs Wainscott was instrumental in helping Rowena find suitable accommodations, and as soon as she finished her course at the unit, Rowena was offered a maisonette not too far away from that famous, or infamous, St Saviour's Road. It was a new start.

Guy went along with Rowena to see the liver specialist in Camberwell, and he was a gentle and considerate man who spoke kindly to Rowena, who was still in a vulnerable place in her heart, which felt at times that it was about to break. When she saw an

X-ray of her liver, she was so frightened that she never touched another drop of alcohol. Now she would be able to let her liver regenerate, as it is the only organ in the body that can do so.

When they came out of the specialist's consulting room and headed off down the road, Rowena linked her son's arm, looked ahead and said rhetorically, "I've been very selfish, haven't I?"

Guy did not reply, and let the impact of what she said grip them – and grip them it did. Yet somehow Guy knew that Rowena had turned another corner.

Paul Koble's deed was returned to him some time later when he administered an intravenous injection to a patient incorrectly; he was not qualified or experienced to do it, and was dismissed without any further ado. When Guy was doing some agency work, he happened to come across Koble working as a security guard, and he looked forlorn and dejected.

Coincidentally, he moved quite near to Rowena, and called one day. Guy answered the door. "What do you want?" Guy asked bluntly.

"I've come to see your mother. Is she in?" Koble had what looked like a bottle inside a carrier bag in his hand.

"Don't call here again, Koble, or I will call the police. Do you understand?" Koble left without saying another word, but with more of a flushed face than usual.

Guy was naturally protective of Rowena and felt that he wanted to hit the man full in the face for his machinations against her, but the force of what he told Koble kept him away and he never called to the house again. Guy told Rowena who had called and what he told him and she thanked him. Learning about his demise gave her some comfort that there was some justice in the world.

Life on Prince Street was fairly comfortable to begin with. Rowena had the upper floor maisonette, and an elderly married couple lived at the bottom. They were Victorian terraces probably built for local workmen, with three steps leading down to both the lower and the upper apartments, with the two front doors adjacent to one another. After a short entrance hallway inside the front door, there was a flight of stairs to the upper maisonette. They were comfortable, though not built too strongly; all the living noise was quite audible.

Bert and Nora Tremble naturally took to Rowena. Nora was a controlling type of person, and so she and Guy were wary of one another. She intuitively knew that she could not control him, and he was wary of being governed by her, but they lived amicably. Guy was polite, but did not answer any of her prying questions.

With some of her and Joseph's superannuation money, Rowena bought furnishings for the maisonette. Bruce helped Rowena with putting up shelves and other chores, and it was about this time when he borrowed money from her, as he was going through financial troubles.

Bruce would often visit and he and Rowena would talk at length about things. Guy remembered the time when Barbara visited from Berlin and went to see Venema at her home in Gloucestershire. Again, Barbara enjoyed talking, and many a time had talked at length with Bruce, but it seemed that Venema was jealous and left Barbara alone in her kitchen one night when she stayed over, punishment no doubt for Barbara's rapport with Bruce. Barbara came back to Rowena, shaking with anger and indignation at being treated like that, and Rowena reflected on yet another poisonous act that her eldest daughter had willingly committed.

Before Rowena had turned the corner from drinking incessantly to not touching another drop, there were some amusing experiences, which of course at the time were not quite seen that way. It was at this time when roles were reversed and Guy felt more like Rowena's father and protector than the other way around. Was this a past life resurgence being acted out?

The manager of the co-op superstore that was nearby telephoned Guy one day soon after he had got in from work. He asked him if he could come down to the store as soon as possible because, as the manager said, "We have your mother here."

When Guy got to the store, there was Rowena, totally inebriated and sitting in the front window on one of the garden furniture chairs on display, eating a cooked chicken that she'd bought and drinking from a bottle of gin. When she'd been approached by the security, she said that she had bought the chicken and gin in the store; they could not help but smile at her sheer barefacedness and lack of guile. Although concerned, Guy tried not to be angry at her. Her daily drinking and lack of a constructive drive made him fear that she might be destroying her mind.

There were other times when she was nowhere to be found in the home, and Guy usually found her under the trees in the park, feeling quite consoled by them. She faced a shoplifting charge for taking something she did not even need. Guy remembered when he tried to tell Barbara about it that she was more concerned about her own reputation and how Rowena's misdemeanour would affect that. There was judgement all about, and what would have eased the burden would have been a sympathetic ear or an empathic response, but then children, later becoming adults, can often reflect how their fathers have been, and in this case only one word really sufficed – absent.

But the trip to the specialist that day convinced Guy that Rowena had made the decision to change. He had seen her through the tumultuous and unsettled time of her life, and he felt relief as the burden of responsibility was lifted from his shoulders; she owned it again for herself. He could also not help but think that he was addressing now how he had been when he was a naughty child – a Karmic return perhaps?

Just when Rowena had conquered yet another one of her Herculean tasks, another one unfolded before her. The couple who lived below her moved away, and the maisonette was empty for a while, and for some reason the windows were boarded up. Then a young woman moved in with her little daughter, and Rowena's life at Prince Street took on another twist and turn.

Joanne's day began at four in the afternoon when she started playing heavy bass music from her stereo, which seemed more like disco club equipment. The father of the child, who was West Indian, visited at times, but Joanne was totally in control of the whole scenario, and she often put him out when she'd had enough of him. Carl appeared to be quite a reasonable man, yet Joanne wanted to live her life irrespective of anyone else, especially her child.

When Guy came to visit one day the music had just begun, and he could see that Rowena's nerves were getting frazzled again. He feared that she would head straight for the bottle, but on the other hand he knew his mother, and realized that she was made of stronger mettle. When she made a decision to do something, she did it, and kept her word whenever she made a vow.

Joanne was unapproachable. Guy called at her door with Rowena to ask her to adjust the volume on the stereo, but she just slammed the door without acknowledging that she was causing any disturbance. In fact, she said nothing but just stared in a contemptuous way.

The process went on for a while, and the council was informed of the situation, including the constant rows between Joanne and Carl and the night club setup with music thumping through the walls. Joanne had not even taken down the boards from the windows. Rowena felt mostly for the little girl who was in the midst of all the utter chaos. Joanne had made it clear one day as she shouted at Carl that she had had their child, not because she had any strong feelings for him, but because she wanted a flat, and now that she had that he was redundant in her life. She was going to live a she pleased.

After a great deal of mental anguish, Rowena was offered an apartment in South Norwood, which was a purpose-built flat in a block of about 35. After a huge amount of unrest and unnerving discomfort, Rowena breathed another sigh of relief and turned another corner to start yet again.

When she was alone she sometimes yearned to be able to sit down with her daughters and have a heart-to-heart talk about each other's lives and share their philosophies about life in general —just share some girl talk. It's said that we cause ourselves pain or unease by wanting what we don't have instead of making the most of what we do, but there were times when Rowena observed other people with their children – and even their grandchildren – being close, growing together, or just having light-hearted fun, and could not help but feel a deep pang of loss and emptiness that her children and grandchildren were strangers to her.

How she missed Joseph, and often in quiet moments alone she suffered brutal attacks of remorse at how she treated such a loving and devoted man. These things tortured her mind and heart, yet she had the consolation of Joseph's son, the twin who lived, and he tried in his own way to be the same rock that Joseph had always been, although he was world weary of the injustices and treachery he had witnessed and experienced in his family and would not tolerate any more crap. He could be quite forceful and to the point, and in this she knew that he had been blessed. Blessings are not always gift wrapped in pretty paper;

often they can be plain brown paper packages without any frills that contain a powerhouse within.

Rowena seemed to be destined to live and work for many of her years in flat-roofed apartments. This purpose-built block in South Norwood was a two-storey building, not unlike Addington View and Mooreland Rise. The council probably used the ideas of similar-minded architects who designed buildings focussed on bland practicality rather than fusing them with aestheticism – the type of building you find everywhere in the country, reinforced concrete, suspended flooring with cantilevered balconies fronted with concrete and wood-panelled fascias, the latter often painted in a single colour.

Rowena's flat was at the end of the block, and there was a concrete stairwell on either side of each block to access the upper floors. It was a comfortable one-bedroom apartment on an east-west axis – her kitchen and front entrance faced east but was at the rear of the building – so she got the sun there in the early morning and it's setting in the evening at the front of the building. Rowena recalled Joseph telling Guy about the same east-west axis being the ideal situation for churches and cathedrals.

It looked as though the council had placed Rowena on this site purposefully, as the block was housed with people over age 50, so her fear of hearing another's boom box was dashed when she discovered this –relief indeed after living above Joanne's Night Club.

On the odd occasion, Rowena met up with Mrs Wainscott, and learned that she too had retired, but Rowena found that being with her felt strained. For although the latter had asked her to call her Nancy, Rowena could not do so out of deference – that was an intuitive characteristic of Rowena, not to cross boundaries, even though now they were no longer in the hierarchical structure of work.

About five years after Rowena left the borough council she heard that Mrs O'Hanlon had died of a heart attack. It appeared that she did not ease up on the drinking, which did not help her weak heart condition. Rowena reflected that it could have been her own fate, considering how much she drank each day, but she was not destined to end her life that way it seemed.

She remembered how she had seen the demise of Nora Skane, and somehow knew in her bones that it was a dress rehearsal for her own downfall. She could not help but feel that she was being shown how she would stumble and fall from grace. Rowena remembered the many times when she had fallen before in different situations and for different reasons, but surely for one cause – to learn and readdress elements from her past existences. Somehow knowing that she had come through them, not unscathed but scarred, proved to her that she was indeed a warrior of life.

As she sat in her kitchen looking out of the window, the one thing that she longed for was to have her beloved by her side. Even with that great cavern within her, she still felt a sense of achievement, crowned with the emotional scars of overcoming many tough battles, and overriding the metaphorical earthquakes and tsunamis that had come her way.

She often reflected on the gems that shone in her heart, those few people in her travels who brought grace and peace to it – her father-in-law Ricchypal, Benny, Mahatma Gandhi, and of course her beloved Joseph. And as they shone so brightly, now they overshadowed the dark and despicable characters with whom she had had to deal. She had no illusions that all would be well from now on, there was still a path to tread, but she would carry herself along it with the dignity and decorum that was intrinsically hers.

Chapter 18

She kept the details of the business between her and Bruce to herself, but there came a time when she discussed with him a return on her loan to him. Guy had been saving drastically for his deposit on his first flat and needed a little more to facilitate the transaction. Rowena secured some of what she had lent Bruce and loaned it to Guy; this then enabled him to go ahead.

He got a mortgage on a studio apartment in Norwood not too far away from Rowena, a Victorian conversion, built for the up-and-coming businesspeople and middle classes of the time when the area was called Northwood, about 1890. They were actually two substantial houses converted into one, creating eight flats altogether. Guy was interested in the ground floor to the rear of the building, which offered a veranda which overlooked the rear grounds.

The transaction actually went through just before Rowena moved to Norwood herself, and before she had stopped her drinking, and there were times when she had let Guy down in arranging to meet him or be there to have something delivered.

There was an occasion when Guy was very angry with his mother when she was to be there to receive a delivery of a cooker. As everything was still new and exciting, he had not had time to get a new set of keys cut, so had left the original set with Rowena. He was returning about two in the afternoon that day so that she did not have to wait too long, but when he arrived he could not get in. After ringing his flat doorbell several times and looking through the outer front door letter box, he eventually saw her scrambling to the door on her hands and knees – she was clearly drunk – and his heart sank. Eventually, Rowena dragged herself to the outer front door and just about managed to open it. Naturally Guy was fuming, but he helped her back into the flat.

"Couldn't you have left the drink alone just until I got here?"

"Well, I went to the shops and got talking to someone, and then we had a drink together."

"I wish *a* drink was the truth; it looks as though you've had many."

But he had things to organise and see about Rowena, who was not really able to stand. The cooker was not delivered, as Rowena was not in when the delivery man arrived; he left a card stating this.

Guy was exasperated with her. He had not yet connected a telephone line, so he went to a local phone box and called a cab to take her home. Rowena was being her obstreperous and argumentative self, but he was not going to hear it.

The taxi came and he helped her into it, giving the driver the destination and money for the fare. Guy had made it crystal clear to his mother that he would not be a whipping boy for her excess baggage. She learnt that that day with a heavy blow, even after she threw recriminations at her son afterwards for his actions. However, she knew in her heart of hearts that it was probably the best course of action, even though it meant bruising her pride.

Later when Rowena was ensconced in the alcohol unit she came across a little book about what children become after what they've been taught, which gave her food for thought. She copied down what inspired her so much and kept it with her for the rest of her life.

*When a child grows up with criticism he learns how to condemn;
with hostility he learns how to fight; with ridicule he learns
to be shy; with shame he learns guilt; and so with tolerance
he learns patience; encouragement leads to confidence; being
praised from time to time leads to appreciation; with fairness
he learns justice; with security comes faith; with approval he
learns to love himself; and when he has known acceptance
and friendship he learns to find love in the world.*

Rowena wondered where she was in the course of all those things, and how she had been with her children. Of all the things that she knew she had not done, she did know that she tried to accept her children for who they were, and disowned the destructive things that they had done. She was glad that she could separate the actions from the person, and therefore did not condemn them. But condemning herself was another matter, and that took a great deal of training to stop doing.

Sometime later Rowena was looking for something to fill her day, as she was hungering for activity again and to be needed. Guy went along with her in search of a job, and she saw one that she took a liking to. It was cooking breakfasts for workmen on a labour site, and it was local so she would have no travel expenses.

Guy went along with her whilst Rowena went in for the interview, and she was successful and was going to start the following week. That raised her spirits immensely, for things looked like they were turning a fresh and positive corner, something that she'd experienced many a time before. Now that she had moved from Prince Street above Joanne's Night Club to Norwood, and had become settled without the prop of alcohol to support her, she was ready to walk another path in her continuing journeys.

She and Guy had been to see the specialist, and Rowena had made the decision that day to stop being selfish and give up that which would undoubtedly kill her within months if she continued. As she linked her son's arm, she was guilt-ridden that she had also put him through so much, but Guy did not belabour the point, and just let her feel her own feelings without trying too hard to assuage her. He was hurting too, and had not had the time to really grieve for his father, since he had to protect Rowena through her travails and put his own feelings on the back burner.

But they got through it and moved on, and then one day after Rowena had been working at the building site for some months, she told Guy of Michael Murphy.

Rowena got into the role of cooking for the men quickly and effortlessly, and it was a small makeshift kitchenette in a trailer on the site. It had adequate cooking facilities, but the area was cramped and the cooking section was at one end of the cabin, with seating at the other for the men to eat. The dining area could only hold so many men, so they took turns having their breakfasts.

Rowena was aware that there was one man who had watched her quite intently from the start. She felt that he was a protecting force about her, because he was always the last to leave after the men. She did not feel threatened by him, but he emanated the ethos of a young boy who hung around mum whilst she cooked.

He had asked her out for a drink something like three months after she started at the site, but Rowena had declined. It was as if she needed Guy's approval somehow, because she asked him what she should do. Guy answered that she clearly didn't feel any adverse vibes from the man's attentions, so why not go out for a coffee with him?

Rowena understood the irony in the suggestion, and added that he was not a coffee type of man but a Guinness drinker. He had shared that with her when he had asked her out. Anyway, she did go out for a drink with him one evening, and there were no ill effects. Rowena discreetly had soft drinks without going into any detail why.

Time went on and Rowena asked Murphy and Guy over to her flat. Conversation was always a strained affair with Murphy, but Guy felt that the man was inoffensive enough and genuinely liked Rowena. Guy was pleased that she had met someone, as he knew that his mother was an intuitive caregiver, and he sensed that Murphy was in need of a mother figure, and Rowena needed another child to take care of and nurture.

Rowena confided in Guy later on that the relationship was purely platonic, as Murphy had no sex drive, which suited Rowena. But of course to the world he was a man with his girl. Guy could not help but feel that there was a similarity between this man and Zoot the Cat; the reader will learn of him later.

Over the course of the next couple of years, Murphy came to live with Rowena in her flat. Firstly he would stay over for a weekend, and then they decided that he should move in and give up his flat near London Bridge. This filled a great part of the emptiness that she felt after Joseph died, someone to cook and clean for and take care of.

So in the eyes of her judges, she had found yet another man. *They are attracted to her like moths to a flame; she is never too long without one.* But how easily judgement without knowing the facts can condemn – and how often it does – for those who judge so readily do not really want to know the facts, because knowing them would take away that habitual trait which they've so grown used to belabouring.

One day Venema paid her mother a visit when Murphy was there and asked her to lend her thirty thousand pounds. Rowena retorted that she did not have that kind of money, so Venema asked Murphy; he also declined. "Insufficient funds," he said rather enigmatically in his broad western Irish brogue.

Venema's visit was short and not necessarily sweet, and that was the last time she saw her mother. What did she think as she left Rowena? "She's got another man in tow now. Dear God, she can't leave them alone?"

As her eldest daughter left, Rowena wondered how they had grown apart instead of growing together, which she had observed does happen with some mothers and daughters, but Rowena's life had never run along those lines, so in a way she was not that surprised at the end result. It was useless hoping for anything different, or comparing it with others whom she saw having interactive relationships with their children; that would only bring her grief. Instead, she mused on the tapestry that was her life whilst she washed the dishes and looked out of the window.

Guy had chastised himself for treating his mother that way, but he just wasn't going to indulge her drinking anymore. He intuitively felt that some tough love was needed. He felt that after she got over her wounded pride and indignation at being treated thus by her youngest child, she would come to terms with it. But then, he did not intend to mention it again; rubbing salt into her wounds was not his technique either.

Deep within her, Rowena respected Guy for his actions. When she looked at the situation objectively one day after she parted company with her false friend alcohol, she admired him for his quick thinking, which was not as it could have appeared, done for totally selfish reasons. Then again, in just getting a new flat, who would want neighbours to see a drunken woman crawling to the front door?

Rowena knew what she was capable of putting people through, and the closer they were to her, the stronger her ill-treatment of them – how bizarre are the workings of the damaged mind. It was as if the brutality that had been done to her was in her veins, and she then became the torturer of those she loved. What better way to inflict the pain that was thrust on her than to wound those who relied on her for emotional support? Many a moment alone was she tortured by the things that she had done to innocent parties, whereas the guilty bastards who had done her wrong went away scot-free. She lamented those actions to the day she died, and accused herself of being a coward in hurting her most beloved and their son.

The way Guy would not be controlled by anyone, and the sure way in which he challenged her fired her soul. For here was someone of her own bloodline who had strength of character, to the point of being ostracised for his opinions and actions. She knew that he did not want to truly hurt her, but would if it meant that she might learn to address her destructive ways. Perhaps he was her father or mentor in a previous existence, because the force with which he chastised her sometimes surged through her soul in an earth-shattering way. She naturally rejected it, as she was his mother, and that action seemed incongruous with that reality, but she intuitively knew that he was right.

From a Karmic point of view, they could have had many things to readdress from a past existence, and Guy felt absolutely sure that by the end of Rowena's days on earth he and she had faced all those past issues. But what a road it had been! Sometimes there were heart-rending confrontations with one another because she would not listen to reason, as alcohol played too strong a role in her life. He was also very harsh at times, but he intrinsically knew that he was not just being reactionary but proactive in his dealings with his mother, a compulsive drinker. However, he did not know all the answers, and at times got things radically wrong. That was why he needed her to get her professional help, which in the long run helped him to cope with her unmanageable behaviour and focus on his own life ahead.

Another fascinating paradox about Rowena's life was that she was excellent in advising others about their problems, and was usually right, yet she fell short of her own prognosis. The forest was most definitely too thick to see any trees, and Rowena was assuredly a wood nymph who transmuted at times into Medusa herself. Perhaps that was how she gave birth to the Cobra Queen of Poison, issued forth from one of her own poisonous snakes that writhed about her head.

Rowena would most definitely have been a first-rate hypocrite if she was to say that she was the innocent party in all of her dealings with people in her life. Yet on the other hand, she was not wily and scheming, because she did have a pure heart underneath her ravaging tirades that she threw at Joseph and tried to unleash on Guy. Even though he had become much more resilient to her ways, Guy could still be affected by Rowena's nihilistic outlook on everything –especially when she was loaded up with booze.

So when she thought about her children and saw them leave her, like this last time with her eldest daughter, she did not look at herself as blameless in the way that they behaved or the way they saw their mother. Rowena knew that they had grievances against her, which they wanted to hold onto as if that was all they had. They were negative and destructive, but were also concrete in their memories, like bad habits that are familiar yet damaging to us. Yet we still do them, enslaved until we change the pattern.

Rowena often thought of how beautiful her eldest daughter was, especially when she helped her with the fetes at Wynberg High School – how her green eyes glistened when she smiled, and her pure olive complexion shone in the sunshine. Rowena wondered where Venema had learned to be so Machiavellian, and yes, she must admit it, cruel. Her tongue had become a honeyed, double-edged sword that sliced through people, flattering on the upper thrust and cutting them down with the retrieve. Were these survival tactics that she had to fashion in order to live in a cruel world? Or was it to do with bitterness and the regret that she never had her rightful inheritance?

As they never spoke at length, Rowena never knew, but then Venema could very seldom talk to her mother without saying something cutting. So heart-to-heart communication was never really possible, and Rowena carried the hurt all of her life, which wounded her deeply. In that Venema succeeded; she hurt her mother to the heart.

Guy remembered Venema's question at Rowena's funeral as they both looked into the aviary with the zebra finches chirping and flying about. "Do you think she is there, Guy?" she asked, looking into the cage.

And his reply, "No way! She has flown and is now a free spirit."

No longer chained to useless recriminations and a slave to others' blame and resentment, she was a free spirit to return to her beloved so that they could play like two childlike spirits at the leisure of their own wills. Free to let others think and feel what they choose to, and free of all derogatory thoughts and feelings towards her. She no longer wanted anything to do with useless and unnecessary baggage that people chose to carry. Those who wanted to weigh themselves down with it, that was their business.

Chapter 19

Guy had often thought that for a great many years of his life he had been living in an altered reality, because it seemed as though he was an observer who bordered two worlds, one reality and the other a surreal dream state. He crossed over from one to the other to take mental notes and observations, and never fully felt part of either plane. It was as if he had no claims to having any personal relationships, as they all diminished into the horizon as soon as he made any effort to build on terra firma. He was reminded that all there was was sand on which nothing could be constructed, because anything that was built on it would crumble, fall and blow away in the winds. Perhaps the cause of his unhappiness was that instead of going with that flow, he wanted it to be different, and wanted what was not destined for him to experience.

Then the day dawned on him that he had played his part regarding his step relatives, but now he had the prerogative to choose another path, which did not include them. Now he knew that he would not carry any excess baggage, especially someone else's. It is said that when a man's mother dies he grows up. Guy went around for about a year like a wraith when Rowena died, as he now had the impact of the loss of both his parents, which took its toll on him. Here again, it would have been comforting to have been able to talk over things with a loving brother or sister – even quarrel and then grow together as a result – but this reality was not there for him. That was when he stepped into the surreal plane and looked across at his grief and loneliness. Loneliness is a human condition that has actually been known to strengthen our mettle in the long run; although, at the time of having such feelings it can seem like we're in a vacuum and it's hard to breathe.

When he was able to breathe in the air deeply once again and hold his head high in order to see the sky by day and the stars by night, Guy realized that he had lost his parents but that he lived on in the flesh, and he actually enjoyed this dual existence of living in the reality and the surreal. *Just don't start wanting things Guy* was the message that came to him from an ancient Buddhist teaching, as longing for things enslaves us and blocks our evolution. After he had come out of his chrysalis casing he felt stronger than he ever had. The shaman calls this a rebirth.

Guy had received some letters from Reynald, who was now back in Barbados and running his beautician business. What he missed the most was their lengthy talks about the *raison d'etre* of being, which got expensive over the telephone lines. Then in a telephone conversation one day, Reynald asked Guy when he was coming home, which led him to believe that Reynald still hoped that they would be together, possibly in Barbados. The irony of the situation was that when Guy wanted to put out a hand in friendship it was often rejected. Yet when others did the same to him, there could be ulterior motives, which Guy did not see because he approached the offer with an open heart. How rejection can dull the senses and make us distrustful of all humankind!

Guy realized that he was a warrior, and he remembered his Ghanaian friend, Asieu-Du-Mensa, saying to him one day, "Life is war, my brother, and we as life's warriors must live to overcome, not fight, the many obstacles that come our way."

Guy made that mistake many times. Instead of working to overcome obstacles that seemed insurmountable, he would try and battle them, causing an internal war, instead of finding an armistice that would give him firm ground on which to build a strategy.

Guy established himself over time in his studio apartment in Oliver Grove. One day when he had the veranda doors open and he was reading inside, a small kitten as big as his fist walked in and squeaked at him, baring his small mouth and needle-like teeth. It was a warm afternoon on a summer's day in July, and this small kitten sat down by his side and looked up at him, still squeaking. Guy asked him where he had come from, and it looked quite plain that the kitten wished to remain where he was, for he was a bold young tabby with white down his front like an apron.

Guy went out to look from the veranda, and noticed one of his neighbours who lived in a garden flat diagonally to the left of him.

"Have you seen a small kitten?" Ian asked.

"Yes, he's just sat himself down in my flat, and by the looks of things he has no intention of leaving," Guy replied as he glanced back into the apartment at the kitten still sitting in the same position.

"Did you want a cat?" Ian asked.

"Well, I hadn't really thought . . . well . . . okay, I'll keep him. It looks as though he's chosen me, to be honest," responded Guy. And that was the reality. The tabby, who then became Felix, had made up his mind to live with Guy – and he did.

Felix never grew to be a large cat, but his face could win any human over, and his pugnacious ways with the other neighbouring cats made him quite a formidable tom. Guy spoiled him at times with fresh fish or chicken hearts that he'd secured from a sports club in Beckenham where he worked at the time.

Guy and Felix had quite a union, which became a fascination to others. Whenever Guy would leave the flat, he always looked back and said to Felix, "See you later." Felix would always answer in his own way, just as he remembered him when he first came to stay.

When Guy secured a job as a chef-manager for the local Department of Work and Pensions, which was walking distance from where he lived, he got friendly with one of the workers who used to come up to the staff restaurant for meals. Jane had told Guy that she had a cat which she'd been trying to get rid of for some months, because she lived in a top floor apartment and it was difficult for the cat to get out. She would take the cat in a cardboard pet carrier and then try and leave him somewhere some distance from her home, but the cat always followed her back.

At first Guy was dubious, because he knew that Felix was territorial, but somehow the story of this cat seemed to pull him in. He went along and saw him after hearing about him for some time. The cat was the bushiest black creature that Guy had ever seen, with stunning, large green eyes and a totally docile, yet frightened, manner about him. As Guy set eyes on him he told Jane that he would take him there and then. He used the same cardboard carrier in which Jane had tried so many times to abandon him, got a taxi and took him home.

Guy knew that there were going to be fireworks, especially because both cats were males and neither had been doctored. Felix was the most challenging, and naturally hissed at the new arrival, arching his back and going straight into attack mode. The black cat Guy named Zoot, and he watched the latter arch his back but then just stand still.

It got better over the next few weeks, but Guy had to get them both on neutral ground, and decided to have them both doctored at the same time, which would give them something in common.

The vet was a fair walk away on foot, and again Rowena had promised Guy that she would be there to help him carry the two cats to the vet's. She did not show up, but Guy had to keep the appointment. He walked to the vet's to get there for 9am; it was a busy road and it was rush hour. Zoot was doing his utmost to break out of the carrier, clearly thinking that Guy was trying to get rid of him again, and no consoling words would appease him. Guy was fortunate that he just about reached the practise with the two cats still in their respective carriers, but only just. Zoot's was badly damaged from where his snout had pounded the carrier – and no doubt his snout was the worst for wear too. Felix had been howling all the way along the road. It became quite an ordeal, and Guy was livid with his mother for letting him down again.

There was a minor issue to deal with later. The veterinary nurse telephoned Guy to say that one of Zoot's testicles was actually in his stomach, and could they operate to remove it. Guy naturally said yes.

After the day of their de-balling, the friction between them seemed to lessen, but Felix would not accept Zoot, and whenever the latter tried to lick his head or was affectionate, Felix always hissed at him and went out of the cat flap. Guy understood that the way Felix saw it, this was his pad and any other cat was an intruder. But Zoot was another story.

It looked as though Zoot had no sex drive, because in the flat he followed Guy around everywhere. When he did go out to do his business, he ran back in immediately afterwards. It was clear that Zoot was a lovable ball of fur, and a very unusual cat indeed. Perhaps that was why Guy felt such an affinity with him even before he met him; he had sensed his need.

When Guy slept at night he would find the two cats curled up in each of his arms that were positioned above his head. In order to let the blood flow again he had to move them, but it sadly disturbed the cats from their deep slumber.

There was a time when Zoot was not seen for days. Guy was deeply concerned, because he knew that the cat would never wander anywhere outside of the flat. There was knock on the veranda doors one summer evening, and the daughter of a neighbour from a block away asked if Guy owned a black cat.

What had transpired was that Zoot got confused as to his whereabouts and mistakenly went through the neighbour's cat flap of her veranda doors, which was an identical set-up to Guy's, although she had a larger apartment altogether, and the back room was in fact her bedroom. Flanking one of the walls of the room were fitted wardrobes, and at the back in one corner there was a gap in the wall that reached all the way to the floor. Zoot was trapped at the bottom of the shaft. Totally disoriented, he must have tried that last aperture as a last resort for freedom.

When Guy eventually climbed onto the wardrobe and looked down, he saw a frightened Zoot looking up at him. First they tried to lower a basket so that he could climb into, but to no avail. Then Guy just called down to the cat and coaxed him up as best he could. What followed was incredible. Zoot clambered up the back of the wardrobe shaft, which was a good twelve feet, clawing into the wood panelling and gaining momentum. As he reached the top he clambered up to Guy, putting his two paws around his neck, bringing relief to both himself and his owner.

The owner of the flat, a rather flirtatious, yet clearly irate woman, was naturally concerned about the area at the bottom of her wardrobes that had been fouled by a frightened cat, but it always remained a mystery why there was a shaft that went from the top of the wardrobe to the floor, instead of the wardrobe being fitted right up against the wall like the others.

Zoot's future trips to do his business outside were much briefer, and he ran in hurriedly lest he got lost again. He also followed Guy about the flat even more after the incident, waiting outside the toilet door for example when Guy was inside. Guy understood the cat's insecurities and never scolded him, but had to scold Felix, who naturally was jealous of their closeness and was reactionary, or would at times sulk. Felix was no longer top cat, but he was loved nevertheless. Since his castration, there no longer was that rank tomcat odour about him, and he did not disappear on long "dirty" weekends out, yet he still had a face that could win anyone over.

It was about a year after Guy had been in his new apartment when Rowena was offered the flat in Norwood, freed at last from her ordeals above Joanne's Night Club. It seemed a healthy move and a new start, because Rowena had now made the decision to stop relying on her false friend, alcohol, altogether. Guy was relieved, and the burden that had weighed heavily on his shoulders was at last lifted.

The new flat suited her and her needs, and it looked as there was no one under the age of 55 in the block of apartments, which banished the fear from her mind that she might be subjected to someone else's night club. It was also within a short walk to Guy's flat, so that gave her a close link, which prevented her from being too lonely and have thought rummaging set in.

It was some six months down the line when she secured the building site position, cooking breakfasts for the workmen, where she was to meet Murphy. Rowena was ready for a new challenge.

Rowena's other children lived their lives in their respective parts of the globe, and it all remained a fractured affair like it had always been; nothing changed for the better on that score. Rowena had stopped hoping that anything would change by now, and certainly did not long for any closeness that was not really there. She had resigned herself to knowing that people often just do not grow together, including one's own children.

Rowena often wondered if given the opportunity to speak clearly and lucidly, would her children have ever been able to sit down and discuss their grievances with her, the causes behind their resentments, or even question why she did things the way that she had. She knew that there was far too much emotional baggage that clogged up the waterways for the water to run freely. Certainly towards the end of her days, she felt strong enough emotionally to have faced them with their gripes, but she also remembered what supportive words her beloved had said to her about her efforts to do the best by her children. She acknowledged that when she became Medusa, others close to her suffered at her hand. But to be honest, her outbursts grew worse later in her life, and as the frantic activities of her life gradually diminished, and those haunting thoughts began to seep back in – or she was just more aware of them – there was much more time to ruminate and feel the poison of past events that had hurt and violated her.

What her children could say was that she became a disciplinarian, as she felt the protective need to be both parents to them. Perhaps she always had been, owing to their errant fathers, and it became more apparent when she was transporting them from the East to the West in a time of much uncertainty and insecurity for all, the fierce lioness defending her cubs.

The striking irony in the whole affair was that Rowena had at last met a man who was prepared to try to be a surrogate father to the children, but it was too late, and the teenagers of the clan had now become cynical and renegade mercenaries who would not play by any more men's rules. Unfortunately, they never appreciated Joseph's steadfastness and loyalty.

What Rowena did regret most deeply, what plunged into her heart like a sharp rapier, was the years of what seemed like wasted energy on so much strife and emotional harangues that did not get anyone anywhere. Her children still wanted to remain in the mire of resentment and cast recriminations at a woman who never claimed that she had all the answers or did not always get things right. Perhaps if she had been seen as a violated girl who was constantly tortured within, they might have understood her better. If the essence of forgiveness was first understood, it might be put into practice; but those things that have fired us negatively usually wield a great amount of power over our psyches, to the point of blinding our senses to anything that is whole or true.

Chapter 20

Guy had begun to put his energy into his playwriting, and the one that he had just finished was to be used by the drama company that he was involved in. He was naturally delighted that it had been chosen, and helped in its production.

The play follows:

Esoteric Timescape:

The Soul Connection

Cast of Characters

Ancient Egypt

Mahathanna Ra	Pharaoh
Queen Biditita	His queen
Egypt Phast	High Priest
Patakh	Overseer

Rome

Creditus Caesar	Caesar
Pratus Valus	Senator
Approximatus	Senator
Lustus Lufus	Senator
Bona Botanicus	Senator
Sanctimonious	Senator
Ancient Greece	Gladiator

Renaissance – Florence, Italy

Eduardo Grecelli	Painter
Piedro Pantalones	Performance artist, Commedia dell 'arte
Giovanni Arlecchino	Performance artist, Commedia dell 'arte
Niccolo Bagliatella	Smith
Two nobles	Patrons

Berlin in 1923

Edgar Schlast	Elocution and drama professor
Heidi Greckman	Undergraduate
Johannes Greckman	Undergraduate
Hans Zimmerman	Aufbahn Zoo Cabaret Proprietor
Klaus	Aufbahn Zoo Cabaret Proprietor

Roses lay strewn across vast beds of silk, with kyphi and patchouli interlacing the air, carried on the gentle breeze from the west.

Sand intermittently blows and forms dust storms.

Reverberations of chisel on stone resonate within the quarries, interspersed with the crack of a whip and groans of weary and sweaty slaves. Many gods were invoked by the supplicating men; their pleas were universal and fervent, and burned within each man's heart – freedom.

Scene 1, Act 1 – Alathabhad Quarry, Ancient Egypt

Set deep within an ancient and grand civilisation, our initial scene opens in the sun-drenched planes of this

North African land. We are in ancient Egypt midst the reverberations of chisel on stone, and for any slacking slave there was a steel-tipped whip ready and waiting to flay their backs to the bone.

The one-eyed overseer, Patakh, whose breath always reeks of garlic and stale wine, mercilessly, and without compunction attacks his slaves; for him they were naught but filthy, yet useful, swine.

The noises that resonant within the quarry are from enslaved mortals' groans and the hammerings of metal upon stone, interspersed with the lashes of Patakh's whip, often mercilessly flaying the skin to the bone.

Once the blocks had been fashioned and cut to the required size, dragged by oxen sultry and submissive, they were to be hauled up and positioned, for "More pyramids" was the directive.

There were slaves of various races and creeds, Nubian, Neapolitan, Mesopotamian and even some from Crete, each with their own faith and belief in their own god; they were nourished solely on corn cakes, kamut bread and sun-dried meat.

In the distance, the pyramid site was about 500 paces to the northwest, and this heterogeneous collective from the quarry to the site had these blocks conveyed, by the royal architect's behest. Huge rollers made from cedar and sandalwood trees were used as transporters of these gargantuan, carved pieces of stone. And a lengthy and arduous process it was indeed, requiring much endurance, toil and skill, each man watching themselves carefully, lest any weakness be shown.

Each day was always long, repetitive and sultry under the blazing sun, for it burned eternally. Yet what kept the men as a team was an underlying sense of fraternity. Being owned by another man, each slave was possessed, seemingly body and soul, and each regularly supplicated to their respective gods to relieve their huge burdens in this dole.

Scene 2, Act 1 – The Pharaoh's Palace

There is a chorus of softly chanting male voices in the background, "Mahathanna Ra, Mahathanna Ra, the son of Isis and Osiris."

Mahathanna Ra sits on his golden bejewelled throne, draped in his white linen gown, with his cortege of attendants to act out his every whim all positioned around – fan-bearers, scribes, men of the cosmetic box, his high priest, and his chief architect are awaiting the living connection to Osiris to direct their injunctions.

Mahathanna Ra, in peremptory tones, enquires of his architect, "How fare the constructions?" To which, he replies obsequiously that all is going to the pharaoh's edicts. After requesting that some Nubian slaves to be brought to him and castrated for his harem, Mahathanna then dismisses his cortège, save his high priest and trusted confidant, Egypt Phast.

Of all of the Pharaoh's attendants and obsequious and devious ministers, he knew in his heart that his high priest was no sycophant. Egypt Phast stands tranquil and tall, with deep-set eyes that reflect many gates to unknown regions that could reveal all, wherein the pharaoh would often peer for enlightenment or to instil peace in his soul.

Phast had always had the ability to infuse his pharaoh with inner strength and tenacity.

Scene 3, Act 1 – The Courtyard of Fountains

Queen Biditita, slender and statuesque, through the gardens of the palace takes her guests, via the lime groves and the Courtyard of Fountains, wherein the ponds are garlanded with many lotus blooms, a flower fest.

Exotic fish swim therein, whilst the odour of kyphi and patchouli waft gently through the air, intermingling with the aromas of orange and lime, softened with pear.

In the distance is heard the accelerating and approaching patter of feet upon stone of the maidservants and attendants around, with the tintinnabulation of their anklet bells resounding, interspersed with fits of giggling, always to great mirth bound.

Queen Biditita negotiates with her guests the cost of selling to Syria and Tyre her most precious limes. She alone prefers to take on this task, for she finds that she enjoys this lucrative pastime. In doing this trading *par excellence*, she is greatly revered in business as a woman astute and shrewd, and even the pharaoh has no say in the matter, for the queen would consider it most rude.

A figure was reached and settled on, and then the queen proceeded to trade with Syria for spices and herbs. It was not too long before another deal was done; in this one, the queen and the Syrian ambassador agreed and no one's feathers were ruffled or perturbed.

Biditita pledged kyphi and cedar oil to their aromatic spices and grain – naturally depending on sufficient rain.

Now with all negotiations at an end, the queen escorts her guests to the palace, where she and her king, with their hospitality, their needs will tend.

Scene 4, Act 1 – The Roman Senate

In the marbled interior of the house of the ancient Roman senate they sat in their togas, beleaguered, well-coiffured and vociferating. Over the mighty bawd and wail a fanfare resounds, heralding the approach of Caesar.

Creditus Caesar, wan and frail, thin-lipped, alabaster skinned and feverish, swans in, endeavouring a flounce, yet truly has no real charm or charisma ounce for ounce. His voice is whistling and shrill, one certainly not of a great orator, and his elocution instructor had given up all hopes of improving his voice; poor Creditus lacked style still.

In stature, Creditus was unathletic, and of complexion pallid, apropos of alabaster. He walked with the hesitancy often found in a man of later years, unconvincing of an emperor of Rome, and definitely no Caesar.

The chief ambassador and envoy of Creditus was Pratus, a wily, short, stocky, devious and sanguine man, with a stentorian voice and a head through which many machinations ran. He then, with ease, silenced the muffled prattle from the senate with a booming "Hail Caesar!" and all seat themselves awaiting Creditus' decrees.

Valus of the seventh legion, and also commander in-chief of the cavalry, begins by asking Creditus why he withdrew troops from Macedonia, which caused great losses to the infantry. Creditus announces that he needed further help with the transportation of wild beasts for the games. Above the guffaws and loud retorts, Approximatus asks of Caesar if the games will win Rome further honour and victory.

Sanctimonious sycophantically supports Caesar with his ridiculous and idiosyncratic whims, whilst the whole

177

senate reverberates with acrid remarks. The atmosphere is tense, whilst each senator is sedentary.

To add insult to injury, Creditus then announces that he will raise the levy on all landowners and merchants and place a higher tax on all trade, the overlay of the special games he is to put on for the Egyptian pharaoh being so high that he needs to recuperate it back for the state purse to aid.

Two senators huddled together in the back row talk under their breaths to one another so that it does not show. One says to the other, "For the love of Jupiter, this wretch falls short of all reason. No doubt he wants to go down in history for putting on the most spectacular games – for in all else the man is assuredly lame."

Scene 5, Act1 – The Circus Maximus

And so the one named Ancient Greece from gladiator school did graduate, and thence into the Circus Maximus he was put to entertain the mob, they now hungering for blood, and Greece their bold bait.

H was armed with javelin and net, and trident and sword if he thought fit, and protected by his hide-thonged skirt showing off his Olympian torso; his radiant physique need not be covered with shirt.

The mob's excitement was growing by the second, and then a tumultuous roar came forth from the auditorium as an Ethiopian warrior enters the arena and antagonistically to Greece does beckon. Into combat they then fly, javelin soaring through the feverish air, with the Ethiopian bellowing to Greece that with his bare hands he will the limbs from Greece's body tear.

Indeed, it was to be a long and captivating battle, for both men are virile and alert. The mob, now in an orgasmic fury, for Ancient Greece they cheer, yell and blurt.

The two warriors had been in battle for over two hours, and now their bodies are much fatigued, bloody and worn, when Greece attracts his opponent's gaze with his javelin, with a plan to use his net, which is still intact and not torn. As soon as the Ethiopian's concentration does lapse, Greece, using all his conserved might, around the ankles of his foe his nets wraps, and with one straining heave forces this black giant to come crashing to the ground. The mob issues a unanimous gasp, for the outcome of this man-to-man combat is soon to be found.

Greece straddles the black, and with his shield gives his opponent's temple a severe crack. His body gives one last desperate lunge, struggling in the blood-soaked sand. Then Greece with a downward stroke, his short sword into the Ethiopian's heart does plunge.

The mob's unanimous voice is at fever pitch at the furore Greece had caused. Greece, receiving an adulatory ovation, bows and then does pause. He then gallantly and ceremoniously makes his exit through the gladiatorial door, with the crowds of frantic people screaming for an encore.

Scene 6, Act 1 – The initial meeting of Ancient Greece and Egypt Phast

Creditus had planned for some months with Mahathanna Ra that they would hold counsel in Rome, for both lands needed better trading relations, and so via a major distraction such as the games they were to this end prone.

The day of their arrival was to be one of great celebration and hearty feasting, all of Rome resplendent with ornate filigree and eye-catching displays of coloured bunting rippling in the morning breeze, and many crowds of the populace were eager to of the Egyptian party a sighting seize.

The excitement was rife when the Royal Egyptian barge was spotted heading into port, with high white sails all at full mast, with attendants holding them taught.

From the design house of Osiris and Isis stood two magnificent figures carved to perfection along the prow, before which the Pharaoh and his queen before leaving the vessel give a ceremonious bow.

Coming into port then Caesar's finest trumpeters blast a royal accolade, and then the walkway towards the boat is bedecked with the royal burgundy carpet as it is ceremoniously laid.

So they approach, this Egyptian royal house, with many slaves bearing gifts and coiffures of gold, caskets of jewels, and ornately decorated urns. Rolls of the finest silks, unguents from far eastern lands, exotic palms and architectural ferns, which had all travelled far by camel across many desert sands.

Caesar had organised an especial games to honour the pharaoh's visit – the cost from the state purse was phenomenal, and Rome would most definitely suffer from this deficit.

For this had been the most expensive games in decades, and as a result of this flagrant extravagance, Creditus would not make an appearance at the senate in fear of hearing the senators' tirades.

Mahathanna Ra and Biditita watched the games from the emperor's lavish box situated high above with the gods, and out of reach of the hoi-polloi, whilst there was much activity in the arena below, which was for Creditus his new manipulative toy.

In every way the Games was excessive, even an affront to the senses, a visual goring.

As in all Roman endeavours, egos were foremost, and energies and resources were stretched to the limit, whilst no modesty was shown or demonstrated, as the theme was not to all sense and sensibility inhibit.

Often the grandeur and atrocities performed in the arena won for any budding emperor his victory with the mob, whilst people went into orgasmic furies whilst for tortured Christians there was no one to sob.

So after long and eventful games, when the final chariot race had been seen, Creditus leads his guests to the royal chambers, where they can all be pampered and preened.

With the Egyptian entourage walks Egypt Phast, frowning and feasting his eyes on the extremities that had lay before him, and beyond this visual tapestry his eyes rest on Ancient Greece, whose body is pungent with blood and sweat.

Yet still from his victory in the arena over the Ethiopian Greece is glowing, yet looks at the high priest, and Phast looks at him too.

From somewhere deep within there rises a connective link that soars through the warrior and the priest, for their eyes meet and stay linked for a while, Greece being absorbed by the high priest's deep inviting eyes that remind Greece of the Nile.

Phast too is pulled straight into the Mediterranean blue sea of Greece's eyes, and this connection fires through their hearts and souls that this connection could never be denied.

Somehow midst the blood and gore of these seemingly barbaric games, these two souls had reconnected with their eyes, the mirrors of the soul, and in the purity of this union the inner force did not feel tame.

***

Part Two: The Renaissance, Florence

Scene 1, Act 2 – Florence, Italy, Eduardo Grecelli's studio

Travel with us for some centuries in time to the Renaissance in Florence, when the families of Borgia and Medici were in their prime. Rife with much Machiavellian ruse and ploy, yet the focus on art and music was abundant and rich, giving many much joy.

Pavannes and Rondos danced to the music of Terphiscore, the rampant and often disturbing predictions of Nostradamus coexisting with the creative flow of da Vinci and Galileo. In an era where art, philosophy and cultural development enriched the globe, and in the annals of time many centuries later many historians would into this fascinating time probe.

Our opening scene is in Florence in the studio of Eduardo Grecelli. He is a perceptive, sensitive misanthropic man of profuse talent, who lived not in luxury or any great comfort, for his frugality was ever salient.

His artistic works were vast and varied, and his dexterity was renowned and revered, and always when commissioned to paint a picture, his work on time he always delivered.

He socialised little, for he trusted few, save his small circle of close friends and confidants, whose company he enjoyed and whose opinions he closely reviewed.

Grecelli lived in an attic room overlooking the main town square, serving him both as living quarters and a studio, ample yet bare.

He had always desired to live high alongside the gods, a position wherefrom he could get an aerial view of his world, with all its odds and sods.

The room was brimming with canvasses, sketchpads and wooden easels, bottles, feathers, flowers, and in a distinctly classical style urn (awaiting a still-life sketch) were some rather impressive teasels. On his bed there was a fine rug of Aztec geometric design of orange, red, black and oatmeal cores, complimenting further the intrigue of his apartment, for nothing in taste seemed mediocre.

On canvasses already finished there were paintings of still-life, portraits, and a profusion of landscapes – in the latter Grecelli excelled – expending many days and nights in rural parts, where nature would inspire him to fashion his works, here was a true artist and no Jack o' Napes.

Scene 2, Act 2 – Art and crafts exhibition at the Plaza Centra

It had been arranged by one of the families of great influence that an exhibition of arts and craftwork was to be held within the Plaza Centra.

Pantalones had persuaded Grecelli to attend after much deliberation, as the latter always thought that exhibitions were vulgar and course, he naturally feeling precious about his own fine works. Yet at this time Grecelli's morale was at low ebb, and funds were desperately needed for materials and other living perks.

It was a bright spring morning and great excitement filled the air, and people had begun early to decorate the town square. Craftsmen from neighbouring towns, and from provinces further afield, were to grace this town with their talents, all for aestheticism they would their creativity yield.

Potters, silversmiths, craftsmen in pewter, painters and sculptors congregated in the Plaza Centra this morn, firing the layman and peasant onlooker with profound feelings of awe. A richness of atmosphere did abound, the amalgamated creative power of these doyens could easily the simple mind confound.

Before it was midday many works fashioned by these artisans were on resplendent display, colonnades of canvasses whereon coloured images coloured the square, with their respective designers all awaiting to see how they will fare.

Tables of goblets all made in different metal ores sparkling in the midday sun. Objects of wrought iron, some utilitarian, some macabre, and some made in fanciful fun.

Puppets on strings dancing in time with the gentle breeze, musical boxes and an assortment of canisters and trunks, all with intricate designs and motifs, which to the artisans this fine talent came to them with comparative ease.

The nobles who had arranged this fayre did then arise and amongst the artisans did fraternise, and being confronted with so much visual splendour, they were assuredly taken aback and wanted more about certain craftsmen to discover.

It became a gargantuan task to select but a few. Of the many talented entrants they resolved to select three, for they had a political need to patronise men of the arts, and by this help them to politicians be.

So three were selected to be under the patronage of these two noblemen who wanted to their political seeds sow, one of whom was Grecelli, the other a superb smith, and the other was a recruit to the Commedia dell'arte, Giovanni Arlecchino.

Scene 3, Act 2 – A centenary celebration play

In the environs of the university an awning of broad strawberry coloured stripes overhung the stage, a canopy supported by stilts and the like under which there was much haggle, garp and gripe.

Preparations were now underway, scaffolding being erected, boards and planks being hoisted, all contributing to the ethos of this centenary and festive play.

There was an antechamber wherein the performers were preparing for the act, donning their face pieces, lavish gowns, and costumes for this splendid cavalcade. With rehearsals now fully completed, from this performance hopefully no actor would retract, for it was a celebratory play commemorating the centenary of the university's birth, and today's celebrations intended to bring much enjoyment and bags of memorable mirth.

The intended tale was written briefly to entertain the academics, not a play for comedy or farce, but one of tragedy and loss.

The dons and undergraduates were to be ceremoniously attired, and this especial event was not open to the general populace, for as it was to do with a specific mien, apropos of the study of some of the academics, it was possible that the general throng would not be fired.

And so the play was toward a classical theme bent, and the writers had on it much time and toil spent. It had been rehearsed indefatigably, for to put on a play of sheer perfection was their driving intent.

The play was scheduled to commence at two in the afternoon, and the pillared theatrum would hold up to a hundred people, who could be seated amply and comfortably with ample legroom.

It began with three Zanni standing alongside one another announcing the oncoming scene. Pedro Panatalones was napping under a willow tree engrossed in a mid-afternoon dream – which was portrayed by the Burle, one dressed as a woman.

It was a prophetic reverie wherein Pantalones is told by his erstwhile mentor, now dead, that he will be a famous artiste, and of this particular troupe of the Comedia dell'arte he would become the leading head.

He was to have a magnificently talented protégé, Giovanni Arlecchino, who would too attain national notoriety. Together they would work constructively as a team, increasing the entertainment value of the show.

But despite this troupe's efforts, a noblewoman, Cassandra Da Bologna, wins the heart of Pantalones, and she being possessive of him demands that he renounces his art for her; otherwise she will be gone and leave him to be a loveless loner.

Torn between his art and his heart's pangs, he becomes morose and his remarkable performances consequently deteriorate.

Arlecchino, deeply concerned for his fellow performer, invites Cassandra to a small informal banquet unknown to Pantalones. He poisons the wine she drinks, which kills her instantly. On hearing of his enamorata's demise, Pantalones wastes away and he himself dies beneath the willow tree.

Arlecchino then endeavours to continue on in the same vein, but the entertainment value and magic that these two thespians were together on stage, could no longer be captured on one of them alone, however dexterous, and so his popularity wanes.

It ends with Arlecchino wrapping himself in his renowned all-encompassing black cloak and black mask, and with a full moon rising at his rear, lamenting the loss of his dear friend, gesticulating the action of wiping away floods of tears, the merge of the Harlequin's vibrancy into the moon drunk and shadowed Pierrot.

As the curtains were closed, the academics and dons roared their ovation, bellowing "Bravo, Signores! Bravo!"

Amidst the scholars, sitting aloof, invited by Pantalones as a friendly gesture for the artistic cause, Grecelli was to meet backstage with his friend, which they duly did, to share some time and his critique and opinions expend.

Over a goblet of wine, Grecelli was introduced to Arlecchino, and once again through their eyes ocean met ocean, and into each other's dived they then.

***

Part 3: Berlin, 1923

Scene 1, Act 3 – The Aufbahn Zoo Cabaret, Berlin, 1923

Now we travel to our tertiary and final stage in our journey through time. Still in Europe, but we go to Berlin, when underground cabaret was most defiantly prime.

Our initial scene is in the Aufbahn Zoo Cabaret situated in a backwater Strauss in the basement of a brothel. Hans Zimmerman is behind the bar, which he has just opened, it being around 9pm, ensuring that the varying shaped glasses, from champagne flute to brandy roundel, are all polished well.

It is autumn and there is an early winter chill already interspersing the air. With it now being Saturday night, this modest sized venue will undoubtedly be packed to the brim, for it is an especial evening with some celebrities billed to perform herein.

A small performing stage had the Zoo, whereon many had had the fortune to perform, for the management chose quite discriminately often from the controversial few.

On this particular night for the clientele, the event was more than a misdemeanour, for Lottie Lenyer and Bertold Brecht were to appear in all their creative splendour.

Scene 2, Act 3 - Edgar Schlast's apartment, Schlagenbader Strasse

In the Schlagenbader Strasse there lived a dramatist and teacher of this art, Edgar Schlast. He had a large apartment, of which there was one room that was reminiscent of that Phast. Egyptian hieroglyphics adorning the walls, with the multitude of mirrors carefully situated to reflect its mystique, and sending any newcomer aghast.

Schlast gave private tuition in elocution and drama, earning him the reputation of being Der Grosse Meister von Schlagenbader Strasse.

At this moment in time the professor was holding a class. Some of his students were studying for an oral examination, and part of their recitals today were firstly from Schiller, and then Goethe, and Shakespeare last.

Then the clock struck four, and all of his students automatically knew that that was their cue to pay their dramameister, and take their leave via his chamber of hieroglyphics then through the heavy and beautifully carved sandalwood door.

One of the professor's outstanding students was Heidi Greckman, who had a brother Johannes, a student of the history of art. Heidi had told her brother often of the professor's great knowledge, and had suggested that for his thesis Schlast may some invaluable information impart.

It was arranged, therefore, that a meeting should take place, so that the two students of life could share thoughts by meeting face-to-face.

Scene 3, Act 3 – The Aufbahn Zoo Cabaret

Now we return to the Zoo where the atmosphere is smoky, dimly lit and very alive.

At one particular table to the right of the entrance sits a slumped figure of a withered man, intermittently playing a harmonica and cradling a glass of schnapps, momentarily to the music playing in the distance his foot erratically taps.

Many bottles lay before him on the table, and his companion (one of the flamboyant barwomen) grows bored with the man's inertia, returns to the bar in order to find another man to pay for her drinks.

Sitting around the crowded room there were the Zoo's clientele seated in threes and fours, and a great majority of the rest were chiefly from the university's academic cyclone. City workers, who by day were imprisoned behind white stiff collars and positioned behind desks, fulfilling society's stereotyped slot for them, office drone.

They were all here to feel a sense of recalcitrant freedom, which the Zoo exuded, and no one expected a conventional evening, for at the Aufbahn Zoo Cabaret by respectability no one was deluded.

Hans Zimmerman and his beau, Klaus, were the main say as to who would enter the club, and they both arranged all the entertainment. It was their venue, and they had earned for themselves the reputation of running a decadent yet captivating establishment.

Their arrangement of acts was always innovative and unique, ever satisfying their cabaret clique. Yet keeping a steady balance of acts, with never too much focus on one particular theme, that was why it was always packed.

The harmonica player was now fully satiated with schnapps, and no longer has the breath to blow into his harmonica or imbibe his nectar. So he resigned to tap its spittle and then put away in his pocket. Then he hazily peers around this underground haunt by the sultry lights' flickers.

A young male singer has just finished a song, "Die Glauber Menschen," and was descending the stool whereon he was sat.

A group of four then enter the door after a resounding rat-a-tat-tat. Knowing them instantly, Zimmerman nods an approving glance over to Klaus and he lets them enter, the club now full to the brim with laughter, smoke and endless banter.

The collective comprised Heidi and Johannes Greckman, and two other students from the university who were being brought to the cabaret for the first time. A Saturday evening was not complete without a visit to the Zoo, and everyone lost all knowledge of time.

Heidi and Johannes sat their friends down in their usual corner, adjacent to the stage, for tonight Heidi was going to recite some of her poetry; in this field she was renowned to be quite a sage.

Between each act, Klaus would master of ceremonies be, and now he announced another act, this one being the third of the Cabaret's repartee.

Two female performers who called themselves Aggressive Earth, who used fire and water and salt, "Sister of the earth," they did vociferate and chant, adding indeed a different nuance to this cabaret session, and they by day were both practitioners in gestalt.

Scene 4, Act 3 – The room of Phast, Schlast's apartment

Heidi had informed Schlast of her brother's desire to meet him apropos of his studies.

Johannes had been in contact with the professor, and an afternoon had been arranged for their rendezvous in Schlagenbader Strasse.

It was a Friday afternoon, the autumn air was decidedly dank, and the temperature was getting colder. Johannes duly arrived, and Schlast's valet showed him into the room of Phast, wherein a strong feeling of déjà vu came over Greckman, yet it did not last until he met face-to-face with the professor. Then that resurgence of inner knowing returned to him and soared through his inner ocean, confusing his head with strange notions.

The professor did not look up from his desk at first, for he was engrossed in a dramatic piece that he wished to complete. "Please do come in, Johannes Greckman, and take a seat. I will be with you shortly; allow me to complete this final dramatic feat."

Johannes seated himself with a perplexed frown, for he felt that he already knew Herr Schlast, whereupon the latter looked up from his work, and upon Greckman refocussed his eyes.

Again it happened – ocean met ocean, and into each other's dived they then, continuing their bonded ties.

On his return trip from a drama rehearsal for the play, Guy was walking home one autumn evening in late September when he met up with a man going in the opposite direction. They exchanged looks and both smiled. Soon after, when they both looked back, they stopped and began talking to one another, initially about topical things and then where they had been that evening.

Herve Black was as a thickset man with a full black beard, yet Guy had sensed that he was an individual-minded person, which was always a point of attraction to him in anyone. Guy also sensed that the man had a capricious way about him; he just did not look run-of-the-mill. There was also a playful glint in his eyes that emanated a powerful sexual energy, which Guy was later to discover had many more depths, twists and turns.

Herve had changed his name because he felt it gave him an edge on his original name, which he considered quite ordinary. He was born in a small place just outside of Glasgow called Airdrie. He was the only child of Euphemia and John Black, who had come to England when their son, Billy, was a teenager. Guy had gathered snippets of information from the Blacks and Herve during the time that he knew them, and those details were not at all pleasant. There was definitely no bond between them; it seemed a clear-cut case of Herve seeking to be understood and his parents never really being able to, as they considered their son mentally unstable.

Herve worked as a social worker for a drug dependency unit in a London hospital. It seemed evident that he thought that by following such a career he would not only be helping to solve others' problems but eradicate his own psychological quirks that troubled his makeup.

Herve seemed to have an extremely strong persona, and a voice to match that smacked of obsequiousness. He came across as being too helpful, and definitely left any perceptive person questioning his motives. Guy was to see the other side of this, which was very different indeed.

Guy had lived at Oliver Grove for some four years and was glad to have made this his first flat, as it was full of character. Next door lived a Norwegian woman, with whom Guy struck up a friendship. They did many different things together like go to jumble sales, take trips out, and often have a meal together.

Liv had initially come over to England to work as an au pair, and then had a stormy marriage to an Englishman. Liv was an outspoken person with a strong sense of enjoying life, which was probably why she and Guy got along, until one day when her ex-husband called to see her.

Guy happened to be at Liv's flat, which faced the front of the property, and she actually saw him approach the front entrance. Liv immediately went into a panic, as she never wanted Brian to know where she had moved to, as she was frightened what he might do.

Guy tried to console Liv by saying that he would stay, and it might be a good idea to see him and try and be adult about it. Naturally, Liv knew Brian much more intimately than Guy did and had forebodings. But Liv was not a timid kind of person, and so went to the outer door, greeted Brian and asked him what he wanted.

Thinking that she would stave him off and tell him that she was busy, she instead asked him in, and then introduced him to Guy. Brian naturally thought that Liv and Guy were having a relationship, as Guy sensed Brian's furrowed brow when he looked at him, clearly with a mind racing and having made the wrong conclusion.

Conversation was strained at first, and Liv asked Brian various questions – who they once knew and if he was doing the same kind of work – in an attempt to break the ice. Guy told Brian that he was Liv's next-door neighbour and that was how they met. He also intimated that they were not a couple after Brian asked how long they had been seeing one another.

Liv looked perplexed, because she told Guy afterwards that she wanted Brian to think what he liked, which would be that they were a couple.

"Why did you want to do that, Liv?" asked Guy

"Well, because he would think I have somebody else and he would leave me alone."

"I am not happy with that, Liv," responded Guy. "Maybe I sensed that was what you were doing, and that was why I put him straight. I don't see why I should lie for you."

"Oh enough, enough now!" shouted Liv. "I have had it with you men. Get out of my flat!"

It was some time before they actually came across one another again, and being face-to-face prompted them to speak, but it was strained. Something had been lost that Liv did not seem to want to repair, because she mentioned nothing about the evening when Brian came around, and an apology would have eased the waters. Liv clearly did not think that she had done anything untoward.

Some months down the road Liv sold her flat and Guy saw no more of her, until one day when he was in town and came across her. "Hello, Liv. How goes things with your new flat?" he asked.

"Oh, you know how moving goes. It's all so hectic for a while, and then it gets sorted. Would you like to come and see it one day?" she asked.

Guy gave it some thought and said that he would. Liv said that she still had his telephone number and would call when things were straighter in the flat.

Guy thought no more about it, but then got a telephone call from Liv about a fortnight later, asking him to come around and giving him the address. Guy agreed to go along.

When he saw the block it was a similar design to Rowena's, again with a flat roof. Liv had bought the penultimate flat on the first floor. Inside it was of a similar layout to Rowena's, and she had two bedrooms.

When they sat down with a drink, and after she had shown Guy around the flat, Liv began to speak, which was in a reflective even contrite way.

"I did want you to see the flat, Guy, but I also wanted to apologise to you for my behaviour at Oliver Grove. I was very wound up, and seeing Brian again just threw me into a panic. I was clutching at anything to keep him away from me, and so I used you. I am sorry.

"It's also difficult because I have strong feelings for you, and I just could not get to grips with them then either. So you see, what Brian believed I wanted to be true, and I got very frustrated and angry when you put him right. It shattered my illusion that I was holding on to."

Guy had never heard Liv talk so eloquently, and told her so. Because Brian had told her many a time that she was a thick Norwegian whore, she began to believe that she was, which brought tears to her eyes. However, Guy was compassionate and thanked her for her honesty, but they both knew that it would be difficult to remain friends after knowing these facts.

So Guy left eventually, wishing her the very best in life. He held on to the fantastic memories of the many things that they did together, and would always remember Liv's indomitable spirit.

Soon after this Guy wrote another play:

Turbo and Giggle's Marriage in Paradise Island

Cast of Characters

Turbo
Miss Giggle
Colonel & Mrs Giggle
Fatman
The Boy Blunder
Ms Claude Winnie

Petunia
Dy Guzzler
Little Rita Riff
(Scrummy Ha Ha)
Filip Finance
Desmond Deale
Simon Stock-shares
Reverend Rey
Sister Sugar Lee & her Gospel Choir
Claudette Calypso
Royston (Roly-Poly) Griffiths
Lorris Laughilia

Act 1, Scene 1 – Introducing Fatman and the Boy Blunder

Fatman and the Boy Blunder (who could send them asunder) through the English countryside, in their Porschemobile they would plunder.

Aiming for things higher and higher, never mind the palpitations, it's my heart's desire! Their aim was for a penthouse, which ruled out all country shires. For certainly at heart they were no respected squires.

It was their intention to reach Wall Street and be, before their twenty-first birthdays, millionaires, getting caught up in the neurosis of their daily bread being stocks and shares.

So endeavouring to impress everyone with this fascia of the financial dynamic duo, beyond the curtain calls the truth unfurls, to expose them as a pair of pseudos. No need for Holy-Cow or X-ray specs, for they would rather analyse the Dow Jones index.

For the Boy Blunder as a child, a day out meant a Red Rover on the buses, to go and explore wherever he desired. And now later on beyond his teens, in working for Fatman – who fostered his big car dreams – his pull for big and high was fired.

He had saved for years; life became a squeeze, living on bread and cheese. He'd stay at home rather than go on holiday, having absolutely no wish to join a safari, for what he aimed for was a brand new red Ferrari.

And so, zooming through the villes and towns, much like a fox pursued by hounds, drove they, this financial dynamic duo, the Dow Jones boys in their Porschemobile, accelerating through the countryside with rapid speed, going along so fast that of road signs and speed limits they took no heed. On now to their destination, it being an executive mission, for they accrued their earnings solely on commission.

The Porschemobile was well-equipped with worldwide communication, it being fitted with state of the art technology. So with all this addenda they would for business rout and roam.

Today they were on a special assignment, where with a positive attitude great financial benefits they would incur. They were off to see Ms Claude Winnie at her country estate in Abergavenny, Publicans Pride Grange, with the intention to her financial matters disassemble and then rearrange.

So stopping at the Pump House Lodge and speaking to Dy Guzzler, the gate man, he directs them to go along the gravel drive, for to make an enticing greeting and fab impression is their plan.

Arriving then at the grand entrance to this estate, they glanced at their digital time display and hoped that they were not late. Being late was for them an anxious thought, for this formidable beldam would flog or flay any latecomer, so they were acutely anxious of their fate.

The great oak door was opened and they were met by Claude Winnie's companion, Petunia, who led them into the vast drawing room, displaying many art nouveau artefacts and wartime memorabilia.

"Please wait here, gentlemen, and I shall inform the mistress that you have arrived."

And as she leaves the room, Fatman and Blunder nervously rearrange their ties, brushing down their lapels, and on the back of each calf vigorously brush their shoes to all scuff marks repel.

A distinguished mahogany grandfather clock then chimed twelve, midday, and on the last chime entered Ms Claude Winnie without further ado or delay.

"Now, gentlemen, let's do business, Please take a seat," she said, directing them to a table.

Furtively glancing at their glassy, shiny shoes, they prepare for the financial feat. And from their executive cases some documents sadly tumble, and then they across the parquet flooring fumble.

Fatman, being an astute solicitor and having a secret desire that this great dame would one day be his benefactor, got down to the business at hand.

Claude Winnie went on, "Now, what I want to do is rearrange my will, which to all my blood-sucking relatives will come as a bitter pill. To Petunia I wish my entire estate to be bequeathed, and dear old Dy can keep the

GUY JONES

lodge. Of course, of nothing will my dogs be bereaved, so hopefully this will eliminate all bureaucratic stodge."

And so Fatman and the Boy Blunder, after finalising the arrangements, drive off once more to new adventures explore.

Behind the wheel of the Porschemobile, Fatman drives with enthusiastic zeal. Of road signs, pedestrians and speed limits he is heedless, for he thinks that his driving technique has met no match. And so he goes on, foot down and fearless, Formula 1 at Brands Hatch.

On to a gift shop now to buy a wedding gift for a colleague of theirs, Mr Turbo, driving through the town's roadways, horror upon horror, they had to slow down.

It was a quaint country place, but for Fatman and the Boy Blunder its staid and ordered movements were well out of their pace. They really wanted to drive in and out, pick out the gift and be gone, with the intention of gaining points for knocking down potential lager louts. But alas, such things did not exist in a town like this, as everyone was enwrapped in their rural bliss.

With the gift wrapped in a box of ribbon red, back to the office they duly sped.

Stopping off at a greasy roadside café, grabbing some meat and bread – this was Fatman's only bill of fare – they hurriedly ate with gusto and lots of tomato sauce, eating so fast that others would at them fix a steady stare.

So with this fibreless snack filling their bellies, on the road again they watch *Batman* on the car telly.

They were zooming off to themselves prepare by showering their bodies, and of course gelling their hair, for it was their intention to after dark go to Turbo's stag

200

evening in Holland Park, and would arrive there well after dark.

Scene 2, Act 1 – Giggle's hen night

In a twenties mansion block, with a concierge and the rates for living the highest in the land, Miss Giggle was in her boudoir getting ready. Selecting dresses and adjusting her curls, trying to choose the right necklace – the rubies or the pearls? This was for the knees-up night with the girls.

Many frocks and gowns were strewn across her bed, all of many designer labels, strictly haute couture it must be said. For her to choose any one for this occasion was such a difficult task, as she wanted this night to sail her ship at full mast.

Looking at the sea of couture, the pink, the off-white, the red or the rose, or indeed the rue blue, darling Giggle's mind could not be made up; that was true. Eventually, the coral pink she did pick, hoping that it would just do the trick.

To over fifty friends and acquaintances she had invitations sent, mainly in Sussex, Berkshire, Hampshire and Kent, hoping that they would all come and on having a whale of time were decidedly bent.

In a trendy wine bar not far from High St. Ken was to be the rendezvous for this complement of hens, because this place Miss Giggle knew very well from her shopping sprees. From the couture houses she would often pop in here for a cocktail spell.

Daddy had often promised her a soft-top MGB, but mummy inhibited him by saying, "Really, darling, she will look just like a dame from a James Bond movie. I really wanted my daughter to be a recognised member of the arts, but now she's got tangled up with one of those Wall Street financial farts. When I think of my little girl, I really feel at the end of my tether, so I'm off now to the roof garden to water my heathers."

Scene 3, Act 1 – Henry's Wine Bar

So now at the wine bar rendezvous, Giggle is awaiting the arrival of her girly crew. Sipping a cocktail through a fluorescent straw from an elegant slender glass, watching the clientele as they wander in or pass.

Rita Riot (Scrummy Ha-Ha) then appears at the door, saying goodbye to a colleague, after the mwah-mwahs on cheeks, she screams ta-ta.

"Giggle darling, hi, how are things? How many are coming tonight? This is going to be a fabulous evening, so that you can ride off into the sunset with your knight."

Giggle returned, "Well from Cheltenham there is Sissy, and from Berkshire there's Bettina, and do you remember that rather exotic half-caste girl called Thomasina? From Kent comes American Brent – probably Dallas sent. From the Sussex coast comes that delightful treat, Amelia from the family Smitten-Boast, and daughters of gentlemen farmers, some of whom are terrific charmers.

"Horsy types, and of course Sloane Rangers clad in their liberty scarves, and those who will sleep in only silk pyjamas. Some barrister's nieces and dull debutantes with huge allowances, from broken homes and all sort of other dramas.

"So here we have this gathering for tonight, and, Rita, if all goes well it's going to be ripping and out of sight!"

Scene 4, Act 1 – The Boar's Head Inn

Not too far off the beaten track was a pub called The Boar's Head Inn, and the proposed stag night was to be held herein, a quaint place with oak and beams, where one could easily picture medieval scenes.

The inn was redolent of mulled wine and mead, the sort of haunt where one would find a Nell Gwynne or a Madame Bovary type, and where bawdy and raucous romps might breed. On the upper floor the stag was booked to be a many bed-roomed level, but a leaded, windowed gallery was to be the venue for this revelling jamboree.

A Friday night was booked, of the clock eight, and a huge collective of the Dow Jones brigade would fill this place till late. Now the clock had chimed nine, and our gang are swilling down their pints of ale, already burping and farting and making the air quite stale.

The intention was to keep the evening in a medieval vein, and so they had all come dressed in like costume, with the hope that this would the object attain. Boy Blunder dressed as the court jester –some would say how apt – and Fatman an obese squire with gout, not too unlike the real him too. Garbed in many buckles, much velvet and many pearls, he was akin to a prune shaped lout.

As a scribe came Filip Finance, armed with a pen and not a lance, for this was no jousting match, he being worried, naturally, about his financial despatch. Desmond

Deal, looking not unlike Quasimodo, lurched about, mumbling, "Quo Modo." Simon Stock-Shares, dressed as a cardinal in red and ermine, vociferating about the plague and all its vermin.

The star attraction of the night was Mr Turbo in all his might, for he was dressed as a king armed with orb and sceptre, coming across as a regal spectre.

So here were the stags for a night of stags' frolics, and no one this eve was to accuse another of being an alcoholic. And for no rhyme or reason, spirits were high as in the rutting season; they were wont to throw their codpieces to the winds and explore each other's genital domains.

This developed into some primeval rugby scrum, and they grew more and more desirous of each other's bum. For restrictions on mead and genitalia there were none, and with this rustic rutting scene things were wild, untamed and rampant to the core. For beginning the evening as stags, during the night they graduated into wild boars.

So here we'll end this bawdy brawl, for there is no need to write more. Yeah, you've concluded right, that they all ended up prostrate upon the parquet floor, and 'twas no pretty sight.

Scene 5, Act 1 – Giggle's apartment

Being such a delicate flower, Giggle could not drink too much, for her easily confused little brain, alcohol would influence easily by its touch.

Here she was again in her apartment, moreover sitting at breakfast without a hangover, picking at her pink grapefruit, not knowing that her husband-to-be was stranded elsewhere as pissed as a newt.

This day she had no time to glance through fashionable women's' magazines or haute couture dress journals, for Daddy was coming shortly. And as always, his punctuality was pinpoint perfect. After all, he was one of the Foreign Legion's excelling colonels.

Giggle had wondered if with him he would Mummy bring, and to this morning her little girl's praises sing. But in all truth, of late Giggle had her doubts about seeing her mama at her pad, because Mrs Giggle had been so lachrymose and sad. For, after all, this was her baby gal, although not of the arts, she was today to be flown off to foreign parts.

So then at the final chime of nine of the clock, Colonel Giggle arrives without Mama, having had polished and waxed every inch of the car to drive his gal to a major airport, where she and Turbo were to fly to a tropical isle, there to be man and wife by linking matrimonial arms, beneath the profusion of gently swathing palms.

Yet there was a rat-a-tat at the door, and it was Mrs Giggle after all; she had decided to have a few stiff drinks before she came, then bid farewell to her little gal. And this all happened in the hall, for mama again got lachrymose and had to leave, to return to her bevy point, her favourite cocktail, Autumn Leaves.

Scene 6, Act 1 – The airport lounge reception area

In the airport reception lounge daddy was worriedly looking at his fob watch with a frown. After all, he would tolerate anyone being late, his philosophy being "If you make an appointment, by Jove, sir, you make sure you're punctual on the day and date."

Meanwhile, in the half light of Boy Blunder's apartment on the bedroom floor, Turbo could regurgitate no more; grey of complexion, stomach gel-like and pappy, for a doting and very late groom-to-be, he did not look at all happy.

It wasn't a case of get me to the church on time, but the thought of flying that made him want to throw up more mulled wine. Without any frills, his friend would no doubt have very high cleaning bills.

The time was now approaching ten fifteen, and Turbo knew that he had but half an hour to catch that aeroplane. Without any further ado or delay, he dressed hurriedly into his modern garb. With much discomfort of belly and heady pain, he headed for his turbomobile, which was not parked too far away, and within minutes he was to the airport well on his way.

Colonel Giggle, in the reception lounge, is now quite irate, for in his valid opinion this young man is far too late. Then rushes in Turbo, looking dishevelled and burping profusely, having discovered that mulled wine gives him dyspepsia.

Although Colonel Giggle endeavoured a blandishment, after an imploring glance from his little girl all he mustered was a mild and good-humoured chastisement.

It was not too long before they boarded the plane, setting off for their tropical paradise, saying goodbye and waving farewell to this English terrain.

Scene 1, Act 2 – Paradise Island

At a small hotel known as Sunset Walk, Turbo and Giggle were to stay. It was situated not too far from the beach, near a beauty spot known as Calypso Bay. It was a comfortable, clean and exclusive resort, recommended to Giggle from one of her debutante's reports.

Their room was small and bright, and for them this Tropicana scene was to bring them many new sights. One indigenous sound in the backcloth was the resounding chorus of birds of paradise, and in the evening the breeze would waft in from the gentle sea as they supped their Caribbean iced tea.

Sunday was set for the nuptial feast, Turbo now the man again, shedding his skin of the wild beast. Giggle was in readiness for the ceremony, hoping that all would go well, with no tensions or hang-ups, just pure solid harmony.

A dress rehearsal in the small church was arranged for Saturday evening, where Reverend Rey would be there in full display to take them through their moves.

"Reverend Rey is here today to marry you on this fine and beautiful day, hoping that love and happiness will with you forever stay. For after all, you are in Paradise Island. How can it be any other way?"

Then from the back of the church, a gospel choir led by Sister Sugar Lee started chanting, "Oh glory be . . ."

Of course, this was just a dummy run, for the real thing was to be out in the Sunday sun, with much steel band music, and punch made with pineapple and pure tropical rum. On the night of the proposed wedding a celebration had been planned, to be held at the Sunset Nite Spot, hosted and owned by Claudette Calypso, a woman whose reputation was *hot, hot, hot.*

Now with rehearsals over, the betrothed couple ventured down to the silky white sands, looking romantically at one another and holding tightly each other's hand.

It had been organised that Giggle's wedding gown be made by hand, of pure course wild silk, crafted by the couture doyen of this isle. This dress, it must be known, had taken several days to fashion, being designed and perfected by this expert's skill and devoted passion.

As an additional personal treat to this haute couture array, this designer had interwoven handcrafted silk peach blooms into the dress and bridal bouquet.

Scene 2, Act 2 – Wedding day bliss

For Giggle, Sunday could not have arrived any sooner, for it had been a day which had filled her dreams, and all her reverie hours, on daddy's fine schooner. She had been preparing herself from early morn, for the ceremony was at twelve. Her chief desire burning within her was to be a blossoming bloom and no wilting flower.

Turbo was to wear a bespoke double-breasted suit of beige mohair, very well cut and superbly hung, to be adorned on the right lapel with a specially grown bloom of peach petals giving off a striking perfume.

So on from the sun at twelve of the clock, their friends gathered for a great ceremony, the atmosphere already charged and alive with the voices of the gospel girls of Sister Sugar Lee. Through the congregation then walked Reverend Rey, equipped with Bible in hand to join this couple in wedlock as planned.

Giggle was agog with it all, and Turbo also looked nervous, yet this time under the influence of the punch he would not fall.

After they both had said, "I do," everything was then rounded off, and the Sister Sugar Lee Gospel Choir led them all into song. Knowing the song, Giggle and Turbo sang along.

Ceremony now complete, the complement of guests head down to the beach for an afternoon wedding-day treat, with much steel band music, rum punch, and many Caribbean delicacies on which to munch.

Scene 3, Act 2 – The Sunset Nite Spot

So now with the nuptials and afternoon treats at an end, the guests all go off to their respective apartments to take a siesta and change. Later they will on the Sunset Nite Spot descend, owned and hosted by Claudette Calypso, to make this an altogether fun-packed weekend.

Royston "Roly-Poly" Griffiths was on the door, wearing his white tuxedo to match his teeth, which could shine no more. "Good evening to you, good people. Hey, hey, hey, Mr and Mrs, I dare say come on in and enjoy de night, for we are goin' to give y'all one hell of a time.

"We wanna see y'all dancing and having a great time, as this will be an evenin' y'all will never forget. So come on, and don't let anyone fret!"

Now into the Sunset Nite Spot where the music was calypso and bluebeat, Miss Claudette was in charge of the show, and under her supervision the entertainment was just neat. Every now and then she burst into an unforgettable song that always entertained the wedding throng.

So in came the wedding throng, all feasted and rested after their siestas and fiestas, Miss Calypso then coming and introducing herself as the club's owner-organiser.

As you have heard before, Turbo could not really handle much booze, but here it was different, as he did not have to impress his Dow Jones dudes, so he had nothing to lose. Here he did not want to appear droll, so did indulge in a lot, but no way would he turn into the wild boar drunken sot.

The boom of the bass was now permeating the air and getting thick, which got heavier the more they drank the Caribbean bevies. It bore no comparison to mead or mulled wine, and for the present Turbo's thoughts were for his wife, not for codpieces, rear ends or swine; so he was light and not at all heavy.

The beat slowly softened and the bass goes down, to reveal Lorris Laughilia, the biggest bombshell in town. Singing many lovers' rock tunes, thereby enticing Mr and Mrs to smooch around the floor, with their heads in the clouds with excitement and rum, eyes a-twinkling they were truly having fun. This was indeed a marriage feast in a paradise isle that they would never forget, even if their marriage was ever done.

Chapter 21

Guy saw quite a lot of Herve over the next months, and they seemed to have things in common. Herve had also bought an apartment in Norwood, but it was an extremely small, purpose-built studio flat, and Herve had said that he felt claustrophobic living there.

Herve's work was exceptionally demanding, and he suffered bouts of depression from time to time and wanted to see no one. Guy understood this, and usually waited for Herve to call or get in touch. It never was too long, because they seemed to enjoy each other's company, but Guy sensed that there was a dark side to Herve's nature, which had not revealed itself just yet.

Guy decided to sell his apartment, and was very happy to learn that it was easy to do. In the time that he had lived there he had made a considerable profit; buying it for fourteen and a half thousand pounds, he sold it for twenty-nine thousand.

He found a very large basement conversion, again in a Victorian house, in Anerley, very near Crystal Palace. The landlord, who lived in the flat above, was a wide boy, who gave the impression that he was a fly-by-night. He had inherited the property from a benefactor – he was an in-law – and converted the four flats into saleable properties, which brought him quite a profit. Naturally, he had had the conversions done on the cheapest of budgets, and so the quality of the conversions was debatable. Guy paid the asking price of thirty-five thousand, putting in a substantial amount from the profit he had made on Oliver Grove.

As he got settled, his relationship with Herve was getting more serious, but Herve seemed to be changing – or showing more of his true self – which Guy did not like at all. He advised Herve that they stop seeing each other for a while, but the latter at first said that he would find that too difficult. However, Guy stepped back from their union and Herve got the message at last.

After what seemed like a healthy break they started seeing one another again. Herve was even more charming than before, which won Guy over and made him believe that Herve had just been going through some problems before.

One day Herve broached the subject of then moving into together, and wanted to hear what Guy had to say about it. Guy was not sure to begin with, but looking at practical issues, they both having separate mortgages and relative expenses with separate properties, he thought it might be more economical to pool resources. Guy eventually saw the logic in this and agreed, but before that, a major fracas that happened one evening.

Guy and Herve often had quarrels, and Guy was beginning to feel that he wanted to be away from the situation. Herve did not want this, and was so manipulative that he always managed to win Guy around. On reflection, when Guy thought about those days later, he acknowledged just how naïve and pliable he must have been in Herve's master plan.

After this major disagreement over something which was of no real importance, Guy had arranged to go to Camden Lock with a friend of his. Joe was always late for things, but Guy had waited half an hour for him and finally decided to telephone him to see if he had left his home.

Prior to this, Herve had telephoned Guy and pleaded with him not to end their relationship. As Guy had nothing more to say, he told Herve that he was putting down the telephone. When Guy went to call Joe some fifteen minutes later, Herve was still on the other end of the phone. Guy remained firm in his resolve to end things between them, and put down the receiver again.

Within the next twenty minutes Joe arrived, and following him was Herve. That day there was no trip to Camden. Herve was exceptionally attentive and made lunch, almost fawning over Guy and Joe.

Joe had never trusted Herve, and had told Guy that one day over a drink they were having together, but being subjective about something or someone is a totally different ball game to being objective. An outsider can often see the truth, whereas the insider can be blinded by their own feelings. Guy's other few close friends at the time were of the same mind; they did not trust Herve, as they found him to be unpredictable, and even went as far as believing that he was mentally unstable.

Perhaps Guy knew it but did not want to face it, or he might have gone along with the belief that love heals everything, even deeply disturbed people. Clearly, this was foolhardy arrogance that Guy had to pay the high price for later on.

So, even with his own instincts warning him, and his friends having strong reservations, Guy agreed that Herve buy into the property, putting down the same deposit that he had after he sold Oliver Grove. That was when Herve revealed who he really was. It seemed time now for that dark demon within to unfold itself.

"Now I am in. You can never tell me to get out again, can you?" he said to Guy one day with a gleeful look of supreme achievement on his face.

Guy thought quickly and retorted, "Just because you've bought into this property with me, it doesn't mean that we're suddenly joined at the hip, Herve. If things work out, they work; and if they don't, they don't."

Herve was lost for a riposte. He desperately wanted one, but could not think of anything to say. Instead, he seethed within and thought of something else destructive to do at another time.

If a person in a relationship likens that union to scales and weighs up what is negative and destructive on the one hand, and all that is constructive and uplifting on the other, there is usually a result – and it seldom weighs out equally. It's safe to say that when the scales tip to the negative, it's not a healthy union. Although there were times when there was some laughter, sharing, and growth together, Guy always felt that he returned to the beginning without having evolved with Herve as a couple.

Felix and Zoot had coped with the move and were settled in their new home, but Herve was seriously jealous of Guy's union with his two beloved cats. So one day Herve got rid of them; Guy was to see them no more.

Guy and Herve had a few friends around one evening, and Herve made an announcement when there was a silence that he had found the two cats dead in the gutter when he arrived home one day. No one believed him, and there was a chilling silence the rest of the evening, which prompted people to leave.

Guy had begun to drink Colt 45, and it was becoming his best (false) friend. It flashed through his mind that he was going down the same road as his mother; he felt terribly trapped and cornered.

There was such an irrational side to Herve's makeup that as soon as Guy thought that a compromise had been reached over something, Herve would sabotage it ruthlessly. An example of this was when there was a dispute about having ventilation coming through the sash window in the bedroom at night. Guy thought it always wise to have some air coming in; Herve did not, for security reasons. So Herve bought locks that enabled the windows to be locked but remain slightly open.

Guy thought that this solved the problem. Yet one day when Guy returned to the flat, the windows were all smashed and there was a note left from Herve that he now had permanent ventilation. Herve then went to stay with his friend who lived by the coast, who he claimed was madly in love with him. This was his bolt hole every time there was a drama – which was often.

Another time he destroyed Guy's possessions in a fit of rage, shouting that Guy had taken his home away from him and he was not going to let him have one. Guy answered with logic that no one took anything away from him, but that he decided to buy into this home.

But the most classic story to tell was when Guy went to use his vacuum cleaner one day and found the cord cut to about a foot from the source. Herve had a cylindrical vacuum cleaner, and Guy had an upright one, and it seemed quicker to use the latter. Herve's was called a Goblin, which coined the name that Guy gave to him, Goblin Black, which inspired another play.

When Herve came home that evening, Guy asked him if he knew what happened to his Hoover lead. Herve answered, now in a low and pathetic voice, "Yes, I cut it because I was going to hang myself with it."

Guy could not muster any sympathy, for he was now used to Herve's games. He retorted, "And why couldn't you use your own Hoover wire? It's much longer."

"Why are you so cruel? If they had found me with your Hoover wire, you would have felt guilty."

From this time on, Guy realized that everyone was right about Herve, especially his own strong gut feelings that were urging him to walk the other way. Although he was angry and hurt, especially knowing that Herve had got rid of the cats, he flew into a verbal invective, which naturally led Herve to get quite violent.

The adrenaline was pumping so fiercely through Guy's veins that he did not realize that there was a knife buried deep in his back. It was only when he looked back from the front door, exclaiming, "I'm getting out of this madhouse," did he then see the trail of blood behind him, with Herve looking on with a smile.

Herve then telephoned Rowena and announced that he was killing her son, and with that he quit the flat post haste. Rowena soon arrived and dressed Guy's serious knife wound, and even though she insisted on him going to hospital, he refused.

"Maybe *now* you'll realize just what a madman you've got mixed up with," Rowena chastened.

After this episode, Guy knew that he had to do something about his violent and disturbing relationship that was unhinging his equilibrium. As the adrenaline ceased to flow, Guy could now feel the pain in his back, and Rowena insisted that he lay down. It had been a phenomenal day, but then life with Herve was always that way; there was always a new drama to fill the day.

Herve disappeared for a few days and went to stay with the friend who adored him by the coast in Hastings. Guy now knew that he needed to talk to Herve when things were calmer – well, as calm as would ever get with him – so he waited until he returned and broached the subject.

Naturally Herve was penitent, yet blamed all his adverse and extreme behaviour on Guy drinking too much. Guy ignored that, as he did not want to get into any more quarrels, especially with someone who did not use much logic, but precipitated emotional war games, into which Guy had made the great error of getting hauled into in the past. Guy was now objective, because he had come to the realization that living with Herve was not a healthy option, and it would not change because Herve was fundamentally disturbed.

One day, Herve's father was helping repair a window that his son had smashed in rage, when he said in his heavy Glaswegian brogue, "I should have had him locked up years ago."

Guy felt sad both for Herve and his father after hearing this remark, but there seemed to be no way of broaching the wide gap between them. They were like parallel lines that would never meet.

And of course there was the dog that Herve had bought one day in a vain attempt to replace Guy's cats. But the real reason was that Herve wanted a dog, so he went and bought a piebald sheepdog puppy when they were out for a drink in town with Guy's friend, Joe.

Herve was behaving like a child who was attempting to get what he wanted, and would not be silent until he had it. He left Guy and his friend in a local pub and went off, saying to them that he would be back in no time at all. He returned with this puppy, which was adorable, but was not a practical proposition, as both Guy and Herve were out of the flat all day.

As they walked along the street, Guy asked Herve to take the dog back to the shop because it would not get the proper care that it needed. Herve would not listen, and walked ahead of Guy and Joe. In utter exasperation, Guy gave Herve an almighty kick in his rear, and realized the phrase "you need a good kick up the arse," which sadly ended up in a street brawl. Guy named the puppy Kik after the event.

They kept the dog, because again Herve won Guy around after pleading with him in his obsequious way. Guy took pity on the poor creature because the pathetic little dog's first day out of the pet shop was met with violence and discord. Yet Guy's predictions came true. The puppy kept getting out of the cat flap, and was often found in neighbours' gardens. One day as he came in from work, a haughty woman who lived nearby told Guy that a man had taken the dog for safekeeping until its owner came home, leaving his telephone number.

Guy had warned Herve that if he left the dog alone with him for another weekend whilst he visited he who adored him, he would give him away. So he took action and followed through with his promise. Guy telephoned the man who had rescued the dog from the street, and told him that if he wanted the dog he could have him.

Guy was not prepared to argue about it when Herve returned, but Herve wanted the man's telephone number in order to retrieve poor Kik; in the end, his parents took the dog.

Herve did not want to leave, and naturally wanted them to give the relationship another go, but Guy was now adamant that it would never work out between them. Before this decision was reached, Guy made a trip up to Edinburgh – it seemed the farthest north at the time, and a means of escape – to check out the prices of properties, with a view to buy there.

Their flat had been on the market, and it was not long before interest was shown in it, as all the floors had been sanded and it was decorated to a classic and neutral standard – Guy and Herve shared classic taste – and it was also a spacious flat. The entrance door led into an L-shaped hallway, with the kitchen off to the left and the scullery to its right, beneath the outer staircase that led up to the upstairs front door. To the right from the hallway was the bedroom, and then to the left the lounge, which was a good twenty by twenty-five feet.

On his return from Scotland, Herve informed Guy that there were people due to visit that same evening who had seen the flat once before, and the estate agent had told Herve that they were prepared to make an offer of the asking price. Herve did not want to see them again, and asked Guy if he would tell them that their plans had changed, as Herve now wanted to buy out Guy's share in the property.

Guy faced them with a heavy heart, for he could see that their spirits were high about buying the flat. They went away, bearing the news badly, and Guy remembered the estate agent in Edinburgh who had told him that "yes" must not be said when viewing a property, because that would then be considered legal and binding. So the plan then was for Guy to move on and Herve to remain in the flat, after having bought out Guy's share, but the process was not short of obstacles.

Simon Rawlings, from whom Guy had bought the flat and who lived in the flat above, had used a company to do the damp coursing of all the properties. When Herve had had the flat surveyed, the damp coursing had not been adequately carried out, and now the company had gone into liquidation; all guarantees were null and void.

Herve seemed to take pleasure in telling Guy this, for he had a pleasurable smirk on his face which implied that Guy was stumped at the first run. Herve added that he would not continue with the sale if the two and a half thousand pounds was not met for the damp coursing. Guy was forced with an obstacle. After he gave it some thought, he decided it was not insurmountable, but he said nothing to Herve about his plan.

Guy met up with his building society manager to discuss this possible loan on his mortgage, as he was able to put a substantial amount down on his next property, which was to be in Lewes – although he told Herve that it was Reigate. Mr Bolton, after considering the facts and figures, sanctioned the loan, which was to be added to the mortgage. Then, at Guy's request, he prepared a money draft for the two and a half thousand pounds. Guy felt jubilant and proud of himself for using his own initiative, but was going to play a little game with Herve.

Herve was now staying with friends, and Guy was paying his share of the mortgage, as it was impossible to get along when they were near one another. Guy asked him around one evening to talk about the damp coursing, but put on a face of anxiety. Herve looked happy, and was exceptionally buoyant, believing that Guy would not be able to come up with the damp coursing fee.

So, after asking Herve about things with his work, Guy casually remarked, "Oh, by the way, that business about the damp coursing, I've got the draft for you." He then handed the draft to Herve.

Guy felt pleasure at seeing Herve's face, for it took a sudden dive right down into the doldrums, and all hopes that he harboured that they would remain together were totally dashed.

Guy had seen a cottage in Lewes which he immediately felt a strong affinity for and made plans to make an offer on it. This also had its fair share of obstacles, but through sheer determination and perseverance, Guy got through; Herve was powerless to thwart his plans.

The one thing that Guy wanted to keep from Herve was the fact that he was moving to Lewes, just in case he decided to follow and stalk him, so he decoyed him away, saying that he was moving to Reigate.

Unfortunately, this ruse was foiled one day when Guy left his briefcase out when Herve had come to collect some clothes, and he naturally rifled through the documents. Herve began making exaggerated gestures, saying, "I hope you'll be happy in *Reigate*."

"Okay, so you know. You've had a good look through my papers and you've pilfered the information." Guy was careful not to say more. He wanted to say something to the effect of "and don't even think about following me there," but thought twice about it, because that might certainly have put ideas into Herve's mind, and the mere force of its challenging directive could precipitate delinquent action from him.

Guy had to put this development out of his mind; it was only a grain of dust on a beach of warm and soft sand. Guy even overlooked the rather pompous and cutting way the owner of the property in Lewes dealt with him. It was not personal, or Guy chose not to see it that way even if it was, but this man was the developer of the property which he had clearly made a substantial profit on and wanted a quick sale with no hassle. Herve had tried to hinder the process in whatever way he could, but failed.

The sale went through, and after the removal men had gone, Guy sat down in his lounge on the floor and put on the radio. The song that came on was "Don't Worry, Be Happy," advice that he valued and remembered.

When he had got settled, Guy made a trip back to Norwood to see Rowena and drop in the keys to Herve. Herve did not come to answer the door, but Saul did, a friend of Herve's, who thought that he was Joris-Karl Huysmans, the French novelist with a handlebar moustache. It was just like he had stepped out of a West End play as a 1920's dandy, precious and delicate to boot. Saul had always wanted to come across as being an authority on antiques, and got irritable with people when they did not know certain things.

Guy remembered once when Saul had come around and they were talking about glass. Guy liked a certain one that Herve had bought, and Saul had to say, "Do you not know that it is Lalique?"

Guy had a quick retort. "We are not all experts like you, Saul."

Guy greeted Saul and asked if Herve was there. Herve appeared behind Saul, and the latter retreated into the flat.

Herve looked devastated and dejected, and Guy felt a pang of compassion surge through him, but he needed to remain objective. He handed Herve the keys and wished him the best of everything. Herve said "Bye-bye" in his own pathetic and lost way, which was intended to promote sympathy from Guy, but it was wasted this time and Herve knew it.

Guy remembered the quote from the New Testament, "Shake the dust from off your feet," and that was what he did mentally as he walked away, feeling a wondrous sense of freedom and empowerment. Herve and Guy never saw one another, or had anything to do with each other, after that day.

The cottage in Lewes was actually on four levels, as the builder had developed out the basement room, which was extremely cool in the height of summer and was an ideal dining room/study.

Guy felt like he had been through a washing machine, and he felt an emotional mess after his tumultuous relationship with Herve. Lewes gave him time to convalesce and give his heart time to heal. On reflection, Guy understood what it was like to be in lust with someone, as the physical side of the relationship he just emerged from was powerful. But when that is the only force, fierce as it can be, it soon peters out.

When Guy gained some inner strength and began to laugh again about things, he wrote another play, inspired by this last experience.

The Goblins Gathering, A Gregorian scene

Cast of Characters

The Social Worker Set
Millicent Minority-Group

How-Do-You-Feel-About-That
Sally CQSW (Clever Questions Solved Whenever)
Edna Ethnic
Goblin Black (Double Agent)
The Goblin Gathering
Slimy Seethe
Walter Mulch-Wart
Gavin Gribble
The Gregorian Congregation
Jeremiah Pope-Aspirant
Brother Bender
Monsignor Vice-Closet
Father Felatio
Max Machismo (Owner of El Cruiso Bar)

Scene 1, Act 1 – The El Cruiso Bar

The El Cruiso Bar, packed with denim boys, varied coloured handkerchief men, with chained caps and mirrored shades, and queens who spent their lives in shopping arcades, a smattering of waifs from other zones, and the usual quota of moustachioed clones.

Seated on a high stool at the bar was Goblin Black, sipping half a pint of lager and looking at the mirror on the wall before him reflecting all that was beyond his back. Not far away was Jeremiah Pope-Aspirant, scotched as usual, although not yet sozzled enough to be on his final sway.

After a while their eyes meet, both fired by one another, and then grabbed by the idea to give each other's bod a treat. Hot and sultry glances did they pass from one to the other, and before too long they were in deep conversation, seemingly as happy as sand boys rolling in clover.

Goblin Black, trying to portray his caring approach, concealed behind his convincing mask, curtaining only malice and harm – a trait he claimed that he inherited from the funny farm. Together then they both decided to leave, to look for an off-license to more alcoholic beverages retrieve.

Pope-Aspirant of emotions was a hollow wasteland, and so resigned to scotch was he, that it had become his life-giving potion that helped put his sordid desires into motion. Spirits he would drink from a bowl, for radically he desperately lacked soul.

On the other hand, Black drank little, for he needed to impress upon the world that he had no substance misuse tendencies, preferring rather to ruminate on his own spittle.

The connection linking these two creations was that they were both from Scottish shores, Pope-Aspirant being of Gregorian bent, and Goblin Black, the social worker who thought that he was heaven sent.

Back now to the Goblin grotto, in the suburban dusty "countryside" amidst the middle class homeowner hype, there was still room for Goblins to fester and hide.

For often from the bowels of the earth you could hear, but only with an acutely tuned in ear, the Goblin song. "My name is Goblin Black. Goblins, Goblins, Goblins are back; dark and desirous, we like to live in shacks. Although we might live in yuppyville, into the seething darkness we prefer to go, where we can get our thrills. Perhaps we could be used in some horror eclipse by Cecil B. DeMille."

Scene 2, Act 1 – Goblin Black's grotto in Subterranea

Amidst the William Morris wallpaper, Black and Pope-Aspirant into the grotto for a sexual experience came, to lustily share each other's bodies.

Pope-Aspirant, the worst for excess whiskey – although initially at the bar had found himself feeling frisky – now found himself feeling guilty. Then into the greying sheets did they then retire. This scene was not fulfilling, or pleasurably nice, midst the dandruff stains and pubic lice.

Although there was some mutuality in a combined ejaculation, Pope-Aspirant was eagerly awaiting his next confession. It would run something like this:

"Bless me, Father, for I have with another man sinned. It was last night when he had me on his bed pinned. I didn't enjoy it, Father, no, no, no. For in moments through our union I was haunted by the compunction that I had to make this confession, and then felt shameful of the sacrament that I would have to take."

On the other side of the confessional sat Father Felatio, a hirsute man of ample proportioned ratio, who replied thus, "Think nothing of it, my son. Human togetherness is a human need, and sometimes necessary fun. I wish myself that I could indulge behind this cassock; my dear, I wish you could see how many times I have a loaded gun.

"When these beautiful men come to me with their confessions, I regularly fantasize about other sexual sessions, for this in reality I know I can't achieve, so that is why I keep a vibrator up my sleeve. And in this confessional to conceal my enjoyment many a time, when I hoo ha and hum, this is when I slide it up my bum.

"And furthermore, between you and me, my son, when I have finished all my ecclesial chores, I do it with a candle, but then on all fours. So you see, we all have desires and feelings, my son, so try not to feel so glum."

Monsignor Vice-Closet and Father Felatio to a number of seedy joints were wont to go, putting on their jovial charm and discreetly linking arm in arm. A neatly folded copy of *Gay Views* had they, over which they would later ogle and peruse, for as their reputations were at stake, they carefully concealed it beneath *Church and Diocese News*.

Jeremiah Pope-Aspirant, Father Felatio, Monsignor Vice-Closet, and Brother Bender had all studied at the same Jesuit college, accruing much catechism but little general knowledge. They all enjoyed the high camp of ecclesiastical hierarchy, and of course the garb, begowned in robes and tassels, and all men to boot – what a patriarchy!

These four would once a week meet, to share their gripes, desires and inhibitions, each relaying one to the other sins that they had perpetrated at bedtime in horizontal positions. They claimed that the devil reigned from 12 midnight till the early morn three, during which time they could enjoy an action packed sexual spree.

Enjoy it they did, but lo, to confession afterwards they always had to go, for they were guilt-ridden according to the Catholic doctrine, of indiscriminately letting their semen flow. Fumbling with public hairs and KY jelly, with eyes cast down they dared not look at the Virgin Mary.

Scene 3, Act 1 – An office of social workers

Of this particular social services scene there was a joint supervisory committee, apparently an excellent team. But as councils and boroughs with each other compete, organisation within these departments was quite a feat.

The supervisory collective were Edna Ethnic and Millicent Minority-Group, How-Do-You-Feel -About-That, and Sally CQSW (Clever Questions Solved Whenever). This group's motto was "a problem shared is a problem halved. Oh, and we forgot that double agent Goblin Black is another employee of this team, whoopee!"

Goblin Black, a social worker with motorped wheels, was wont to travel through the borough's council estates, endeavouring to do community deals.

Trying to patch up family warfare and smaller disputes, he, after often doing a computer analysis of the family's roots – he distrusted his own brain's statistics – he put complete faith in the computer's floppy disc, CD-ROM and hard drive's logistics.

"Oh, let's be an enigma, look at me. Could anyone else such a computer genius be?"

How-Do-You-Feel-About-That, being a bohemian type with flowing batique cotton skirts, her hair always hennaed, and her face, although comely, was inclined to resembles a peach, but overripe. Having gold-rimmed, Lennon-style glasses, she's subsidising her social work pay with giving evening classes. Her political leanings were feminist, advocating Germane Greer, and from lesser spiritual mortals she could often get a sneer.

Now, Sally CQSW was of an entirely different ilk, being a devout born-again Christian who enjoyed Soya milk. She had had an austere Anglican upbringing, which did prevent her from going to raucous parties or any late night singing.

From a tender age she had always been an avid reader, often to be found in the park or library with her head engrossed in a classic or encyclopaedia, often staying well into the early hours of the morn, and often all other means of enjoyment scorn.

Millicent Minority-Group, of West Indian descent, was on multiracial integration bent, for she was of the belief that all nations and cultures should unite, and that all could live safely together without friction or any threat of any fight. These views she had construed by reading many sociology books, and these same views she would often try and put into action, despite opposition and ostracising looks.

Edna Ethnic was of sociology the revered and respected doyen, for her years with social services exceeded more than two times ten. As a student, she had been the founder member, and was now the chairwoman of Liberation Lesbian, and often in her time off from work she was dab hand at being a thespian.

She was still wont to slap the girls on their rear ends, protectively treat them as baby chicks and she the mother hen. Her hair was always short and was characteristically greying, but to her political activities and beliefs she was never swaying.

Scene 1, Act 2 – A monthly meeting

At the MGM, this collective of social workers did gather for a talk. To discuss the matters of the month was Edna, at the ancient blackboard, just like some school ma'am equipped with pointing stick and chalk.

A film show there was proposed to be, to be shown via an archaic projector faulty and worn. Yet Edna was never defeated, and continued on smiling and never forlorn – because of the cutbacks they were not allowed at present to buy new projector parts, which did restrict their instruction of the visual social work arts.

Thus we learn that their social work education is inhibited, with all of these otherwise functional items, which because of major departmental cuts were prohibited.

Then during their sharing of case histories, coming in late was Goblin Black, looking dishevelled and with an air of puzzled mystery. Carrying his crash helmet and files by the stack, he endeavoured to take his place in the social worker pack.

Yet being sympathetic creatures and not hungry wolves, at his tardiness no scowling looks were given, so consequently he did not have to give them any polite hype or bull.

Murder and mayhem had entered into their social work scene, and Black had brought in all the info, which he had word-processed on his computer machine. Before all his colleagues he felt like a shining star, because after all, he thought, they all did not have their own computers, rah, rah, rah!

Another one of his Goblin chants was, "You put the left disc in, then the right disk out, and programme your computer without a shout. Arrange all the data and tap it with the mouse, and don't I look an enigma; that's what it's all about!"

Scene2, Act 2 – The staff cafeteria

In the staff cafeteria, How–Do-You-Feel-About-That and Goblin Black were having their caffeine fix and chocolate-coated wafer bix, discussing the weekend's events.

Black started, "Well, How-Do-You-Feel-About-That, at the weekend I met someone special in the bar, and took him where we took our sexual enjoyment very far. Although he may well be an aspiring bishop or some kind of official in the church, I wouldn't want any harm to come to him and knock him off his churchly perch.

"I met him on Friday night, and he stayed over till Saturday evening, where we shared so much in my William Morris'd bedroom."

With this, How-Do-You-Feel-About-That asked Black if he would be seeing him again, for it was apparent to her that for this churchly man Goblin had a strong yen. The Goblin replied that her instinct was right, and that he liked him much, with every hope in the world that they will keep in touch.

How-Do-You-Feel-About-That then shared with Black the account of Friday's events, teaching her social science at the poly. It had left her feeling tired and distraught, for there were a few students in her class who were clear-cut wallies.

"They weren't there to learn anything, but simply wanted to waste my time. So, with this in mind, I brought the lesson to an end sharply at nine."

Black and How-Do-You-Feel-About-That were bosom buddies, confiding in each other their innermost thoughts, and Black for his friend had devised a computer game, which would be a useful visual aid for her studies.

Scene 3, Act 2 – The fund-raising function

It was a fine autumn Saturday afternoon, and people had gathered for a fundraising event in the social services function room. Most of the social workers were there, drinking tea and laughing without a care, doing their utmost to raise funds for whatever cause they deemed it fair.

There was one major raffle, for the first prize there being a fortnight of social worker calls; second prize was the automatic allocation of officer-in-charge of the multiracial wherewithals.

There were various stalls, selling a heterogeneous selection of eats and goods, from obscure collector's musical vinyl to Mrs Beeton-type cakes and homemade foods.

Goblin Black was hovering behind a trestle table laden with wild mushrooms which he had grown in his grotto garden. For him, the cultivation of different mushrooms occupied a lot of his leisure time, and on these dark and dank morsels he would in the evening voraciously dine, making him belch vociferously and all done without a pardon.

How-Do-You-Feel-About-That had a very colourful stall, displaying many materials of batique design, over which any sixties beatnik would pine – coloured beads and wooden bangles, Egyptian henna, which instil in anyone's hair quite a sparkle without any tangles.

Millicent Minority-Group was engaged with a client, and over her pamphlets that she had processed she stoops, standing there with the hope of selling them all, with advice too, just like Marjorie Proops.

Edna Ethnic, wearing jeans and a collarless shirt, would to any clients her political views express. "Sexual freedom and the abolition of clause 28" would eventually come booming out, whether they were gay or straight.

Scene 1, Act 3 – Gregorian and social violence

Back at the El Cruiso Bar, which was wont to smell of leather and poppers, the Goblin's teetotalism had become quite slack. He was no longer abstemious, slugging back the brandies and the rums, for he had a burning desire to have Pope-Aspirant back in his William Morris'd shack.

They had arranged to meet at the bar a little after ten, with the hope of having an ecstatic evening. Pope-Aspirant was now on his umpteenth scotch, and the mixture that Black was drinking had turned into a real Goblin's hotchpotch.

So they were no longer talking amicably, for they had really ruffled the feathers of those in the vicinity, to the point that Max Machismo had asked them to go, whereupon Pope-Aspirant revealed his dog collar in full show.

Max then exclaims, "Look here, Father Creep, you could be the Queen Mother for all I care; now you and your pickup get yourselves out of here before I really go spare!"

Pope-Aspirant and Black then quit the joint, calmness frayed and tempers raging to boiling point. As soon as Pope-Aspirant was outside, Black grabbed him and pulled him down to the floor. Pope-Aspirant then grabbed Black's legs and pulled him down to the gutter's dregs. Both bloody nosed and tearful with some teeth missing, both still tight, they really were no pretty sight.

They both said that they would never meet again after this night, and now that this brawl was over they both disbanded and then took flight.

Scene 2, Act 3 – The Goblins Gathering, Rehearsal for the autumn resurgence

In the dank dripping chambers of the Goblin's grotto, murmurs could be heard as they chanted their motto. Linking hands and standing in a ring, they were stepping ante-clockwise and chanting, "It is way past the midnight hour, as we like things dark and dour. We hate elves and fairies – yuk! For us their musings comes unstuck.

"We've no time for poetry and rhyme, for we feel happy in our mulch and slime. We loiter in a random church cloister, when the church bells have chimed, awaiting another opportunity to commit another Goblin crime. Ya ya ya, rah rah rah!"

An earthworm wriggles through the earth, and Goblin Black sucks it up with a slurp. Then chewing on his juicy snack, he pats his Goblin chums on their backs.

They that made up the Goblin gathering were Gavin Gribble, the elf hunter; Slimy Seethe, whose habits were so foul you wouldn't believe; and Walter Mulch-Wart, a fretful sort who made the mulch for the 'shrooms and 'stools. And of course, Goblin Black, that serious double agent who presided over them all and made their general rules.

This was their favourite time of year, approaching late October. And in this leaf mould, half-rotting decay they would find good cheer. But with that acutely atoned ear to the bowels of the earth, you would hear, "Ya ya ya, rah rah rah."

So, beware if you hear these muffled noises and chants from over ground, it could well be the Goblins Gathering, chanting and mulching underground.

Chapter 22

Guy related to the tragedy and humour of life, which is so well reflected in the two theatrical masks that encompass both these things. He related to the Commedia dell'arte, and had studied theatre design and costume. When he remembered himself as a young boy, amongst so much activity, hostility, aggression and reactionary behaviour, he slipped into his surreal world and watched from afar. He realized now that his mistake was to ever hope that there would be strong ties between his stepfamily and himself.

It was as if he was the court jester who was laughed at, ridiculed, or even discarded as a nonentity. Yet from this vantage point he watched, observed, and assimilated everything that he saw. Not that he understood it all, but logging it to memory was sufficient, and he intuitively knew that one day he would understand it all. *The brick that you discard will be the cornerstone of the building.*

Murphy lived with Rowena until she passed away, and she again fulfilled her need to be needed. Murphy had two sisters, who were staunch Catholics but were loath to meet Rowena because she was not married to their brother. They did, however, turn up at her funeral, sobbing profusely into their handkerchiefs, and Guy always wondered why on earth two people would weep over someone they never really knew. The lamentation could well have been for their brother, who they knew to be a simple man and was alone again. Nevertheless, it struck Guy that they looked like anonymous extras on a movie set.

The build up to Rowena's demise started one very cold November evening, when her next-door neighbour, Hilda, had fallen ill and needed some help. Rowena did not wrap up as well as she should have, and although she had found something to throw about her shoulders, her midriff and back were not sufficiently protected against the wintry north wind that blew that night. The result was that she picked up a severe chill in her kidneys, which later turned to pneumonia.

When Barbara and Guy saw her in the hospital, she was no longer responding to treatment and was being kept alive by a respirator. After discussing it for a time, they both agreed that it was time to let Rowena go, so they instructed the nurses to disconnect the machine.

Guy went into a vacuum for some time after that, and slowly over the course of a year he let his feelings out – the anger, grief, pain and sorrow – for all that he had lost, his father, his cats, and his mother.

Barbara went to her own inner place, but shared nothing of it with Guy; perhaps she did not know how to. But they were the only two of Rowena's children who dealt with all the funeral arrangements, and Barbara notified her stepfamily. There were no replies or telephone calls. Is that strange, knowing this fragmented family? Yet they all appeared for the funeral, except Gerard.

To Guy, the funeral was another surreal adventure, something like Magritte would paint on a summer's afternoon. The fragmented picture of the dismembered family had no sense of unity even at their mother's funeral. To be honest, it was a fascinating surreal farce, with the characters playing anonymous parts in the play. Who were they? Were they the children of the woman whose body now lay dead in the coffin that was to be burned – it was Rowena's wish to be cremated – or were they actors in this drama of the fragmented family?

Guy wanted to be the objective master of ceremonies, because he felt that he owed it to his mother to keep the conversation light and topical, just like a gentleman's club room. Yet he watched Barbara as she blanked everyone and stood on her own against one wall in the antechamber. Venema was chatting to Guy, and he felt, as he always did with her, a heart connection, but it was always so phoney and acted out like a dress rehearsal in a play. He learnt not to distrust his feelings, just his step-relatives; they said that they would do things, but never did them.

During the service Guy awaited expectantly for one of the elders to stand up and say something about their mother, but perhaps they did not feel that they wanted to honour her. If so, then they were being authentic, but where was what Rowena always called backbone or any strength of character?

When he knew that it was not coming, and he thought that it was not his place to take the lead, Guy drifted back into that surreal world and watched with a vacuous heart. He had no feelings for any of them, which left him as empty as a dried out well.

However, when he saw Venema standing alone and watching the zebra finch in the small aviary outside when they all left the cremation service, he felt something for her. Perhaps he touched her sense of loss, but it was fleeting, as were all the experiences he had with his step-relatives.

Then those words of hers, which again raised some hope in his heart that she did want to know about him and his life, "Now remember, darling, keep in touch, because we only have each other left."

Guy knew that he would take her up on that offer, and he did. He telephoned Venema a few times, but got the brush off;

her interest had waned again. She told him one time that she had put his number in a bureau that she was stripping down to wax and then sell, and had left it in there when she sold the desk. Oh Venema, how the poison still strikes! This was the final time that it would spurt out at Guy. After hearing that, he cut any fond feelings that he had held for her and saw her as stranger.

This was now his reality. There was no surreal existence, not one of either the Singh's children, Chunny or Raghubir, wanted to know Guy; so now he knew. It had taken him a long time to realize it, or did he really just hope that it was not so? The decree nisi existed for some time, and now he had the decree absolute.

Guy kept Rowena's ashes, and he and Gerard were to take them to Rottingdean one day and throw them high up into the wind. It seemed so fitting that it should be the fate of Rowena's ashes, as she loved the sea and the winds, and now she floated on them.

There were times when Guy connected with Gerard, but most of the time it felt discordant and distant because he blocked all real closeness. The rare occasions that he did were momentary and fleeting. Knowing the Singh's were the most confusing and conflicting experiences that he had undergone throughout his life, but that would be no more, because Guy had decided that he wanted nothing more to do with them. In fact, he had not one more word to say to any of them; all the fractured threads that ever connected them were now frayed completely, and all the weak links were severed.

Guy actually questioned whether he was being melodramatic. However, he needed to worry about his own equilibrium. Knowing them brought nothing but heartache and strife, and he was no masochist.

Guy's main outlet to express his surreal world was to write plays, and Lewes inspired him greatly, as the reader will see:

A Time Sketch of La Rue de Soleil

Cast of Characters

Ned Rise	Baker
Will Smythe	Blacksmith
Aycres	Farmer
Leonard Arch	Cobbler
Jethro Pyke	Inn Keeper
Edmunde Wakefield	Printer
Simple Garthage	Village Idiot
Master Tim	Ferryman
Alfred of Alfriston	Squire
Jeffrey of Berwick	Squire
Jeremy Turnpike	Solicitor
Hugos-There	Sergeant-at-arms
Robert Upstart	Brigand
Sil D'arblay	Travelling Minstrel

Scene 1, Act 1 – A medieval scene in Lewesville

On a bright, dappled autumn morning, when one could smell the dankness and chill permeating the air, we will portray for you a medieval scene and unravel an entertaining play of fayre.

So, thus it was back in Lewesville, a time when you could hear no car clamour or police sirens shrills. Instead, around about was the sound of horses' hooves on cobbled streets, and the pungency of wood smoke interlacing the air would a quivering nose greet.

The laborious turning of wood on stone of the carts drawn by those magnificent beasts, the horses of the shire, their colossal strength carrying them through each day from morning until dusk, they would labour on and seemingly never tire.

Many cartloads were drawn in at this time of year, it being the harvest gathering, fruits of the forest, and produce from a season's toiling in the fields.

Simple Garthage, unsure of what to do, kicks around a battered swede with a much worn-out shoe. Tall and ungainly with a toothless grin, and on seeing him one would ask, "Where has he been?"

Dirty faced, snotty nosed, barefooted urchins garbed in ragged raiment shriek and mock our village buffoon, who lived in a shack-like tenement.

Aycres yelled, "Oy, Garthage, get out of the way! If you want somin' to do ye can help me unload these trays!"

With more jeering and laughing from the street waifs, Garthage puts sacks to shoulder and moves the load as heavy as a boulder.

Little brain power had he, but his body had much strength and fortitude, living off market scraps and handouts, this being his staple food. He knew nothing of etiquette or manners, for no one had taught them to him, so he could never differentiate between polite or rude. However, there was always an odd job to be found for him by a carter, farmer or innkeeper in this bustling little town.

Not too far afield, gliding downstream in a cargo boat laden with timber, lead, and iron ore – there was so much ballast within the boat's hold that it was barely able to keep afloat – was Master Tim, the ferryman, a jovial, hail, well-met type of man. He made this journey from Haven Harbour every day, ensuring that all went according to plan.

When he reached Lewesville Harbour, not too far from the fosse, an old Roman camp site, he made sure that the boat was tied to a mooring hook, securely yet not too tight. Proceeding then to unload the cargo with a set of block and tackle, relieving himself of this burdensome load – which if the truth be told he found to be a cumbersome shackle.

Once unloaded he would go to Ye Old Sunrise Inn for some refreshing ale, to share with Jethro Pike, the inn keeper, from his travels another interesting tale.

Passing by the inn some horses hooves on cobbled streets did resound; it was yet another cart driven by farmer Aycres, who from his farm with grain for Lewesville was bound.

From the rear of his cart a trickle of grain had fallen for some time, leaving a trail like a paper chase, and gobbling this up with great gusto was a gaggle of geese, flapping and screeching with much haste.

Aycres then on to the miller did proceed, up through the town via the path to the windmill, to sell to the miller his valuable grain and seed.

Scene 2, Act 1 – An afternoon's entertainment

Down near the willow trees where the river bends, a crowd had gathered with many friends. Laughter and mirth were the general rule, for here stood the ducking stool.

All and sundry were wondering whom, today into the river would be plunged, and then pointing fingers and a fixed stare was at Isabelle Lockwood lunged.

As she was strapped firmly to the seat, the mob then rose jeeringly to their feet.

There she waited with matted hair, and owl-like eyes that did nothing but glare. Then a roar from the mob as she was plunged into the water, and a louder one still when she was lifted up and was gasping for air.

Now that they had had their fun, with the afternoon ducking session being done, they unstrapped the wretched wench, and then going on her way, she dried herself off with dry clumps of hay.

Some light music was then heard from lyres, timbrels and viols, and children danced giddily around the maypole, with spiralling coloured ribbons wafting in the breeze, just as this way and that their feet stole.

A trio of travelling minstrels who were passing through stopped this afternoon to recite a play, which they had construed. Ending their piece with a madrigal sung in pleasant and sonorous harmony, one of the band went amongst the crowd with his upturned hat for their performance fee.

Three dwarfs, with marmosets initially perched on their shoulders, did a tumbling act along with the monkeys, a bit or roly-poly and head over heels along the riverbank, and some doing leap frogs along another flank.

Great cheers were coming from the crowd, and the festivities were growing increasingly loud. The afternoon's entertainment then did go down well, which warranted them all to go down afterwards to Ye Old Sunrise Inn for a refreshment spell.

Scene 3, Act 1 – A further backcloth of Lewesville

The following morning with the grain ground down, the miller comes with his wagon into town. With many bushel sacks of flour, with the odd peck thrown in for good measure, baker Ned Rise will use to make bread, rolls, cake and pastries with much pleasure.

Ned the baker had been working since five of the clock, with his freshly milled grain, which sustains well the digestive system, giving it no untoward shocks.

One of Ned's specialities was his "Nourishin' Ned's Journeyman Cake," which on long journeys and travels the carters with them would take.

Another popular treat he would always make was his renowned game pie filled with rabbit, pheasant and grouse, and with a pastry that would neither crumble nor melt, but flake, coming forth from many hot ovens in the kitchens of many a house.

Now we will take you to the forge, where hard at toil is Will Smythe. A burly mammoth of a man, who in height and girth was some six feet up and around, he was always duty bound to finish his many tasks, the sound of his hammer on anvil would through the town resound.

A heavy worn cowhide apron clung to his deep hirsute chest, for working continually in this heat he needed no vest.

The anvil whereon he worked, moulding and shaping the ore, was a family heirloom and object from which Will would seldom be apart, positioned in the centre of his workroom. It had been gnarled and well-beaten for many a ten year by his father and father's father, done always with seeming good cheer.

In the centre of the town, near an inn called The Rose and Crown, was the cobbler's shop of Leonard Arch. A leaning bay frontage did his shop have, past which in the morning and afternoon at three soldiers would march on manoeuvres from the castle keep, garbed in their leather jerkins and chain mail from their heads to their feet.

Leonard Arch, a slightly short man of wiry frame, the making and mending of footwear was his game. He was no apprentice, but a great master with hides and skins, fashioning shoes, boots, belts and slippers for all and sundry, from beggars to kings.

An irascible misanthropic man who liked to be alone, left with his work and orders midst the cutting shears, sewing thongs and lasts strewn pell-mell over his worktable, by the light of a single tallow candle would he arduously work his fingers to the bone.

Edmunde Wakefield was the town's printer, using a William Caxton press on which he would print works of religious, political, and romantic themes. He supplied to many squires, monasteries, parliamentary clerks, and the local magistrate, even some royal queens.

His books were exquisitely bound, often with gold-embossed endpapers and strikingly coloured kid leather, the pages being of onion skin as light as a feather.

Now to Jeremy Pike, he'll take you to his office, up the staircase to the top, overlooking the goings on down in the street. Clerks on conveyancing business would often be up and down this oak staircase, it being above the milliners shop.

Pike's stature could be described as rotund maxima, distinctly a man who feasted well on his food; ruddy faced and quite bawdy, garbed in lavish raiment, but concealed beneath his lawyers robes, this was a man who had travelled the globe, an amiable, jovial fellow overall, yet shrewd in business and figures, a trait he had inherited from his patron Tumlin Spall.

The Pikes were renowned throughout the shires as being doyens in the legal field, after their reputation had been established, when they did from ruin an important personage shield.

So here you have now a general backcloth wherewith to appreciate our play of fayre, set with the pillars of our community.

So now we will continue to further scenes with you share.

Scene 1, Act 2 – Mutiny at Lewesville Castle

To the castle keep now, where the sergeant-at-arms, Hugos-There, a man no one would easily insult. There were 500 infantrymen, 500 cavalry, and a smaller number of reconnoitre scouts based at the keep. Guarding its surrounds were men with crossbow, bow and arrow, and catapult.

There was an allotted area where the soldiers lived in barracks, yet not too far from the frontline of any imminent or unexpected enemy attack. Life at the castle was fairly waged; all duties, routines and battle training were strategically staged.

The sergeant-at-arms, Hugos-There, would rise early every day to see if his troops were in tone and on fine display, checking that chainmail, jerkin and helmet were all to standard, for he had no time for slackers, misfits or dullards. A matter-of-fact, straightforward type of man, for any serious misadventure he would have anyone mercilessly hang.

On this day extra attention was given to overall turnout, as a collective was visiting them from Arundel Castle's keep.

Up river they came, being transported in a longboat with twenty oarsmen sound, two hundred men for mock battle training, all to Lewesville bound. The portcullis then went up and the drawbridge down, and many more marching feet were heard throughout Lewesville town.

Immediately then to the mess rooms they were led, where they were given warm milk and freshly milled bread. With them thus nourished on the victuals, they were instructed on the day's rituals.

Flags waved fiercely from the battlements, winds were blowing gustily this day.

Now into mock battle and into teams they were formed, hoping that with these lethal weapons no man would be deformed.

For there were bludgeons, ball and chains, maces, axes and javelins, clashing mightily against one another in this the keep's courtyard.

So midst this seeming chaos and roaring battle cries, to hear a man's voice above this din was very hard. Activities were brought to a standstill, with the sergeant-at-arms bellowing, "Halt!"

A stentorian voice had Hugo, which was clearly needed above this battling jamboree.

All iron on iron ceased, yet the echoes reverberated still, and from some neighbouring oak trees many a crow did flap and squawk with a piercing shrill.

Said Hugos-There, "You men have been invited here today to be trained further in battle manoeuvres and tactics, you being infantry and being used to terra firma. Brave bold and forthright I hope, for we want no squirmers!"

He did then proceed with his corporal-at-arms to check body tactics, general gait, battle deportment and correct foot positioning, instructing where needed, and to some giving more sound conditioning.

Hugos-There now calls to his corporal-at-arms and says he, "I'm not too trusting of these Arundel men, I get a gut feeling that something's afoot. It's these furtive looks I see pass from man to man. We shall see after manoeuvres where their loyalties lie, yet to the root of this I will assuredly get before I certainly die."

Then Hugos is prompted to look yonder, and an entourage approaches all on horseback. He makes his way to the lookout tower, peers ahead, shielding his eyes from the sol's glare then bellows, "Drawbridge down without any delay, for the king approaches the castle this day!"

Before too long there were men lining each flank of the keep with trumpets ready to make a fanfare, with instruments pressed to lips and awaiting the call, they all make a fanfare for the king as he passes the great hall.

So being thus honoured by his sudden appearance in their humble little town, the king about to dismount with his many attendants by his side, looks up and sees an arrow that just misses his majesty, all are dumbfounded at this most serious travesty.

Yet the arrow went not amiss but hit one of the king's trusted courtiers, killing him dead. All rushed to the king's side and he took his leave, brushing their attentions aside.

Hugos-There saying to himself, "When I catch this brigand, he will be glad to die after the torments I will see him through."

Scene 2 Act 2, Confession and Conviction

So beyond the chaos and storm that this event had caused, the perpetrator of this attempted regicide, a Roger Upstart, for his thoughts to collect did pause, throwing his high bow into the trees, causing the crows once again to jabber and squawk.

By this moment's loss of control and indiscretion, Upstart had realised that the plot that had been planned for weeks, nay months, had been ruined by his impetuous longbow session.

Three of the Arundel men made up the conspiratorial complement, now deep within the dungeon's hold, where after a while Upstart would his grizzly confession unfold. The wheel, the rack, the whip and irons were used mercilessly, until they extracted from him, from what seemed like his last breath, the names of the other three.

Yet the punishment of this miscreant was to be a gruesome affair, for on Hanging Hill just outside Lewesville, Upstart was to be hung, drawn and quartered without a care.

Scene 3, Act 2 – The execution on Hanging Hill

On the day of the execution it did not rain nor pour. It drizzled and heavy with the elements was the grey, murky sky, on the afternoon when four were to die. The gallows looked menacing and dark as the condemned in the drizzle looked criminally stark.

For the rabble, an execution was an entertaining feat, for so little else was in their lives, that for them this human slaughter was the most macabre yet satisfying treat.

So to the gallows the four are drawn in the solitary death cart, pulled by one of those magnificent horses of the shire. With hands roped together behind their backs, with frightened eyes, battered bodies and sunken hearts, the rabble about them fit and dart.

For these men there was no escape, and awaiting them is the executioner garbed in black cloak and black facemask. He then removes the cloak to leave his hands free to do his gruesome work, so prepares he his knives in order to make them croak.

Midst the throng are the usual vendors selling their cleverly construed pull-string puppets designed to look lifeless and lope. With one pull of the string the puppet would do his death dance at the end of the rope.

Moments before his demise, Upstart a speech had comprised, "In this now my final moment, I am not despondent, dull nor dour. For although I failed in the act of my mission, the seed is sewn for it to one day blossom into fruition."

With this he then yells, "Down with the king; the king must die," inciting the rabble to much hue and cry.

The warden then wrenches him to the gallows steps, with his broken black nails tearing his shirt, giving no heed to the man's treasonous words or concern over whether he was hurt.

The nooses are tied around the prisoners' necks so that they will be partly hung, and then be sliced open from the throat to the genitals, and their intestines drawn out and flung.

With the stench of faeces, urine and blood, and the sight of innards pulsating in the mud, the mob was crazed by this heinous scene, but quickly disperses as the drizzle becomes torrential rain, falling abundantly over the planes.

Organs of four corpses lay strew across the gallows on Hanging Hill, sufficient carrion for the hovering crows and rats to eat their fill.

Scene 4, Act 3 – The king died not, the king died not . . .

The two squires, Alfred of Alfriston and Jeffrey of Berwick, had briefly witnessed the execution as they rode back from a day's hunting in one of their shires.

Alfriston had commented to his companion, "Look you yonder at the rabble and some miscreants getting their dues."

Yet Berwick said no words, just a wry smile appearing upon his face, which he hastily hid with his gloved hand, feeling that it could be seen to be out of place. Alfriston noticed not, and the squires continued on to Pheasant Wood through Hawthorne Lane.

They were to their abodes bound there in La Rue de Soleil. Substantial property had they, kept well by their servants and maids, very sunnily situated in this street on resplendent display.

Meandering along La Rue de Soleil was that renowned travelling minstrel, Sil D'arblay, always at work forming lyrics to his strumming, laughing and humming, and of the Hanging Hill was singing:

"Deep within the castle's hold there was a surreptitious plot, and an arrow sped by, but the king died not, nay the king died not . . .

"An Arundel quartet made up this band of men, and they were hung, drawn and quartered on Hanging Hill, giving the mob a mammoth thrill. Rumour did fly that there was a local squire behind the plot, but the king died not, nay the king died not . . .

"The corpses on the gallows were left to rot. Will the squire then find another wretch to fire the mortal shot, but the king died not, nay the king died not."

On hearing this, Berwick, with his eyes narrowing and an expression upon his face, which was cruel and stark, resembled an eagle ready to prey upon a lark. And so to the minstrel he voices this remark, "Get you hence, travelling minstrel, go you and entertain the rabble, for we are weary of this futile babble!"

And so to end our medieval tale, our wandering minstrel steps lithely on the cobbles, taking his leave of this eventful town. Resplendent in his harlequin suit, he being no tawdry clown.

Bespeckled by the evening sunshine, he plucks the strings on his lute with the same haunting melodic tune, and later on beneath the moon-bathed countryside he'll be playing it on his flute.

So off he strolls to encounter other folk, and to find other interesting places to explore, this colourful, magical, mysterious, disappearing troubadour.

Chapter 23

La Rue de Soleil of Lewesville (Sun Street) was a quaint little one-way street situated in the middle of the town. Guy remembered visiting Lewes with Joseph and Rowena on one of their trips about, when Joseph had passed his driving test and the open road became his oyster.

Guy had been visiting the Bexhill Belles in Bexhill, whom he had met through Herve, and happened to be looking through a local newspaper when he saw the listing for the cottage for sale in Lewes. He knew when he laid eyes on it that he would be going for that very house.

What Guy had learned about himself was that he had steadfast determination. Coupled with the motto of his school that he used to wear on his school badge, "Tenacity," he got through, leaving Crystal Palace and making a new start in Lewes. It also gave him first-hand training in living the now, as Guy had no job to go to. He felt confident that he would get work with another branch of the same agency he had been with for some years.

Things fell into place as they do in time, and Guy became quite established in his new home. He was also healing well from the tumultuous relationship that he had had with Herve, and he was beginning to feel stronger emotionally. "Being hung out to dry" was something that he now understood the meaning of. He felt that he had been in the long wash cycle and was now drying off in the Sussex breezes – another rebirth would say the Shaman.

There was a cavern that never really got filled again, and that was the loss of his cats. He never knew what Herve had truly done with them, and he wondered if it would play on his conscience. Yet Guy still held them in his heart, because the relationship with them felt so pure that it was impossible to ever forget; that could never be taken away from him.

Guy also stopped feeling the need for vengeance or throwing recriminations at Herve. He had to get over the anger and the hurt at first, which then helped him go a stage beyond, and that meant letting go of any attached feelings or blame. Herve was who he was, and he had his own Karma to deal with; it was never anyone else's burden, and was certainly not Guy's.

One of the Bexhill Belles, Effra, had known Herve when she had been a man, and told Guy quite a lot about Herve's background. He had never got along with his parents, as they never really understood him, and had always been involved in counselling of some kind. It was as if he wanted everyone to be gentle with him, and would not tolerate anyone being direct and to the point, which Guy was, and naturally drove Herve to violence.

However, the strong persona that Herve portrayed of the eccentric individual who had a kind heart had fooled Guy, and he realized that the first part was correct, yet the eccentricity had macabre connotations. Herve harboured a huge amount of vengeance, probably for his parents, and it came out in ways which made his reactions to things disproportionate. A prime example of this was when they had had a quarrel over something simple in the home, and Herve had gone to see he-who-adored-him, leaving a message written in his own blood on the wall. This was after the episode with the smashed windows to give

Guy "permanent ventilation." The issues that he had not been dealt with created poisonous residue that seeped out in response to lesser experiences.

That relationship would certainly be one that Guy would never forget, and when he was able to relate tales about it in a light-hearted way, he knew that he had moved on and away from it.

There were some shared moments when they came together, which were also memorable, and the physical side of the relationship was powerfully charged, evidently through the negative electric powerhouse that existed in Herve, but it was unpredictable and could lead to violence. Herve's lack of inhibitions unlocked the door to Guy's sexual freedom. Guy also realized from that that love is powerful, but it does not instantly eradicate hidden demons; he had learned that that arrogance had no leverage in their exorcism.

Many of the characters whom Guy came across he put into his *Caustic Collections*. Quite a few of these are actually used in the plays, so they can act as a sound introduction to the reader.

The Caustic Collections

A Ballad to Jean the Surreptitious Snipper

There was an old woman, who we named Snipper,
Who discarded her shears, but kept her clippers.
At 6am sharp, in guise of the winter dark,
She would sneak out and snip in her slippers.
The snippings she let fall to the ground,
And no one would tell that,
Jean had snipped with the clippers.

Yet shrewd she was not,
For one day with eyes askance,
She was seen snipping the architectural plant,
Knowing she was seen she hurried away.
So with a sprint in her gait,
This time she was caught by fate,
And being seen, she no longer felt safe.

The plant looked poor,
As she slammed her front door,
And that night 'neath her sheets she felt a pang of guilt,
But her clippers she could leave no more.
These clipping bouts she did,
As a means of escape from her big boys' tantrums,
Of these you'll hear more later, in our poetic landscape,
Which may well take you out of the doldrums.

Cutting Edge and her family come to call

A woman of the arts was Cutting Edge, who endeavoured to live life beyond her privet hedge.

From Lewesville where she was born, to Canada had she flown, to lace her feet on more fertile earth.

'Twas here she did university attend, and here also she met a special friend.

One raunchy night feeling no ill, she forgot to take her pill, and this relaxing fashion she was to have a night of passion.

On waking up the next morning, she was left with more than a yawning.

For here to finish her course in the arts she would stay, even though now she was in the family way.

255

Nine months later Brat appeared, midst anxiety, stress and tears.

The man, who sired this unfortunate waif, seemed meek, mild-mannered and safe.

Whilst in Canada everything seemed cosy, but then later back in Lewesville, life did not turn out to be rosy.

Life at home was never easy, for living with Cutting Edge, Grown Up, and Brat was indeed sleazy.

Every room in their corner-situated apartment was chaos, with toy trains and building blocks, and in all the carpets there were trodden in jelly tots.

Through this muddles of household duties, Brat screaming, and furniture cleaning, Cutting Edge strove for a deeper meaning.

One Friday eve, with the intent to the stresses of living relieve, the Boy Bombshells asked this couple around to dine.

Then larger than life, at the front door were Cutting Edge and Grown Up once more.

With them was their bane, for they could find no babysitter sane to watch this little terror for the night, the mere thought was a disturbing fright.

On filling up our glasses with wine, Grown Up suddenly ejaculates, "When are we to dine?" For no social etiquette, you see, had he.

And so the evening went on with five in the throng, and as usual with this mismatched couple and their bane, everyone was wondering if anyone was sane, as with them things usually went wrong.

As usual, totally out of control was Brat, squirming around like some sewer rat, and even though he took the stage, alas we could find no cage, for in answer to his constant din we desperately wanted to lock him in.

Then the conversation took a nostalgic turn, and stories from our childhood we were to learn.

On one topic was to grasp, like a bramble from the past, the tale was told without a stammer about a misdemeanour with a hammer, and Cutting edge could not leave this tale alone, for with thunder thighs and flashing eyes, she'd always find time to criticise.

Yet deep rooted within this negative plight, we all knew that in her home life things were not right, of this we were about to learn, for mention and hint of it came out at every turn.

Grown Up's conversation lacked any imagination, and it was also splintered with shards of degradation.

Little had he to offer, for no constructive talk had he to give. His parents, being the puritans that they were, had brought him up to have tunnel vision, yet his brain was like a sieve.

It was duly vowed by the Bombshells that night, that to avoid and further occurrence of this plight, they would simply not ask Grown Up to dine.

Yet merit there was in Cutting Edge, which could be seen much more when she was alone, for she was really an all-rounded gal of the arts, who would not gladly tolerate any prissy old farts.

Sue Slovenport and Pete

To the ice-cream parlour one day we were took, 'twas a warm Saturday eve and we went along to look. There was Cutting Edge, Grown Up and Brat, and the Boy Bombshells.

Then all on a sudden, tearful and befuddled came in Sue Slovenport. Her boyfriend we were to meet in this parlour; he was called Pete.

Our ice creams we licked whilst our topics we picked, but Sue and Pete could not respond. Instead, we heard of the death of her cat, of which she'd grown fond.

So with a lick of her cone of iced vanilla, she truly looked like Godzilla, whilst Pete sat with a permanent grin. As it was the original plan to go home and watch Roseanne, and when we our ice creams finished we did.

To view their flat at first, the overall impression was bland, and the dominating colour a very heavy blue, for clearly it reflected that they had no penchant for using hues. How the atmosphere was bitter, ranking strongly of very soiled cat litter, and this ghastly perfume permeated every room.

Other cats were seen, and it came over that being neurotic was their mien, and Sue's views on cats were unclear for they would not come near. To stroke them there was no chance, for they all vamoosed into a corner in total fear.

It became increasingly plain that to live in this vein, would drive any normal person barmy or insane. But their insanity only matched their inanity, and by this they would eventually find fame.

To add a touch of class, Sue would intermittently munch Shanghai Nuts, and on these morsels she masticated until her hunger was appeased. Often feeling morose, she would change all her clothes, and in the breaks from Roseanne her man would make tea.

Stumbling in with a grin, then the fun would begin, for Pete would keep Sue's mind on track by feeding her many snacks, and these were out of party packs.

Employment for Pete was quite a treat, for at the abattoir he did his work neat. One day on a slicing edge he once lingered, losing a finger. He tried to remedy the accident by using a sticking plaster, and this tale became his party piece.

Kaz and Effra, the Bexhill Belles

From Brighton came Kaz and from Streatham sauntered Effra, and together a semi in Bexhill they bought.

You see, we'll let it out from the start, for it comes from the heart, and it is to be deemed they were not what they seemed. Really, Effra had been Fred, and Kaz had erstwhile been Chas.

TS's they were, not genetic belles you see, once pre-op and now post-op, and together they lived in Bexhill-Boulevard-On-Sea.

Effra, ash-blonde, in dresses she would not be seen, for above-knee-length skirts and tops were much more her scene.

She drove a Cortina with a grip like a vice, yet in this car there were to be seen no furry dice. And careering around corners she felt in control, and betrayed her delicate persona, for she could look like a frightening Desdemona.

For cigarettes she had a strong penchant, smoking one and many, and by the end of the week she would not complain if they burnt out her last penny.

Another one of her penchants was bric-a-brac, and of ornaments and household sundries she would never lack. Her eagle eyes were never far from a jumble sale table or boot of a car, for with ferocious stealth she would hone in on any bargain, although it often emptied her purse of everything but her lucky inherited farthing.

And now to Kaz we go to unveil another show, which we know will entertain.

Kaz's pick-me-up was homemade wine straight from the vine, and only too often she would gulp it down without a frown, belching profusely without any care to tide and time.

In the main the dress sense of Kaz was plain. No collars of lace or feminine grace were to enhance her whole pace. On her eke there was no slap, on legs no slacks, and on her feet she wore only little brown shoes. Whatever the weather she would always endeavour to wear her long brown overcoat too.

With her hair style there were no limits, for Kaz would let no barber trim it, and being fuzzy by nature, it looked like a cross between an afro and a perm.

The high-street fashions were no her passion, so to charity shops she'd go. To Oxfam for blouses, where she might contemplate trousers, and to cancer research she would wander for shirts.

In common, the one thing they had was T. S. Elliot. Now was this so bad? Mutual hobbies could not be shared, for deep down within her, for them, Kaz did not care. Apart from homemade wine, life was too much strife.

One day the Boy Bombshells took her to British Rail, for here there was a job for sale.

Kaz then, making her own hangman's noose, hit them with a volley of trivial excuse, and so this opportunity she missed. For really her one drive was to on that homemade wine and get pissed, rendering herself again to be of no use.

At home in the bathroom stood products from Vidal Sassoon, enhancing and beautifying this private room, a chaos of loofa and lampshade, toothpaste and brocade, and a cleanliness that would banish a broom.

When mutual harmony between the Belles sank – this was a gradual process, for Kaz could not help but slurp and burp on her homemade wine – Effra went out and bought the most stubborn dog of all breeds, a Staffordshire bull terrier, which she named Tank.

To be far from the home malaise, Effra would sail casually out of drive in a haze, with no thoughts on her mind bank save those of her new companion, Tank.

Then it came to pass that Effra's mama did pass away, leaving her a substantial inheritance to line the clouds with silver another day.

And so now being able to escape all domestic traumas with Kaz, Effra bought another bungalow, wherein she could flounce about in front of many mirrors, and live a happy life with Tank.

Sadly, for Kaz her operation did not quite do it for her – she thought that it would be the answer when she was Charlie – because she wanted to be a genetic woman, but sadly, ole girl, this would/could never be.

Life apart from Kaz for Effra was now the thing, for Effra knew that Kaz could bring no sunshine in. To her new abode she was wont to spend most of her time, taking tea at the De La Warr Pavilion Café in thirties splendour, after all she was a new woman in her prime.

Then as time went on the Belles were to part. Effra had established roots elsewhere, yet Kaz sadly left the fold, and no one heard a word about her again, but we hope that she found an acceptable place to live and peace in her soul.

Patels's Palace

Easter was early this particular year, and Patel's Palace was open to sell food wine and beer. A handpicked selection of staff was employed, a manageress named Migraine Miranda, whose dress sense was so lousy you had to hand it to. In clingy man-made fabrics she would waddle, most definitely not this season's top model.

Cheap perfume and strong body odour would waft from her head to her toe, whilst her smileless and pained expression would turn friends to foes. She was aided by a winning pair, for all their meagre efforts, everyone would fall short of despair.

Karen Konstipation's unwelcoming deadpan face was assuredly a front-of-house disgrace, whilst High Anxiety's demeanour was one of total anaemia.

And with these their stern looks, you could read them as open, unwelcoming books. Yet any intelligent self would leave them on the shelf.

Two accountants were the Tanzas, who owned the Palace, full of false smiles with an underlying malice. They had said in a sickly turn of phrase that they wanted to start a commercial "family," evidently with much conviction and great gravity.

But in hindsight what a travesty, for in most families is there much harmony?

Much hair had Kakatita (Mouth-On-A-Stick) down to her waist, yet in dress sense she had no idea and seriously lacked taste.

Jirito Lank-Look, bespectacled and lank, smelt of curry and his breath often was rank. For numbers and figures he had a strong bent, but as a restaurateur he was as foul as Migraine's scent. In all things he was limp, acting and dressing like a wimp.

A brother had he, bespectacled too, employed in a bank as a clerk – by this in life he aimed to make his mark. Unfortunately, for his personality there was no hope, so he was nicknamed Dope-On-A-Rope.

His conversation was unsteady, and all anyone remembered him saying was, "Is food ready?" It came as no surprise that his voice was not hoarse, for bottle after bottle he'd guzzle chili sauce.

Into the kitchen would wander Jirito clones, his sons Cummin and Coriander, and in their greed would take no heed of the kitchen's danger zones. Always waiting for their chili-topped pizza and chips, they would be told, "Stay away from the fryer, for it spits."

Their mother, Kackie, who was also known as Mouth-On-A-Stick, a probable member of a witch's coven never, told them to beware of the oven.

A chef was employed, the Patel's blue-eyed boy, yet in the kitchen he had no culinary merit, so he got named Caroline Credit. In growth he was stunted and by nature insipid, much resembling an underfed whippet.

Living no by the sword or pen, he lived by the credit card alone, and often boasted of evenings at home with his palone.

In his desire he could never come clean, for deep down he was a rampant closet queen. Masquerading in chef's garb, he tried so desperately to look macho and hard, but in reality he was such a drag, and had a secret penchant to look for white stilettos and a matching handbag.

This foul little bore would make any sensible being throw up over the floor, boring them to death with his Lanson champagne and lobster thermidor.

Of the sauces on the menu, Credit always found solace in the one named Calvados. For this tired little queen would gleefully sing with a scream, "Calvados, Oh Calvados," whilst adding the cream.

Now onto a great hat trick called Patrick, of Gaelic descent, the Palace's porter, probably Paradise sent. 'Twas his intention to do his daily work without mention, for he was not of the mob and clearly enjoyed his job.

This was our cosy family at the palace, but where things mattered, some illusions have to be shattered. The truth then being our main intention, for of these sordid things we must make mention.

So gather around and join the throng, for by what you've read you'll understand what went wrong.

Frau Frown

We knew of a girl we named Frau Frown, living with her parents in a nearby town. Now here was a girl who had travelled far and wide, but she had an innate ability to get you down.

She would think and think and think and think, until her contact lenses popped out and fell in her drink.

When everything was set out on the table, it is true that she was unstable, for she was prone to irritate everyone, and at parties she was definitely no fun. She would never enjoy a drinking spree; often favouring many cups of herbal tea, for her only leaning was in analysis, you see.

In the kitchen of a famous opera house she came to work, and by her constant neuroses and stress she made herself look like a right burke.

Her smiles were very few and far between, and with her dope she was very mean. Being of a delicate mind, she would hate any bad atmosphere, as being in one would leave her in floods of tears.

Out in Bangkok, in an opium den in Bali she once sat, and a penchant for this opiate she discovered thereat. Drawing in the smoke to relieve her fears, she was even able to annoy her foreign peers. So did this opiate relieve her fears, for she was ever reduced to shedding more and more tears.

Now back to the nearby town where she lived with Ma and Pa, for back in the family nest she thought that she could give her troubled mind a rest. But alas into the void, Frau Frown did gradually become more paranoid. Analysing her navel was the new trend, this she did with loads of herbal tea and like-minded friends.

The afternoon thing at Riah RADA's

To Riah RADA's the Boy Bombshells went, for a midweek afternoon thing. Frau Frown was already there, alongside Zag and Pieman. Riah was her usual self – talk, talk, talk and not much else – prancing about in her nostalgic dress.

Riah was really a total riot, and she had serious plans to go to RADA. For the dramatic arts ran through her veins, and in everything she did it was to impress, so she went to extreme pains.

This was a small gathering, not intended to be quite a party, Riah carrying on having every intention to appear "arty." A natural girl of the arts you see, and to meet her we think you'll agree.

Frau Frown was for a change in a party mood, and trying her utmost not to appear rude, for she had made contributions to a table of food.

In the middle of the sofa sat she, with a plate of snacks and vol-au-vents, whilst drinking her fruit punch and regularly going for a pee.

After she'd eaten, she perched herself on the sofa's edge, then her photographs of foreign lands she did show when she smoked so much blow. Zag and Pieman passed them round, and we saw them all, especially the one with Frau Frown sitting atop an elephant looking starry-eyed and tall.

Zag and Pieman for another beach party left, and Frown deigned to furrow, causing herself much pain and sorrow, for they did not want her to follow!

In the meantime, the Boy Bombshells and Riah were getting along fine, from her lips words and eccentricities would spout without any danger of drying out.

Her head she would often toss about when she wanted to scream and shout. She needed to use no ploys, for she was once one of the boys.

Working down in the local pub worked Riah's boyfriend, who we named Snub. For when he from work came back, his greetings to anyone were none, and his manners were decidedly slack.

This was indeed a confusing thing, for Riah had always put it about that Snub was a wide-seeing and intelligent sort, so it prompted the Boy Bombshells to leave, and they hoped to their heart that Riah did not grieve.

Jean Snipper and her boys

You've heard us mention about Jean Snipper, well two boys had she, and they all lived together in a cottage by the sea.

There were many times on a Saturday morning, quite a while after the morning's dawning, when Jish and Jash would have their usual bouts of shouting about and throwing tantrums, then they would be of their cottage in and out.

You see, Jish and Jash were big boys, late forties and early fifties, but with money they were never thrifty, as Jean Snipper took care of it all.

So often on a weekend, when they spent together the most time, they were wont to scream and shout. This was often about chocolate cake, because if Jean bought the wrong Swiss Roll the boys would in temper roll and rout.

Then Jean would with clippers armed, roam about and cut off neighbours plants, leaving the boys to sort it out.

Then there would be slices of cake thrown over their wall, for the Swiss Roll was not their brand, and as soon as Jean re-entered the bedlam – having had her cutting spree – she would see the entire cheaper brand Swiss Roll over the floor sprawled.

Of this choccy fury any local rag reporter would want to report, for the one thing that resounded through Jean Snipper's home was that the wrong brand of cake was bought.

Then Jash, the bigger boy, quite rotund for over the years he had eaten much Swiss Roll, would go to his car for solace and then it thoroughly wash and wax, often repositioning his disc for road tax. Then the younger Jish would from the home storm out, and go walking on a total roustabout.

Yet later when choccy fury had died down and they were all in front of the TV, it never dawned on the boys that their boyish mentality was about me, me, me.

This did prove a point about chocolate cake to Jean, that it's best to get the right brand and not settle for fakes.

Elegy to lost sales

There were times when we would to the local off-licence go, to buy sparkling wine with which to recline. The manger and his wife, always with faces full of strife, would come out from wherever they hid, much like wood lice but not so industrious.

Their complexions were pallid and gory, and they reminded one of some dire B-movie. Served they the public nevertheless, but it always seemed under complete duress, for their expressions were always an unwelcoming mess.

As retailers no business acumen had they, and definitely no sign of any dignity or poise, no sense of humour, so they could never play.

Although there was one day, when she served in the shop alone, she announced that she was with playing the guitar quite pronounced, but this story seemed irritatingly trying, for it appeared clear that she was lying.

Her nails were bitten down to the quick, yet when she saw the Boy Bombshells he eye lashes she did flick flick flick.

One day this poor wench, to her face tried to apply makeup, and did it look out of place, for the hairs upon her upper lip there much more than just a trace. She certainly had no tan, and in some light looked like Desperate Dan.

The Bombshells had sussed her out, for in true light she came across as a dykish lout, and it was easy to see her routing for truffles like a wild boar with its scavenging snout.

Bureauport and Robust

On coming to this small town, we would often visit the job centre with a frown.

Positioned well in the corner sat he, Robust, who was in charge. With no *joie de vivre* upon his face, he was the hapless manager of this place.

Quite pigeon-chested, pen-tapping and woollen-vested, he did not look like he would make a huge mark, and he dressed like a fourth-rate office clerk.

Within this field he sought recognition, and was already up for promotion.

On another side of this dismal place Bureauport was sat. Before her was her pile of paperwork, of which procedure she was off pat. With her facial muscles inert, and without any twitch, she really came across as a mercenary bitch.

We could guarantee that at school she was teacher's pet, and she would gladly squeal on others without any regret.

So in the office she was conditioned to do her job with gusto, but she emanated this aura of being a latter day, flag-flying member of the Gestapo.

Mr Turbo and Ms Giggle.

Two great friends had we, whom we called Giggle and
Turbo, who whenever in his car would never do a go-slow.

Giggle was a Far Eastern gem, an exquisite blossom
on the top of a tall stem. With a face as sweet as Turkish
Delight, and eyes like almonds, brown and bright.

Sometimes her nervousness got her into a serious
giggle, so she became quite a laugh, and Miss Giggle
would probably be her epitaph.

Now we'll zoom on to Turbo, who enjoys his fast
cars, putting down his foot to the sound of the music
heavy metal. He would zoom here and there in the time
it took to boil a kettle. He was never really a drinker, so
seldom frequented bars.

He was devoted to Giggle and had known her since
the age of nine, and one day with the Boy Bombshells
they all roared with laughter watching a film with Divine.

Their company was rich, their laughter deep, and
often with them we'd all memories reap.

To their wedding the Bombshells were invited along
with two others, Jollity Hall and Appetite Plus, and
during the ceremony Giggle got into a giggly fuss, which
everyone picked up on and giggled to, for it was a fine
day for them to be married, this bright and lovely two.

Draughtsman and wife II

Draughtsman had been wedded before, and during the
divorce was glad that public was made of her many flaws.
So off to pastures new did he roam in order to find a love
that was true?

He came from a public school, self-discipline and loneliness often being the guiding rule; ruddy, bloody and possibly bally were the swear words he would use in his vocal rally.

Often getting carried away with forced social gatherings in the garden, he would nonchalantly toss his cigarette butts over the wall without a pardon.

In the summer Pristine, wife II, would enjoy the occasional barbecue, and really Draughtsman wanted to opt out, and from his house he wanted to these people rout.

For deep down a loner he wanted to be, as this was very obvious and plain to see.

From his former marriage he had had one girl, and he would bring her home at alternate weekends to give her a twirl.

Pristine, although a pleasant sort, if ever found herself with child would undoubtedly abort, but to her stepdaughter she would try to support feelings of love and all that sort.

Joan Sussex and the Inventor

Just over the way in the Old Coach Inn, lived a man and his wife and their next of kin. An inventor was he, of portly frame, and with the Greenpeace movement the lady had found fame.

Early mornings when the curtains were drawn, you could often see the inventor looking forlorn, being consoled by his ponytailed son, who would wrap his arms about his dad's portly tum.

On the fascia of the house much ivy grew, giving all around a picturesque and rustic view. Not long ago this was a famous inn, and many a smuggler and highwayman was found therein.

Returning to this interesting pair, both highly intelligent and of judgement fair.

An active life Joan Sussex lived, for she had a generous heart and truly liked to give. She would travel about daily without a fuss, in their orange and purple minibus. The petrol they used was naturally lead free, which took them on their country jaunts and picnic sprees.

It was good to have these people around, for they emanated a good vibe and were quite sound.

Vaudeville's Vault

There is a quaint little wine vault not too far afield, a cold shadowy musky smelling place where larger than life characters are revealed.

The owner of wines knows very much, for when asked about them he will converse on their origins and such and such. We named him Cecil Seysell, after a bottle he one day to us did sell.

A man with no dress sense, bespectacled and old fashioned, yet without any pretence. In shirts of yellowing nylon, Seysell would often appear, yet he always wore a tie, and sold some very interesting beer.

An assistant had he who we named Vera Vaudeville, probably in her mid-sixties, yet having great charisma still.

She was wont to wear vermilion nail varnish on well-groomed nails – the brightest of orange reds – carrying on in the vaudeville tradition it must be said.

She had a cockney voice that was quite hoarse, through many decades of smoking fags, but she just

oozed with girlish charm and often was seen out with
Cecil arm-in-arm.

Always hankering to be centre stage, Vera could do it
always with that sparkling smile, for people to come and
see her perform used to come from many a mile.

Karmic Awareness

Thee in robes of faded orange sat she we called Karma.
Her main aim was to show everyone that she worthy of
the Dalai Lama.

In amongst the crystals and gems she'd speak on the
blower, whilst keeping her customers waiting her service
became increasingly slower.

If asked for the incense of the moon, she became
befuddled with excesses too soon. Yet there were often
many calls asking for her advice, and it was unbearable to
watch her aspiring to be sickly-sweet and nice.

She thought that she was inspiring you with calm,
yet underneath you feared that she meant you harm.
Speaking to her clients with that awful pseudo-smile, it
lingered not even for a short while.

To the perceptive ones she had no charm; it rated
for nought, yet naturally she adored her impressionable
ones, over whom she could pull the wool, for they were
truly caught.

Sheila at Rainbow's End

One day a trip on the train took us to Seaford-on-Sea, and
discovered that it was not all that it was made out to be.

On the way down towards the front there was a
small shop which caught one's eye, for it was laden with

antiques, second-hand furniture and bric-a-brac all seemingly baked in a pie.

And this abundance of bric-a-brac would have brought Effra and Tank to sniff out the track. Sheila was in her paradise sat, and Rainbow's End was where it was at.

Walking opposite the road, it was clear to see that she had in the window an original 1930s sofa and chairs, making us smile with glee.

Yet from the distance the price looked too high. We thought it said eight hundred, yet on getting closer the sum was just eighty, so we looked in and spoke to Sheila about the price.

It transpired that Sheila was closing up shop, for the goodies she had within it for high sales had made a flop. No connoisseurs there were here you see, so with her lease running out, Sheila had to vamoose, and so in her shop one could have gone on a wild spending spree.

Sadly, lacking any comfortable chairs on which to sit, we heartily took up the offer of this original set, which was in pristine condition; in the sofa and chair world they were really fit.

How the dye was cast between the Boy Bombshells

In a small backwater by the sea in Brightown, a very small hotel did stand. The hotel was grotesque, an artefact from Norman Peake's *Gormenghast*, and its décor was flocked-wallpapered walls and far from grand.

Its proprietor was from a Far Eastern land, and its manager we called Fob, and by his insipid demeanour and dress sense everything about him appeared second hand.

Even if he had made a trip to Rainbow's End, he would have been fitted out better, for Sheila would have kitted him out to the letter.

Then one day into the doldrums of this dour domain came a chef to work one day, Bomb, an attractive guy who needed work, so about the booking did not delay.

The Far East owner, Wad – as his pocket with bank notes was always laden – but his knowledge of being an hotelier was limited, and his manner was brusque and brittle, that he was of the same ilk of the great Fagin.

To this dump there came another chef to work, Shell, another beauty, who looked like he was from Olympian stock.

Then a great charge of power filled the air, for a great union was formed between these two, and it was in such a dump that they found such something so fair, that only those who know how to love would know how the story to construe.

They were here to prepare and serve a Valentine's dinner, yet Wad was convinced that after the table was set for the banquet, a few pounds of money would buy the flowers for the centre table runner.

Bomb and Shell vociferated together that at least twenty pounds would do the trick, so from his wad, Wad came up reluctantly with twenty, and it looked as though it made him quite sick.

In that backwater hotel in Brighton, Guy met up with Jacques, who stormed in one day through the swinging entrance doors. Guy had arrived just about five minutes before, and was talking to the hotel manager named Fob. He was a tall, rather spindly German, always clad in a badly fitting pinstripe suit, and often prone to looking at his fob watch, which he housed in one of his waistcoat pockets. He had a wan, almost alabaster, complexion, and his gold-rimmed spectacles he hoped gave him an intellectual mien, but they just intensified his rather intense look.

So Guy was talking with Fob as to what was expected of him; it was a Valentine's function, and naturally he wanted costs to remain within a very tight budget. It looked as though Jacques and Guy were to do the catering for the function.

Jacques was quite Olympian; he was thickset with tight, thick, curly, blond hair, deep-blue eyes, and a full mouth. Hitler surely would have wanted him to be his prototype of the Aryan production line.

Jacques also had an aggressive air about him, which Guy at first put down to his problems that he was going through at the time.

Guy and Jacques went out for a drink after work, and found that they had quite a lot in common. There was clearly quite a powerful attraction between them. When they left the pub Jacques was going in the opposite direction, and Guy spontaneously said, "Walk with me." It just slipped out, and Jacques did so, to the station where Guy was going on to Lewes.

As time went on, after their booking at the hotel – they were called back to do another function another time – Jacques told Guy about his current life and why he was so angry.

Jacques lived with another man who had been a priest but was on a serious guilt trip about his own sexuality and his loyalty to the church. Their relationship had gone sour, and Jacques was looking for somewhere else to live when he met Guy.

One day Guy was with Jacques, who decided to take him on a tour of his regular haunts. When they arrived at one of them Jacques partner, Lionel, was seated at the bar with glass in hand. As soon as he saw Jacques he said something sneering and sarcastic, for he had heard that Jacques was seeing someone else. Guy observed Lionel but said nothing to him; it did not seem worth the effort.

Before long, Lionel had goaded Jacques enough for the latter to want to hurt him, and Guy pulled him away, saying that they both need to quit the joint. Guy could see that Jacques was at the end of his tether with his domestic setup, and told him that he was to come home with him to Lewes.

Guy and Jacques went to his flat to collect together his belongings, when soon after Lionel arrived, shouting abuse. It was a difficult scene to handle, because Lionel was not going to ease up on the verbal abuse, which naturally goaded Jacques to violence. Guy tried his utmost to persuade Jacques to ignore the flying invectives and pack his stuff as quickly as possible so that they could get out of there.

Jacques nearly held out, until, at the bottom of the flight of stairs, Lionel roared out "AIDS," which was prompting Jacques to hit Lionel hard in the face, but Guy intervened and pulled him away. The taxi Guy had called was waiting outside, and they hastily got into to it and left for the station.

When they arrived at Lewes, Jacques broke down into floods of tears and was silent for a while afterwards.

When he talked about it, he related that he and Lionel had shared some good times, but Lionel started to get possessive and jealous of anyone Jacques talked to; they both knew in their hearts that their relationship was over.

Guy let Jacques talk, and shared some of his own experiences with Herve. It was not too long before they were sharing laughs about their respective experiences, and because both of them shared a kind of gallows humour, their rapport blossomed.

Another play followed:

Vaudeville's Vault:
The Labyrinth Beyond

Cast of Characters

Vera Vaudeville	Star of stage and wine vault
Cecil Seysell	Wine vault owner
Plaza	Performer
Ventura Vick and	
Sambo Cotton	Performer
The Great Mephisto	Performer
The Boy Bombshells	Themselves

Scene 1 Act 1, Vaudeville Vault's wine cellar vault

There was this wine vault as you came in the door, where there were wines of all types, classes, and vintages all lining the shelves from ceiling to floor. And with a proprietor like Cecil Seysell, it was much more than your average shop, and the articles therein were much more than theatre props.

Cecil was a man whose knowledge of wines and the like was not nominal, and he would freely share his wine wisdom with anyone who asked; some said his know-how was phenomenal.

He was not a man who had much dress sense, as he wore his yellow, fraying, nylon shirts daily, never giving the impression that for sartorial splendour he had any desire or pretence.

On a particular day way past the month of May, the Boy Bombshells went to buy some wine. Riah RADA, Pieman and Zag were coming over that evening, so they wanted to ask Cecil for some advice on what wine to use when they dined.

They became engaged in conversation with Vera Vaudeville, who was looking radiant with her vermilion-varnished nails, a woman, like Miss Jean Brodie, who would always be in her prime.

Only ever seeing the front fascia of the vault – with a small anteroom behind – it was always thought that there was nothing else beyond. Yet on this particular day, Vera showed the Boy Bombshells through to the back and they were invited to stay – clearly of one another's company they had all grown fond.

Vera Vaudeville, in her distinct cockney brogue, said, "Look here, me duckies, cum an 'av a look be'ind." And with many golden bangles a-jingling on her wrists, and dressed in her polka dot gown, she did look very fine.

Passing then by the first door, they were to discover that they were to see much more. It was quite dark at first, but after their eyes had adjusted, as for this intrigue they had quite a thirst.

The corridor in which they stood was long, nostalgic and pungent of the past, and they wondered just how long this unfolding intrigue would last.

Vera, like a jailer with a huge bunch of keys, opens a heavy oak door, asking the Bombshells if they care to look.

They were uncertain as to what to expect, as Vera was keeping this all as an utter surprise, and the Bombshells looked from one to the other whilst Vera continued on in the same guise. So, with a welcoming grin and eyes a-sparkle, she ushered them in.

Then down a narrow wrought iron staircase did they go, not knowing what lay before them, what they were to discover, of whom they were to know.

Yet they feared not because they trusted Vera Vaudeville, the cockney gem, and she strutted on, leading the Bombshells with her silk scarf streaming behind her like some elegant mother hen.

Lo and behold! What stood before them was a voluminous stage with vermilion-painted wood. This to some could sound tacky, but with Vera's theatrical sense it really looked quite wacky.

Then up to the platform she did ascend, and out from the shadows appeared her trusted friend. For as soon as she stepped onto the stage, Cecil hit the lights ablaze. And now whilst on this elevated plane, they could clearly see how Miss Vaudeville had captured many a heart, her performances wild but never tame.

With a tap of her foot and a clickety-click, arms outstretched, embracing the world, and Cecil ensuring that all the correct lighting illuminated her vermilion lipstick, she displayed a brief but vivid sketch of some of her vaudeville acts for them to see, from the days when she was a rampant and notorious showgirl and would fill all music halls to full capacity.

Some people in whatever they do are true veterans at heart, and they know from an early age that they're theatre professionals right from the very start.

Then the Bombshells sit down in the comfortable maroon velvet seats, being captivated by her sheer presence, which did all senses pleasantly greet, enhanced all the more with Cecil's lighting technique.

Vera Vaudeville sings:

So cum on all ye toffs, let's go down to Bow St Church, coz we don't wanna leave any of yer in the lurch.

I'm a vaudeville act and a vaudeville dame, and consider me wild, for I'll never be tamed.

Red lips, red nails, and cha-cha heels is me game, and petticoats twirling through storms 'urricanes and rain, coz, you see, show biz runs thru me veins. And the rains don't fall on Spain, but only on my plain.

With this sung, she then flew into dance, doing her renowned tap routine, ending up in her famous Vera Vaudeville stance, hands on hips with head held back, ready to confront any hecklers with a good hard slap.

On entering the vault that sultry afternoon to buy wine, they hardly imagined that they would be transported to the music hall era by Vera and losing all knowledge of time.

So there was Cecil waiting in the wings, like some devoted puppeteer waiting to adjust the strings. In total adoration of Vera on his face, there was always a smile, and for her he'd travel the globe, in his fraying, yellowing, nylon shirts, from the North Sea to the Nile.

All of a sudden Vera's act came to a halt, and the Bombshells wondered what then was to happen in the vault. After taking her bow Vera had disappeared beyond the curtain backstage, lights then went low . . .

And from the darkness beyond the stage could be heard a slurp, and then a burp. Cecil's voice said, "What a good vintage."

This indulgence would him greatly please, for he carried with him his small Tupperware box with biscuits and mature cheddar cheese.

All of a sudden lights then came on again once more, and it was clear that Vera had more in store. Now from being a solo act, she became the compere supreme. Dressed in a lavish Chinese gown, she looked like an elegant oriental dream.

Partially hiding her face behind an exotic fan, she then announced that the next act would be a mime man. Then, with a gracious pirouette, she turns and heads for the velvet drapes of the curtains of the set.

After a clever lighting change Plaza did appear. He portrayed buffoons, balloons, kings, queens (both varieties), court jesters and jokers, daffodils, tulips, and even red hot pokers.

Speaking not a word, but speaking much with his silent act, his choice of costume was very precise, and at every moment exact. Although his act was short, his presence was magnificent, and in these minutes he could lifetime experiences relate.

Now to introduce the Vault's ventriloquist, Vera is garbed in yet another lavish gown, which could never ever bring to any one's brow any form of a frown. Then to the auditorium she addresses a humorous soliloquy.

So with much smiling and laughing, and slapping her thighs with ease, she portrayed the epitome of the cat's whiskers and the bee's knees.

Another act there was to come, intended to add some more humour and fun, a ventriloquist act called Vick Ventura, along with his little man, Sambo Cotton, with his sugar cane stick.

Then with a flounce and without much more ado, Ms Vaudeville leaves the stage and Cecil Seysell merges the lights to blue. Now onto the stage comes Vick Ventura, dressed in faded cotton dungarees and a faded weather-beaten straw hat, carrying little Sambo Cotton in top hat and tails.

Sambo Cotton, hello everyone, I'd like to introduce to one and all, to the ladies and the gents at the back and all of you in the stalls, Vick Ventura my reputed house boy, who when they're short in the cotton fields I allow him to work. He's a grafter, is my Vick, and never been known to shirk. I'm a Cambridge man myself, me name's Sambo Cotton, and I think you'll agree once seen and never forgotten.

I am a man of independent means, and I will go on to say I'm full of beans. I've been invited out by many a queen – the royal type you know. Doesn't it show?

I've travelled the world far and wide; now I'm living comfortably on my estate along with all our family pride.

As we haven't got very long, let's launch headlong into our song. Vick Ventura and Sambo Cotton then duet:

All day long in the sun picking cotton like candyfloss, answering the masser's beck and call, Yes boss, yes boss!

We're men of varied talents, honest worthy and sometimes gallant; sometimes a cad, why can't we all be, by gad!

As I don't like the cotton fields, I'm working wit masser on stage fer dem higher entertainment yields. For a-cotton pickin' life ain't much fun or good. I'd rather be up here with masser where I is understood.

Vera Vaudeville then comes on stage, again looking an alluring sight, announcing that a short interval will follow, pointing the Boy Bombshells to the wine cellar and admonishing them not to get too tight.

A spotlight then on a huge archway beams, and through yet another door we were to go it seemed; with keys a-jingling, Cecil opens this oak-laden door, revealing a cobwebbed quarry tiled floor, an ancient and intriguing wine store.

But what a superb collection there was therein, of unique and full-bodied wines, at which the Bombshells could only hastily glance. Through the centuries these wines had been laid, and for their acquisition much money had been paid.

Cecil Seysell, what is your choice? As you can see, we have quite a wine jamboree.

Being so spoilt for choice, the Bombshells stood there at first aghast, then they asked him if they could have a white sparkling, still feeling that they were in Gormenghast.

Gladly did Cecil oblige, and into two flute glasses he dexterously poured them their wine, which was ideally chilled and had a taste that was just sublime.

Way in the distance they could hear steps pitter-patter on stage. It was now Madame Vaudeville in leopard-skin tights and vermilion taps, doing a tap routine wherein any less energetic dancer would surely collapse.

To Seysell the Bombshells then handed back their glasses, and on those plush velvet seat they did plonk their arses.

They watched the vaudeville dame glide from left to right, then right to left, their heads going likewise fashion just like an umpire at a tennis match. So captivating was Dame Vera Vaudeville that eyes that had fixed on her could not be detached.

In using up of the stage, any good choreographer would have been amazed, carrying on a-twirling, with her abounding talent unfurling.

We know that about her we go on and on, but how do you dull the light of a star that has so shone?

Now this tap extravaganza came to its end, and we heard Cecil slam the great vat door – the boom resounded throughout the labyrinth – to return to his lighting, to perform once more.

Spotlight then on centre stage, Vera is turning yet another page, and reveals another act, a psychic and occult adept, who in some parts of the globe was revered as a great sage.

Vera Vaudeville says, "An' now, me dears, ere, ere, ere and oh, oh, oh, (cos I like to drop me h's), and now for your entertainment I'll introduce the Great Mephisto.

The lights dimmed quite low, and through the atmosphere dry ice was released, giving a chilled effect, and for a while we wondered where everyone did go.

Through the murky blue shadows, echoes of the past would resound and reverberate, and there was the distant sound of a cello solo hauntingly played, and into the audience's minds did infiltrate.

Mephisto, shrouded in subtle lights and wearing an all-encompassing black cloak, suddenly was centre stage in all his might. Dry ice surrounding him, adding to the air of mystique, his presence did captivate the Bombshells and they saw him as someone unique.

The temperature within the auditorium dropped to a much lesser degree, now to experience a chilling experience and an incredible and memorable performance see.

Mephisto then, with outstretched arms, requires of the audience their desires. And blow everyone down, voices were heard from various parts of the labyrinth hall, each stating their wants, that for the Great Mephisto orders were wide and tall.

From one came a request for Mephisto to tell all, of what he carried in his pockets, whereupon the latter recounted in every detail, even down to his food voucher docket.

From another a plea came in a strong cockney brogue, "'Ere, I'm in an un'appy plight; I lost my man the uvver night. Tell me if 'e's happy."

Great Mephisto replied, "Your husband died suddenly in bed, Madame, after you both had to each other many harsh things said. But blame not yourself for your husband's death, for his body was destined that night to breathe its last breath. He, however, in a happy vein exists contentedly on another plane."

Then the dry ice did evaporate, and with a dramatic wrap of his cloak about him, Mephisto did disintegrate before everyone's eyes, lighting changing once more to reveal Miss Vaudeville to do another musical score.

Dressed this time in a resplendent vermilion silk gown – clearly her favourite colour – one could just imagine the furore this would cause when tell-tale of its story got handed around.

Then she announced that this song was the final act of the show, and hoped that everyone would return to see more acts of her vast repertoire that she would show.

Then without further talk, she drifted into song, and from the pit came the musical accompaniment. And with the correct lighting from Cecil, she looked just so in her very fine raiment.

Roll out the bottles; let's 'ave a bottle a gin.
Roll out the bottles; are we glad you bleedin' came in.

Roll out the bottles, 'cos Cecil's doing me lighting again.
All we can do is perform up 'ere and roll the bottles,
'Cos we'll do vaudeville through thick and thin!

After the final curtain had come down, the audience found themselves once more in town.

Everything seemed chronologically out of mode, and when they looked at the clock, to their consternation, no time lapse showed. It was the same minute and hour as when they all first went into the vault, and they wondered if it was all in their imagination, or if it was Master Time's fault.

Being entertained in the music hall vault and the labyrinth beyond, it seemed as if a day had passed, being under the spell of this music hall cast.

In leaving the labyrinth and entering the front of the shop vault, there was some faint hurdy-gurdy music, which it seemed an organ grinder did flaunt. In looking about, no one saw anything, which added further to this mystique.

So through the town the Boy Bombshells walked on in a dreamy haze, feeling rather out of place in these modern days.

One thing though that was most definitely certain, the Bombshells were captivated by all who performed beyond the Vaudeville's Vault's magical curtain.

Chapter 24

After the sudden move of address and change of circumstances life naturally grew into a pattern, yet Guy started to realize certain things about Jacques. Guy did not necessarily understand it at the time, but in hindsight he realized what it was to be infatuated with someone.

Jacques was actually quite stunning in appearance, but what Guy discovered was that he was someone else who glittered but was not actually gold underneath – how he thought of Venema! As Jacques became settled, he began to show parts of himself that were not very endearing.

Unbeknown to Guy, Rowena had spoken to Jacques over the telephone one day, and he basically told her that he was broke and that it prevented him for looking for work, etc. His plan continued – to extract as much money from every source possible. Rowena, in all good faith, sent him one hundred pounds in the post, which Guy later learned that Jacques banked. Jacques also had a maternal grandmother with whom he got along well, and she naturally added funds to his new bank balance too.

Jacques applied for housing benefits and got a payment which he paid to Guy for his rent. So in the long run, Jacques was living off as many others as he could – probably what he did with his erstwhile lover.

It appeared that Jacques had an intense relationship with his parents, and a doting mother whom naturally considered him to be her blue-eyed boy who could do no wrong. But it looked as though she smothered him, for when he returned from a visit to them in Norfolk, Jacques was quite morose and withdrawn.

After one of these visits he was so pent up that he put his fist through a wall in a rage one day. Now Guy was starting to read signals very clearly, and realized that two ships don't sail together, the personal relationship on the one hand and the landlord on the other. For his own protection, Guy decided that the latter now took prevalence, and he asked Jacques to use the spare bedroom as his room from then on.

Purely by chance one day, Guy opened a letter which was addressed to the house, but the addressee's name was not visible in the envelope window as it had ridden up in the envelope. Guy was astounded to see just how much Jacques had built up his bank account, especially after telling Guy that he was struggling financially.

Then Guy saw the light, after taking off his rose-tinted spectacles, and understood that Jacques was using him as a stepping stone for other pastures. Guy thought that he had crossed this stile, but things would be changing from now on.

Guy was forthcoming in apologising for opening Jacques mail, explaining the error, yet Jacques knew that he had been rumbled, so Guy played a calm and steady game of endurance and tenacity.

He gave Jacques notice to leave. Jacques had mended the two holes that he had put in the walls, but Guy understood violence, and although Jacques had hit the walls, Guy had seen him hit his former lover. Where would Guy stand in one of Jacques's outbursts one day? Guy remained composed, and Jacques seemed contrite, for he did genuinely care for Guy, but the road pulled him on too strongly for him to be loyal to anyone for too long.

Jacques was also extremely volatile and petulant, which Guy had witnessed himself after working and living with him. There was a time when Jacques had secured a position in a restaurant which had been opened by a mother and her daughter in Hove. Jacques was actually quite condemning of the two women, telling Guy that they were rough trade trying to sell their food ideas which were rubbish. Jacques ended up stealing their knives, which did not please Guy when he Jacques told him what he had done.

Jackie, the mother, telephoned Guy at his home, asking for Jacques. Guy would not cover for him and said that he was not home. When Jacques spoke to Jackie, she more or less said that if he returned the knives she would say no more about it, but Jacques told her that she had no proof that he had taken her knives and put down the phone. Jacques had already sold the knives for a fair price.

So the time came when Jacques, with a good seven hundred pounds behind him, left and went to Norfolk – at least for a while.

Guy had now become objective and matter-of-fact about things, and put out his hand to shake and wish Jacques good luck with his future. Jacques pulled him in to hug, but Guy remained statue-like and unresponsive. Guy had no more respect for Jacques and needed to show him that.

When the taxi pulled off with Jacques in it, Guy breathed one of those long deep breaths of relief that he had come to know so well.

He put himself into another play:

Raffles Rendezvous
A Haunt of Jingle and Monkey

Cast of Characters

Melissa Monkey
Jessica Jingle

Rupert Rife
Maud Monsoon
English ladies in the Rendezvous
Army officer and lady friend

Act 1, Scene 1 – The Raffles Rendezvous Teahouse

In the 1880s, a quaint little teahouse did stand by the name of Raffles Rendezvous. In India it was, and known by its clientele as being rather grand, unostentatious, an ideal place to meet, to sit down to tiffin and teacakes, or to merely one's acquaintances greet.

The interior was pleasing and the atmosphere warm, the décor was in traditional Indian design. The staff were amiable and welcoming, giving and bringing to all their customers a smile.

The aromas, perfumes and varying *eau de toilettes* were pungent within this great teahouse, the fragrances of Parma violet, lavender and English rose lingered here, yet seemed to always stay.

Blending with these aromas was also ginger cake and freshly brewed tea, so thus was the atmosphere convivial for all to see.

Maud Monsoon had worked here for many a moon, and her position as head waitress was quite flowing, for she took her work seriously, enjoyably doing everything in her stride, seemingly all-knowing.

Serving people at the tables and welcoming them at the door, always looking fresh and elegant in her starched pinafore. Her voice was warm and welcoming, a perfect hostess one could say, and she never bemoaned one minute of the hour of any day, as her nimble fingers cleared away the trays.

In little groups of twos and threes the "English ladies" would take their refuge in the Rendezvous from their shopping sprees to catch up with local gossip, and with news from home for them to bemuse.

Prissy Pollys and bright-lipped Dollys with their parasols and crinolines would flounce in; regularly getting the vapours, for those corsets had been pulled in so tightly about their waists in order to make them look thin.

So here they would sit, each one hoping that they were the talk of the town, but quite candidly they would make any beautiful woman frown, chatting endlessly about banal inanities, and competing with one another as to who had the best gown.

"My cotton is from Cashmere, my dear!"

"Oh really? My silk is from Singapore, with hand-painted designs from Bangalore. You see, I would never deem to wear any mass-produced thing." (For really she wanted everyone to her looks praise and sing)

"Well, my Cashmere cotton is really for my safari suit. I have to look my best of course, because at the weekend I'm off to a tiger shoot. The cotton is so light; it will reflect the sun, and I will make sure I am away from the gun.

"It starts at two and ends at four, and then we stop to have a hearty glass of Pimms No 1, or for those who are more staid, a long glass of cool lemonade."

So in the Rendezvous life was seldom dull, for there was always a wide mixture of folk, besuited always in light tropical wear, massed produced or bespoke. Some sat with their polished walking canes in their neatly pressed trousers without any sweaty stains.

Just like Ascot, there was always a profusion of headgear to be seen, from fedoras, panamas, bonnets and bows; the female contingent wearing all-engulfing cottons, and of course their rather elaborate pantyhose was well concealed.

Uncles in monocles and spats, nephews and nieces garbed in sailor suits, the latter sometimes screeching when boys pulled their plats. Occasionally you would find the scruffy anthropologist or writer at his plot, often in his haven, clean but unshaven, never remembering to after his long paragraph putting a dot.

So clearly our Rendezvous is open for all to see, reflecting a wide cross-strata of society.

Now at a table situated at the end sits a certain Melissa Monkey, adjusting the sugar cubes with the tongs, clandestinely scrutinising the faces in the throng. She has chosen a piece of banana cake, and is having another cup of tea, which she likes to be hot and strong.

Across the floor towards the door she hears Maud, Jessica Jingle welcoming in, and in she comes looking sprightly, statuesque and thin. She then sits down and joins Jessica for their rendezvous at the Rendezvous.

Melissa Monkey: "Hello, my dear, how goes it with you today? I hope I'm not too late, for through the market I came, and around the mass of people I had to steer."

With bags laden with interesting goodies, she places them on the floor, and Melissa orders more tea and Maud then places it down with a smile once more. Above their heads a rotary fan rigorously rotates round, cooling off the heated shopper with its muffles beating sound.

Jessica: "Well, Melissa, I saw the usual amount of smart alecs today thinking that they would swindle me. But I their plans waylaid, for I am used to their cunning pleas, and what then baffles them is how au faire I am with annas and rupees.

"And of course they never think that I can speak their tongue, so you can imagine how it is for me, pure unadulterated fun. Although I have relatives in the army, I can speak fluent Hindustani. So tell me, my dear, what kind of day have you had? Have you heard from Hyderabad?"

Act 1, Scene 2 – Jessica Jingle's home in Bombay

To certain respected customers, the Rendezvous would reputable Sudan chair owners entreat, to save them unnecessary aggravation and preserve their tired feet.

So across the thickly populated Bombay streets these close companions were flown, to relinquish the shopping at Jessica Jingle's home.

Melissa Monkey: "Well, let me tell you, my dear, I have heard no news for so long I am beginning to wonder what's wrong. The last time I heard from the man he was in Dehra Dun on an assignment with his platoon.

"After all, you really would think that he would send me a word. How I wish sometimes that I were a little bird, able to fly off at will to receive a comforting word.

"As for this morning, I was off to the milliners to have a new hat fashioned, for as you know hats are one of my driving passions. This one, Jessica, is powder blue, without any frills or plumes."

Jessica Jingle: "How lovely! That hatter is really fine, and I feel sure that with this new hat you will look just divine."

Melissa Monkey: "I found a new ayah, my dear, and in manner she is so sweet; her little face is quite a treat."

A small, sparse yet tidy place had she, bedecked outside with many a palm tree. And adjacent to her home was a full laden conservatory, crammed with brightly coloured and exotic blooms, with which Jingle would enhance her petite rooms – all furnished with chairs of Bergere and Lloyd Loom.

That afternoon they both reflected on the walk that they had made when they did by the Ganges stroll, being aware that many a body had into the crocodile mouths did roll. They had been told this by their gentleman friend who was with wildlife photography a genius, and one day he would to worldwide notoriety ascend.

This man's reputation had already travelled far and wide, for he also sold pictures to *National Geographic*, often giving picture shows. After all, why should he his talent hide? He had begun with the daguerreotype mode, and then went on to master his style, showing them off at his own abode.

It had been one afternoon in the Raffles Rendezvous where our two dames had seen the photographic gent, pipe in mouth looking rather blasé and cool. They knew intuitively that he came across as no fool.

They all eventually got chatting as the gent was doing some sketching of wildlife, and they gathered that he was of an intellectual and creative bent. So they all exchanged many anecdotes and nostalgic tales over many glasses of port.

They were all from different parts of England, but had chosen to live in Bombay, originally intending to travel about and then deciding to stay.

Rupert Rife was the photographer's name, and in England had found no wife, so he had in India decided to make his life. Fairly affluent and comfortably off – he was the son of a prof – lecturing in some 'ology of some sort in an English port.

Scene 3, Act 1 – The market place

Now we'll take you back in time and show you where these two great ladies met.

Conjure up if you will a busy bustling market place where calm people could easily fret, and by the heat, pandemonium and bedlam, they would undoubtedly sweat, the colourful, ever-ebbing sea of merchants, vendors, beggars, cripples, and playing orphans and waifs – no one ever trusting another, and no one really feeling safe.

Near a material stall resplendent in colours and designs, above the shouting and many gesticulatory signs, the two ladies did by chance meet.

A coin from a merchant's purse did accidentally fall at their feet. For the coin each lady did deign to stoop, and for it both their hand did grasp, banging together their heads, which then made them both laugh.

Then one tossed it up in the air, making people stop and stare, and the other caught it as it fell, like a pair of jugglers at a country fair.

And from this moment on, as sisters they would carry on; in each other's opinion the other trusted much, and when alone they were synonymous to two school girls talking double Dutch.

Often they would tour together the market, and be to other places bound, for they had in each other a true and lasting friendship found.

When market perusing through the stalls and trestle tables they would fumble and for goods barter. And if disagreeable merchants came their way, they would not hesitate to show how they could be right tartars

Sometimes their faces were out of place, yet they carried on regardless, and of hesitation or shrinking there was no trace.

Although they were both of English stock, they had a penchant from eastern food, and in choosing herbs and spices they were liberal, uninhibited and certainly no prudes. In both having a command of Hindustani, they ordered with gusto the spices for their favourite dish, vegetable biryani.

By frequenting this marketplace, celebrities they had become, for to and fro they were wont to go, and they were really very easy to know.

Scene 4, Act 1 – Melissa Monkey's apartment

Not too far away from the market, just on the outskirts of Bombay, was the little house where Melissa Monkey was wont to stay. It was situated in a pleasant spot, where she had a picturesque patio, whereon there were many fine shrubs in terracotta pots.

She employed a little gardening boy called Richy, who her plants did tend well and in the evenings did water them with aqua from the well.

Her little home was comfortable and quaint, and never needed a touch of paint, for Miss Monkey was house proud prone, and all the colours on her walls and furnishings were of matching tones.

Over the way there was a park, where lovebirds courted and cooed after dark. It was a lovely spot to spend the day, and many a time Jingle and Monkey had gone that way.

They would often with them a picnic take, and watch the guileless children playing around the lake.

One day in Melissa's home, Jingle and Monkey were together talking endlessly as they were used to do, when the mood caught them to go to the park, so they prepared all their victuals – a grand selection of creative food.

Scene 5, Act 1 – The enlightenment in the park

This was during the season of the monsoon, yet the rain had eased, so the ground was sodden, and they expected the rains to begin again quite soon. This they thought to be an unusual feat, to get soaked in the warm, heavy rain they saw as a treat.

There was a certain army officer who caught Jingle's eye that made her heart beat and dart. She saw that along with this army gent was a foreign female, linking his arm, and she looked assuredly towards coquettishness bent.

Jingle's manner towards her friend did change, for she was protecting Monkey from seeing this couple, lest this scene might her derange.

This was the same officer of whom Melissa had so fondly spoken, and as she had received no word from him, was heading to be heartbroken.

Yet Monkey, who was an astute being, noticed her fiend's demeanour, and asked her outright, "Whatever is the matter with you, my dear?" with great fervour.

Whereupon, Monkey saw the sight from which Jingle had tried to shield her, and Monkey realised that for Jingle's friendship she felt much more than fleeting affection that she had felt for this man, whom she now saw as an upper-class, caddish bore.

Monkey then took her trusted friend back to her fine little abode, where they enjoyed good strong tea from decorative teacups from the best Spode.

Whilst they drank tea, shared tiffin, and looked out from Monkey's decorative patio, Jingle felt quite content that she had been spared from this rampant Luthario.

***

Rowena appeared to get along with Murphy, for they evidently lived a stress-free existence. Murphy seemed quite possessive of Rowena. Guy also noticed that whenever he visited his mother when Murphy was there a force that could only be described as jealousy coming from Murphy.

Rowena had made friends with another woman who lived in the same block as she, but towards the north side. Like Rowena, Joan was from Wales, so they had this in common to begin with. Joan was the only one of the neighbours who went to Rowena's funeral. Hilda, the neighbour who Rowena had rushed to tend to that cold winter's night, did not come. When Guy knocked on her door to tell her when the funeral was to be held, she immediately said that she was not going.

So, it seemed that Rowena had another child to care for in the last lap of her life. She was a woman who desperately needed to be needed. Perhaps this counteracted, but never eradicated, all the feelings of deep-rooted shame that ate away at her core. How she yearned for respite from all of these nagging hindrances.

Then the day came when she said to Guy during one of his visits that she did not feel that she was going to be here much longer. Guy knew, yet he played along and asked her if she was moving home, but he knew what she meant, and maybe the prophesy made his heart ache.

That was actually the last time that he spoke to her, because when he rushed to see her when she was on a respirator in the hospital, she could no longer speak. However, in his own way he sent her his thoughts, but did not have the faith at that time that she picked them up.

"Turn off the machine, Doctor," were Guy's words as he looked at Barbara.

They had discussed it, and after being told that Rowena had not responded for days, it seemed the right thing to do – to let her go.

It was as if a lifeline had been cut from him too. Guy now felt the loss of both of his parents, and he had to be strong for no one else, but could not muster any strength for himself. For a while he entered a twilight zone of his own, which seemed to go beyond his surreal world that he often drifted into. And feeling no links or any sense of connection with any of his step-relatives, he felt very alone.

But after this deep mourning period, Guy seemed to go through another rebirth and came out of it stronger and more focussed. The Hades that he descended into had been a continuous trial of endurance and tenacity, and he'd wondered at times if he ever would surface from its depths.

When he finally felt the sun on his face again – this time with more refreshing force – the changing of the seasons which had always been a comfort to him continued to remind him that he lived in England. He had always relied on the seasons, for they never had let him down. Spring and its smell of rebirth and renewal; summer with the sound of the blackbird in the evening singing so sonorously; autumn and the smell of dank leaves; and winter, the great sleep.

After giving it a year after Rowena died, Guy now felt that she and her beloved Joseph were together again. This gave him a freeing sensation, and he actually felt closer to his parents now than he did when they lived on earth. They had to endure no more pain and mental anguish, or worry about what was said about them. This was his belief anyway, which comforted him during his sense of loss.

Again Guy put his energy into another play:

Patel's Palace: Along the De La Warr Pavilion
A Midsummer Night's Feast

Cast of Characters

Kakatita (Mouth-On-A-Stick)	Patel's Palace Owner
Jirito Lank-Look	Kakatita's husband and joint owner
Dope-On-A-Rope	Jirito's brother
Migraine Miranda	Palace's Manager
Karen Konstipation	Head Waitress
High Anxiety	Waitress
Caroline Credit	Chef
Nicalas Nervus and the	
Dykish Lout	Brewers
Effra and Kaz (the Bexhill Belles)	Transsexuals
Frau Frown	Complimentary Therapist

The Frau quartet:
Brenda Breakdown
Angela Agitation
Hilda Healthrisk
Polly Paranoia

Jerry Hardcore-Camp	Bondage bistro proprietor
Stu and Happy Girl	Boring financial farts
The Boy Bombshells	Just that
Riah RADA	A budding actress.
Zag and Pieman	Dope fiends
Instant Karma and companion	Buddhists
Sheila Rainbow and Piers Pisces	Hippies
Cutting Edge and Grown Up	System Analysists
Sue and Pete Slovenport	Abattoir workers

Scene 1, Act 1 – Patel's Palace along the De La Warr Pavilion

Along the De La Warr Pavilion there rests Patel Palace, where it was said there lingered there a great deal of malice. And now the scene we must set for you well, for a bizarre and intriguing story is ours to tell.

It was party night on midsummer's eve, and the doors of the Palace were open for guests to receive. Many celebrities had booked to come, and the bar was bursting to sell the punters cocktails, gin or rum.

High Anxiety and Karen Konstipation, as we know, were not atmosphere makers, for they had no cocktail shakers. They certainly gave everyone a rum deal, for their faces were forlorn and smileless, with no front-of-house appeal.

The décor at the Palace was not a disaster, for there was no flaking plaster. The efforts of the lighting were quite sound, giving off an ambient glow all around.

On entering the front door there were two flanks left and right, affording quite a pleasant sight. The bar was semi-circular and quite long, offering ample room for a drinking throng.

The wine list was varied and vast, which would leave an ignoramus looking aghast. Of the wines that had a sparkle, the favoured one was Henkel Trochen.

The wines and beers were brought by Nicalas Nervous and Dykish Lout. They would supply most things except Irish stout. In the through the side door they would with boxes stumble, leaving an invoice and a goodbye, see you soon, they did mumble, for it was there station to be meek and humble.

Frau Frown had booked not to come too late, for on social occasions she was prone to hesitate.

With her this eve she brought with her the Frown Quartet: Polly Paranoia, Angela Agitation, Brenda Breakdown and Hilda Healthrisk. No one could blame it on the weather, birds of a feather must stick together.

Over to the palm-laden corner by Migraine Miranda they were led, where after she seated them she maintained that they had a bowl of bread.

But High Anxiety took over the scene, offering them melba toast with a face as white as a ghost.

Choosing from the menu was quite a feat, for Frau Frown could eat no wheat. This was for her often a sad tale, for she had noticed that her friends had nervously gobbled up the bread before it had a chance to go stale.

Kakatita (Mouth-On-A-Stick), the wide-mouthed hostess, comes over to the table and asks the quintet if they would like a drink. All of them except Frau Frown, who is undecided, gives their order.

Then, after much deliberation, she decides. "Frau Frown, er . . . I'll have . . . Oh no, I won't. Oh, I don't know! What have you got?"

Kakatita (with head moving from side to side): "We've got the lot."

Brenda Breakdown: "Oh, I'm having a pick-me-up."

Frau Frown: "Er . . . I'll have a treble vodka."

One of Kakatita's major noticeable traits is that, after taking an order for drinks, she would always bare her gleaming teeth, asking "With Ice?"

Frau Frown answers affirmatively then proceeds to peruse the menu for her food order.

Migraine Miranda then brings over the drinks to the table, looking flushed and rosy cheeked, establishes which drink is for whom and then places each one down respectively.

Kaz enters wearing her long brown overcoat and matching brown walking shoes; she resembles a librarian of the 1930s. Kaz has come to "check it out, guy," and the surroundings she finds appealing. Awestruck and standing nervously, she looks studiously at the ceiling.

Effra was parking the car, and she found a spot not too far, waiting for Kaz to give her the "go ahead" remark, but also trying to quell that bull terrier Tank's barks.

But nothing this midsummer's night eve was going to inhibit this caped and dolled up transsexual exhibit.

And so, on entering the door with a smile and a toss of her hair, everyone put down their drinks and turned to stare. Effra was then directed to the window where she would be on full display, for there she knew that her ashen locks with the light behind them would be in full array.

Then when settled down, into her evening bag her hand did glide to reveal a silver cigarette holder there inside. Indeed, this very successful transsexual, erstwhile Fred and now glamorous Effra, sat in the window spot looking a dream, or like a larger-than-life movie queen.

Kaz settled herself down to dine, but alas for her there was no homemade wine. Kaz then settled for the cheapest on the list, with every intention on this eve not to get pissed (as she was wont to get drunk every night of the week, you see, and Effra would spend more and more time with Tank).

Effra: "Er ... Kaz darling, would you be an angel and find me a light, for I must use this new cigarette holder, a gift from my new bomber pilot friend."

Kaz: "Alright, Effra, right you are. I'll just get one from the bar."

She strides off to the bar and buys a box of matches.

Effra: "Well, I didn't really want that many, Kaz. Did they not have any little books of matches with their name on it?"

Kaz: "Well, shall I take these back and ask?"

Effra: "No, don't bother, darling. I'll be content with this butch box instead; it may give me a rough and basic edge."

Scene 2, Act 1 – The Bondage Bistro

At the Bondage Bistro adjacent to the boulevard, Jerry Hardcore-Camp was working very hard, dusting bottles and polishing glasses, intermittently snatching glances at other men's arses.

Jerry was of the limp-wristed variety. No one could call him mister, as he was Caroline Credit's big sister. Unable to make a macho stance, but often he would snort poppers and to high-energy dance music he would bop and dance.

Now back to the bistro we will tell you this tale, of how Miss Hardcore-Camp would behave whilst serving his ale. Fosters, Heineken or Carlsberg would roll off his tongue with ease, for it was, after all, the well-hung clientele he was ever ready to please.

An all-white Alsatian was wont to appear in the bar, and when Jerry wore his black, skin-tight pants he would threaten to the dog from the bistro debar. For Snow's hairs would cover Jerry's trousers from head to foot, and thus ran the little ditty from this troubled queen who was being too prissy:

Hardcore-Camp: "Snow, Snow, Snow, get down girl, for you're sending Auntie Jerry into a whirl. I have told you over and over again about your white hairs, and I wouldn't mind if I had on my old flares.

"But with these skins on I am much more alluring and fit, so piss of upstairs, Snow the Alsatian, and leave me in my men pit."

And so, back to the Bondage Bistro where every cigarette was sold except The Old Mephisto . . .

It was basically a sleazy joint, and not the sort of place where one would want one's gods to anoint.

Yet in came beings from various planes and walk of life, with strange and common names. To name but a few, there was old Stu, and Happy Girl as his bride, her waistline being forty inches wide.

Well, in your excitement don't miss the bus, for there was also one called Appetite Plus. Stu was on the whole really quite rude; his two interests were work and food. He would thrash his gears through heaven and hades in his brand-new red Mercedes.

So into the said bistro they came for a while, discovering that the bar was not their style. Stu did not want to play wine bar games, as he was having hunger pains. And in wanting desperately to look like a tease, he reached for and then dangled his Mercedes keys.

And now three beings wandered in, hardly heard above the camp din, Tacky Jacky and Margie too, with an acquaintance who they vaguely knew.

Tacky Jacky: "Give us a drink, luv. What yer got? 'Cos we feel like havin' a lot."

Hardcore-Camp: "Now then, girls, don't burn out all the oil you get left in your lamps."

Margie: "Look, Ginger, we're not 'ere for the food, cos we feel in a drinkin' mood. So get those gin optics down, 'cos we feel like goin' to town."

Then the Boy Bombshells with their small group come in through the door, and Hardcore-Camp's eyes went from the floor to the ceiling to the floor. His lemons he had always cut prissily right, but this midsummer eve's night was not his night, for he hungered to be the centre stage all night and every night, but he knew that when the Bombshells entered eyes would to them turn, and Jerry would feel so spurned.

So, sadly, from finely cut demi-slices of the citron fruit, they had become unsightly wedges, for his main thought was to give the Bombshells the boot.

In with the latter came Riah, Zag and Pieman. The Bondage Bistro was a new venue, but they had said, "We'll try it, man!"

But really the Bombshells had decided not to stay too long at this venue, and so they agreed that after their drink, and the sour looks that Jerry aimed at them, they would find pastures new.

On this then they were all agreed, and trusted in the Bombshells, for them all to the Palace lead.

Scene, 3 Act 1 – Patel's Palace

Again we return to Patel's Palace. The atmosphere has now grown considerably, as there are many tables occupied with people eating and revelling.

Frau Frown and the quartet are still seated in the same spot beneath the palm tree, all now quite inebriated with their continuous drinking.

Still positioned well in the corner is Effra, with Kaz sipping her wine slowly so as not to irritate her companion with her slurring and burping.

Effra, still with holder and cigarette burning in it in hand, was posing dramatically as if in some commercial for a renowned fag brand.

On the other side are Shelia Rainbow and her beau, Piers Pisces, she being dressed in a nostalgic thirties-style dress in black lace. Pisces has made no effort to dress for the occasion, and is prosaically clad in sweatshirt and jeans, still clinging on to his misspent teens. They are drinking champagne in flute glasses.

Opposite their table is Karmic Awareness, as usual endeavouring to look as if she has all the clues to life's eternal puzzle and maze, whilst her companion seated opposite her is reeking of Estee Lauder's Youth Dew.

Migraine Miranda and Kakatita are both looking flushed and bothered, trying to look attentive and keen, but they ask customers too many times if everything is alright, proving that they're an overactive team.

Tacky Jacky, Margie and Sandra shuffle in after drinking in the Bondage Inn.

Konstipation: "A table for three, but have you booked ladies?"

Sandra: "No we ain't, luv, but 'ave yer got a free one, cos we're that empty we need to fill out tums."

Miranda finds them a spot and the gin gang all sit down and look at the menu.

Tacky Jacky: "I fancy a steak and chips."

Sandra: "Yeah, and wiv a green salad and onion rings."

So now the tapestry within the Palace is getting rich, for the noise and din is reaching fever pitch.

The Frown quintet is slurring their words, and Kaz and Effra are looking around at the other birds. High Anxiety brings forth some food, and Kaz covers up a burp, not wanting to appear rude.

Effra from her cigarette holder pulls another drag, dropping that butch box of matches back into her bag.

Then the Boy Bombshells enter with their throng, making the place even more alive, voices could be heard, "the Bombshells are here." Subtle looks and glances were thrown at them, and many over their wine glasses peered.

For they both as usual cut a dashing silhouette. With the midsummer evening turning dark behind them, they looked like a pleasing vignette.

Karmic Awareness naturally ate no meat, so on this eve she thought that she's be in for a vegetarian treat. But greatly disappointed with her meal was she, and then announced, "The chef I must see."

Then Caroline Credit flounces through the swing door, making his debut on the restaurant floor. He had had much instruction from his brother, Jerry girl, on how to get noticed and to do a memorable twirl.

Prancing about in his newly bought whites, wearing this garb he thought that everything would have to be all right. But being neither a creative nor a diplomatic type, he really gave Karmic a load of unconvincing hype.

Karmic Awareness: "I've had one of the vegetarian options, and I am not impressed. In fact, considering how much it costs, I feel quite distressed. We had thought that by coming here tonight you would have offered us a tasty bite."

Caroline Credit tried to explain, but his feeble whimperings were all in vain. Karmic Awareness and her friend vowed never to return to the Palace again.

So onto the Bombshells and their little company, all coming out with the intention of being hap hap happy!

Despite what obstacles might be in the way, they were of a mind to let nothing their enjoyment waylay.

Over to their table came Kakatita, Mouth-On-A-Stick, who offered them not Bombay duck but Bombay dick?

Kakatita: "Have you tried this new house recipe? With big bookings it is a real necessity."

And Riah RADA, being a right Eliza, rattled off the ingredients, and did it surprise her. This came to Kacky as such a shock, and she spilt chili sauce all down her frock.

Not to waste this valuable essence, her brother-in-law, Dope-On-A-Rope, was soon in her presence, armed with a spoon and a bowl and much zeal, all this chili sauce from her dress did steal.

Then he came out with his usual question.

Dope-On-A-Rope: "Hello, Kakatita, is food ready?"

"No, now go inside," she said with much force, "and see if Caroline Credit has finished the curry sauce."

By this time the Frau quintet had grown very drunk and had a craving to hear some party funk.

Frau Frown had grown increasingly decisive, and her companions had become decidedly derisive. Brenda Breakdown after her final pick-me-up had been sick on her sleeve, and earlier Kakatita had asked her to leave.

So it transpires that the Bombshell gang went to the car, for beyond the Boulevard the beach party was not far. So on their way out they did to Zag and Pieman call, for with all their combined dope they were planning on having a midsummer eve's ball.

After all, it was midsummer's eve, so why not make this an evening of fantasy and make-believe?

Instant Karma, growing tired of this restaurant role, glides out with her companion, and so not to get an evening chill wraps about her shoulders an imitation mink stole.

Standing there on the pier with the sea beneath her feet, she stares up at the stars showing everyone that she's having a cosmic treat. Swaying there in her high heels, she has the expression of regurgitated jellied eels.

Passing by this cosmic pair, is Helen of Troy (Cutting Edge) and her little boy. Grown Up had made no effort to look neat, this was for him too much of a major feat.

It was their plan to be with them Sue Slovenport and Pete, but this arrangement was changed to "Let's later at the Palace meet."

Coming in and sitting down, Cutting Edge was hastily peering at the menu, but with a searching look, because on banoffee pie she was seriously hooked.

On the upper flank were they seated and over to their right was that wonderful Bexhill sight, who with a grand smile they, Cutting Edge and Grown Up, greeted.

Jirito approaches their table to hear these two practising jump rope chants and rhymes, and he had the look on his face which said, "Hey man, don't waste my time."

Cutting Edge then says, "Please give me a while, for we await our two Newhaven friends."

Whereupon, onto the Palace the two Slovenports descend; no tears did she shed for no more of her cats had died – they were dropping like flies over some virus they had caught – so this put Sue in a better frame and she was no so fraught,

Tonight Mrs Slovenport looked like an elephantine babysitter, reeking of an eau de toilette that seemed like eau de cat litter.

She was wearing an ill-fitting evening gown, for which she made it known to everyone that for it she's searched all over town. But if the truth be known, she had a mate who worked in the local haulage firm. He was a transvestite, and had many things that he'd got from charity shops; this dress was his favourite, yet on Sue Slovenport no beauty could anyone discern.

Now onto Pete Slovenport, the grinning wonder, who was eager with tales from the abattoir to send everyone asunder. He could not sit still and would often fidget, for he had recently lost another finger digit, for this track-suited twerp had had another accident at work.

From the waitress they would take no buts, for they wanted to munch on their favourite Shanghai nuts.

Grown Up brought up the topic, that while he was their car parking, he had seen in another car a dog frantically barking. On hearing this, Effra's ears were cocked, and enquired of Grown Up if this car with dog a-barking was a white Cortina.

To this he answered affirmatively, adding that he saw the dog also rummaging through the car assertively. He then offers to be the gallant knight, to escort Effra to her car this night.

Then when they reach the car, when Effra opens the door, Tank friskily jumps to the floor. Grown Up tried not to the dog excite, but, alas, Tank tore round him, giving him a mighty bite.

Here it must be said with haste, that in the mouth of Effra's canine companion there was left a bad taste. So back to the Palace with a mighty limp and much regret, he was eager to bandage his hand with a serviette.

Cutting Edge remarked that this sight would not make Pete's eyes blight, for at the abattoir he was used to seeing many bloody sights, blood and loads of innards and guts; so here, dear, have some Shanghai nuts.

Scene 4, Act 1 – Still at the Palace, the kitchen

Now of that swing door between the kitchen and the restaurant you've heard before, and if you care to come with us you will certainly not be bored. For now we enter Caroline Credit's domain, that prissy little thing and tired bane.

More entertainment nevertheless for your ears, so on then, draw back the drapes and into this world let us peer.

Caroline Credit was rather flushed, for on this eve he had most definitely been rushed. And then with the scene with Karmic Awareness, he really thought that life had lost all fairness.

But even when things may run smooth and easy, Credit would still complain in that peevish whimpering voice ever so squeaky. It does make one wonder if anything will make him content, as he is so far along the pessimism road bent.

Even Hat-Trick (the kitchen porter), although a man of sound values and healthy stock, at times in frustration at this tired little queen almost puts him on the butcher's block for Pete Slovenport to finish off by tearing out his spleen.

So Caroline has another coffee and then smokes another Camel, praying that there are no more complaints, for he is not up to giving any more flannel. For really he cannot lie convincingly well, and basically wishes that they'd all go to hell.

In through the door comes Konstipation and High Anxiety, and now you will learn that Migraine Miranda is not of their sorority. For behind her back they spit out all forms of abuse, saying that she is of no use.

They say that she cannot do the simplest thing without getting into a mucking fuddle. On top of that she looks like the bride of Frankenstein's double.

They thought that Kacky and Jirito had better taste, for giving her the position of manager was such a waste.

Just here Credit interjects with an inane remark, all three of these tired little things looking like pariah dogs with vicious and poisonous barks.

So you see, this is how it was with Kakatita's "family." And it was when you heard them talk backstage you learnt that they had no breeding or inner security, for they were adept in gossiping and vilifying everyone, trained at an early age in the art of backstabbing.

The two waitresses promptly return to the restaurant as Jirito Lank-Look comes in. On his face there was no smile, let alone the faintest grin. He had that look of perpetual worry, and his head numbers – he being an accountant – did spin in a flurry.

Jirito (to Credit): "How is going, man? What are you cooking? I hope we get some more bookings.

Credit: "Well to be honest, Jirito, I want to get home to my respected palone, there with an open door, and of course my lobster thermidor.

Scene 5, Act 1 – The Palace again

And so now, alas, we must let the curtain fall upon our little show, for to their respective homes each of our celebrities must go.

On their exit, Kaz and Effra pause to receive their due applause. Together, Kaz and her companion, the caped Bexhill Belle, wander slowly to the car to career around corners and give the roads merry hell.

We'll let you into another little secret here; after her wine, Kaz had had some beer, so she could not with the car career. So from the Boulevard they did glide, in the Cortina to take another death-defying ride.

Sheila Rainbow had by now become quite loud, which seemed out of character, as she always wore a shroud.

To the car park she then with her beau ran, like some aging Peter Pan. Because all the midsummer's eve wine and food had put them in a horny mood, so they headed to romp about in their furniture van.

There was a content gleam in Cutting Edge's eye, for she had consumed many helpings of banoffee pie.

Grown Up had all evening desired to go home and tend to the wound from Effra's hound. When it came to pay the bill, Cutting edge handed it to Grown Up at will. For this we knew he had to fork out the dough, for if he didn't later he would bruises and blows know.

For Cutting Edge on a full stomach of banoffee pie could pack a punch, and send anyone to the sky.

It was with great difficulty that Sue and Pete were able to rise to their feet, for the rate that they been accustomed to eat made it a surprise that their arses were not glued to the seat.

So they all slouched out, one with probably a rabies infected cut. And of course they were still sharing their Shanghai nuts.

Chapter 25

Guy did quite a lot of DJ work with his close friend, Flyn. They shared a lot of the same taste in music, so got a reputation as being quite a dynamic duo. Flyn had had issues with substance abuse, but had decided that it was of no beneficial use to her, and the paranoia that she suffered as a result just was not worth it.

Guy always found solace in being creative, and some of his best work was the result of his most painful experiences in his life. He had been through many things, overindulged in many others, yet he always fancied that in hindsight it was a necessary journey in giving him first-hand knowledge, rather than seeing things from an objective stand all of the time. He understood that to feel something is to know it, yet not necessarily understand its dynamics at the time. Being an observer has its uses, but it never feels the heartaches and the twists and turns of life as much as the liver of life does.

He had been through changes of behaviour too; sometimes he could be withdrawn, and at other times vociferous and even cutting. But what he was searching for was his true self, not a picture of it that these learned external behaviours had given him.

When studied psychology, it became a long process of opening up that can of worms and searching through the debris that lay therein. It took time, a great deal of work, and soul searching, but he was convinced that he was not a bad person with malice in his heart, but one who had love there, because he had been conceived in the mutual love that his parents shared. It was all of the tirades and travails that he had to sort through in order to understand his own behaviours at times, especially why he reacted as he had to certain things.

If he had caused any harm to his step-relatives than he was sorry, but something rang in his heart and head like a nearby church bell. He had not intentionally done any harm to any of them; he had been a precocious boy growing up amidst their battles, and was a confused civilian who got caught up in their crossfire most of the time. Does not the child blame himself for grownups' quarrels? Guy did for quite some time, until he realized that they were not his battles, and he wanted to have no part in them.

Often we have to find the forgiveness for ourselves within our own hearts, because it is so easy to carry self-blame, guilt, and even shame all of our lives, not realizing that these things are eating away at the core of our well-being.

Guy lived in Lewes for some four or so years. When costs began rising, he sought to re-mortgage, but there were problems. A certain amount had to be met each month to the mortgage company until a part of it was returned, so if Guy did not earn enough to cover the overall payment it went delinquent, which caused problems. Guy asked the company if they could put the collection date to later in the month, but they would not oblige and he went into arrears.

His home was eventually repossessed, and for a while he faced being homeless, but after some searching he found a studio apartment in Brighton on the main street. Lewes council could not help him at all, as he came nowhere near their criteria for emergency housing, but it was worth a try, just to find out more about their protocol.

In a way he was sorry to leave Lewes. However, he felt that his sojourn there had come to its natural end, and he looked forward to another turn on the road in his journey.

Guy remembered Barbara asking Rowena why Guy wasn't more upset about losing his home, and she answered that it was just bricks and mortar – something that she knew Guy would say.

From the rustic and semi-rural environment of Lewes, Guy was now in the heart of the metropolis living in a flat above a busy, even frenetic, main road. How he noticed the energy switch from a more subdued, even lackadaisical modus vivendi – which he needed after the tsunami called Herve – to a more highly strung city energy that resonated movement all day and night.

He worked for the same agency, whilst doing DJ gigs with Flyn around and about Sussex. Then another play was born after he went somewhere unusual with the agency.

Basherbill Hall

Cast of Characters

Vanoga Bog	Manager
Quamdam Quodo	General handyman
Miss Tortoise	Resident
Miss Jenno	Resident
Mr and Mrs Snake	Residents
Pettsie Poise	Worker
La Lugubrious	Worker
Bella Boom	Accountant
Huntley	Resident
Miss Conno	Resident
Alex Mex	Chef

Boozie Cue	Kitchen Asst.
Gabbler	General hand
Lacuse	Asst. Chef

Scene 1, Act 1 – Basherbill Hall, an introduction

Along Belvedere Way by the sea stands a building called Basherbill Hall where retired clergy live and breathe.

Many different characters in this gall live and toil, and we will open up our stage to show you much more, how the workings of the religious minds can throw dark shadows on others who are easily foiled.

Running the religious joint is one Vanoga Bog, a woman short and peremptory, yet when fired up charges like a wild hog. She accommodates well those she considers to be in her domain, and for anyone who she perceives to have insight, she considers to be a total pain.

Quamdam Quodo, the general handyman and Vanoga's spouse, although an industrious man, has the permanent expression of a troubled grouse. Although he does have acute perception sense, he desperately lacks social skills, which leaves him aloof and looking dense. He is pretty sharp, but plays no harp, for he looks just the devil's advocate.

Bella Boom is the fat accountant who has no time for anyone, for she thinks in only figures, yet has no control over her own shape, for it is rotund maxima up from her feet to the nape of her neck.

A woman who claims to be a Christian, but lo, she seems like a result of something Faustian. No compassion had Bella Boom, for she claims that every

man is for himself, and if a kind word is needed, Boom
will disappear, the needy party unheeded.

Now let us some of the residents within this retired
churchly arena unveil, for you will undoubtedly be
enthralled by the denouement of this tale. For the front
of house persona can easily have you fooled, when you
see how convincing is the façade, and how thoroughly
their training in hypocrisy is schooled.

There is a strong dichotomy between the resident
folk, between Evangelism and the traditional Christian
approach. The former believes every word from the Bible
and believes that the word must be spread abroad, and
the other faction believes that each man is answerable to
his own conscience; this in itself is the heavy load.

Many a heated debate about the rudiments of the
Christian faith has passed in Basherbill Hall, for such a
line of debate will always be there, surely to either repulse
or enthral.

Scene 2, Act 1 – The kitchen at Basherbill Hall

So to our kitchen where all the food is prepared and
cooked, and often some of the residents will have guests
stay over, when it has all been properly booked.

Alex Mex, the head chef, a creative man in his own
right, yet never really thought that he'd ever stay too long
here, as for him it was not real delight.

Vanoga Bog would be prone to interfere too much in
how Alex ran his catering ship, putting her nose too far
in into matters that weren't her concern. Because another
one of her renowned traits was that she would on anyone
suddenly turn.

One of his assistants was Boozie Cue, a Slavic wench who knew just how to sue, for she had lived with an Englishman, Dew, but found that he was not rich enough for her desires, so sued him and moved on to pastures new.

Her next intent was to marry a rich man from the United States, so to this end she went to do a tourism course, thus hoping that she had planned her fate.

However, in the time that she worked at Basherbill Hall she was really quite a Madame, and not a person to be trusted, for many a time she would carry tales and spread gossip, to the point of getting someone from their job ousted.

Then there was also Gabbler, who talked and talked and talked and talked, all of nothing in anything particular.

He had come to the joint on a work experience from school and had stayed, as elsewhere he would not be employed, as his social grace and learning had never been much deployed.

A sad waif from a broken home, whose parents for him cared naught, and so he had no grounding for living in this world, but tried and tried, forever getting fraught.

After alleging that he had secured a loan from the bank one day, he put it about that he had found a flat of luxury and was going to live in absolute splendour. Yet it transpired that this was yet another fantasy, for there were unsavoury characters looking out for him, and these had been his lenders.

Then one day our very own Gabbler did not appear, and no telephone could even reach his ear, and not another word was heard about him; it looked as though he wanted to disappear.

Now there is also Lacuse, the trainee chef, who although with catering is very able, his relations with other are fundamentally unstable, for he would withdraw into himself and making contact with was impossible, and at times he could be quite irascible.

His mother was from a West Indian isle, yet sadly had passed not onto him too many rays from the sun, for at times he was inclined to be dull and puerile, and definitely nothing like fun.

Yet talent he had, and far in the catering world he wanted to soar, for he was but nineteen and had rougher seas to sail once away from the shore.

Now Pettsie Poise, who came from a good home, was another tale, but of personality was frail. She, although was comely, was also a taciturn wench and went about as if under her nose there was a permanent stench.

La Lugubrious was apparently her friend, yet would always the negative side of life defend. Of the things she watched on TV, she had an obsession to watch *EastEnders* all day, for this was how she saw life, a medley of all trouble and strife.

These were our workers at Basherbill Hall, where one might think from seeing the impressive façade that all morals and values were nothing but tall.

Yet lurking beneath, like in a dark and unpredictable lagoon, were many monsters with many issues, and connecting most of them was a mentality of doom and gloom.

Coupled with the persona of the religious mob, some of whom followed the teachings of the Bible to the tee and really had no idea of living in the real world, for they had eyes but seldom did truly see.

True, they had lived their lives and functioned of a sort – mechanically so – having children, living abroad, believing in hell and damnation, but really having no insight into what life is about, and thought that it was evil to talk of Darwin or reincarnation.

Scene 3, Act 1 – The residents at Basherbill Hall

Now we are going to portray but a few of the many varied characters at the Hall, and we think that you will find them intriguing, so why should this play not be just a ball.

Let's introduce you to Miss Jenno, who was at one point a Poor Claire nun, and gave this up to live her twilight years at Basherbill; she loved it there. A creative woman with horizons fairly wide, she was also a keen crafter and made cards and such like, being her delight.

Then along the corridor on the next floor we have Miss Tortoise, who walks and talks just like her name, always wanting to engage in evangelical theory, and others would think, "What's her game?"

As with all humans, there always seem to be different factions, and especially in a living, community this seems to be more pronounced, for Tortoise and Jenno would often be at it at the dining table, debating on what Christianity – or rather, man's corruption of it – has announced.

Many people will use and abuse a theory in order to satisfy their belief, and often the very essence of what it represents changes, like the truth has been stolen by a thief.

So asks Miss Jenno one day, "Explain to me what Christ meant when he said that in the face of adversity you should turn the other cheek? Did he mean to look a fool without any pride when someone else insults you?"

But this was too profound an opening gambit for the mob at the Hall, for they wanted to tuck into their dinner and get all three courses withal.

There was a grump, and across her table there came a resigned sigh, but the food was too much of a pull, and over philosophical debates it took precedence, and with mouth-watering juices dripping, the mob in delight slapped their thighs.

Miss Jenno realised that her opening to a possible debate had fallen on deaf ears, and too joined in the mob for eating, putting all thoughts of any more talk aside, lest in sheer frustration she may shed a tear.

Now there was also another inmate of this place, a Miss Conno, who would have everyone believe that she was a walking advertisement for the young at heart and the modern woman. Wish it were so, for in appearance Conno looked hale and was active and also went much a-walkabout.

She liked to have literary friends and people who she thought would impress the ecclesiastical mob when she talked over her day's happenings, which no one really listened to, and frankly she was labelled The Snob.

Conno had an extremely strong persona, which was so convincing it could lead you to believe she was a freethinker, yet see the other side of her and you would be mercilessly sunk – hook, line, and sinker.

When the persona is so overpoweringly obsequious and sweet, watch out, we say, for the sting is in the tail, and like our Vanoga Bog can with poison lash out, neither subtle nor discreet.

Then there is Mr and Mrs Snake, two slitherers who know just how to crawl, for through their obsequious natures they can bring about another's mighty fall. They gather information with a teeth-baring grin, yet behind the mask they have a malicious streak, sharing their day's conquests over many a tonic with gin.

And then we have Huntley, who with his beautiful wife lives on at the hall and hates every moment therein, for Mrs Huntley is deteriorating mentally, and Huntley is there to nurse her confusion midst all the ecclesial clatter and din.

But you see, Huntley's true nature is not inclined towards women, and he'd rather bed a prospective male than be in any witch's coven. Many a heartache had Huntley with men he would casually meet, and then he would fawn and falter after them, becoming a slave to kiss their feet.

Huntley was definitely under a male spell, which had him mesmerised all the while. The irony of it was that he was never short of an offer for sex, that tabooed word in this ecclesiastical setting, and to some brought up just bitter bile at even the mention of simple petting.

But Huntley knew exactly where to go to meet his many male beaus, who always kept him busy, and he was sprightly on his toes.

Often he would be in a dale or dell with a builder or decorator too, where they'd often be down to it, stripped to their very shoes.

Oh, Huntley was a randy devil, often seen in a vicar's collar. Yet for his male pursuits he never went so dressed, for only guilt would follow.

Huntley also kept his proclivities under cover, yet to the perceiving eye his bent was easy to discover, for his fey ways did show more than just an expressive man of the cloth. It rather portrayed outright campness, although he would describe himself not so much the butterfly but more of the basic moth.

Yet a lot of the time the mob would be fooled by a person's convincing front, because if a man is married with children, then he is an upright pillar of the community and not some deviant runt.

So Huntley lived on taking care of sickening spouse, and in times of libido need – which was often – up in the hills he would rout about like a horny grouse.

Then the day came when sickening spouse grew worse and needed even more care, yet Huntley would wait till she deteriorated – as he did not want to carry the guilt – so her needs would demand more intensive care.

Such a man was our Huntley, that he for himself had no esteem, and guilt and shame had haunted him all his life, especially when he played for the home team. His proclivities were strong and directing, and with men he thoroughly loved to be physical, and he seemed to be in love with love, and his pursuit of beauty was quite ethereal.

His spouse was a woman who had loved him with an unconditional heart, and she had been his mainstay throughout his life, even though he had his affairs with men, which did not lead them to part.

She loved in Agape and he loved in Eros, and how we know the pangs of pain those arrows cause and drag us down to all human dross.

But sadly Huntley kept no friends, for he always expected someone to chase him up. His friendships were always a case of loose ends, for he made little attempt to keep any fires burning – after all, this kept him free for his men and kept that wheel a-turning.

In the course of the life of Huntley many diverse things had occurred, as with all things by which we can be judged and putting on our name a slur.

Years ago, Huntley had fallen in love with a man whilst he lived with his comely wife. And she accepted the situation, for she was never one to instigate strife.

She was a woman who loved unconditionally, never expecting anything with glee, and never judging husband Huntley when on his man-hunting sprees.

This time, though, for Huntley it was more than just a random encounter, for he fell for this man full hook, line, and sinker, and then they all lived together happily?

Yet throughout this entire rather unorthodox ménage a trois, Minnie's love for Huntley never turned to hate, notwithstanding Huntley's major faux pas. Minnie was an angel, you see, who loved absolutely unconditionally; she was not under the influence of Eros, but bathed in the light of Agape.

'Twas sad that the relationship between Huntley and his paramour was not destined to last, for tragedy struck and the latter then passed from some sudden illness that seized him by storm, leaving poor Huntley to weep wail and mourn.

Yet Minnie knew just how to hold it all together. This she had always known how to do, even though there were times when with Huntley she was at the end of her tether.

Then there was another time when Huntley had a live-in lover. Yet this time there was much more that was under cover, because as time went on, his lover wanted to change his gender, for being a transgender was his goal and not to remain a bender.

This was not an easy situation for Huntley, or indeed his spouse, and again lived they altogether in this one vicar's house.

Naturally, in Huntley's day it was not the done thing to be openly gay, for it was not the social thing, but Eros again struck the heart of H with many arrows, for again this was no casual fling.

Yet the sex change was not for him, and it was a most difficult blow, for H did not want a surrogate woman, and so did find it harder and harder to his partner know.

So Minnie, as supportive and caring as always, helped this man through his travail, yet could not change Huntley's malaise, for he just could not cope with where this ship was to sail.

Huntley had many a story to tell of when he and other priests were able to come out of their shells, for they saw each religious service as a performance on stage, which would always entertain the congregation of any age.

For at High Mass, Huntley would all the others surpass, as he was a showman. "The show must go on" was his renowned adage.

One of his colleagues remarked to Huntley one day when they were all enrobed and cassocked, "It's just like a performance of Aida, my dear," and that was Father Vivien from Hassocks.

Huntley would often reminisce of these many varied and colourful anecdotes, even though he was always in search of his male partner on whom he would want to dote.

But later in life when Huntley and Minnie lived in Basherbill Hall, Huntley's meanderings for men still drove him on, and his lust and guilt still made him feel ashamed with it all.

Not much esteem had H for himself, you see, and he seemed to be in search of an unattainable dream – the perfect relationship – but what an illusion, and such a topic over tea.

Huntley of the Basherbill Hall crowd stood out with his radical views, often leaving some of them fuming, and he then left them alone to stew.

H could be a rampant agent provocateur, for he had little else to entertain him, so enjoyed being the Hall's court jester, the eternally pained farceur. Is this not the destiny of the clown, that he is the first to take away everyone else's frown?

Yet behind this rather see-through curtain (to the perceptive eye), his own thoughts and fulfilments are seldom fulfilled and never always certain.

Miss Jenno's life had been much more staid, for she had lived as a poor Claire, and all secular trappings had been waylaid. In a haven like Basherbill Hall, Jenno found great solace and respite, for herein in her self-contained flat, she revelled in its luxury, it being airy, south facing and bright.

Jenno was a crafter and enjoyed making handmade cards, and she would often be engrossed in reading plays, and she liked especially ones by Shakespeare, the Bard.

Jenno and Huntley would often in lengthy debates about religion be engaged, and at times they would be quite heated, H often leaving J somewhat enraged.

Whilst Huntley stood out from the mob, Jenno found it easier to integrate. And Huntley revelled in the fact that he was seen to be the outcast, yet also had the facility to be able to himself ingratiate.

Miss Conno now was a totally different kettle of fish, always bearing a toothy stage-like smile, and definitely wanting to always take control – this she did with utter relish.

How her smile would wane when she could not get her way, which left everyone in complete dismay, for Conno's motto was, "Conno says and others do."

And the only time she was forced to relax from this governing mien was when she was seriously struck down by an epidemic bout of the flu.

She wanted it put about that she was a spiritually superior being, yet her persona was strong and could easily fool the more susceptible of the mob. Yet those with perspicacity clearly saw through our devious Conno, but so easily she could fool any Tom, Dick or Bob.

Scene 1, Act 2 – The summer fete at the Hall

Now that it was in the height of summer when the nightingales and blackbirds would sing at dusk, Vanoga Bog, with some of her acolytes, a summer fete had arranged to put on in order to raise funds for the trust.

Watch out there, for Vanoga Bog is in full flight, she might suddenly snap at you if you did not please her, or send you to the tower with all her managerial might.

Of course she protects her little "family" gathering – ugh! And left alone with them, all you would really rather pull out is the plug.

Guy Jones

So there was to be stalls for cakes, stalls for tea, and definitely ones for all and sundry. Miss Jenno had made cards for all occasions, which were to be on open display. Conno made her jams and conserves, but boy did she make people pay!

She always claimed that all the ingredients in her jams were organic and pure, and they were popular and sold very well, which left her looking demure.

Huntley had a picture stall on which there many of his works of art. He used to paint in watercolour, but now has branched out to gouache; he is definitely no posy-painting fart.

In fact, his works always raise interest, and of course he likes to chat with the men. And if the chemistry is right – which it usually is – he will ask them back to his den.

Vanoga Bog thought that she for making cakes was some kind of wizard, for she always overcooked them, and without tea to wet the whistle they tasted like dried lizard.

But could anyone tell her about her skills, which needed a serious upgrade? Oh no, Vanoga Bog knew it all, and she would often, if anyone suggested anything to her, go into a raging tirade.

So the sun shines bright and the breeze is just a fine southerly on the day of the summer fete. With people's heads agog with ideas, and some in serious tête-à-têtes.

Being held in the rear garden of the grounds of the hall, it was accommodating and picturesque, and perhaps at one stage later there was to be a group of girls from the local Catholic school, who from their ballet training would demonstrate a pirouette and an arabesque.

Also, another group of locals with their Morris dancing skills would prance and jump about, giving many some rustic thrills.

Overall, this was jam-packed day, and for the amenity funds was to raise some dosh, and most certainly a great proportion of this money was raised from the abundant nosh. Lacuse and Alex Mex had done themselves proud, for praise for the bill of fayre was resounding, and compliments to the two gentlemen were distinctly profuse and very loud.

Scene 2, Act 2 – A major burglary at the Hall

As we all know, there are people who are prone to bear a serious grudge, and when they have been unfairly treated they take it upon themselves to be the adjudicating judge.

One day there was a major break-in at Basherbill when there was much damage done, and the perpetrators from it all appeared to get a great thrill. For much was stolen that contributed to the running of the ecclesiastical joint, that everyone was in a prolonged state of shock, and naturally wondered why this had occurred and what was the point.

The more investigations were made, the more it looked like a clear cut case of an inside job, for the perpetrator(s) knew exactly where particular things were kept, and where monies were stored so that he/she could them rob.

'Twas a case where everyone was numbed by the impact of the event, and there was a grieving silence that pervaded the air at Basherbill Hall, and it brought about an abstinence of all camaraderie, as if they were all in a prolonged state of Lent.

Now it came to pass that Gabbler, who once toiled at the Hall from his work experience time, had been seen hanging around with some others who looked like they were in their most criminal prime.

After many investigations in the source of this grand larceny, it became clear that Gabbler and company had committed this felony.

It was not too long before the police caught up with the felons, and Gabbler, for once, had little to say at first, but after much questioning started to release his venom.

He stated that as they were all people of the church, they should not have left him in the lurch, especially when he needed help the most. But it was put to him that it was he who had suddenly vanished from sight, so how, because of his actions, was anyone to help him out of his plight?

But sadly, Gabbler was of the sort who blames everyone else for his own shortcomings, that the world owes him something because of his parent's lack of parental care and all their bizarre doings. So compunction he seemed to have none for his premeditated act of theft, which left him of sound friends or even acquaintances totally bereft.

His only known comrades in crime were dark and suspicious untrustworthy folk, and it appeared that he wanted to remain in their company, as he was a vengeful bloke.

So after this misdemeanour he spent a spell inside, to see the freedom again but to plan yet another heist. But little did he know that his modus operandi he could not hide.

From an early age you see, had Gabbler been involved in petty crime, and his actions had been for long monitored by the Old Bill. Very little seemed to want to sway him on the straight and narrow, yet his cry for normality was an inner wailing shrill.

Rowena's funeral promoted some action in Guy's mind now that he could see it all objectively.

So You Did Show Up at my Funeral
A play in one act

Cast of Characters

Veda
Pierre
Ronnie
Aaron
Blanche
Johnnie
Shamus
His two sisters
Geraldine (friend of the deceased)
Jim (Johnnie's partner)
Officiating minister
Undertaker

Scene 1, Act 1 – The crematorium waiting room

The opening scene is in the waiting room of the crematorium. Just arriving through the door are Blanche, Johnnie and Jim.

Blanche is smart woman in her late forties, dressed in a well-cut, navy, double-breasted, skirt suit, beneath which is a classic beige blouse with a black bow tied at the collar, and fine black patent court shoes on her feet.

Her younger brother, Johnnie, is dressed in a double-breasted navy suit, a slate-grey button-down collared shirt and coordinating tie, and a black Fedora hat. Jim is wearing a grey suit; both men are in their late thirties.

Blanche sits down in one of the chairs in a row; Jim looks through the half-glazed door opposite the main entrance, then opens the door and looks over the garden. Johnnie looks through the entrance door.

Johnnie: "Blanche, Ronnie is here."

Blanche looks at her brother nonchalantly and resumes her blank stare. Ronnie enters along with Aaron, his son. They both shake hands with Johnny, and the latter thanks Aaron for coming.

Ronnie sits down beside Blanche; they do not acknowledge one another. Aaron sits down on a chair at a right angle to his father, and Johnnie sits down adjacent to him.

Johnnie: "How is your wife, Aaron?"

Aaron (In a heavy Yorkshire brogue): "Aye, she's alright, thanks Uncle Johnnie."

Johnnie: "Are you ex-directory, Ronnie? I haven't been able to get through to you?"

Ronnie: "We've . . . been having funny phone calls."

Johnnie: "Everyone was informed; Gerard couldn't make it because of his court case. I don't know about Pierre."

Ronnie: "Pierre is here."

At the last remark, Blanche turns and looks at Ronnie, then gets up and walks to the window, through which can be seen the car park.

A black car pulls up outside, and from its steps out Shamus with his two sisters and Geraldine, a fresh-faced woman in her sixties. Shamus, a stocky man dressed in a dark suit, gives the air that he has no time for fools or time wasters. Both his sisters have tried to look smart, but there are some people who cannot succeed in that. They all look and smell like they've been drinking. They enter the room and stand in one corner.

Soon after, Veda and Pierre enter, the two elders of the family. Veda is a rather tall and distinguished woman in her late fifties. She is dressed in a black-and-white, hounds-tooth wool skirt suit, with black patent knee-length boots, a matching black-and-white chequered floppy brimmed hat, and a roll neck black sweater.

Pierre has the characteristics of a heavy drinker, with a bloated face, bloodshot eyes, corpulence and a general sluggishness about his actions; he also makes jittery erratic movements. He shakes hands with his younger brother. Johnnie then embraces him. Pierre then shakes hands with Ronnie and his son.

Pierre greets Blanche, and she nods to him superciliously.

Veda makes it quite plain that she wants nothing to do with Blanch – and vice versa – for the former walks to the far side of the room. Johnnie follows her.

Veda: "Why weren't we informed earlier, Johnnie? The entire short note from darling over there (pointing her head to Blanche) said that mother died after a critical illness."

Johnnie: "That's what happened really. The last time I spoke with mum was about a week ago, and she sounded in pain then. After that I saw her . . . (*He becomes tearful and his voice quivers. Veda pulls him to her in an embrace*) she was in hospital in intensive care."

Veda: "What was the problem, Johnnie?"

Johnnie: "Mum had a punctured stomach, which they operated on, but she then became too weak after the op. Her kidneys and lungs stop functioning. Blanche and I had to make the decision to have her taken off the life support machine, as she was not responding at all."

By now Pierre, Ronnie and Aaron had joined them. The room is quite clearly divided into three groups, Shamus with his sisters, Blanche on her own, and the other group with Veda, Pierre, Ronnie, Aaron and Johnnie.

Geraldine was a neighbour of the deceased, and Johnnie, who had met her before, went over to her, and also to introduce himself to Shamus's sisters. Johnnie felt irritation at the two women, as they both had handkerchiefs to their eyes, yet seemed to be faking the grieving. After all, they had never met the deceased, and would not because Rowena would not marry Shamus; they were staunch Catholics. Geraldine was a woman who Johnnie's mother spoke highly of, and she and Johnnie shared some pleasantries.

Johnnie then returns to the group.

Pierre: "How did you get down here?"

Johnnie: "Jim brought Blanche and me. Jim, come and meet my eldest brother and sister. (*Johnnie beckons to Jim from the garden entrance.*)

Jim: "Have you had far to come?"

Veda: "Pierre is staying with us in Evesham; he arrived from Canada yesterday. It wasn't too bad a journey down."

Whist they are all thus engaged, the minister puts his head around the corner and nods an affirmative glance to Johnnie that the service is about to commence. He then asks them if they would make their way into the crematorium.

Act 1, Scene 2

The scene opens in the crematorium courtyard, with the door to the chamber ajar. The sound of Mozart's "Laudate Dominum" is heard in the distance, and as it comes to an end the mourners make their way into the courtyard.

Once again they automatically fall into the same groups, other than Johnnie who tries to integrate and put aside any family squabbles for the sake of his mother. Blanche stands at a distance looking at the flowers, and Johnnie stands with her for a while. They share some tears together and then hug each other. Johnnie looks over at people leaving,

Johnnie: "I must just say goodbye to Shamus and his sisters."

They both exchange an understanding smile as they look together at the three, and the wicked shared humour lifted their grief somewhat. Johnnie goes over to them as they get into their car. Geraldine is returning with them, and Johnnie says goodbye to her as well.

Johnnie: "Goodbye, Shamus – and thanks to you all for coming."

Shamus: "Okay now, lad. You take care, you hear?"

They smile and the car pulls off. Shamus speaks in his strong western Irish brogue.

Johnnie then walks over to Veda, who is in the courtyard in front of a small aviary and is peering in reflectively.

Veda: "Do you think she is in there, Johnnie?" (*She remains looking at the birds while she speaks.*)

Johnnie: No, never – Mum was always a free spirit, and if she knew she was cooped up in a cage she would never be happy. Mum has truly flown and is free."

Veda then links her brother's arm and they walk towards the others. Ronnie is crying profusely and embraces Johnnie.

Ronnie: "If only you knew how much I cared. I brought you up . . ."

Johnnie: "Well, why don't we see you anymore?"

Ronnie: "You know you're always welcome to come to Yorkshire anytime."

Somehow Johnnie did not believe him. Since he had become a Jehovah's Witness, Ronnie had changed a great deal. He did not even want to know his brother, whom he said he loved so much, because the latter was gay. But this did not seem the time, situation or place to broach that subject. Johnnie felt the insincerity of Ronnie's words, yet he also wondered why he was really crying.

Pierre: "Well, old son, I hope we meet in different circumstances next time."

Johnnie: "I'll write to you, Pierre."

Pierre: "Well if you do, I'll reply."

Everyone is gradually getting themselves ready to exit.

Veda: "Remember, Johnnie, you are the only link we have left with Mum now, so keep in touch."

Johnnie: "I will."

But he thought I knew in his heart that she would not. All exeunt, except Johnnie who walks up to the central fountain and sits on the wall surrounding it.

Act 1, Scene 3

The scene opens with Johnnie by the water fountain, sitting on its edge and looking reflectively into the water at the fish.

Johnnie: "Well, Mother, what do you think of it all?"

Moments after he asks this, a figure appears beyond the fountain. Johnnie looks quizzically up at the figure with a fixed stare.

Johnnie: "Mother, is that you?"

Figure: "Yes, son, it is. Don't be alarmed; I am fine, and just as you said, I am free as a bird and happy, more so than I have ever been. I believe that the tears were not for me, son, but for their crying consciences."

Johnnie: "I didn't want any scenes, especially at your funeral, so I tried to be a neutral force."

Figure: "And that you were, son, thank you. Saying anything to any of them would have been wasted anyway, because they cannot see what is the truth, only what they want to believe. Let their consciences be their guide.

"Do you remember just a week before I passed over that I felt I wouldn't be around much longer? I was called after the critical illness. The nurses were so very kind. I knew that you and Blanche were at my side, and Shamus too.

"I want you to know, John, that I am radiantly happy and at peace, because I am with your father – and I'm still driving him mad.

"Those other men I knew, the children's two fathers, had to incarnate again to recompense for what they had done. They are here now, but we have little to do with one another. There is no animosity, hatred or grievance; if you want to see someone, you do. Otherwise, you just get on with your life.

"You carry on the way you are, son, because your father and I are proud of you."

Johnnie needs to wipe away the tears from his eyes, and as he does when he looks up the figure is gone. Blanche joins him by the fountain,

Blanche: "Johnnie, are you ready to go now? Jim is looking for you and is eager to set off."

She sits down beside him compassionately looking at him.

Johnnie: "Blanche, I saw Mum. She was just standing over there. She says that she is happy."

Blanche: "Come, John, let's go."

As Blanche puts her arm around him and they both walk towards the car, Johnnie looks over his shoulder at the spot where he saw the vision. For a moment he sees his mother again, and smiles to himself.

About the Author

Guy Jones was always an observer of life and the many-sided ways of human beings. From a small boy he watched and assimilated everything around him, which naturally gave him a powerhouse of information and a sound backcloth for his writing.

Struck by the strong paradox of the tragedy and humour in life, represented by the two dramatic masks, one with upturned lips and eyes representing light heartedness, and the other with downturned features representing gloom, he uses this premise as grounding for most of his written work.

His prolonged studies in psychology and psychotherapy have given him understanding behind a lot of the diverse and often confusing ways of human beings. He agrees with Shakespeare that the entire world is a stage and that we are the players who perform upon it.

Yet he sees a difference in that. We as the players have the right to alter or change our scripts; they are not written in stone to be followed and obeyed, just used as guidelines for our many journeys and experiences through life.

Also by the author: *The Journeys of Rowena Sunita Singh* (The precursor to *Demon Seed*)
   Upcoming: *Omina Uvorix*

Review Requested:

If you loved this book, would you please provide
a review at Amazon.com?

CPSIA information can be obtained
at www.ICGtesting.com
Printed in the USA
BVOW08*0945191217
503201BV00002B/3/P